LIFE AS A PROTODOG
By
PANDABUTT Mackin
Princess Windy's
Directors cut

DEDICATED TO All the Kindergarten Teachers out there who have laid down their lives or sanity to raise our children as we are too lazy too anymore!

TABLE OF CONTENTS

FORWARD:

Hewwo! Is Windy again! My Gweat Beast means well but it is hard to type with a pencil held in your mouth. So I fix this story like I fix everything else. Once again do not tell my Mama I read this as I is not old enough. She would get sad if she knew. My Beast is gweat and I love her so much but she mess up a bit. Is getting better and I may not have to fix much in book thwee were we fight Awiens and save Universe. In this book I just take over Earth. Oh and save Monsters! And ride a tank! We meet Awiens and visit Poophole Planet. My Beast pooped on it so she owns it now. Make new fwiends too but we have little time so I must teach them the hard way. We get Coliseum and Lions! Make Pope feed them. Is much fun in here but also so much sadness. People and Awiens can be so dumb and mean. They be glad I am not!
"Treat Monsters nicely! Or else!" Princess Windy.

INTRODUCTION:

I'll apologize now as I am not going too later! If I have not offended you with this one I am sorry! I'll try harder in book three. What you hold now is the surrender of the human race to her Highness Princess Windy! She is such a cutey. If you think anything in here is wrong I have news for you. IT AIN'T! There will be a book three! All things are answered there! Nothing in here is illegal! Except the Killing. But that is for the public good! Unimaginable horrors await inside! Are you ready? Are you wearing a diaper? My editor says I must ask these things for safety reasons. Pammy the ProtoDog.

"There's no place like home!"
Dorthy
"Then go back there and get your immigrant ass out of our country!"
Republican National Convention

CHAPTER 1 PIMPED OUT
Saturday September 25th

Woke in a darn good bit of pain really! Definitely had a lumpy problem going here. Well Becky was it turns out an extremely bony Tiger and she was under me! Had to fatten that bony Girl up a bit and soon or I'd get myself some nasty bruises before long! A problem with the cage here at the compound it turned out. Well it was bloody not here, Robert had loaned it to Doctor Lucy I was told, so I bravely volunteered to sleep on Becky. Had to keep her safe you know. Us ProtoDog's are really into protecting endangered species after all you see and Becky was a Tiger! She was wearing a Tiger costume and that is more than good enough for a ProtoDog! Don't make me bite you! Look at her cute naked butt quick and check the bullet hole. Ignore the teeth marks! That butt was mighty fine, the bullet hole looked like it was even healing already as well. She had not gotten much of my milk but it seemed to be doing something for her already. Impressed me. Brutus was pissed at me though ya know! He was mad at me because I had never licked his butt after he was shot. Yes I was a bad Girlfriend and I knew it! Had to lick his butt often now to make it up to him! Wanted too anyway! So I'm a perv! Also a Dog so there! He had a sweet Doggy butt too. Very tasty! Don't give me that! You'd beg me to lick yours!

Was gonna be in more major pain than just what I was getting from a bony Girl Tiger soon however and I knew that one as well. There was close to a hundred pounds of poop ready to come out of me damn it. Felt like it at least. No we never weighed it. Too scared of the truth I think. Pretty sure I had eaten over fourteen hundred pounds yesterday however. No idea how that worked so do not ask me. My body was like a Black Hole! Speaking of black holes? My butthole was gonna hurt after I pooped. Knew it! That I was taking in more then came out bothered me of course. Had no idea where the heck it was going as I was still very lean looking. Svelte even! So sexy too!

As I stood on the bed though Girls began waking around me. Off the bed I slunk and stretched quickly. Going up to the outside door whimpering. Girls gladly helped Becky up and out of the Tiger costume. No idea why as I preferred her as a

Tiger. She was breathing well but still kinda quiet. No real symptoms of Methane poisoning that I saw so I assumed she was just processing things or still dealing with the drug. Well drugs. Swear I have no idea what she was injected with before they extracted the bullet fragment from her butt. Not a whole bullet at least and only a ricochet so it had not been deep. Still certain it hurt like Hell for the poor Tiger. Had been a lot for that poor Tiger Girl to deal with this week. Raped, Caged, Shot, Father murdered! That was a definite murder! And I didn't feel bad about it in the least however. Damn good about it to be honest! Maybe angry that he died to quick though! If you read that diary you would throw me a parade! That BASTARD deserved to DIE!

And once again all my fault she got shot! Okay it was partly Teela's fault she got shot. Liked Teela a lot however so I would except all the blame myself. Us ProtoDog are such noble creatures! Her raping and caging were honestly my fault! Admit I enjoyed both at the time too. Not denying anything here! Felt bad about them now though.

Sabrina mused out loud as she squatted in the grass to go potty. My fault again as I seem to have housebroken them. It is nice to just go and not have to run to the toilet and wait so I understood why the Girls did it. "I wonder if Becky is still suicidal at all?" Sabrina's voice was very gentle as she spoke. Sounding only curious really I thought.

No one answered as they all squatted as well. Was a valid question after all though and I think even Becky was not sure on that one and only time would tell. This was not my fault though! Well I did not say anything to her about how if I pee or poop on something I own it! At least I hope that was why she did what she did because if not it was a Bad way to die! As I hunched to go poop you see Becky lunged quickly and dove beneath me! Plenty of room under my butt for a skinny human as I was big. Kimmy was closest and luckily she just reacted by grabbing Becky's ankle very fast and falling backwards pulling Becky from under my butt barely in time. This all took place in less then a second or Becky would be dead. No way to stop now as it was coming out! As it was it was close to her unimaginable death and I howled my pain as my asshole tore open. That is a lot of shit! It hurt bad. There was blood too! Well I smelled it. Fucking damn Kevlar!

Tammy with tremendous awe in her voice as well as some laughter said. "Looks like she is still rather suicidal! Anyone got a front end loader?" Seriously! I was ready to bite Tammy till I turned around and saw the awful truth. Oh My God! I just gave birth to a Poop Elephant! We needed a front end loader bad! No wonder it hurt so much! That was a freaking amazing poop pile. The embarrassment I felt equally tremendous!

Becky just stared at the pile with her mouth hanging open with fear in her eyes now. Should have wondered just how the hell Tammy knew how big it was!

Thought she must have untaped her eyes or something. Maybe a trick of some kind. Peepholes or something similar. She was very smart and could have rigged a way or two I was certain!

Still, I ate a lot yesterday! Felt better now mostly that it was out at least. Butthole still hurt!

Kimmy started it! Grabbing Becky in her arms and holding her saying. "Please don't kill yourself Becky! We want to love you!" Tammy and Sabrina joined in rapidly. No idea if they thought she was trying to kill herself or just wanted to hug her for a while. Not sure it really mattered. Becky never made a sound though. Probably still in shock! All the way to the kitchen too. They dressed themselves and her in the bedroom before coming out. Hugging her all the way to the kitchen table even. Not a sound yet. This oddly enough attracted attention! Go figure. So I turned and went back out into the hall to wait. Well I didn't feel like being stared at while they discussed my bodily functions. Again! Big topic around here it seems. Not that it was any of their business but that never stopped any of them now did it? Probably talking about my weight as well. The shame of being a ProtoDog!

Windy found me first in the hall and hugged me sweetly. "I Love you my magnificent Beast!" She said that with feeling. Aww! Teela was next to come out and said how she loved me as well and wanted me to go on her chest like that. What a perv! Nasty, Nasty, Nasty, Girl! Knew that now didn't we. Still loved her anyway. Maybe even more because of it. Okay I so totally wanted to go on her like that too! Give that Girl a poop bath! Her Sister had one before but Teela wanted it all the time.

Third to come find me however was Becky herself. That kinda raised my eyebrows a bit. She came and hugged me saying thank you for not killing her when she asked me too. For now she wanted to live it seemed. See if it truly was worth it. Telling me I gave her something wonderful. HOPE! Then she blew it. "I know I may never be normal!"

That did it. Oh I was laughing my ass off! Could not help it. Found it very hysterical for some reason. Wonder why? Becky looked like she was about to cry but I could not stop laughing. Maybe I needed THIS! Luckily Sabrina who had been watching from the doorway said gently as she went to Becky. "It's fine Becky! Don't be upset by this! She just doesn't like normal it seems. Too boring perhaps. Frankly I don't think she knows a normal person. Or even wants to for that matter. I'm not normal! None of us are. She will always accept you as you are. Just be you hunny and she will love you always. I'm now a 'PooperScooper' after all! Pammy has taken a big liking to you fast Becky but Dogs do that ya know. Friend or foe instantly." This statement was so true.

Pushing Becky to the floor I nuzzled her and licked the tears from her face. Tammy asked really smiling. "You know where that tongue has been don't you Becky?" Becky nodded still smiling! Definite good sign there. Tammy just snickered. She knew she had no room to talk. She had gotten plenty of poop breath kisses too!

Things looked good then but things got real awkward at breakfast when they asked what plans us Girls had and Dean Kelly said like it was an everyday thing. "Twenty four hour Lesbian orgy." To my MOM! Awkward! Especially that smile on Mom's face! A couple people had parts of breakfast fall from their open mouths onto the floor at that. No idea why their mouths were open? Brutus and I were all over that food fast though. Snack! Do not give me that gross shit! My tongue had been up over half the people present's assholes. That truly puts things in perspective now doesn't it? The life of a Dog is always gross!

That was nothing however as when they asked for an explanation of that statement, and Windy gave one! Talk about looks to kill! Oh I was getting several and I had not set any of this up. CRACK! SMASH! That little Girl is hard on the furniture. Well I was just glad it was not fancy plates as several broke when they jumped off the table and hit the floor. Surprised she did not break the table. More Snacks! Windy's voice was stern! She is adorable when she does that. Just saying! Scepter is so totally dangerous! "My Beast! Leave her alone. She must learn to hunt better! School not teaching her good!" Windy had not said anything about sex and only about hunting Prey in her explanation and they still glared at me. However when she said. "I need a shovel!" I almost shit on the floor. If anything was left in there I would have. Trust me. Possibly not the only one came close. Better check!

They quickly tried to talk Windy out of going with little success and I understood why and hoped they did as well. She had to protect her "BEAST" after all she said. Which meant burying the evidence of course. Really I felt loved so I was okay. That Scepter bloody hurts too!

The General came to the rescue however. Well he tried at least. Was really a good idea however and I was even mad I would not be able to go with. His voice so sweet he said. "Windy hunny you don't want to spend all day digging in the dirt do you?" Thought he was nuts there. She was only five! And nodding her head! Then even sweeter. "Wouldn't you rather ride in a tank parade and wave at the peasants? I'll teach you how to drive a tank!" She was five! Problem solved. Like I say who could turn that one down?

If only it worked!

Nodding and grinning now Windy said commandingly. "Teela get a shovel and bury evidence deep!" Oh, the looks that statement generated. Not at me for a change! Mom and Mrs. Gonzales got along very well as they both liked to watch the same real crime shows and everyone knew it! They both mumbled sorry. All you Moms out there who watch those raunchy lame soap operas with the kids playing in the same room need a spanking! If the idea of getting a spanking is appealing, Please, call me! Teela was on the floor nicely leaving a puddle for me to lick up. Yes I did, I'm a Dog and Teela pee is damn tasty. In truth I had thought getting permission for Teela to go along with us would be impossible. Adults knew it was a trade off however and the lesser of two evils, so to speak so caved! If Teela saw something that she needed explaining about it would be a lot easier then explaining anything to Windy! Maybe? Frankly I was just wondering who was going to explain things to me? Had no idea what we were in for now did I?

Once breakfast was done, floor was licked clean, plates licked clean, Staff liked me, beats washing them before putting them in the dishwasher now doesn't it. They get sanitized! Besides my tongue has been down half their throats already. With poop breath! Nasty People! But I like Nasty People! What do you expect from a species that rolls in dead things? Was a Dog! Mostly. The General went to try and arrange a quick tank parade. Her royal Highness got a makeover. So did her Mom and the Dean. Well if we let a five year old ride on top of a tank without an adult up there we would be all over the news networks in an hour and not nicely now wouldn't we? Oh yes that would get attention! Even Fox News would express outrage at that.

Ricardo was apparently giving Teela proper grave digging lessons out back. He never dug a grave I was told but how different can it be between a grave and a latrine? If I ate them and waited twelve hours, NOTHING! Pretty sure they were just humoring Windy but I knew it would not work. So I plotted with the blind Albino and the Tiger. Don't ask me! Tammy had taped her eyes up again it seemed. Something was off about Tammy and I knew there was but you try and deal with all this crap and focus on everything? Becky actually liked wearing the Tiger costume I found out, and after she found out that I didn't care if she did and actually liked weird people she put it back on again. Well they did for her. Certain she wanted it on however. Yeah I understood a bit more. No idea about what. She had so many bad memory's in her head it was nice to just embrace her inner wild animal and let those things go. She was so darn cute in it too and they were feeding her well here. She was eating well too and I thought that was a good sign. Eating disorder was a real possibility I had felt before. She actually had a thing for Tigers too it seemed. An odd twist of fate isn't it? Was wondering if the penalty's were the same for unlicensed medical procedures on an animal as a human! Important stuff ya know! Well I was thinking of doing colonoscopy's on this Tiger soon. Had no idea I could do other procedures yet the Dog in me liked poop.

Knowing I was going to be doing all the work later I went looking for Brutus. Get me some sweet Dog-Cock for a while! Did not realize Becky had followed me and watched us till he had already made the tie and I was just a drooling Bitch. She could see I was happy so she did not freak about it but she looked nervous none the less. "It's okay." Breathlessly I growled out. "It is very nice if you decide you ever want it." Sure I understood her issues. Sometimes things that scare us or hurt us normally can be nice or more under the right circumstances. Pain and pleasure are two sides of the same coin and that is true! But also true, a coin is not very thick now is it? Seriously? You're gonna bitch about that? You're just jealous.

However I was certain she was ready to bolt after a few minutes as I could sense her tensing, but then Kimmy walked in and smiled at her nicely. Kimmy just walked over to me and looking at Becky said sweetly. "Here Kitty, Kitty. You can pet the Doggy's while they stand here. They don't mind. No one is being hurt sweety. No one is going to hurt you. Come here." Kimmy's voice was so gentle and compelling. Kinda understood why some may fear Kimmy. Very charismatic Girl. Becky stood there on hands and knees like an animal for a moment but slowly she came over. She was nervous true, but curious. Kimmy stroked her back as Becky sniffed at us and I just thought it was cute of Becky to act like an animal. So I had no clue yet as too what was going on. Like I did anything else? You can know two plus two equals four, but, if you are doing the math in your head and not watching as you cross the busy road you still get SPLAT! Kimmy explained to her simply why we were stuck together in such soothing gentle tones. Yeah she lifted the tails and showed Becky what she could. Becky was in awe of what she saw and looked closely. Very closely. Snickering Kimmy said sweetly still. "Don't get to close though, Becky. They both fart!" We did! Well if you had something that big swelling in you it would push your gas out too. BRRIPT! Becky actually sniffed at it to my amazement! Interesting!

Her choice though! That was the difference now and she was realizing it. She had a choice in everything now. Scared her a bit I think but I understood that and most did too so we were very kind and caring with her. Kimmy sat next to her as she watched. Becky gasped as Brutus finally came out of me and spoke. Her voice shaky as she looked at me and asked. "You had that whole thing inside you?" Oh I would have bigger in me before too long but I nodded smiling. "And you liked it?" WOOF! With a nod. She hugged me. "I love you, Pammy, but you scare me." Her voice was barely audible but I heard it.

"I love you Becky!" Growled to her and really meant it.

Kimmy snickered and said sweetly. "We all love you as well Becky! Just watch out for the Dean however. She has a riding crop collection." The look of horror on Becky's face meant this carpet needed steam cleaning! After a moment Becky was peeing while rolling on the floor laughing. Fear can be funny. Not to be left out Brutus lifted his leg and peed on Kimmy. Well I had lots of times. That pudge loved it! All that hot yellow goodness. He lifted his leg and she scooted under to get it all. SEE! My kinda Girl!

Becky laughing hard said trying to sound serious. "You're all freaks aren't you?" Hey! She was getting it! Yeah it took her a while but it had been hectic so I understood.

Sabrina came in and never batting an eye at what she saw she smiled as she spoke seriously. "You might like to know I've been on the phone with Miss Winters for a bit. She is quite cautious about us taking Becky along with us today so I explained to her we could not watch Becky otherwise. Says it should still be her choice to go though. It may help and it may make things a lot worse she said. We talked. She told me what to watch for if Becky goes. Might have another problem however as it seems that Tammy is just been going around raving about Tiger blood! Honest I have no idea what that's about."

Kimmy now asked gently sounding just curious. "Becky when is your next period due?" Lots of stuff was going on so I understood accidents happen. Not Kimmy's fault here.

But that was not a good question though! How fast Becky's face went from a smile to hatred was astonishing. Becky began bawling so hard as reality came crashing in on her and I was thinking she was having a seizure. "A-a-about N-n-nine m-m-months!" She stammered out. Oh Shit! The Tiger was pregnant!

Kimmy was very upset at her own mistake as she realized it instantly and you could see it on her face as she said almost in tears herself. "I'm so sorry Becky! I Forgot what we heard." You could see the distress on Kimmy's face at her mistake. She truly cared for others. Then very hesitantly Kimmy asked. "Do you want to keep it?"

Kimmy's voice had been gentle. Becky's voice however was demonic and starting to scare ME! "NO! I WANT IT OUT!" She began punching herself in the stomach. Violently and hard. We all went to hold her quickly before she hurt herself and let her cry her pain. A hug is the best way to restrain someone. Kimmy just had to look at me over Becky's shoulder and I understood why so I nodded. Sure I could! Knew I could do it. Sabrina sighed when she got a look. Nice to know they could read each others minds and not just mine! Kimmy got up and went to the wall by the door and pushed a button.

"Nurse Teela, nurse Tammy to surgery!" Kimmy looked at us cutely and shrugged saying. "Operating room is down in the basement." Sabrina looked at her kinda scared now. Kimmy just smiled at her and said. "Like fifty illegal colonoscopy's and you get scared over one abortion?" The ChewToy had a point. Pretty sure her estimate was way low though. However I think it was the thought that they had an operating room here that bothered Sabrina myself, but I was not saying anything. Life is so much easyer if you keep your mouth shut. Hey I never used to shut my mouth and look at my life! Was learning however. Enjoyed where my life was too but it was hectic.

Oh and you human MEN should be thankful some Girls don't shut their mouths! The thing I missed most about being human was sucking cock! True I only had done it twice but I loved it! That thick warm throbbing thing deep in my mouth and the sounds you guys make is priceless! Impossible with floppy lips! Licking a Man off is fun but just not the same. My troubles were all just so earth shattering weren't they?

Becky was both terrified and in shock I think. Which worked fine for us now. Never even struggled as they pushed her onto my back. Oh I felt her trembling up there however. Might have been excitement at the idea of getting it out I guess. She needed my help now and I would do whatever I could for her. Felt so sorry for her knowing some of what she had lived through but a part of the Dog said she was a true friend! Yeah the nose. Loved her as a friend and possible family member. Maybe more! Have you been reading any of this? Not a problem fucking my family! Kimmy led us along a hall to an elevator. This place was absolutely freaking huge. Like a major resort hotel. Over two hundred rooms! Down we went. The two Girls were speaking to her very gently telling Becky she had nothing to be frightened about. Mostly she didn't I thought but what did I know? I was cutting nothing, so no chance of infection. Figured she had, had enough of my milk in her too to guarantee that much. Pain may be possible still but I had ideas about that too. Yes I was taking this seriously and thinking. Hopefully if there was any pain for her it would be no worse then period cramps. They suck sure but they are manageable. My worry as we were led down another hall was could I actually do it successfully. My tongue was amazing sure but would it work. Was it long enough! I kinda knew what I had to do in theory, however I was just not sure how far I would have to go. How big is a womb?

Yes my lack of medical knowledge was a problem for me. Maybe we could get some books for me however. On tape of course! Hey it might be helpful! Do you know where the easiest spot is in the neck to rip the head off? See! Neither did I. Wanted to work on speed and points for style so knowledge may help. Well when head removal becomes an Olympic sport I want the Gold!

Then we went into a room and I thought. OKAY! It was a full operating theater like in a real hospital. State of the art too. Heck yes I was impressed! Maybe we should explore this place and see what else is here one day. Teela, Tammy and Anastasia came in before we even got Becky on the table and things went very bad very fast.

You know I really have to bite Tammy and soon! "Who am I operating on today?" Tammy said quickly bobbing her head. Really? Scared me and I was not the one being operated on! Was not joking when I told you the Albino was crazy! That her eyes were still taped up is what scared the Tiger!

Becky was no longer in shock at least. She was now screaming in absolute terror and trying to escape quickly. Did not blame her! PHUMPH! Tranq dart in the ass. That it even penetrated should have told me something. Frankly I thought Anastasia shot the wrong one as Becky was still trying to get out of the room! Still a very quick draw for an older lady.

Then again? Maybe it wasn't a Tranq. Tammy was sitting on the floor trying to catch her own hands in mere moments. Very strong and quick stuff whatever it was. Considering Tammy could not see a thing I was impressed by her behaviors then. Someone had done a great job of taping her eyes shut for her this time. The staff here were all multi talented and more than helpful.

Teela went to Becky concerned quickly and said gently petting her like she was a real animal. "It's okay Becky Tiger. The blind one is not operating on anyone and if she does not knock it off she may get a really bad colonoscopy. It's okay for you sweety. Pammy likes you a lot and will be very gentle with you. You are such a brave beautiful Tiger. Here Kitty, Kitty." It actually worked. Teela is a natural at that. Something about her put animals at ease.

As Becky got back on the table, by herself this time making it her choice, Anastasia asked gently. "What part of the Tiger are we operating on now?"

The General really needs to invest in major industrial strength Baby gates around here. Windy's voice was cold as she entered. "She has the spawn of Satan in her and it must come out!" Thought she was being silly at the time but now I wonder! That Girl knows things she should not! EVER! Becky was just a nodding in agreement and I farted. Windy spun on me! "No pooping in the operating room!" Like that was gonna prevent it. It was so close! Positive I could not blame this one on the Discovery channel though so I blame it on the Sci-fi network now! Windy went to the head of the Table and began petting Becky's hair sweetly saying nice childish things. That child was truly amazing!

And you know what I say? FUCK REALITY!

The scaryest thing is you have read nothing yet! Oh it gets worse. Much much worse!

Anastasia only smiled at Windy's presence and her outburst as she quickly got the ultrasound equipment ready. Disturbed me a lot! "She reminds me so much of Kimmy when she was that age!" The scary sweet old Lady said. Kimmy blushed as we all looked at her! Oh I try not to think about it personally. Once Becky was exposed the Nanny looked at me. "It won't be easy to do Pammy. You will have to curve your tongue and push through the cervix if you can get the leverage! It won't want to open either. A kind of mucus plug in there. Once through you are going to have to stretch and scrape around with your tongue as far as you can. That should be enough to abort the Satan Child if nothing else." Windy now smiled up at her. And you wonder why I found that sweet Lady scary? Humoring the Princess may have been a smart move but still? Not sure anyone was! "I will try to locate the Devil's Child with the ultrasound. If she is not very far along however it may be difficult to find. There will be a bit of blood most likely, Pammy. Like a heavy period at least."

Tammy screamed sounding drunk from where she sat on the floor. "Save the Tiger's blood and we can drink it later!" There may have been snickering. Not saying for sure. It was a twisted time.

Now I did look up at Anastasia curiously though. Could be important to know this. Her sweetly smiled response was. "Retired Military Doctor." And professional mind reader. See both good information to have.

Maybe I should have gone to med school I thought once done. My first abortion was a resounding success you see. Okay sort of. Well read! Becky bit her own lip as I got close to her Girlhood and she could feel my hot breath on her cute Tiger privates. Told me to do it still and I was gentle. Not a fool however and my nose was pressed against her clit just in case. Orgasms are the best painkiller ever! Got a Migraine Ladys? Do not grab the Tylenol, grab the Vibrator! Slowly I stuck my tongue inside her vagina feeling around. Keeping it as nonsexual as I could. Hardest thing I ever did! Found the Cervix easy though. Usually I was just rabid in there but this time I was careful and felt what was there. Kinda cool really. Cervix was tough but I pushed through. The problem for me was, by going slow, I tasted every single individual flavor. There are many. No joke as a Dogs tongue is something amazing! Ha, ha, ha! Sorry just read! Oh there were different flavors in there too. Past the Cervix was WOW! Took a lot but I controlled my instinct and desire.

As I twisted my tongue scraping slow, Anastasia said. "I have it. A little higher Pammy. To the left. Just knock it loose and it will come out." Yeah easy for her to say as it was not her tongue in there doing the work. So I pushed as hard as I could though. When I pulled back out there was blood. A bit of it. Was tasty. Tiger Blood is yummy.

Sabrina finally asked the question I dreaded after a minute as she had been watching closely for no reason I care to mention. "Where's the fetus?" Crap. BURP! Well I didn't mean to do it! So I got stares! Lots!

Becky raised her head and looking at me asked nervous. Not sure which way she was gonna go there. "Did you just eat my Baby?" Oh I could not lie to her! Really I did not intend too do it but it just happened. Slowly I nodded sadly. Linda Blair imitation. That voice sent chills. "Good now it will be shit just like it's Father!" Our Tiger had some anger issues it seems. Scary anger issues. Could be fun still. Never know!

Windy patted her head cutely and her voice grew cold. "Yes Kitty! The Demon Spawn is poop soon!" Like I said about kids before. They know way too much! That said I will deny the existence of a cup with Tiger Blood in it to my grave! The Tiger got herself a diaper put on. Understandable really. She would bleed for a while after all. Instant period! Strong one as well. Did not get upset about it. Anastasia explained it to her very medically yet nicely. That Woman does a mean diaper let me tell you.

Then I got a Tiger shoved on my back. She could still probably walk but I liked being ridden and why take a chance! Sabrina snickering said. "Come on Charlie, I mean Tammy!" Kimmy helped get the Albino upstairs. Okay she carried her. Tammy fell out of her chair when they sat her down she was so out of it still. Didn't feel a thing either.

So you may ask why in the Hell they let her drive an hour later? Valid question I felt as well. So why you may wonder didn't I ask it? Well I was afraid to know the answer! Sure I questioned their sanity! Everyone's! Even my own! When we were getting ready to go Teela shoved Becky in the back seat, grabbed Windy, jumped in herself yelling. "Gun this Bitch!" And Tammy did! So much for a tank parade or my nice plan. It had been a nice plan. Maybe I could use it some other day. The dumb Mayor had denied the Tank parade anyway. To short of notice he said. What a party pooper. So we probably saved a life or two this way! Well when that Girl found out there was no parade and they did not let her go with her Beast there would be blood shed! Theirs!

Tammy laughed manically the whole way into the city too. Well I think she was practicing. Changing tone and pitch to see what sounded best. Okay I hoped. We pulled into the driveway of the address we had been given at eleven forty five and a very cute short familiar Blonde pudge ran out of the nice green house looking very upset. Almost in tears she whined. "We can't have a party now! My Mom is making me watch my little Sister for the weekend. It's not fair! They always do this to me! She was supposed to go with them but they changed their minds at the last minute." Looked like her world was ending! Tears were definitely on the way the poor Girl.

Teela just smiled and snickered at her. "How old is your little Sister?" True, we had one as well didn't we?

The Blonde looked flustered but said all whiny. "She's five! What does it matter? We can't have fun! The weekend is ruined!" Teela held up Windy who waved so cutely.

"We have our own! This is her Highness Windy. The new Princess of the World!" Sure I was good with it. Think the rest were too. Teela said to her little Sister. "Want to go play with this Girl's Sister? What's your Sister's name?"

"Um Emily. I'm Krissy." She still looked confused. Tasty to I remembered now. Yummy plump Kitty on her.

Teela had an idea and went with it. "Windy want to go play with Emily?" Windy was nodding so Teela set her down on the ground outside of the car.

Windy looked up at Krissy smiling cutely and asked. "You got shovels?" Krissy nodded. "Two?" Krissy nodded again. "What does your Sister like to play?"

Krissy looked terrified at this but spoke. "Rabid Barbies!" Windy's laughter was diabolical at best. What's not to like about Rabid Barbies! She ran in the house. In a panic Krissy added. "Don't let the…." Too late!

Becky went "Umph!" As the big Saint Bernard just leapt into the car and landed on her. It rapidly began licking the Tigers face happily. A very friendly Fluff Monster.

Kimmy just snickered ignoring things like they happened all the time. Did pretty much! "Is the pool heated?" Krissy just nodded in heavy shock. "Nobody else here yet? Let's go Girls."

Sheila Winters pulled in the driveway at that moment and my Girls looked at her worryed now. "I'm the Chaperon!" Miss Winters said so sweetly with a smile as she got out of the car. "This is my Sister's house, Krissy is my Niece." She was smiling big time now! Oh I had known it was a set up. No! Did not care but still. Everyone had tasted great and I am always up for second helpings! "If anyone asks. We are an official study group!" Yeah studying the effects of multiple orgasms on college Girls. Valid medical research! Honest! Since I had been skipping my Raping I mean Counseling sessions I now knew she wanted me as she quickly groped me! Pretty sure this was mostly Miss Winter's idea but Krissy was truly upset thinking it wouldn't happen. Maybe she had few friends in high school or they had gone away to other colleges I did not know. Sweet Pudge. A van pulled up out front and about twenty Girls I recognized slightly piled out. The van left laying rubber the instant the doors closed. The Woman driving the van was screaming she was free the whole way down the street! Might be a bad sign.

Tammy squealed at the new Girls grinning and pointing in the backseat. "We have a Tiger!" That car was surrounded in a second or less. Once we got the fluffy Dog off Becky those Girls still went Aww a lot even if she was not a real Tiger yet. I didn't say nothin. Ignore that! She was so adorable. The costume fit her very well now. Frankly I hoped someone had actually altered it last night. Darn right I got lots of hugs and thank you's quick. I'd just growl at these Girl's and they would get shivers. Such fun! Still they all introduce themselves to us and each other. The College was not huge but still kids from across the state and other places came and few knew each other yet. Hey that was what the Dog was all about! Love and friendship! How many friends do you have? And I don't mean on social media! If you were in a car accident and hospitalized how many would come see you? Yes I know it is a sad thing but you can have more. Trust me on that. Be friendly and they will come! (Okay not you Steve! No one wants to hang out in your Grandmother's basement. With Grandma.)

Kimmy was sweet and smart and knew we could not eat this family out of house and home. That she knew we not only could but would was a great sign of her leadership skills! So Kimmy made some calls. Pizzas arrived about forty minutes later. Forty of them! From ten different places. One for each girl and a few for me. It was a nice two story house and looked like this family had money but still I could eat. Thirty of us! Frankly I felt it was not set up properly. Well they had no where near enough food to feed us here. Did Miss Winters plan on ordering some? Would be a very expensive raping for her then. How much would you pay for a good savage raping? Some of you would too! I'd bite Kimmy but I do that all the time so how would she know I was upset with her? This was Miss Winters idea. She loved her Niece and knew Krissy had few friends so she wanted to help the Girl. Well her Mother was the prosecuting attorney and had put many kids her age in jail. Problem was her parents were clueless about their children's lives. They had almost no friends. Miss Winters had decided she was finally going to help that. With Kimmy's help! Tall reddish wooden fence around the backyard for privacy was perfect for nudity and raping however. Hey I might be delusional at times but nudity was guaranteed! Some may be naked all weekend!

Big driveway too. Might seem unimportant but it was actually useful. It was very warm weather lately but the forecast was for a big change tonight. Bathing suits were donned and Girls got wet once done eating. Okay wetter. They all knew why they were here and were expecting savage rapings! OH, I could smell them all and I was drooling. They were all hoping for a weekend to remember and the time of their lives. Pretty sure most did have one! Hey I was horny too. It was a big pool. Krissy seemed a bit upset once both Dogs were in the pool. The Saint Bernard was a female named Heidi! Fun Dog. What? You have something against Dog on Dog Lesbian sex? Okay I won't tell you about it then! Yes there was some. Not passing that up! She was a cute Fluff Pudge and I made her howl! Kimmy said not to worry about the Dog hair as she would have the filters cleaned by professionals on Monday to get all the hair out. Weather was still unseasonably warm which was nice. Late September and eighty three out! It's important! So remember that. Hunting began quickly!

That Goth girl hanging onto the side of the deep end while she treaded water could scream! Black bikini bottom was a tie on. Can hold my breath for a while it seems. Long enough to rape her good! She tried to escape but the walk around the pool was too wet to get a grip as she clawed at it and no one would help her. After her fourth orgasm a couple Girls finally grabbed her arms and held them. NO! Why would they pull her out? Just did not want her to drown! Bikini's came off easy and I was hungry! Miss Winters looked so darn amazing in her bikini. Looked better when I got it off her. She's nice naked! Okay there are probably a few people in the Universe I would not want to see naked but the rest of you? I'd look!

Probably should tell you this. Okay I certainly don't have to tell you watching sex gets you horny. Well some heavy petting was going on around there as well. Even Teela! With her Sister! Many were watching that one. True Sabrina may have teaching her how. Frankly I hoped Tammy got it all on video as I wanted to watch later. Yes the Blind Girl had the video camera! It was hers!

The RAPING, I mean PARTY was in full swing when a few hours later a wave of sudden silence brought instant terror to the party goers. All heads turned toward the house as Windy came out riding Becky with little Emily walking next to her. All looking so serious. So everyone heard what was said! Even Miss Winters who would have pooped herself if not for the recent colonoscopy. Hey I had frozen in my tracks over a non-albino redhead pudge with nice bouncy booby's. Windy spoke sweetly patting Becky. "Emily? This is my spare Beast. My royal Beast is over there making another kill. My Beast loves to hunt! Look at all the freshly killed prey!" The raw emotion and pride in that Girls voice might have been the scariest part. Yes I did look around and it was impressive. Looked like a slaughter ground or something.

They were walking past a naked drooling brunette laying on the ground as Emily said just nodding. "I see what you mean Princess. I'll get the shovels. We can bury the bodys back by the fence." Not sure which semi-naked Girl did but one farted and everyone heard! The silence was terrifying. We watched the five year old's go to the shed get two shovels and head for the back fence happy. Oh screw this! Now I hunted for the one who farted! Found her. MINE! Oh the screams were glorious!

Well why not? Shit! They saw everything already! They were digging graves and enjoying it. Other than the nudity it could look like I was killing them the way they squealed, screamed, and moaned flailing their arms about begging for their lives as I was ferocious between their legs. And that last loud gasp! Sounded like a death rattle to me! You lot are naive. I suggest you put the book down and watch three hours of the best of the Discovery channel! Miss Winters asked those two Girls later what they thought was going on earlier? Scared of the answer I think. They both said the Beast was hunting like animals do on TV. When I was five I would have said the same thing. It was not like we were making out first. Not a penis in sight either. I'd ponce, they'd scream, looked like a savage Beast attack after all so what would they think? Well you're a pervert! It only lacked lots of blood. Still some blood as few liked it very rough. Even the Discovery channel did not cover this kind of behavior in nature so they did not think it was anything but. Frankly I don't think Porn Hub covered this even! Might be problems when they start Sex Ed but that was years away! They just played Rabid Barbies for Gods sake! Oh you've never played Rabid Barbies? You lead a sad, sad life! Bet you never even stripped your GI Joe's either. Stripped your Sister's Barbie's though! Yes I know who you are. I see all.

Fine! Becky was with them and said they seldom looked over even. A few fist pumps and high fives may have taken place at the sounds of a particularly savage kill! But nothing else. They had shovels and holes to dig. Becky had told me she would go keep an eye on them before the rapings began earlier and I understood. She needed time and it was good for her.

A little after five Anastasia not so surprisingly walked into the back yard in her granny dress and yelled. "Supper is ready!" Startled me for a moment I admit. If my nose was not full of pussy juice I would have smelled the food. Of course I was snorting it! It's Pussy juice! Besides! We were outta Tiger Blood! They had a big catered buffet set up out in the driveway. Very impressive spread too. The large kitchen staff at the Compound loved a challenge. Not fools they had burgers and nuggets as well but fantastic extravagant foods also. The Girls were all amazed. Me too. Most even put their suits back on or at least a towel. Windy and Emily came out with Becky who had been staying with them. Becky was not ready to join the hunting yet and had said as much. Offered to watch the kids for us instead. She showed no signs of any disturbance by what was going on around her and I should have understood! She was already changing at that point. Almost freaked when a Cop Car came by and slowed. That plump red head with the nice tits waved to them enthusiastically! Her nice naked breasts still just a flopping around. They waved and left. There were other half naked Girls in the driveway! Not just boobs! We were all Girls! Go the public pool and look in the Girls changing room and see how many naked Girls you can see before some one hits you with a Taser!

"And what have you two cute young Girls been up too?" Anastasia asked the five year old's so sweetly. She understood.

Windy gestured toward the back yard.

Emily spoke happily. "We played Rabid Barbies for a while then we dug graves! Want to see our Cemetery?" Oh I suppose you never dug a Cemetery either? What a sheltered life you lead! Go find a shovel!

Anastasia laughed. "Sounds wonderful. Let's eat while the food is warm first and I can look at your Cemetery afterwards Girls." We did eat with very little peeing. Anastasia was having fun now I think as we played int her delusions. She explained the General had told the police to not bother the party or he would declare martial law. The Mayor had pissed him off and he was gonna get revenge! They were driving by every half hour or so to make sure we were safe that was all. Show the neighbors they were aware of us and not interfering.

Was a nice neighborhood and bloodcurdling screams may possibly be reported. My neighbors never would! Oh I had not forgotten them either! On my list still the Bastards!

It was a very fantastic meal however and everyone enjoyed it. Well until Becky died! That kinda sucked a bit! Put a damper on the festivity's.

Well I had to assume Becky saw the muzzle flash before she leapt in the path of the bullet meant for Kimmy. I'm afraid of the truth to be honest. She had only gotten a little milk. How she knew the bullet was aimed at Kimmy is beyond me. Then again the shit Tammy and I could do was beyond me as well. It tore through almost the center of Becky's chest shattering ribs and still struck Kimmy high in the chest by the shoulder where it actually penetrated her skin knocking her backwards and down with food and blood flying. Girls dove for cover. Anastasia spun dropped to a knee pulled her cannon and fired into a tree in the direction of the shot about a half mile away. Yeah right I know what your thinking. A pistol could never be that accurate at those distances. Well hers was a fucking cannon and she had very impressive bullets too. Probably an alien design on those bullets. Probably in case she had to shoot me too! She did not need to hit the sniper either now, just make him stop shooting and move! Believe me on this! That tree was definitely fucked up! Might have been Alien explosive bullets.

Fast I went to my Becky Tiger in absolute terror with my heart breaking and lay my head on her shattered chest tears starting to flow. The damage she sustained was quite extensive, massive amounts of blood pooling under her and I thought I was watching her die in my paws. Her heart was still beating but barely and growing weaker. Mine was definitely breaking in half! She did not have enough of my drug in her to heal this much damage! My despair here was tremendous. She needed more drug! WAIT! Could do something about that now couldn't I? Windy was just there fast, like she just appeared, looking at me proudly and I had a great idea. What's another Illegal medical procedure. My claws go through metal so her chest was nothing. Windy was nodding her approval like she knew what I was doing. Did not have to go deep but I needed to find a good one and the bullet hole was too damaged for some reason. Then I slashed my own shoulder. Blood was everywhere as I pointed and Windy got it fast! Might have known before hand but that idea scares me too. Maybe the worst transfusion ever but it worked as I leaned down and that little Girl got her hands between us and held vein and artery together so my very life blood was pumping into Becky's body now. Windy was the only one with hands small enough to do it so I was glad she was there now. Hey I had to be close to Becky so there was no room for bigger hands. Felt Becky's heart stop but knew the brain was still alive. Someone gets shot through the heart or their head ripped off they all say he felt no pain as death was instantaneous!

Bullshit! The brain is still working for a minute. Knowing this I closed my eyes and concentrated hard feeling the connection being made.

Also I was silently apologizing for my anger at Mrs. Gonzales TV viewing habits. Sabrina was the first one tending to Kimmy. Whether she understood Becky was beyond her or not is unclear. Some of us just reacted and did what had to be done, consequences be damned! Perhaps she had written Becky off or just had tremendous faith in her little Sister and me! Kimmy was hit true but not bad enough to die at least. That the bullet even penetrated her skin at all was totally astounding to me later. No time to think of anything then. Just save my Tiger! MY TIGER!

Anastasia had explained earlier that morning that the Tranq darts she had used were of alien metal and origin. The General had gotten them in case you see. To use on me as well I am sure! Oh I understood his concerns for Kimmy and they had helped us so far. He knew I was no threat anymore. That said this bullet probably had alien origins as well I already suspected.

Then I felt the miracle happening beneath me and knew someone was going to be pissed. Just hoped she was no longer suicidal! As we both healed I pushed away fast leaping backwards twelve feet. Hey I was trying to save her not absorb her. Knew if we stayed connected I would have. She was not strong enough to resist yet if ever. As I looked up I saw tears in Windy's eyes where she still knelt beside Becky. She pointed and in a voice so cold that five year old Girl passed a death sentence and EVERYONE knew it as she said. "BEAST KILL!" That little Girl was full of love too! Still a five year old so blood-lust was there as well! Ask a Kindergarten Teacher.

Now I was just a blur of tan fur as I tore out of there! Nothing mattered to me except my Princess's wish! After all I was her Beast and her command was MY law and would be carried out with extreme prejudice! Yes, I was the five year old's EXECUTIONER!

Finding the tree was easy. The scent he left easier. Did not even question my thoughts and feelings as I hunted. So he had a motorcycle. Big fucking deal! WINDY HAD A BEAST!!!! Caught him in less then ten miles too. It was a fast motorcycle and he could drive but still I was a ProtoDog and he had to swerve around traffic! Sniper rifles are expensive however and long so carrying one on a motorcycle whipping through the city would be noticeable wouldn't it? He foolishly broke it down and stored it in his bike before he ran. That was his first mistake. Second mistake was going in a straight line. Okay his only mistake was pulling the freaking trigger. True he did not have a clue what was coming after him now, no one did at the time but that is later, which told me loads. Oh I was on his ass before he saw me in his mirror. Pounce like lightning and we went down violently his motorcycle breaking in half. Think he was going down anyway as he got very shaky when he finally spotted me in his mirrors. No idea why. I am just stunning and svelte. Cars were swerving out of the way and people were fleeing as the heavy bike slid across the pavement with us sparks a flying. It was awesome!

He was alive when we finally stopped. The bike wedged under a BMW. Not alive for long from the looks of things but breathing at the moment! Grabbing him by the collar of his jacket I just began dragging him back. Who cared if he had another weapon! Like it would do anything other then piss me off more! Had to be careful as I wanted him alive when we got back. No idea why at the time I thought that but I did. Sure we could question him but seriously? They were Dickheads not total idiots! This guy probably did not even know who gave the order let alone why! Still I wanted him alive for some reason. Took a half hour to get back and he never woke. Maybe he never would. That crack in his helmet was probably not a good sign. By the halfway point I did not care if he was alive anymore. Knew why I was bringing him back! My Pup had worked hard digging graves. Be a shame not to use at least ONE right? See I was a good parent and wanted my Pup to be proud and happy!

As I walked up dragging my Prey I saw that Doctor Petrov was already here and standing there just smiling at me hands on hips shaking her head. Damn she got here quick! College was close however and she was staying there, so not really a big deal. Anastasia may be a former Doctor but had no equipment here and the college did. Ellsbeth was smiling so I kept calm knowing no one was dead. YET! Kimmy was sitting up in a metal chair, her arm in a sling. Kimmy smiled and waved at me. Sabrina was sitting on Tammy who was struggling still which was impressive. No idea! Okay I had some and we really need to put a shock collar on that Pup or something strong! Doctor Petrov saw where I looked. "It was this way when I got here. The best I can figure is she asked for salad tongs and this is preventive. The rest of the Girls are in back worshiping her Highness!" There was humor in her voice so I was not too worryed now. She pointed however but not at the house. Now I was nervous!

Becky was just bent and licking herself. Yes there! Like you wouldn't? Windy came out alone not looking happy and nodded at Anastasia.

Apparently Anastasia had reloaded her cannon with regular bullets. Alien ones are hard to come by but she had some. Zombies, Chupacabra's, and possibly Sasquatch were in the area after all! Anastasia stood as Windy came over and told this future corpse why he was about to die! Scary stuff came out of the mouth of that Babe! Ellsbeth looked nervous at those words. But I felt so great! Windy told of her love for me and the world. A barely perceptible nod and Anastasia unloaded! Kneecaps, elbows, groin, head in that order. Probably did him a favor. Some extensive brain damage I figured as he had made no intelligent sound. Now I picked him up in my jaw and headed for the backyard. Nice grave they had dug but definitely not deep enough. They were only five year old's! How deep could they go. Easy fix however. Oh I like my paws! Eight feet should work. Body in. Eat. Fresh liver is tasty so never waste it! Squat over hole. Shit on corpse. Had an audience however. Oh now I started something and they wanted to pay their last respects as well. Yes I know lots of guys would kill to have that many pretty Girls piss and shit on them just to see their pussy's. This guy died to get it. Shame he could not enjoy. Windy patted my head as we both watched.

Doctor Petrov approved of me. Windy too! Still we terrified her. The Doctor told me. "You redeem me you beautiful Girl! Not sure you make up for all the bad I have done but you have made me feel something I seldom have. PRIDE! As for the shooter? Probably not one of O'Donnell's men. Still possible I guess trying to get at the General but Kimmy has lots of enemy's herself who would rather see her dead then reappear as well. How did you know how to save the Tiger, Pammy?"

So I mused a moment. Hard to talk so I wanted the best words. "She bleeding bad. Hospital would do IV add blood. Mom watch true ER shows. I thought transfusion. Windy helped." Doctor Petrov nodded at that proudly, fully understanding what had to have happened. Looked impressed by us!

Scared bad still she asked. "They said you jumped away from Becky like you were terrified. Why?" She asked that sounding very curious as well however. Her eyes still sparkling.

Okay I snickered. "You see movie Akira?" She nodded. "Would have absorbed her." It was all I could come up with. If you have not seen it go rent it now! Becky would have become a part of me and I knew it as fact. How or why was well beyond me.

She knelt and hugged me with such amazement and wonder in her eyes. "Pammy? I have done horrible things in my life and I know I have no right to ask for anything but will you please absorb me one day." Knew deep down I would do it and nodded both of us near tears. Hey the Monster always kills its creator in the end. Ask Victor von! Well I hugged her for now.

Windy came over and motioned me to move. She looked the Doctor in the eyes and the Doctor lowered her gaze. Ellsbeth was shaking as Windy raised her Scepter over the Doctor's head. Most watching grew tense as the Doctor never moved and they had no idea what that Scepter could do. Windy passed sentence! Gently touching each of the Doctor's shoulders with the most powerful weapon in the Universe. Windy's voice was gentle but loud. "I dub thee Lady Bitch!" This was astonishing really as it showed Windy had forgiven her. We were good! Even Lady Bitch! No one was arguing with the Princess!

The sky was quickly growing dark after all were done eating and the buffet had left as it was almost eight by now. To cap it off it began to sprinkle filling the

Girl's with sorrow at the distant rumbles. Water and electricity are a dangerous combination. Still it was almost eight and night would be here soon.

It was still a party after that however as the Princess said it would be still even inside so some Raping still went on inside the house as the rain finally came with the night. Gentle at first but I felt it's intensity building. Needed it really as it had been a fairly dry month last month. Well maybe we didn't need super thunderstorms. Big nasty ones rolled in not that long after both supper and the funeral. Severe storm warnings were issued the radio said after we were inside for a while. Okay it was very consensual sex for a change. A Girl would come make out with me and I would follow her to a bedroom I assumed was Krissy's. Lots of stains on her bed now! Bet she did not change those sheets for a week, as I would have fun with their bodys and they mine. Very pleasant even. Oh I got some too from a few. Most were watching Monster movies and playing Rabid Barbies with the two five year old's while I was busy. Not those lame hack and slash movies either. The only thing monstrous about them is the characters stupidity and maybe the acting! No! These had real Monsters in them. Cheesy mostly but so much fun and it was even cute when the Girls began cheering for the Monsters. Think Windy started it. Such love I felt from these humans. Knew that I was a Monster and was damn proud of it! Let's hear it for Monster Rights! The storm itself was raging outside but we were safe inside for the moment I felt.

Famous last words? Hoped not.

These storms were absolute Monsters as well! Building such intensity while moving in and we did not have a clue as they turned the radio off and the Movies were not on local networks. Hurricane force winds were gusting out there with lots of lightning. We knew almost nothing yet of the terrible damage and devastation it was leaving throughout the area as it came through building in intensity! Sounded bad enough so no one even looked outside. Kept checking the Weather Channel but all they showed were episodes of "Ice Haulers" and "Hurricanes of the 1800's"! just like you can no longer get music on MTV you can no longer get weather on the Weather Channel. Still the air itself felt alive to me and some others. Windows rattled and as no one wanted to get close to them we huddled close on the living-room floor. Tammy seemed to grow weird as the storms drew close, well weirder than normal and I wondered if storms perhaps frightened her! Felt her flinching with every bolt of lightning. Thought nothing of it. The Rapes had ceased and it was a Cuddle Fest.

The power went out in the house just after midnight as the storm only got worse outside and I got nervous quickly. Without the TV you could hear it well and it sounded scary bad. Girls seemed tired however and were not to scared as I wore most out during the day so it was not that I sensed. Still something bothered me.

Some Girls where asleep already Before long all were out and I lay there felling odd but not wanting to wake them.

Well they were asleep until the bright sound shook the entire house like an earthquake or nuclear explosion not much later. Felt as the house shook. No one was sleeping now! Screaming a bit? Sure! Blinding light and massive sound at the same time. So bright and loud! It hit so very close. Most thought it struck the house or a tree in the yard as they were all talking at once. Sure felt like it might have. We cautiously looked outside at the trees in the backyard in time to see the lightning strike down a second time in the exact same spot blinding all of us. Damn that is bright! We could tell where the first bolt struck as that was the spot where Windy was just standing! So lightning struck twice!

Windy!!!

Feeling no fear my mind was racing. What the hell was she doing out there in the storm? Other then getting struck by lightning that is?! The ground around her was scorched before the second strike so I knew where the first strike had hit. And Windy was still standing. Looking up.

One Girl, I think Emily, said slightly concerned after the second bolt and our vision returned. "That can't be good for her." Another added. "Her hair is gonna be a disaster!" Another said excited. "Makeover time!" Practical bunch of Girls we had here! She was still standing after the two hits and we could see again so no one panicked. The ground around that little Girl had been scorched very bad before the second strike and even worse now! No one could hear what Windy was shouting up at the sky above with all the noise from the wind, rain, and golf-ball sized hail but she was definitely shouting something and not nicely! That was one angry child out there! Third strike! That is very bright! Girls all rapidly grabbed sunglasses! Looked to me like little Windy and God were having a not so nice discussion at the time and I felt pretty darn sure God was losing. Another dozen direct hits we watched and Windy was not talking anymore as she just had a disgusted look on her face. She had said her piece it seemed and turned away with one last hand gesture heading for the house. She flipped God the bird! Everyone held their breath at that but I thought good for her. What was God gonna do? Throw another bolt?

My Pup! Felt such Pride about her!

Hey! I did not want to know what she said either as quite frankly it all scared me! That was one intense five year old and I heard the shit she had said at other times. Loved her!

She had some real anger issues too it seemed but I understood her anger! Far too well. It was a righteous anger! Not for herself but FOR the World!

Girls threw themselves on the floor just prostrating themselves in the dark as she came in through the sliding glass doors like nothing just happened. She was not wet either. These Girls had no idea what they just witnessed but knew it was something awesome. Windy was a kind Princess and went among her peasants touching each of them with a gentle smile thanking them for coming to her Coronation. Was that what had just happened? Did God make her Princess or Queen? Then again maybe he tried to stop her and just failed! Had no idea. Had not felt like he was happy. They jumped at Windy's touch however and we saw sparks fly as each Girl was touched. Static I guessed. Could be denial on my part! Hey it was dark so sparks were visible. Well until Windy's Scepter began to glow gently for her. She set it on the coffee table now and snuggled with us. All gentle smiles since coming in. Could feel her joy now. The memory of that anger on her face as she shouted at God helped me know she would rule well!

They all wanted to be by me however. Not easy but we managed. The three plumpest under me, Kimmy, Sabrina, and the Goth girl, a couple on me and the rest all against me so I was freaking warm sniffing Goth farts all night.

Were else would my nose be? Very fragrant!

CHAPTER 2 BECKY TIGER
Sunday September 26th

Windy had peed on me in the night but I didn't mind. She was my Pup! Had drank a lot of rainwater probably as it had been coming down hard while she shouted at the sky! Did not worry either. She may have even done it on purpose which scared me I admit. Nothing sexual however! Had she only laid claim to me? Perhaps? Well I did not think she wanted to claim that stinky Goth Pudge. Had gotten her as well. It had been talked about, far too much, well when I was not raping them they had to do something, how if I peed on something it belonged to me and she was only five! Yes with God like power it seemed! Hey I would wear her scent gladly however. Make this Goth wear it too! Might even add some of my own. Windy was five and had been through a lot of shit though so it may have only been an accident and I loved her so much in such a short time! She was naked again. You get struck by lightning fifteen times in a row and see if your clothes are still there! Sure they were cinders by strike three. Don't you have a clue about Science? If not for the rain we could have gotten her a diaper from the car too. These Girls stunk however. So many different farts to smell. Canine paradise! It is a Dog thing! Nasty or nice does not matter. It is the intensity that counts! Ever catch your Dog chewing on your shoes that stunk so bad last night you almost put them outside? The St. Bernard was with us too and sniffing a lot as well. Laying with Becky Tiger. Tammy was the only one awake as I saw her moving to the chair in the gloom. That white skin of hers meant I had no trouble seeing it was her. Figured it wasn't a ghost! To white! Have I mentioned she was a left-handed Lesbian Albino? Yes she was left-handed all right! Should have known she was up to something though. Did not even connect it to her at first when a Girl got up and left the room. To many fart smells perhaps. High on Methane! About two minutes later that Girl was yelling. "Where the hell is the toilet paper?"

Krissy got up and went looking confused. Sounded more confused when she spoke. "Where did all the toilet paper go! We had lots yesterday!" Great! Girls were all panicking now. Highly understandable. Hey if you need to wipe and there is none do you just pull your pants up? Does it itch later?

Sleepy Teela just smiled and shoved me saying sweetly. "You heard them Toilet Paper you're needed in the bathroom." Teela loved me I knew. Several Girls snickered at that. They were okay with that and had to go too, perhaps! Well I sure was HAPPY. The life of a ProtoDog is hard! Almost all had to shit too. If they didn't I helped. Such flavors! Did not want to raise Krissy's parents water bill either! Not one of them flushed. Did not need too either. No one even cared how all the toilet paper had gotten in Krissy's bedroom closet later but I figured it out! Felt it was Tammy's way of apologizing to me. Maybe to all. Krissy went to get clean clothes on and had found it. Power was on again at least. Had to shit myself finally so I went out back. We hadn't filled in all the holes and with the foot of water in them looked like toilets to me so I pooped in one then filled them all up. Could not leave that in the yard. Enjoyed the hospitality and pooping on the lawn was no way to repay it!

Krissy said as she watched her voice hysterical and squeaky, having come out as well and now looking at the graves in near tears. There were five and they were big. "My Mom is gonna flip!" Well we could not have that now could we? Still watching that Girls butt get spanked was a thought! Very nice butt! Maybe her Mom still would.

Miss Winters came over and put an arm around her Niece's shoulders tenderly. Looking at me but nicely she said. "Tell your Mom it's an early Christmas present kiddo. Let her know we all helped. New flower beds or some gardens for spring! She loves flowers." That would work very good Krissy said with relief. Her eyes were so bright now. It was a pretty yard and they would be a fine addition. Nicely spaced and easy to access Windy had made fine choices so I went and made them look pretty for her. Least I could do. Kimmy said she would have a gift card sent to Krissy's Mom as well from the garden store for the wonderful use of her Daughter. Sure! I knew she meant it. Had used that Girl well too. Teeth marks on her tushy proved it! Wished I could have seen the look on Krissy's Mother's face when she read it and that was what it said! Did get a thank you card back that said anytime! Well after what happens later. Took Kimmy a while to send it.

It had been a huge storm last night and the world was in shut down outside. We were watching the news in the morning and the devastation had been a lot. The footage of flooding and devastation were awe inspiring. Branches from the trees out back were just everywhere in the yard. Not necessarily small ones either. Big perfectly round scorch mark in the grass where Windy had stood. No idea what to do about that! Maybe decorative stone circle. Girls just began cleaning up the yard by hauling brush to the curb. It was cooler outside today and I would have worn a sweater if I did not already have a fur coat on. Fall was here finally. Those pudge Girls all looked so adorable in sweaters I wanted to just eat them again!

May have but I suddenly realized Becky was not here however and I quickly grew scared. She was here when we woke up so she could not have gone that far, right? Well I knew her mind was in a fragile spot before even yesterday! The violence of the storm may have triggered something. Then again I was certain she, like Kimmy, knew she had died! That her and I were now linked in a way that was unbreakable for all time. Now I was afraid of losing her somehow. Did not think suicide was possible now but after Drake the thought she may just go off and be alone in the wilderness somewhere scared me. Had done something to her head and knew she may want some time alone. Any Girl who enjoyed being a Tiger was my kinda Girl however and I wanted to keep her around! Yeah right? Sorry that was a lie! The pain in my heart at the thought of her away from me was so strong! Maybe too strong! Sometimes it sucks to be a Dog.

Began sniffing for her quick in the driveway confusing myself as I was thinking saving her life might be a problem for me yet. Hard to pick up her scent now for some reason however and that bothered me till I realized why. She smelled almost like me now! Oh WOW! Made me very nervous in some totally different ways however! Out of the yard. Sniff more in the road. It had to be here somewhere! BINGO! Found the New Tiger scent and by the direction I immediately knew where she was going. Understood why she left now! Felt like a fool I had not suspected this immediately.

Apparently Tammy also understood as she had watched me closely. Yeah the Blind Girl watched me! Had been all over the place but she was always facing me. That should have told me loads. No idea why she had the keys to the car or was smiling either. She still could not see as her eyes were securely taped and I could see that much. The roads were so full of debris! Still got in the car with her! In spite of being blind we pulled up in front of what was left of Becky's old house without incident. Never hit a branch or downed tree. There were lots of them on the road that we had to swerve around too. Missed them all! Had been a big storm and city crews were out cleaning on a Sunday! Made me nervous still. Scared to ask I guess but knew I had too!

"Can you see?" Growled at her needing to know almost fearing the answer. Okay there was no almost! Scared me bad!

Smiling Tammy said with a sweet chuckle and much awe in her voice. "Not a fucking thing Pammy! But God help me I know where everything is around me! In every direction too! So bizarre but so freaking cool! Can't read a book but the world around me is fabulous now! No color either but graphic detail so accurate, like some kind of fantastic sonar or radar!" Sure I kinda knew how it felt you see as I could sense things around me as well. Not like that but hey, I could sense the pure joy in her as well. Now blind she could see better than ever. Her voice now gentle she said while petting me. "Call for our Tiger Pammy." For a blind Albino she was smart! A bit pasty but so hot naked and lovable. Tasty as well.

Knew Becky wasn't in the house however as soon as we pulled up. Rather obvious really. Nothing was in the house. Except that big ass tree! It had been a really big one and that house was nothing but rubble now. Tree came up roots and all tore out of the ground and slammed down on the house it looked. Kinda like God knew what had gone on there and said never again! Flash back to Windy screaming at the sky! Perhaps God's way of saying sorry? Not as cool as the end of the original Carrie movie but a damn awesome sight none the less! Total destruction! Did not smell much blood though so I was certain no one had been killed in it. Well since Thursday.

So I roared for my friend! A moment later another roar was heard answering me and my heart soared. It was her and loud! She was so close! My fears all vanished instantly knowing she was here now and did not seem sad either so I watched waiting for her to come to me. Giving her all the time she needed for what ever she was doing here. A minute or so later she came just plodding happily from around the house on all fours tail held high, tip twitching. She looked so good. Freaking amazing actually! So hauntingly beautiful! Not human any more that was damn certain! Hey I could tell by the smell alone she was now something different. Something like me! Smaller then me in several ways but still large. Maybe nine feet nose to tip of tail where as I was close to twelve. She came up to the car and sat on her haunches like the beautiful near Tiger she was! Her choice and I knew IT! Might have been my influence but I think she really wanted this form. Her old one held to much pain! Her face was still mostly hers but with a muzzle. She smiled a big Tiger toothy smile at me as her Mom and younger Sisters were coming around the house rather nervously and looking upset! They had lots to be upset about. Unsure when they saw us but they kept coming any way. Understood their reluctance however. Their Becky was a Tiger now! It is a big deal! Their lives had been filled with absolute terror for years and now such wonder? Yes Wonder as that was what it was! It had to be hard for them to accept.

"Had to. See. If they were safe." Becky said her voice all growlly but she was smiling still. Scary smile sure, but I had one of them as well. Hard to talk with big sharp teeth and floppy lips ya know. She had them both now also with a muzzle of a mouth and looked unbelievable! Her face human but not. Furry muzzle and dark black nose in a human shape. Nodded my understanding. Well I'd have done the same. If they had not been here as well I knew she would have gone looking for her family wherever they were. Knew in her past life she had given her Sisters her food on many an occasion as her Bastard had not let them have much. His words, he did not want them to become fat ugly bloat bags like their grotesque Mother! So she was Fat. Still cute. Some of Becky's memory's were in my head now and I knew mine were in hers. All pooped out or that thought may have caused an accident.

Her eyes and cheeks were definitely her own still and it was a beautiful blending. "Am I like you now?"

"Kinda. Your choice to be different though and look like this. Who you were meant to be!" Growled to her. "You like this?" Her turn to nod blushing. "You is Beautiful!" She was. Not quite Tiger but far from human she was beyond mere gorgeous! Her choice how she looked I knew! Could still see it was her in the face. Still had boobs too! Furry ones! Wanted to play with them. All eight! Would wait forever for those. So Fluffy I could die!

Her family still looking scared but not stopping came closer to us holding each other and I was shocked when they walked right past Becky to ME! Oh the hugs I quickly got. They recognized me apparently! Guess I am hard to forget. Had been their salvation and deliverance! Tears flowed as I was thanked for killing the Bastard and saving them over and over. Surely I was touched here. Physically and emotionally. Well I was fluffy! Like a giant stuffed animal. Finally her Mom spoke other than thanks. Her voice getting sad. "We couldn't stay here in that awful house anymore once he was gone and we went to my Sister's that very night once the Police said we could. Lucky we did too it seems. A fitting end to this Hell. Had no idea what I planned on doing with the house. We heard from a neighbor what happened and came to see what could be salvaged. My Sister hates me for not coming to her years ago saying she would have killed the Bastard herself but she is letting us stay. She wants to know if Becky is safe though. God I feel so bad about what he did to us but I was terrifyed all the time." She explained in her own way. Did not have to but it felt that she needed too as Becky's diary held plenty, so I just listened. "He always told me if I ever left him he would find me and make me die horribly after making me watch him rape and kill all my Daughters! He nearly killed me and them several times as it was. Put me in the hospital a few times." She was losing it and her voice was cracking so I had no choice. Oh I wanted to scream my frustration at her but it would change nothing now would it? Sure I can say I would have gotten out of the situation all I wanted but until you are in it you can have no idea what you will do! Lived in denial for years myself now hadn't I? Always loved my Brother! Still do! Oh I knew I could not explain most of what I was going through and I liked most of those things. Instead of anger now I just felt sadness for her and her children.

"Safe now!" Growled out. "You Live!" We can not change the past but the future is not written. Never forget that! Never to late to change either!

In tears again she asked me gesturing at Becky. Her voice strained yet full of love and awe. "Did you do this to my Daughter?" Yes I nodded. Well I had and would not hesitate to do it again! "Is she gonna be okay?" Might be a lie but I thought not so I nodded anyway. Hoped it would work out! When I became a Dog I knew I was different and saw and felt things differently. "Did you save her life?"

Quickly I nodded. No doubt there! More than once as well. "Do you love her?" OH I NODDED! Then with great fear in her voice as her eyes went wide. Hey you can understand she did not see or pay attention to everything at first! Kinda stress filled moment so? "Is that a blind Girl driving?" Hey! No discriminating against the Handicapped. Tammy, Becky and I were all just laughing hard and nodding!

Then I growled out. "Drives better blind!" There may have been peeing. On the seat. Still got whacked with a white cane even if it was true! She can't hit that hard at least. Her cane is not an Alien God Scepter either!

Becky turned to her Mom and Sisters. "Love you all. I call. Maybe visit."

Becky hopped in the car and Tammy yelled. "Come Sancho! I am Don Quixote!" And she floored it burning rubber swerving like crazy around debris but hit nothing! Sure I was just glad we had no windmills around here. Well I think I told you at the very beginning Tammy was insane? Not a lie! Loved her still. It was bad enough we had outdoor cafes around here!

Oh we went for breakfast too!

Those cocksuckers at the McGyver's fast food drive-thru told us to stop wasting their time! We only ordered about four hundred dollars worth of food or so before they said that. Play with us will they? U turn. Park on the sidewalk blocking one entrance. Hop out walk to the other door. In we go with attitude! Customers screamed of course! How I love screams in the morning! Tammy walks right up to the counter reaches over and grabs a big manager by the shirt pulls him close snarling right in his face. "Are you gonna make my food or do my friends need to fend for themselves!" It smelled good in there so Becky and I were both drooling which helped sell the idea it seemed. Smiling too with lots of teeth. Maybe a growl or two as well for the fun of it. It was fun! Bet not one of those employees ever worked that fast in their lives! We even got carryout service. Loaded the backseat. See what kindness can get you? What? We were kind! Well I did not eat any of them! Want me to go back? I can! No problem! That Fat manager looked mighty tasty!

Hit a gas station for six gallons of milk and six of OJ. Sure it costs more at those places but we didn't want the food to get cold, besides the look of terror on peoples faces when Tammy gets out of the car with her white cane is just priceless. Tammy had no problem getting back to the house. Her new senses were quite strong apparently and I was proud of her. Becky rode shotgun and never flinched at anything.

Windy was pissed while we were gone apparently. Saying both her Beasts had deserted her. Such a little drama queen. They had explained quickly to her we had to go out and protect the Kingdom and hunt for breakfast. Hunting Hash Browns is tricky business they told her hoping we had pickcd some up. It really is tricky stuff! They are dangerous and we got lots. Such hugs Windy gave when we returned. This child's love of me could bring tears to eyes and many were. Including me. Yes I was still promised a good spanking later for not getting permission. We ate. Finished cleaning the house. Thought a few of the Girls had found themselves Girlfriends now but I still got kissed by all of them. We even drove a few Girls home by lunch.

Swung by the Veterinary clinic and brought Doctor Lucy some lunch even. Felt the Tiger could use vaccinations and a check up too you see. Wanted to know she was okay. Okay done. No idea if the costume had become a part of her as she was naked now. Well she had fur but the fur was her own. Lucy was just amazed at the sight of Becky Tiger. She was rather impressive and just absolutely beautiful. Using a tablet I typed out as much as I could about Becky and Tammy both. The Doctor was very curious about Tammy and I watched as she picked something small up, I think a Dog vitamin, and tossed it at the back of Tammy's head. Six times! Nothing hit and the Doc was a good shot. Tammy just snickered while she dodged. As for Becky she got a full exam. Yep stool sample for worms too. Both of us had a file here now! No real choice as we were no longer human but not quite a Beast, Becky was astonishing. A little of both really. Still got shots which she wanted when they were mentioned. Doctor Lucy smiled just shaking her head as she injected Becky with Feline Distemper and Parvo shots. "Well this is interesting, Pammy. You got the Dog collar and turned somewhat canine. She wore the Tiger costume and became a Tiger. It would seem the user gets to choose it's own form! At least to an extent." Kinda knew that already but said nothing. Knew I chose the Dog. She had taken some samples from me as well however. Including stool and urine. Thankfully I was worm free! Good to know however I guess, but still quite embarrassing. Dogs feel shame at getting worms! They have told me. Going to put a cap on my urine sample though she spilled some on a tray of medical stuff. Well I pee a lot and that cup was full like she wanted so I expected that much. If I could talk easy I would have warned her. Kimmy had collected it and she did not mind being peed on which is good as I pee a lot. Doctor Lucy got the cap on and began cleaning up the tray quick. Looking down she gasped in a panic. "FUCK!" Never a good omen when said like that! And I just knew I was going to not be happy soon by her reactions. IF I had known right then? Had myself a problem! Tammy was grinning for some reason.

Kimmy in nearly a panic at that tone asked fast sounding scared herself. "What? Is something wrong? Something with Pammy?" It was the tone that scared her now however as they did not completely connect it with me yet. Oh I knew it was me. Always was me!

The Vet was freaking to much so the Girls were freaking as well. There was fear on that Vet's face. Tammy only smiled more. Her voice so strained when she finally spoke Lucy squeaked. "Um Pammy, come with me." So I followed her into what looked like an operating room which kinda made me nervous I admit. Gesturing to the floor by some machinery since I would not fit on this table either, she said. "Lay on your back right here please, Pammy." And she began getting equipment ready. Laid down on the floor and rolled over. Why not? Was a Dog! All were nervous now as they did not understand. Well Tammy was grinning for some reason you see. I'd bite her but I think she wants that. Still it should have told me something and I should have understood! Just far too much going on to think clearly about any one.

Kimmy was freaking bad and so was Sabrina and Teela so I understood the anger in her mighty little voice when Windy snapped loudly. "What is wrong with my Beast?" Becky was blocking Windy's way gently trying to calm her as was Teela. They heard murder in that tone too!

The Doctor just shoved something at Kimmy who looked at it in her hands dumbfounded. "I don't get it? What is it? What does it mean?"

With a sigh the Doctor said and you could tell she did not want too say it but knew she had too. Her voice was heavy as she spoke. "It's a pregnancy tester! That right there means Pammy is pregnant!" WHAT?

Sabrina was in shock and confused but said. "That's impossible! It has to be because she shared blood with Becky! Becky was pregnant!" Made sense if Becky's blood had gone into me but they did not know it hadn't! Storm washed most of Becky's blood out of the driveway. My thoughts and emotions were in turmoil. You understand right?

The Doctor put the ultrasound to my belly and her hand was shaking as they explained about Becky quickly. Yeah, knew what it was she was doing now! My feelings here were mixed. Fucked in more ways than one it seemed. Her voice tense the Doctor said. "That is what I am trying to find out now!" No one spoke for a couple minutes. Than her voice flat Lucy counted. "One, two, three!" She was silent. Finally she looked at me totally unsure of, well, pretty much everything? "You're pregnant Girl!" There were three embryo's well fetuses. Okay? "The question I think is who's the father?" Poor Teela! Well the others all pointed at her fast. Even Windy! Hey! I would have been truly happy with that idea but thought it the most unlikely. Still Teela just blushed a lot! Denied nothing! Naughty Mexican pudge Daddy!

Growling out I asked. "Stone?"

Lucy sighed a not so nice sigh. "That would be nice sure, but what scars me is they all have tails."

Teela said proudly sounding uncertain of her knowledge still. "Well don't all Babys have tails at some point?" Yes I think she was truly hoping she was the Father! Kinda sounded sad she might not be too. Knew she would work hard to be a great Dad to my children.

Doctor Lucy's voice squeaked out. Never a good sign. Poor Doctor! "Well! Yes they do! However not this far into their development or that long. They are big enough to see easy. Look definitely canine as well."

Had to say it now didn't I? Well yeah? Even knowing that it meant nothing. "Lost virginity two weeks ago!"

The Doctor sat back on her heels barely able to speak. "Yeah that is another problem!" Yes that tone of voice made me nervous. The look on her face was kinda scary as well. Everyone looked at her now. Even me and I knew what was coming. "These PUPS? Well, they are further along than that. Look about six weeks at least. Oh FUCK!" She was up and running back in a moment with specimen cups. She had a very scary thought! Well I was just glad I had not pooped when I knew what it was. It was terrifying too but explained things if it were true. Wrong though but the reality may have been even worse. Would definitely poop then! Had not thought it yet personally or there would have been poop. Handing them out she said her voice shaking as well as her hands. "F-f-fill them with pee Girls." Oh she sort of hesitated. Handing her one as well she said. "You too Windy!"

Oh the looks I was getting then could kill a normal Dog! Doc Lucy to the rescue. Maybe? Her voice urgent now. "We have no idea what this drug has and is doing to any of you. I heard what Windy went through!" She did not know the half of it yet. Probably best not to tell her. "Like Stone we probably can't get a needle in Windy to draw blood so this is all we have." Well that made sense at least. Should have checked her sooner really. "It may be the drug itself making you pregnant." Well that was not a good idea! "We need to know even if we don't like the answers." No we didn't! Either need or like the answers! Well that answer!

They all went still. Windy proudly with her head held high! Not sure she understood any of what was said but Windy was finally being treated the same as the big Girls and she darn well liked it! IT is what all five year old's want you know? To be treated the same as everyone else. That and to play in some mud puddles! Lots of them around today. Came back first too and proud she had filled her cup. Doctor Lucy labeled all of them as they came back. We watched nervously as she tested them all as well!

Sabrina said sadly while we waited. "Well I can't be pregnant. The only thing I've had in me besides a vibrator is Pammy's tongue!" POOP! Now I was getting a really bad sinking feeling in my gut! So bad I barely wondered what vibrator? Did she still have it? Was it destroyed in her house? If so would she like to go shopping for a new one? Hey I could not change anything now could I? So I was thinking practical thoughts. Could we both have fun with the vibrator? Felt that would be fun and a real bonding experience. It was practical thinking to me! Also distracting as I needed it! Hey I liked that vibrating Dog penis strap-on of the Dean's you see! So wicked but pleasurable.

The Doctor looked very nervous now, perhaps terrified and I knew I should slink out of the room and catch a ride with a semi headed for the west coast. Well what was left of it! That third earthquake over the summer fucked it up big time! LA did not have a smog problem anymore at least. No smog at the bottom of the ocean! Doctor Lucy asked with fear in her voice. "What do you know about the Octopus?" Huh? Tentacle Sex? Well that was an idea!

Tammy just grinned so badly I knew damn well now she knew something. Maybe I could still make a run for it! Sabrina said now, not understanding yet. Windy probably did as she watched the Discovery channel a lot. Sabrina however makes a great straight man setting up a good one liner. "They have eight arms?"

Oh that look on Tammy's face told me I should have run. Then, before the Doctor could, Tammy spoke. There was great humor in her voice but the words were daggers in my heart. Okay they weren't! But nails in my coffin? Maybe! "Well actually the Males have seven arms as one is a penis!" Glad no one was drinking. Windy just snickered! I suspected at the word. They looked at me and then the Doctor.

Just a fart. Honest!

The Doctor was nodding at this now however. And the bell of Doom Tolled! "The good news at least is Windy is not pregnant so I don't think it is just the drug doing it as I feared it might. The rest of you however are all pregnant including the Tiger." She had peed as well.

Kimmy was in shock but said. "But Pammy just did an abortion on the Tiger yesterday." Seriously? We were already spending half our day explaining stuff to one person or another.

Okay I did not blame Doctor Lucy for her chuckle here. It was impressive what I had done. Even more than all the rest! Yeah all of it! Terrifying to be sure but phenomenal! "Yeah and Pammy knocked her back up at the same exact time probably. Tell me more about this abortion?" Her curiosity was getting the better of her now at least.

Distraction!

Windy with such amazing pride puffed her chest out and said pointing at me. "She ate the Hellspawn!" Shame the Doctor had not just gone to the bathroom like us now. You really can have a look of absolute horror while peeing your pants laughing.

Painful from the looks of it though!

When Teela could talk again she gasped out. "Good thing Pammy is unkillable!" Girls looked at her with fear not sure what she was saying, even the blind one for once! "Mom is gonna try to kill her when she finds out Pammy knocked me up!" Oh God! So true! What scared me is Teela was not upset in the least! Did she like the idea of carrying my Pups? Teela was a very special Girl.

Then Tammy who I think was really enjoying herself reminded us all. "What about the close to a hundred other Girls she's had her tongue penis in over the last two weeks? Think they're all preggers too?" The Tiger was now laughing hysterically while rolling on the floor and I was sticking my snout in butts to see who had pooped themselves. Knew I was gonna be comfy in the backseat! Neither Sabrina or Kimmy moved as I got their pants off and licked their butts clean.

Okay this was bad sure but what could I do?! Sure lots of abortions but I had the feeling they would all want to keep them. Knew I did! Always wanted a big Family.

"I'm driving!" Tammy said as we went out. "Teela let the Tiger ride shotgun! You ride on Daddy with the Princess!" Shirts were pulled off and my naked human upholstery was pushed in the backseat for me. Damn comfy! Windy had seen her Sister naked on many an occasion. Go to the public pool! Are there separate changing rooms for different ages? Hey I kept my mouth closed so no tongue penis was visible here! How embarrassing is that?!

Teela was snickering as I climbed in happily. With a few words she crushed my joy! "I don't know why you're so happy Pammy! When Mom finds out you knocked her up as well you're dead."

OH FUCK! This was beyond bad! Yes I tried to run! To late! They held me down. Did they too want too see me dead? Yeah it was impossible to kill me but seriously this was scary!

However I will say this much. Windy is just too cute to eat! The thought may have crossed my mind at some point I admit. Well it was decided by all on the way back to the compound that we would say nothing about this yet. So when Windy walked in and said right away as loud as she could. "Both my Beasts are pregnant! Isn't it wonderful?" You can probably understand why I thought that. When she said. "Teela is too!" You can totally understand why we all ran away fast! No one wanted to deal with that one!

We cowered out in the woods but we could still hear people screaming for mostly my blood after a couple hours! Certain Windy had explained about the Vet visit right away we knew they had called Lucy already. No idea if that was a good or bad thing! If they didn't have any of them at the compound I was certain someone was making a run to the pharmacy for pregnancy tests and fast! Oh I might have to put my powers of healing to the test. Fleeing the country was actually discussed quickly but I said NO! My father had abandoned us when I was little and my Brother not even born and I would not do that to my children. EVER! Suffer anything for all my children, forever! There was however probably several weeks left and Barbados is wonderful this time of year! If only I had taken a vacation.

Tammy had a very good point when she spoke gently. "I don't know what the big deal is. They probably won't even be human." My first thought was so what? So they would have Puppys?

It was a valid point however! Still made me nervous.

Tempers were understandably high so when Sabrina snapped at the Albino with violence in that tone it was understandable. "I don't know why you're so fucking happy! Your pregnant too!"

Tammy snickered ever so sweetly as she spoke. "I'm just thinking if it is Canine I can try to train it to be my seeing eye Dog." Alright it was a cool idea and we laughed at it. No you can laugh facing imminent death! Recommend it actually! "Okay Pammy go and play with the Bear for a little while. I'll go wave the white cane and negotiate terms for our surrender." Made sense as she was the only one without family of a sorts here. Did not think they would hurt a Blind Girl either! Played with the Bear for an hour. We tuckered it out. Seemed a happy Bear. Even before I made her orgasm. Yeah the others played as well and I hoped the Bear was pregnant too! She was a sweet Bear. We finally heard Tammy yell. "All clear!"

My first thought as I, we, got close was if it was all clear why were there several angry looking people waiting for us? Okay ME! Mrs. Gonzales snarled as we came out of the trees. "I'd Kill you but I won't have all my Grandchildren grow up Fatherless!" Oh I hung my head in total shame. What could I do as I had those same thoughts after all. Well I would never abandon my children. All one hundred and twelve or whatever it ended up actually being. They were mine and I would be there for them no matter what.

Dean Antwerp said sternly waving a finger at me with a glare. "No more impregnating Girls!" Wondered where her riding crop was as I had an itchy spot. Well I was more then willing to accept all of the consequences of my multiple indiscretions and it was an itchy spot!

The look on my face must have been priceless however as the reality of what she said sunk in. No more hunting prey?!

My ChewToy loved me however and understood my concern right away so she quickly asked. "If they are already pregnant by her however can she still be allowed to hunt them?" They had not thought of that possibility but all were nodding quick. Hey I mean why not right? It's not like I could get them pregnant again right? RIGHT? Yes I was still nervous! After all I did not have good or bad luck now did I? No I had terrifying luck! Whether good or bad was up for interpretation. That it was scary was not!

Teela may get me killed yet however. "Hey Mom are you pregnant?" Now I could tell she was just by the look on her face so I pounced on her. Pure instinct I swear! They just said if someone was pregnant they were fair game! She was pregnant after all! MINE!

My Mom, even knowing she could be next, sweetly put an arm around both Kimmy and Sabrina. "Come on girls you shouldn't watch. Let's go teach Windy how to play poker!" They went in just ignoring the screams of STOP, DON'T, and NO!

It is not Evil! Just fun! Extremely intense however. She was smiling after so I was not worryed about rape charges. Just a Mexican as well so they may not even write her complaint down the racist Cops. A sweet naked Mexican MILF! She has a nice comfy body! Knew well where her two oldest Daughters got their beauty! Also knew where those teeth marks in her boobs came from!

Chewy!

By the time I was done with my snack and came in they were about to serve supper. Sandra with a slight smile asked her Mom as she saw me enter quietly behind her Mom. "Mom are you pregnant too?" WHAT? My ears perked up suddenly.

The Dean hissed angrily at her Daughter! Having not seen I was there I presume. "YES!"

Appetizer!

Oh I was hoping to see the Dean spank her Daughter someday soon. Dean Kelly could scream those three words as well! Knew she did not mean them! Hey they both cuddled with me later while plotting against their own Daughters. It was not the sex they were afraid of you understand but the intensity. Orgasming so hard you almost poop yourself is a lot to take. Oh some did poop! Most didn't true but a good colonoscopy pre-intercourse is guaranteed to clean you out and I really need a medical license. Maybe a fake one even. Something to hang on the wall you see. They were all thinking the same I was sure as there was much giggling going on!

Was a little nervous when as supper was finished my Mom said leaving the room. "I'm pregnant!" And she ran squealing! Hunt! So it was My Mom. She deserved to have fun and I was pretty sure that was what she wanted now. Especially after all the crap Stone and I put her through over the years. Besides after the third time raping your own Mother it's pretty normal right?

It was nearly bed time before anyone actually asked about Becky being mostly a real Tiger now. She was stretched out on the floor in front of a TV playing pillow to many. Guess we assumed Anastasia had told them everything but, thinking about it, she probably knew almost nothing about it, which is after all highly understandable. That it actually took that long for them to ask was understandable as well which just shows you how much crap was going on! Not all the violent raping either. Windy explained everything for us once more. Graphically! She wanted too so we let her. Very entertaining too. There were some nods as her use of medical terminology was spot on. Mrs. Gonzales got some looks.

Maybe she should change her TV viewing habits! Then again Becky would be dead if Windy had not seen them. Maybe a few others as well. Funny how little things that seem unimportant effect everything still.

The General just kept snickering away. Had been pretty much since we got home and I think it made some nervous. When finally asked why he just said pointing at Windy. "She will make a fine Supreme Ruler of the World!" He meant it as well. Oh I can tell these things remember? Frankly I agreed with him about it. She would. Probably next week.

Windy stood proudly as she motioned the General over and pointed at the floor in front of her. He knelt with a big grin and lowered his head knowing what was coming. She gently tapped both his shoulders with her Scepter and said. "I dub thee Sir Hammer, Knight of the realm!" One of the servants fainted as he swore allegiance. Swear it had nothing to do with my fart! Cleared half the room but still. You just try being a Dog and see how it is!? Half the servants here were already bowing to that little Girl however. She truly was such a sweetheart. And as the General said a fine future Princess of the Universe!

She waved at everyone as I carried her to bed by the nape of the neck like a Pup still. Oh she loved it and giggled the whole way. Mrs. Gonzales just smiled when she called me Mama Beast! That Woman realized I would die for her children if I had too. She knew far too well I would not hesitate to kill for them either and I think even Sally and Robert Gonzales understood all that. They were getting more time with their Mom out of the deal and they were all still together so it was fine.

The Man, sure it was a Man, who said you can't choose your family is an absolute idiot! You can't choose your relatives but you can always choose your family! You can always sell those relatives that are a problem for medical experiments as well! Have some numbers if you need them. Family are those you love and who love you. Genetics has nothing to do with that. Just like any Man can be a Father but it takes a special one to be a Dad! My Family was growing fast.

Becky followed us to the room happily and got in bed with us. One on each side of Windy. We were the Princesses great Beasts after all and that was our place. Yeah I remembered that little Girls words at the party and wondered if she knew what was coming. Would not be the first time I got that thought or the last! Once that sweet Girl was asleep however Becky gestured with her head. She would watch Windy and keep her safe. Why do you think Becky had stayed and gotten raped and beat repeatedly by her Father at home? She knew if she left her little Sisters would be next! She was willing to submit to anything for them and she would for Windy as well! Had been willing to die for Kimmy and I owed her for that.

Time to HUNT!

CHAPTER 3 MOTHERHOOD?
Monday September 27th

Woke up with my tongue deep in a butt! No idea who's butt! Tasty though!

Pulled my tongue out and my own Mother yelled at me quickly. "Put that back!" Alright I have no idea or excuse! Did as I was told however. Put my tongue back up MY OWN MOTHERS BUTT! My Mom has a nice butt! You would have in an instant dang it! Oh tongue going up my butt too! My lucky day?! Did not care who! My butt has needs!

Tammy asked humorously. "Looking for hemorrhoids back there Teela?" No idea on that but it felt amazing. Talented tongue on that Girl! Maybe they understood my back end had needs too. Got lots of hands back there suddenly. Well I was moaning a bit you see. It is so nice. Sure I can lick my own butt but like the difference between masturbation and Dirty Pig Sex it is just not as satisfying. And I suppose none of you have ever had…..? Um sorry I forgot who I was talking too. Forgive me. You all need to get out more.

They had two hands in my vagina up to the elbows when some blind Girl who shall remain nameless said. "Hey Pammy I bet we could shove Windy up there and you could actually give birth to her!" For a split second I thought it funny. Windy however probably would like it.

Mrs. Gonzales however scared me when she spoke with a voice like a Demon from somewhere in the pile. Hey I did not even know she was in the room. Even though I was laying on a part of her. Laying on a part of several. "Bet I could shove my foot up your ass too!" Why she was looking at me I know not! Well I did not say it! Mrs. Gonzales had big feet as well as big boobs and a big heart. Big hot butt too! Both Sabrina and Teela had mighty whomper's on their chests as well. Sorry I never explained about these things. Why do you think they were just so comfortable? They were dry though so no milk. Not for long though! Butts however always have shit! I'M A DOG! DOGS EAT SHIT! Yeah I ate a tasty dead thing out in the forest yesterday and it was catching up to me fast. Felt the violent rumbles and building pressure. Screaming happened as I farted in Girl's faces and Girls moved fast barely getting the door open before I was out it. Just lucky it was only gas so far. Must have felt the rumbles in there too and realized it was not going to stay gas. Barely in time. SPRRABLE! OH YES!

Explosive diarrhea in an animal my size is scary. Once my ass was turned completely in the other direction they came out and squatted in the grass as well. Not close to me however. Thought a couple of them may puke yet. Stunk bad out here. Needed a hose and quick. It really was a darn long walk to some of the bathrooms here so I understood why they chose the grass as well. Well some of them. A few were just nasty freaks. Loved them all.

There were lots of us in that bedroom also. No idea why everyone had been in bed with me when I woke! Liked it a lot though. Becky took Windy to breakfast long before any naughty stuff happened. Think she had seen where my tongue had been and knew what was likely to happen. She really liked the Gonzales children too. They are fun.

Of course the talk at breakfast was once again about my bodily functions! Always a fun meal time topic. They were leery about letting me even go to school after seeing the awful devastation in the grass from my butt. Did not blame them there though! It was quite horrifying. Felt empty at least so felt I was okay. Was more worried about Becky. She seemed relaxed and all, but? She had been suicidal just days ago and was in flux now. She also had a Counseling Session this morning and I felt she should go but I wanted to be there just in case! True I had a Counseling Raping, I mean Session, as well and that terrified me. So I was mixed on going but knew I had too! Okay I was getting very scared on the ride to school. We had Windy though or I may have bolted. Mrs. Gonzales had insisted I drop "Our" Pup off as I probably only had a few weeks to practice being a Mom before I was one! She had a really scary yet good point. Actually seemed a genuine sentiment as well.

Windy's Teachers were happy to see her again and she them. Some of the Teachers and students alike had seen the explosion and thought Windy dead. Such happy sadness filled that schoolyard. Kids all happy to see Windy and their other friends were safe. They had seen how bad some where injured as well so I understood. Some where hurt bad enough they should have died, but here they were looking fine. Nope! No cobwebs here. No one said jack about that however. Afraid too I think, We were asked by several Teachers to walk in with Windy for support as some kids had already broken down when they did. Kinda understood as I heard some kids crying already. Very good ears. It was gonna be hard for many. They may have barely known her but Mrs. Walberg was loved by these kids. They had watched her die badly trying to save Windy! That was why she died. Protecting Windy! Right in the hall too so they would have to pass that spot everyday. Most were surprised we were there and Windy was still alive like I said and that helped many it seemed. Saw some smiles at her. A teacher was trying to get kids past the spot as fast as possible. Windy went right up to the spot were the Teacher had died and pulled a picture of a heart she had drawn out of her bag and laid it on the ground bringing tears to even some Teachers eyes. No idea when she drew it but it was pretty as she pressed it flat on the floor. Saw her muscles tense. Not a clue what or why yet.

Her voice as she stood again rang out like thunder in that hallway even if a normal tone. "Do not be afraid my people. You are safe here now. I will protect you always! Our friend is gone but never forgotten!" She turned and walked into the classroom. Knew she was close to tears. As she sat at her seat she waved at me. A brave Pup!

Tammy snickered but sweetly. We all gave her a look. It was a sad touching moment and she found it funny? Her voice seemed nervous still but she said. "Some one, some where, is in DEEP DO-DO!" AMEN! Oh I was certain God had already gotten an ear full from my Princess! Hoped that little Girl was done with him. Of course I was very glad that fact was not known back at the compound. They had enough stuff to process now.

As we got into the car to leave, someone somewhere yelled at us. "Don't let the blind one drive!" She was so good with that cane. Why not? Laughing manically Tammy gunned it! She drove over that curb on purpose you know. She knew where everything was. She liked the screaming as well it seemed. My Blind Albino!

It was a damn good thing Girls had dry clothes in the trunk. Or they would be sitting in their own pee all day. We hit a drive through for heavily caffeinated milkshakes. They exist! Tito's, the best burgers and shakes ever! Probably not legal but awesome! They didn't do just breakfast in the morning. You could get burrito's, burger's and fry's anytime. Suddenly as we left it seems Tammy was uncannily struck stupid as well as blind. The damage was not that bad when she shot across the street and hit a sidewalk cafe but still! The worst part was that the Girls and the Tiger were cranking her up the whole trip. Sure those tables and chairs were not cheap! Have to do something nice for this city.

Maybe she was.

Thought we'd never lose those Cops that chased us and get to school. Yes there was a million dollars in a damage fund set up so people could apply for it so that their insurance rates didn't go up but seriously at this rate it would not last long. Maybe Till Tuesday!

School looked normal. Yeah okay we had Soldiers and tanks all over the place still but no running or screaming or… I was just fucked and I knew it! Something was wrong! Just had to be right?

My hackles rose as we headed for my Counseling Session. It's good to have Hackles! Honestly I had no idea why Teela was still with us so don't ask. Well I didn't! The less I know the better. Plausible deniability! A Politicians favorite tool. Teela did make me happy when she was there so was okay. Emotionally you sick perverts! It's not all sex at college! There are party's! The Girls however were giving her the tour it seems as they said what was where as we went past it discussing her education. Miss Winters was all smiles as we came in. Knew I was dead the moment I saw her. Her mouth was smiling but her eyes were ice! Quickly I went and sat in the center of the floor like a good Dog hanging my head in shame! Her words were sweet but her voice was not. Sounded straight from the depths of hell. "And how is the Father of my child today?" Yes I was dead! Also totally hoping it was just one! You get that right?

It was about then I understood why people hate Mondays! We must be trying roll reversal technique in this session I thought. She was the one screaming and losing it and I the nurturing gentle one telling her I loved her over and over. Did. My pudge! Since I was not the only one did not care it seems I refused to limit my love to just one person. Loved them all. A Dog can you know. Once Miss Winters had wore herself out screaming and hitting me, Yes she was, but she ain't that strong, venting her anger and beginning to cry bad, Girls rolled her on her side and shoved her head to a nipple. Why not? No we didn't have tranquilizers. Caffeine would be bad! This truly was an act of pure Madness, NO of comfort, Okay it was Madness but what the FUCK!

So I licked her very Motherly, like she was a Pup, as she nursed on me crying. Sucking on something is a comfort thing. No! Don't get your hopes up straight Guys, Girls do not want comfort that bad.

She was happy as we left her in the care of Becky. Can't say I was happy. There were a lot of Girls in the hallway outside for some reason! Most looked very familiar! They were all looking at me. The Dean who was also out there organizing it appeared was all sweetness and smiles for them! And I got ice dagger eyes! Maybe I went just to far? Not on purpose! True I still would have but they did not know that and I would never tell. Don't let them read this. Maybe the Dean was constipated and needed a colonoscopy? Then again! The Girls were a mixed bag. They looked nervous as they were being handed pregnancy tests first and then taken to the Girl's Room in groups. We sat and watched this procession of Girls as Becky was being counseled. All of them were pregnant! Most put their names on the new list of allowed Prey with smiles! Hunting grounds were redefined fast. Most of the classrooms were off limits now. Damn! Well it can be disrupting to the teaching process I guess. However they got some complaints about this No New Prey policy right away when people heard so by lunch a Prey Application process was setup through Miss Moneypenny who kept blushing when our eyes met, so new Girls could become Prey. My sex life was all they were talking about on campus it seems. Heard a class about me was in the works for spring semester. Must be doing something right! Right?

Got really scared though when child support was finally mentioned! Oh I knew Kimmy was willing to help but I did not think she was that rich! It was looking bad. Girls were just coming up and hugging me telling me how much they loved me. Becky got hugs as well. Kinda disturbed her at first but I told her it was wonderful and to enjoy as it was just hugs and she was a Tiger after all! Who wouldn't want to hug a Tiger? We used no real words between us but we actually communicated. She was not upset after her session with Miss Winters and I thought that a good sign. Becky's schedule had been changed to be the same as mine so I could be there for her. She actually agreed to it even as she had no care what she took anymore. College had been an escape for her more so then me. Maybe that alone drew us closer to each other so I told her I loved her a lot and she said she loved me. She was scared she said as she did not think the way she used to and I told her I did not either. That it was the animal part thinking but it was fine. Just a different perspective. Different priorities. They had asked her nervously if she wanted to abort this Baby as well if she did not feel up to it. She hesitated but shook her head NO as it was mine! Felt glad about that and hoped she would be okay.

True the job market for ProtoDog's and TigerGirl's was probably slim so supporting our kids could be an issue. Yes I had quickly thought about that and concluded most of my classes were still usable as the knowledge was good mostly. Math was always a nice time to nap.

Now all that said Sandra's class was scary that morning. It too was about me! Never used my name but glared at me the whole lecture! Yeah Promiscuity lecture time. About the lack of proper family values and how a child needs a full time Mother and FATHER! (Well I was right here.) How an absent FATHER would effect a child! (Not going anywhere!) All the time looking at me! Oh I was hers as long as she shared me. (And I had to share her with Brutus and Stone so what was the problem?)

At the end of class I walked up and spoke to Sandra. "Wuv You!" Then to her belly so cutely with my snout pressed in. "Wuv You!" Sandra hugged me hard with sudden tears her anger spent. Needed to vent I guess and I even understood that. Once students were gone I just had too ask her. "Brutus want to be Father?" Got hugged again as she nodded snicker crying. Oh he would be so happy when his Bitch had his Pups.

Probably Pups too!

Both our Doctors were nervous about that possibility. Did not blame them. Frankly I was hopeful. Mine were roughly canine but what the others would look or be like who knew. Since mine were so far along ultrasound equipment was ordered for the college so progress could be checked regularly. Doctor Lucy said she would have checked everyone but it could jeopardize her license so Doctor

Petrov agreed to do them weekly at least for all the Girls in the Pregnancy List! There was a List! Well I was fine. Then the Dean's phone rang at lunch. It was the General! Sounded like nothing but hysterical laughter before the line went dead. Sabrina pulled her phone out and began looking around the web and she quickly started laughing hysterically. She showed us what she had seen on her phone. Now we were laughing too. Gasping they told Tammy what was going on. A highly suspicious barrel labeled "Da Bomb" it seems had arrived at Starbucks headquarters that morning. Seattle Bomb squad was called and the Barrel was quickly detonated. That is what they do. Blow up a bomb! No it does not make sense! Like starting a fire to stop a fire! Ask Smokey about that crap. Bomb squad members it said were being quarantined for possible biological attack as all were instantly ill! Oh it was nasty!

We really needed to get Ricardo a present! We all knew it was my shit and he sent it. Got many thanks myself as that spread around campus. Twelve dollars for a cup of Non-Cat-Poop coffee!

Like twelve Girls followed me to Psych class and that worried me as I did not think most were in that class. Mr. Wexall was incensed and talked about how some people were unstable. Yeah he was looking at me! Whole lecture. There was no denying involvement as there was snickering when he mentioned the Barrel! They let him ramble. Still very informative stuff about crazed bombers. Might need one someday. You never know! As class ended Kimmy waved him over and whispered in his ear. Heard he taught the next class with wet pants.

Oh we did not go too far! Twelve bucks for a cup of coffee? Cheaper at Hooters and the scenery is better! Even cheaper at Daisy's Diner and that one waitress has the sweetest butt! Oh it is gorgeous and so fat! Wiggles it well! Want my tongue up that one! Gonna hunt Waitress Rump!

Got a note to go to the deans office. GREAT! What had I done now? Well no! I had no idea what as I had done so many things it could be any of them?! Oh she did not look happy as we came in either. We all sat in silence. Yes they came as well. They don't like to be bored. They all kept looking at me like I had done something wrong! Wondered what! Her voice was solemn. "Now I honestly don't want to do this, as I Like Pammy, but under the circumstances I may have no choice!" Not sure I liked the sounds of that.

Several worried Girls all at once just blurted out. "You can't expel Pammy Ma'am!" Was that what she was saying here? That I was gonna be expelled? Not sure I liked that idea at all. Teela hugged me tightly. Protectively.

Dean Kelly hushed them, her face and voice grim. "I may have no choice Girls! The college is in a very tight legal spot here. We have received official notice from the ACLU this morning that action will be taken against the school if the situation is not remedied immediately."

Sabrina asked hesitantly, confused even. Did not blame her there! Kind of a Huh? "What situation?"

What a sigh from the Dean! That Woman should be running the Drama Department. Could feel she was not lying but still hiding something here. Just hoped I could enjoy it what ever it was. "It seems people are saying that there is some major discrimination going on, on Campus here. On Pammy's part it as well it seems! And looking at all the acquisitions myself I must agree with them. Things are terribly discriminatory." How she kept a straight face saying all this I do not know. Yes! The complaint was real but still?

Kimmy was becoming livid however. Blinded by their affection these Girls did not think. Well I already wondered. Hey!? I was a student, okay maybe a mascot, so how could the ACLU do anything to the school for my actions? "What do you mean, discrimination? We have Hispanic and even Handicapped on the new rape list!" Well Tammy was blind of a sorts and her name was on that list the perv. What else could be the problem?

"Yes! That is true. Well there are no Asian or African heritages on the list it seems! They are the ones making the complaints." Quickly I perked up at that. What was she saying? "Now it has been explained to the ones that are doing the complaining about the consequences of their desires but I now have a list of eighteen new names." Yes! Damn I was beginning to like Mondays again. Just lunged on the desk grabbed the list from her hand and was off. She sounded confused now as she asked. "What does that mean?"

Kimmy giggled. "She likes Chinese food and big butts!" Dry pants were searched for I'm sure. The thing the college needed the most? Washer and dryer! Maybe an entire laundromat! The ACLU could do little as I was a student but the complaint could be an issue if it stayed open I guess. Besides! What isn't to like about Big Black Butts or Chinese?! Still had a problem however.

Where was Windy when you needed a spotter. Yeah I know they say the same about us but it is difficult to tell other races apart and I admit I had that problem. More so now as all you humans just looked like lunch! Now if they had made them all rub pussy juice on their pictures I would have been fine. Track them anywhere then. A small Chinese Girl with glasses went by glancing at me furiously. Check papers. Not easy with paws. There she was. On the list! So I hoped! Yu Yan! Chased her in a building and to a stairwell before I noticed. Pants?! Seriously?! Oh she was dropping her books and pulling them off fast. Cute butt! Greedy Girl. Very accommodating snack. "I am yours! Eat me you foul Demon Dog! Fill me with your Demon seed and give me your Puppys!" She was the right one! Hoped she was in the Drama Department. Maybe the fact Girls were getting pregnant and probably having Puppys should not have been made public. Who doesn't love Puppys? But just try and keep a secret around here! Such a strong voice for such a tiny Girl. What an offer too! Such big passion in such a small body as well! Her screams echoed so well in that stairwell. Was wondering who was raping who here?! Well I was panting when I left the stairwell for Windy's sake. Liked this Girl and would come back for more I was sure. Chinese is always so flavorful! Never get enough!

The biggest problem with Chinese Girls however is you eat one and five minutes later you want something else to stick your tongue in. Might just be me but so what? Sure I really hoped that Black Girl was on the list as I never checked before hand. Might have control issues. But that BUTT was to kill for! Hottest ass I had ever seen! So round and I wanted to taste the Black Moon! She swore at me, and hit me, and kicked me, as I had my fill of her. Had the most amazing ass! Even for a Black Girl. Glad I like it rough as she fought hard! Such language! Not sure what some of the words meant but knew they were bad! Wanted to get my whole head up her ass! Would not fit! Oh it was a savage anal raping! Got the other hole too but we know where my desire was here. Black Girl Shit! I Am A DOG!

She even called me a filthy mangy Bitch as she hugged me tightly after, both of us panting and spent finally. Said her name was Tanya. Gave me her number. Tucked the piece of paper in my collar. Pudgy and beautiful just like I like them. That BIG butt was just a bonus. She was damn comfy as well. That's how they found me you know! On a gorgeous semi-naked Black Girl cuddling in the hall outside of Economics as the class was letting out. She was a dark shade of Black. Many look brown but she was dark. So very beautiful too! The freaking Anti-Albino! Besides I was tired so I had a lie down after that raping. It was agreed by all when they found me that she looked comfy but I could not keep her without asking the General first the Girls said. Understood that line of reasoning however. Was certain that deep background checks had been made on all of us. Not good ones however. Okay they didn't really check. Well I was a ProtoDog Monster! Like anything in our past could trump that. That said the General had no problems with most nonviolent, non-victimizing criminals. Worked with a lot of them it seemed. You beat up old lady's for their money or sell drugs he has a big problem. He still looks at the circumstances.

No! When he did a background check he was looking for anything that may be used against him or worse Kimmy! His love for that Girl was greater then his list of potential enemy's. Kimmy's list was even longer and I was really beginning to understand that. Kimmy's last name held power! My problem was this comfy Black Girl was not on THE LIST! They checked several times. They got her information however and wrote her in. Practical accomplices. They told her about my tongue very nervously. She just kissed me saying she always wanted Puppys but her Mom would never let her have one. Hey a month or two of piddle pads is way cheaper than three years of diapers. What's not to prefer? Sure Teela was still in diapers and probably a smart thing as the laundry was piling up fast around here. And we headed out for the day. Teela was still getting the tour apparently as they pointed and told what things were still. And yes they pointed out the Raping Bushes to her! Did not worry me as much as the look in Teela's eyes.

Teela was scaring me however as I would catch her looking at me all dreamy like. Being very attentive to me as well. Rubbing and scratching me a lot. That was so nice! Quite a bit of affection. Loved it but I wondered what she was thinking. Fine that she was having my Pup most likely.

To the parking lot before the Dean found out what I did. She might get madder! We kinda got nervous as we got there. Hey there were a lot of Army Men nervously standing around Kimmy's car with the hood up looking in at the engine! Could be a problem! What the hell! More Shit? And I was happy! Now this! Kimmy would take no garbage from people and shouted angry and fast as we drew close. "Hey! Leave my car alone!" A couple Men spun and kinda rushed over looking scared. Never a good sign when Soldiers look scared is it? Can be fun though. Always make the best of a situation.

The one in the fancyer uniform went to attention and saluted Kimmy. His junior likewise a second later. Still looked scared. "Ma'am! Lt. Barnes, Ma'am. I am sorry to say this but your vehicle can not be removed from the grounds!"

Tammy and I just kept going. You didn't think a Blind Girl would stop for stuff she couldn't see do you? Yes they meant well but they were mere Boys after all! One of the Men around the vehicle saw us coming and he just freaked. Not at me for once! "Miss! Stay back there's a bomb!" Really? Had never seen one before! What did it look like? Curious ProtoDog's want to know! Tammy was trying so very hard to make a straight face. The Lieutenant turned to see what was happening but Kimmy grabbed him and spun him back. She knew we were starting some shit and she really wanted to help us out! We were just college students! Bored and disenfranchised! Yes, I know it's funny!

"What does he mean a bomb on my car? Weren't your Men supposed to be watching for this kinda thing?" Oh Kimmy's voice held imminent death. She loved that car after all. He began giving her a bullshit explanation. Kimmy listened with arms crossed watching us. We made it to the car. Well I made Soldiers nervous and they moved out of the way letting us in. Was huge you know! Felt if they had seen the videos of what I could do they would be running. Yes, it's true, I, like my idol Godzilla, enjoy the screams of Men!

Pushed Men aside and hopping up putting my front paws on the fender I looked in the engine compartment. Interesting but I had no idea what any of it was. Did not look very normal I felt. A certain General who shall remain nameless was a naughty Boy. Tammy hit a couple Soldiers with her cane in the shins forcing them to move for her. "Where's the bomb?" They looked at her like she was nuts. So hard not to laugh here. SMACK! That cane came down hard and I hoped not on someone. "Somebody point!" They did. Several! Do not fuck with the Blind Girl! Ah so that was a bomb. Not very big was it? Knew the smell though so I knew how strong it was. Had wondered where lame ass Parker Street Boyz had gotten some. Now I growled. "Can your Men remove it?" Tammy snapped sounding frustrated.

"Um, no Ma'am. Dead man switch in there. It will detonate if moved! Once the area is clear tonight we will detonate. No other choice!" Did he think she was stupid as well as blind? Did not feel guilty at all now! No one was blowing up this car! Had fond memories of the backseat!

Tammy looked rather thoughtful. "Is what it's attached to a necessary part of the car?" What did she perceive?

That question took him by surprise but he answered not understanding what she meant. "Um no Ma'am. It's on the exhaust manifold actually. The car can run without the exhaust and it will just be very loud. Potential fire hazard too though!" Doubted that! He seemed to grow less nervous as he explained. "Unique bomb placement. Once the exhaust pipes get to a certain temperature you see the bomb blows! Temperature trigger. Pure genius really. We can't remove the manifold without it detonating either though. Any twisting movement will detonate it." Smart person did this? So I was smart too! Okay I was mostly Smartass! Of course I admit it! Just pulled myself into the engine compartment a ways. His voice in a panic now! "Miss get that thing out of there!" They were all shouting in terror now. What a beautiful sound.

Tammy just smiled saying gently. "Then I'd run!" Blind Albino's are such fun! Even more fun when I raped her later.

Someone screamed. "HOLY SHIT!" Pretty sure a few did as they ran hard. CRUNCH! POOMPH! BURP! Smoking is bad for your health! Exploding bombs in your body? Not so much of a concern if you're a ProtoDog. Maybe I die if I do but I just did. Dogs don't believe in consequences! Just ask someone pulling the Porcupine quills from their Dogs nose for the tenth time! Which may explain why the twenty or ninety life sentences I was looking at if ever charged never crossed my mind. Much!

Laughing Teela sucker punched another soldier who already had his mouth open and grabbed what he was holding. As she ran over she was yelling happily. "Pammy! They let the guy put the bomb on while they planted a tracker on his car." She leapt on my back wildly. Then followed by maniacal laughter. "Try to keep up Tammy!" The happyness that was heard by me in the Father of my children's voice was amazing! Fine by me. Think Teela was feeling left out! That bothered me. Slam that hood! Girls were diving in the car as Tammy brought the engine to life with a roar. Loud roar now! Hey I was off down thc road. Teela lay on me and laughing gleefully said. "Head downtown sexy Mama."

Oh I did and I was!

"He's a ways ahead of us. Keep going straight. Oh Hell! Sidewalk cafe!" Teela snickered as she spoke. You ever wonder about those things? What owner thinks. "Gee let's put tables and chairs out on the public sidewalk so people in wheelchairs have to go in the street!" And what about the people who eat there. Do you think they applaud diversity, or is it more likely that they sit and make fun of those going by? Probably charge ten bucks for coffee too! The BASTARDS!

Besides I like the screams! Shit! Stepped in Creme Brulee! Now I'm gonna have to wash my paws later! Still I bet the waitresses were applauding! Thank Princess Windy, Tammy should be along shortly to finish the abomination off! "Turn left! There he is! The blue car!" Now I put on steam! Must have stopped to eat. Caught up rather quick. In the movies they always show high speed chases in the city all fast and dramatic like. Well they are not realistic and anyone who has watched Cops much has seen the reality! Too much shit to hit! Frankly I wonder what he was thinking as I ran right over his car from behind. Teela slid off onto his hood all sexy and striking a pose. Oh it was so HOT! Give that man an Uzi. Oh wait he has one already it seems. Now his windshield is full of holes and cracks. Teela was still just waving. Fist punched through the busted glass and she yanked his keys. BOOMPH. In through the passenger door I went as he passed. Well I don't have fingers so how am I supposed to open it? Use my head? I just did! Ha, ha, ha! To fast!

Damn it I broke him! Must have been these cheap doors. Should have been driving a '74 Chevy! They don't make them like they used too! So I went all the way through. Including him. Had made a mess again! Not to bad in the car at least. Teela was fast searching first him and then his car. Lots of papers that were probably useless, good bit of cash, locked briefcase, and a gun or two up front. Teela was quick with a search but not good with locks so when the rest pulled up in the convertible a few minutes later she was glad to see them. Kimmy however can pick a lock fast. Her home schooling had some practical lessons in it! Was not lost on me that the Mexican Girls had no real criminal skills. The White Chick and the Whiter Chick had loads! Gee, he had guns in the trunk, a couple more locked cases, and a suitcase with such horrible clothes. He deserved to die just for wearing some of this stuff! Looked like something the Bee Gees once wore! Had hit him hard and what of the clothes he wore we could make out were soaked in his guts and blood.

Some grizzled old Black Guy dressed shabby just walked up beside us without a care in the world and was looking in the trunk with us. "You Ladys looking to sell a gun?" Kimmy picked up a compact weapon with a long clip. Handed it to him sweetly with a smile. Hey, it could be for self defense! Was a pretty shady neighborhood and only a block from downtown. This city was going to hell. And there were Bigfoots around! Can't forget them!

Sabrina looked at him and snickered. Her voice low but sweet. "Actually? Do you know a reputable chop shop? It would help us if this all just kinda disappeared. No traces left." He grinned well now. Liked him!

Took what we wanted quick. Gave the guy five hundred dollars and we piled in the convertible.

Tammy laughed manically as she got in the convertible and said. "Let's go get Windy and hit the drive through!" True I was thirsty so I liked the idea.

Around the corner onto the main street. Shit! Traffic jam? Sabrina stood to see. "Um why are all those Cop cars in front of the bank?" Sabrina asked kinda scared so we all looked. They had the whole road blocked off! Not that she was afraid of what ever was happening. She was scared because she knew me far too well!

Kimmy smiled and shrugged. "Looks like another bank robbery!" There had been a few lately. Well lots of shit was happening and we had nothing to do with it so it's not in here. Not important before either. Still crime was ramping up in the city. Partly why little attention was paid to us.

Sabrina frowned incredulous. "On a Monday?" She had a point there. Bank probably had minimum cash today. No one ever said they were smart! "Fucking Idiots!" She was right with that one.

Teela snickered saying. "Hey Tammy and Pammy up for some shits and giggles?" My tummy was rumbling so I nodded. Hey, i could shit and Tammy could giggle! Moments later a sweet whistling Blind Albino Girl and her trusty Seeing Eye ProtoDog were walking down the sidewalk toward the bank as happy as could be. We'd been milking the Bigfoot story for a few weeks so why not push this one as far as possible as well?

Tammy's voice sounded very timid as I pushed through the crowds pulling her along. Ain't a crowd made I can't push through! "Wow Girl! It's really crowded downtown today." Yeah with all these people waiting to see a shoot out. Maybe get shot themselves in the process! WHY? How the human race has lasted this long is a miracle! Pushed our way through the crowd and past a young Officer trying to hold the crowds back behind a couple saw-horses who looked very shocked at this action to say the least.

Tammy was bobbing her head, wearing very dark glasses and had a white cane! What more can she do? In a near panic he said. "STOP! Miss you can't go down there! Didn't you see the barricade?" Rowdy crowd!

Oh I did feel sorry for him. He was just doing his job. Tammy also felt sorry for him or they would have needed a stretcher. Tammy spun and poked her white cane in the guys face. Such anger for such a small Albino. "WHY?! Because I'm blind? Do you have something against the Handicapped! Or is it because I'm white!" People in the crowd nodded snickering as well. She was white! Very very white! "Huh? You got a problem with me?!" He tried to say something but seriously? How do you respond to these accusations? With mouth hanging open it seems. We turned and left before he recovered.

An older Cop came over and looked at us as we went, but he was checking out my butt, he looked familiar, patted the younger Officer on the back and spoke. "It's okay son. You did good. Run across the street and tell them we need coffee and doughnuts to go." Hey I didn't think this would take that long either. Gasps and snickers could be heard from the crowd as he was not quiet.

Clack, clack, clack, that white cane went on the empty sidewalk. You know I needed a theme song! This Girl however watched way to many Stevie Wonder videos. Her head was just a bobbing away. Cute really! In the bank we went. Like nothing was going on. Very hard not to laugh at this stuff. Everyone inside turned and looked at us mouths hanging open as we entered! Guided Tammy to a teller line my tongue just lolling out trying to look stupid. Right behind a Man with a mask and a gun who stared in disbelief at us. Yes I was looking at the clock so I know! Three minutes twenty seconds of complete silence. "Man this line is slow." Tammy finally said breaking the silence. Than louder waving her cane. "What's the hold up! Somebody wake this teller up!" Okay I couldn't help it. Just had to! Either laugh or shit! Said my tummy was rumbling. Maybe I wasn't hungry after all. Retching and gagging was everywhere at the sight. Wait till the smell hits them! Damn nasty. Tammy never cracked a smile but her voice became concerned. "Oh Girl do you have gas?" Sadly I whimpered. "What? You don't like this bank? Why? They would not open a milk bone account for you? What bastards! Why did we come in here then?" So I whimpered again. "Oh you just had to poop!" A spinning leg sweep and puking began. One robber went face down. In my shit! Sat on him to keep him there. For a Blind Albino she could really move. Like ballet. Second robber lost his gun and got a cane over the head. Spinning fast she just threw it back over her shoulder hitting one in the face. Blood flew. Very acrobatic, she did a quick cartwheel grabbed her cane off the floor and with a flip stood in front of a masked man.

He stammered in fear. "W-W-What are you? D-D-Daredevil?"

With a grin she said. "Nope She-Devil!" She swung that cane so hard when she hit his balls he came up off the floor by a good two feet. Instant projectile vomit! Really this was like shooting fish in a barrel with the grenade launcher. I sat and scratched behind my ear. One felt he was smart and actually grabbed a hostage shoving his gun against her head. Now the problem with that is you can not pull a trigger without a head of your own! No brain, no pull impulse. It was really quite in there when I landed. The last gunman just laid down on the floor and slid his gun away his pants now full. Oh I could smell it. Smell a few of those hostages as well.

Tammy and I just left sweetly like nothing happened.

As we passed the two Cops Tammy said sweetly. "Sorry. My Dog was confused. Not my bank!" They may have snickered. Hostages were streaming out behind us fast. Did stink in that bank. The convertible was parked just outside the crowd. Waiting.

Teela was for some reason standing in the drivers spot. With a big grin Teela said. "Hey Miss! Would you and your Seeing Eye Dog like a ride to the drive-thru?" We would! Still darn thirsty.

As we got close Tammy asked curious. "Why is Teela driving?"

Snickers. Teela said. "I have my learners permit. Have to drive better then a Blind Girl too!" Lot's of heads were shaking now, even Windy's. Looks of terror were seen by me. Maybe she wasn't better! They had run and picked Windy up while we went to the bank. Got in the car anyway! Milkshakes! Windy made them come out side and bow to her. It was that one drive-thru after all and they were scared enough to listen. And get our order right. Really liked the food at Archie's ya know. Okay we were equal fear instilling terrorists and had done most drive-thru's by now. Than over by Pico Mall and hit the Fudge Shoppe as my sugar was low. They made Me stay in the car with Windy as they went into Dark Desire's. Understood that. Took both Teela the Tiger though and that made me nervous. Probably a mistake on their part leaving Windy out here. Her Highness was holding royal court in the parking lot for now. From my back of course. Was her Beast! Many listened to her words and asked her things.

The five year old's advice was spot on however. Yeah SCARY!

Finally a young bedraggled Black Boy of about twelve years old came staggering across the parking lot right up to the car and bowed. Maybe he almost passed out. Looked like he had slept in a dumpster! Smelled worse! She told him so gently to rise and speak in a gentle voice. He looked quite dazed and lost. Not the look you see on a strung out dope fiend. Like he was unable to believe he was still alive. Something was definitely not right here and Windy saw that fast. She has an eye for things and little details do not escape her. A funny smell was on this Boy I detected, besides the dumpster smell, and it reminded me of something I had smelled before. The Boys voice was flat. DEAD! Like he had no emotions left. His eyes were glazed. Not a Zombie though as I heard his heartbeat. Heavy shock at the least though. "A big ugly Fish Monster stole my Mother! Can you help?" There were some skeptical looks in the crowd instantly. Probably thought he was on drugs. Not as many as you would think however. Windy asked him gently to tell us more. That little Girl can be so intense. "I-I was asleep late Friday night when I heard a crash in the house. It was just me and my Mom there and she was asleep. Dad went to prison over a year ago! Scared I went out to see what happened and so did my Mom I guess. It was in the living-room and not looking happy! Seven feet tall at least. It's head scraped the roof and it looked like a Fishman like on the Saturday afternoon Monster movie!" I love those. "He was so tall and angry then he hit my Mom in the head as she came in and she fell. It came after me and I thought it was goin to eat me so I ran and escaped out the bathroom window. Hid across the street in the bushes by the Cutter's house, and I saw it carrying my Mom toward the river when I snuck back. I've been hiding out ever since. I'm so hungry!" He was in such tears. Of course we took him seriously! I was a ProtoDog and Becky was a ProtoTiger! Drake was a Chupacabra! We believed in Monsters! Okay the Girls asked if he was certain a few times just to make sure it was not a Sasquatch when they came out and heard the story themselves. They are real! I'll get there. Next Book! Think we pissed them off as well. They were suing Sabrina and her family after all! His Monster was a Fish for sure!

Windy spoke gently but there was no doubt who was in charge here now and forever. "Show us! Get in young Man. Drive-thru first! My subject must eat." Fine with me. The kid was hungry, that was certain. Frankly I was beginning to think my Girls were evil! Why else drive to THAT fast food place AGAIN! Hey I was Okay with them being evil so it didn't matter but still? No what scared me was Tammy offered to give Teela driving lessons. Don't ask me where that other pair of dark sunglasses came from as I do not know! Hiding in the backseat. Sure I was indestructible but seriously?

He directed us to his house while he ate. And he ate! Four burgers and six large fry's plus a jumbo soda. Told us he had been hiding mostly and had not eaten much since Friday. The way he was going at it I believed that. Hoped he did not get sick. Windy had been the one ordered for him. Wondered what that Girl knew! Again! Barely able to detect it earlyer on the Boy over the dumpster stench that scent was strong here as we pulled up to his house. Damn! His house made our old one look nice! Surprized it was still standing after the storm. Could smell the river close by but that was not what I smelled on the Boy or here. Realized it resembled the dead Fish smell out by the damn dam in a way. Quickly I growled and Teela popped the boot, I mean trunk! Sorry! Forgot I was writing this in American. Has anyone seen a Spanner around here. Rambo would have run in terror if he saw what those Girls pulled out! Their strength too had increased and they could handle the bigger weapons now so had stocked some. Ya never know when you may need firepower. The Boy even stopped shaking as his jaw dropped with his eyes popping out of his head. Still afraid! Just for entirely different reasons now!

Did not blame him for that.

His whispered. "Who are you?" Brought smiles to the faces of the Girls. He was told we were friends. Just not Super Friends! Not going there! Wonder Twins suck! Not in a good way!

Smiling at him Sabrina asked. "Is the door locked?" He nodded quickly and I felt in this neighborhood that was smart yet probably meaningless. He had gone out through the bathroom window he had said. Very smart idea if you fit because Fishmen don't fit easy it seems. They rapidly began discussing some strategy. However Princess Windy likes the direct approach you know and she just walked up and split the door completely in half with her Scepter. Yep I like her! Straight to the solution. And seriously as cheap as these houses were she probably could have done it before she got super powers. "That works." Sabrina said with a shrug. The moment that door was open the hairs on my neck rose though and fast.

Monster stink!

"Call Stone!" Roughly I growled at the smell. Might need some support? He was feeling left out I knew and I felt bad about too. Think he really wanted to be the hero for once.

They called him fast. He said not to go in until he got there. They just hung up on him laughing! "Oh that is nasty!" Teela said sounding ready to puke. It was a bad fart. Had gas again! I really hate Kevlar! Should send those bastards a barrel of shit! Let them know the terror! Who makes it anyways? Dow Chemical? We went in and saw some damage. This place had definitely been tossed, that much you could see. But why? What was the Fishman after? Split up and we searched quickly. Not smart you think? The fire power these Girls carried could completely level this house. Okay a good kick might level it. Only the one in front could shoot if we stuck together anyway, right? Nothing and no one. No idea what we were looking for really but I smelled no dead bodies in here. There was a bit of proof to add to the kids story at least. It had freaking big feet! Claw marks in the floor and walls were as big as my paws. Looked like Fishman feet to me too.

With a snicker Kimmy said. "Becky Tiger stop rolling in the footprints!" She was! Thought it looked like fun so I joined her. "Pammy stop that!" Hey I was a DOG! Her voice grew stern. "You're both getting hosed before you get in my car. Might run you both through the car wash still!" A thought! Becky just snickered. The sliding patio door was ripped off. The tracks were not apparent outside but the storm probably wiped them out. It's scent was still there however and headed straight to the river just like the kid said.

Stone, Sandra, and Brutus came in and Stone said meanly and kind of pouty I thought, looking around. "You Girls suck!"

Sandra hit him in the shoulder playfully. "You Wish! But I will later." Ooh! That put a smile on my Brother's face. Figured she wanted something to do while Brutus plowed her back side! Can be boring after twenty minutes.

Brutus did not like the smell either it seemed as his hackles rose. Stone said. "Sandra take Brutus to the SUV and circle around the block." She began to protest. "Take the kid too. You'll leapfrog as we go because I want an escape plan and get away car." He got some nasty looks now. Girls Do Not run from danger! "Okay then someone to explain to the Cops why world war three is going on by the river than!" TRUE! He saw what the Girls had and it scared him I think! Poor Boy.

Straight to the river the trail led. Windy spoke taking charge as soon as we got there. "The two Beasts will split up! One will go on each side of the river looking for the scent!" Ooh it was a smart idea. The fact that the five year old said it scared me! Wondered where she learned that one from. Did not want to know. She had a great memory though.

"Becky new! So I cross!" Growled out roughly. Made sense to me. Also wanted to protect Becky. She was still learning to trust herself.

Kimmy said with conviction pointing at me. "I'm with her!" Stone was against it of course. He was still afraid for me I knew. Or was it now fear for them? It was decided Sandra would drive parallel to the river. Becky on the waters edge others in between. Well if we found a body and that was what I expected to find people could stay with it while Sandra guided the Cops in.

Good plan!

Do they ever work though? Had a great one on Saturday and they just took the easy route.

They kinda got pissed off fast however when Windy leapt on my back grabbing Kimmy on the way and spurred me on. "Let's go Beast!" There was much screaming behind us as I swam and Windy just smiled back at them and waved. Nice to be the Princess! Was Her Beast to command! Stone did not understand it was not a game! We knew it was not a game! Windy was the boss! Hey I was fine with it. Much understanding came to me as we crossed that river. Mostly I understood what was meant when the Alien had said Tanner chose well. Yes I was a mass rapist and admitted it. But otherwise I cared about people. Especially the ones I raped! These ability's in other hands would be scary dangerous at best. That said I worried someone bad might get some powers from me. If they had been forthcoming with these things I would have been more careful. That said I could not wait to tell that puny Alien how many kids were coming! Evil is up for interpretation! And some beings just deserved to! Shit! Their! Pants!

The problem with our search was that the river was at the bottom of a slope. Only about twenty feet below street level sure but most of it was heavily overgrown with bushes. Some trees. Bunch of garbage. Which made travel extremely hard. Even with the Princess killing plants ahead of us. Don't ask!

It grew dark quick too and no scent yet. Well I kinda caught it at times but nothing strong or definite. Just occasional whiffs. They were calling us to come back finally after three miles. There was a lot of light coming from above us though as we found a clearer river bank. Had been relatively dark for a while so curious I crept up the slope cautiously to get my bearings so to speak. Hoping to take up the search tomorrow mostly using whatever was bright as a landmark. Carefully lifting my head enough to see what I could over the slope however I thought that searching was probably not gonna be necessary. Oh my! This was very interesting! Party tomorrow at the strange prison I think!

Windy said quietly. "Big." It was!

Kimmy whispered. "Looks like a maximum security prison!" Yeah a big one. Where there should not be one! Seven or eight layers of heavy fence sure said it was one. All with razor wire on top too. Men with guns where walking around everywhere. A couple hundred at least. Huge windowless building in the middle! Kimmy got pictures with her phone quick. Creeping back to the river we crossed quietly. For some reason however I was pretty sure if I had gone just a couple hundred yards more I would have found the Fishman's scent. Dogs do not believe in coincidence however! This building and the Fishman were connected in some way I knew!

Tammy said when we got back trying to cheer the kid up. "Don't worry kid we will find your Mom."

He began to cry. His voice pitiful. "Dead?"

Tammy said, and quite gently for a MAD blind Albino I thought. "I don't think so kid. If it wanted her dead her body would be in the house still. That it took her alive is a good sign." Snack for later went through my head. Figured the Fishman had eaten the Boy's Mother by now! Wasn't wrong either. Tammy drove so Sabrina and Kimmy could research this building. Now the Boy was terrified for other reasons at least. We could have told the Boy she could see but we took it for granted and paid no attention anymore. That the building did not even exist was found out quickly. No record of a building there at all! Federal forest land! The compound had been called and told of the little Boy's impending arrival. He refused to get back in the Mustang with Tammy driving so I knew he was not in bad shape. They pulled him in screaming. Had Mexican upholstery so I was good. Where do you think Teela was. Comfy! She liked it! BRRIPT! She liked that too!

That Boy screamed in terror like a little Girl the whole way to the compound! Did not blame him. We were way scaryer then the Fish Monster! He was quickly fussed over and fed again when we got there. After he was done kissing the ground thanking some God that he lived! That got us a few looks. Everyone there seemed too like him a lot. Well he was quiet again. He ate well. May have thought it was his last meal? The General was highly concerned about what was going on with what we found though so being a crazy person he tried to help. One of the benefits of being a four star General apparently is you can have satellite surveillance wherever you want it! Or maybe not?

Of course when that satellite oddly shuts down fast and long before anything can be seen? Even four star General's can get scared! When a strange virus wipes out certain Army computers things begin to look very bad. Those who knew were getting nervous. Except!? Smiling Tammy just went and pulled her laptop out with a giggle. Went to the dining table and sat. Half an hour later she smiled again. That scared me! Well think about it? She could not read a book so how did she know what was on the screen? Not sure I wanted that answer! You understand?

The Dean asked her cautiously. "Did you find anything?" We had all been watching her in silence, utterly fascinated, for a half hour. Her fingers just flew across that keyboard like lightning.

She sighed. "Yeah the land is actually owned by a shell corporation which is owned by another shell corporation which is… well I went through over twenty layers and gave up. Interesting thing is the owner of each corporation is dead. Has been for years. Anyone recognize that Man?" She pulled up a grainy photo of an old man. Doctor Petrov who had come out to learn of the Fishman went almost as white as Tammy and sat down. HARD!

Everyone looked at her waiting. "That is Doctor Charles Whiting. He's a ghost! Certain people only whisper his name. I've only actually met him three times when I was younger. Much younger! Very scary Man! He has to be dead by now! He was older then dirt when I first met him twenty years ago. Where did you get this picture? Has to be old!"

Tammy snickered and I knew it wasn't old. "CIA database. They were investigating a Man down in Mexico who was allegedly selling some biological weapons and doing espionage last year and the Man was meeting the Doctor there in that restaurant. Most of the record of that meeting was destroyed shortly after. There was even audio of their meeting as well but it's gone too. The CIA was convinced the Doctor was a spy also as they traced him and found his birth certificate. Born 1837!" Tammy did not seemed amazed by all this. We should have been? Her eyes were taped shut! Sure she had radar but the screen was flat! No one asked though. Yet!

Oh the General was suddenly turning white now too. But he was looking at Tammy! Interesting! His whispered comment of. "My God! I know who you are!" Full of emotions. Many shades of terror! More than fifty!

Tammy stuck her hand at him with a smile. "Hi General! Nice to officially meet you in person finally." She meant that. "They thought it best if we didn't. For many reasons really."

People here were understandably nervous now. Most of us sitting at the dinning-room table watching this unfold. Had been nervous for a while but this ramped it up big time. The Dean spoke first her voice very tense. She did not like being in the dark about things. "What is going on here?" Shoot! I did not care really. But it was a smart question I thought.

Tammy just snickered cutely blushing. Shyly she spoke. "Well? Back in seventh grade I kinda took over the nuclear mainframe to get all the nuclear missile launch codes and changed them to My Little Pony names. Held the country hostage for three days till the General and his Men tracked me down. If Mom bought me what I asked they never would have. Well they had canceled my favorite TV show and I was mad, young, and foolish. You see I understand machines and their language like no one else I find. Always have. Can't even remember which show it was that got canceled now but I was mad though and kinda left a trail so they found me." Everyone had a shocked incredulous look on their faces and I do not blame them for that. Just yet another unbelievable thing to wrap their heads around. Liked My Little Pony so I saw no problem really.

Mom spoke up sounding rather disbelieving. Don't blame her there. "But I never heard of any of that stuff happening!"

Tammy snickered more at that statement. "Well they sure as Hell were not gonna say it on the news now were they? A little Girl had control of the entire nuclear arsenal? And any kind of trial would be public knowledge as well. Only seven people knew who I really was. Only met three of them. They however threatened to make me and my Mother disappear forever! Like I had not thought of that possibility though and I told them that would not be smart as I had a sweet little virus like program I created. Still do! For my Mom's safety I never shut it down. Took a long time to write it, it was so complex. Very special! Not sure she would work well anymore but she is there. Not sure what she even is any more. Made her actually adaptable and gave her the ability to grow, she has an attitude too. If I don't talk to her every week she will do some very bad things still she says. It was designed to destroy firewalls and tell everyone to go look up their name in the government records. The secret ones. Not important though. My virus is a sweety. As long as I keep contact."

Sandra actually asked something practical but rather terrifyed like most of them. "Were you careful in your search now? Can they trace you back here." Practical question really and it made much sense. Did not think Tammy had been careful though. Okay sure she had not been. We had all been victims of a sort our whole lives and Tammy was crazy. Not a lie!

Also I knew from that smile Tammy was up to some shit. "Don't worry. They won't even try and find us." They all looked at her nervous. "Well I sent them an email after all. Told them we were coming for them at 8 PM tomorrow and sent our yearbook pictures along so they would know who we were when we got there. Did not want them shooting any vagrants." Tammy was all smiles. Happy as could be! Most here however were shocked with mouths hanging open. Even more so when the General actually finally shook her hand.

Obviously I didn't see a problem with any of it. Killing tomorrow night! The only problem I saw here was too many clothes! Humans are quite beautiful naked. It had been hours since my last raping!

Here Daddy!

Teela was mine!

Oh the screams as I savaged them!

Maybe I actually had a problem?

CHAPTER 4 NATIONAL INSECURITY'S
Tuesday September 28th

Woke to the sounds of hard crying. Not a child. They were in the bathroom who ever it was so I went to see. Maybe I could help them? Could be out of TP in there! It happens! Tammy sat in there on the toilet naked just bawling. Bright! Need sunglasses! Went to her and shoved my head between her alabaster legs and sniffed. Well I thought they had gotten more toilet paper in here but you can never be too careful. Might be she was constipated? Better believe I could hope! Well sure I could have looked at the holder to see if there was paper but where is the fun in that? She grabbed my head forcing my snout deep between her thighs and held me there so I was good. Thought she wanted me there and I was right you see? BRRIPT! See? Then she spoke and her voice was breaking. "I love you so much Pammy! I don't want to leave you!"

Just whimpered in her pussy.

Sobbing harder. "But I can't stay here anymore! I'm a criminal! Broke all of the rules they set up for me. Public enemy number one and they will lock me up!" So! Maybe we could get a cell together! Between the rapes and illegal medical procedures I was looking at probably ninety life sentences at least! So what was one more rape? That Blind Albino could scream and I made her do it in the bathtub. She was going nowhere! Told her that too. Windy liked her too after all! Think they all came in and just went potty so they could watch while I raped this quivering mass of brilliant white flesh in the tub for three hours!!! She had a very strong heart! A sight to see naked in sunlight. She did not have to pee or poop anymore! Might have been wearing some of mine. As I got out of the tub Becky who had just come looking for me went in. The screams were glorious! Cat tongue is friggin intense. There was a lot of Cat in Becky now as well which seemed to be helping her. Yes I remembered how different I felt about things with my new perceptions so I was hopeful. Still she had oral sex. The aggressor this time true.

Of course Tammy got me in trouble.

Again!

As I carried a drooling Albino out to the car in the morning they started telling me I couldn't take her to school naked like this as they shaded their eyes from the glare. Sunny outside! Why the hell not? Stupid nudity rules and laws! Shoot! I didn't wear any clothes! Why should anyone else!

Great! Now I had too stand there while they went and got some clothes and dressed her. And here I thought it was going to be a good day.

We had the Black Boy with us so maybe it was a good thing they put clothes on Tammy. He may have gone blind from the glare on that white skin otherwise. There is nothing wrong with nudity! There is something wrong about creating shame in children however! That said public sex is probably wrong! And I should know!

There were lots of good reasons for taking him with us however. He was after all an unknown and he was also a tweenage boy. There was artillery laying all over the place at the compound! Besides he needed someone to talk to and Miss Winters was a wonderful Counselor. Perverted Slut sure but she knew her stuff dang it! Yes I liked her stuff a lot too! Especially that junk in the trunk! See if I were writing this in English that would sound weird. Junk in the boot!? Doesn't even rhyme! Thank God I write in American! We had been rather cautious however and had not pryed to much into his story or life for now. Just tried to cheer him up. Take his mind off things! He seemed a nice kid after all. Not sure anybody knew his last name! Or even his first? So first thing we did when we got to the college was take him to go see Miss Winters in her office.

Sabrina volunteered and went in alone first and told her what we knew of the Boy. We did not want him getting worked up before he went in. Miss Winters however looked almost in tears when she came out and introduced herself to the Boy. She hugged the Boy nicely then each of us. She's a hugger. Liked that in a rape victim!

Okay fine! Listen up all you rapists?! If she does not thank you after or hug you? You did it wrong and need to please her better! If your intention is to just hurt and you think and feel nothing for your victims you are a FUCKING PUSSY and I will hunt you down and show you how it feels! Well I like to EAT PUSSY'S!

Off to Political Science and I grew curious as Tammy came in with us. She did not have this class! Then when she just went up to the Teacher and began whispering I got nervous. It was Tammy you see and she is Crazy! She scared me a bit. More now. Loved her though. The Albino it seems had turned! Not a frustrated and scared little Girl anymore! As class started the Teacher just went and sat at his desk while Tammy stood there and I knew I was gonna have some problems. Should have peed before we came in! This carpet may need some serious steaming soon!

Tammy smiled as she spoke loudly. Honestly she looked good up there. Like she belonged. Dark glasses and white cane in hand. "Can anyone tell me, Who watches the Watchmen?" Even I understood the students confusion here. Well she had dark glasses and a white cane. I had led her in. she used the cane like a blind person would to get on the stage. Looked blind! Well if they raised their hands to answer how would she know? And no one wants to just shout something out and look like a fool if they are wrong! But Tammy did this on purpose. Very smart! That Albino can think on her feet! She snapped with venom and scared a few students. "Exactly! No one is and that is the problem." She paused to let that sink in. "The problem with a government as large as ours is one hand has no idea what the other is doing. Large sums of money are wasted and shuffled around constantly and no one can say where it all goes. Massive secret slush funds exist everywhere! The NSA used to be referred to as No Such Agency! No one knew it existed at one time! There are other agency's and powers out there like that still to this day, and some of you have seen the proof of that here on campus! They may still have spy's around even, might have some in this room even so do not hesitate to report things. The more who know something the harder it is for them to cover up. Too many people want power and will hurt anyone in their way to get it! Her Highness Princess Windy will fix that!" No idea if she knew or suspected but she was right. Knew it in my heart and soul!

As she spoke she hooked up her laptop to the projector and started showing slides. Doctor Whiting, General O'Donnell, and the Burdetts! As she began to tell about clandestine agency's even the Teacher was taking notes furiously at his desk. These kids were in awe of her and what she revealed. Terrified as well because this was very scary shit! Wondered how she knew? She talked about Government sanctioned murder over the last hundred years. Not just American either. Many know who the Tuskegee Airmen were. But did you know in the town of Tuskegee the Government carried out a diabolical experiment letting Black Men die of Syphilis to study the disease instead of curing them? Or about the MK Ultra experiments the CIA did. Did the sitting President know of these things? Most likely not. See what she means? Sure it was for the common good but you can justify anything with that statement! Hell my Colonoscopy's were for the common good! Not just Governments either. Big Corporations are in it too! Like the greedy Starbucks Experiment to see how gullible the nation is! Think about that when you are paying twelve bucks for a cup of coffee next week! If I'm paying that much for coffee it better have been pooped out of a Cat! Kopi Luwack is from coffee beans eaten by a Civet, which is a Wild Cat, and pooped out! Got something against Cat Poop Coffee? Supposed to taste amazing. Think about that next time you get pissed at your job! How would you like to separate Coffee Beans from Cat Poop for a living? There is always something better and something worse so make the best of what you have and stop wasting time coveting thy neighbors Cockapoo!

The class was unusually quiet as they wrote so we heard the sound of nearby gunfire blasts easily as class was just wrapping up. Not automatic gunfire, but three quick loud roaring blasts and I went fast. Opening my senses I went straight toward the Deans office. Hey if the shooting wasn't at me where else would it be?! Dean Kelly had a smoking shotgun in hand and looked sexy scary standing in the hall by the rear exit. Oh I liked it! Explained the blasts too. She pointed to Miss Winters office as she watched for another attack. In the office fast I saw the Blonde pudge laying in a large pool of her own blood and I got PISSED! Barely noticed the Man with no face laying in his own blood against the far wall. The large floor to ceiling glass windows had been broken outwards behind Miss Winters desk.

Quick I went to the blonde pudge as tears leapt to my eyes when I saw the damage to her head and face! It was real bad. Someone had hit her very hard! Shattering her face with a gun butt probably. Her busted eye hung out a little. Could hear her heart still so she was alive still! Barely however! Probably would not even live till the ambulance arrived. My heart was breaking! Tears flowed down my face as I watched her dying. Tammy got there first and never hesitated as she said urgent and commanding coming over. "Pammy! Get your tit over her mouth!" Wrote my fear off as just being upset for the moment. So I got milked! It was fun. Hoped she did it again some time. Tammy held Miss Winters mouth open and squeezed milk out of me. Heard her mumble the cryptic words. "SHIT! This was not supposed to happen!" Knew instantly this was her fault than but waited till I knew more to react. She had I assumed done something people would not have approved of as great risk was involved and it went wrong. Miss Winters was all that mattered to me at the moment though. Could kill an Albino later if I had too! Oh I could!

Heard the Dean yelling from outside. "Strip him to his boxers and drag him to Biology!" Interesting! A live one? Ooh! What fun! Might just be for dissecting I guessed. We were a school and we taught every chance we could and I liked that. Did not think cops would ever be called. Military jurisdiction now! You might understandably ask whose military? Frankly I was leaning towards Windy's! Most had sworn allegiance already! She is so cute!

Kimmy came in the office and saw what we were doing and she smiled sweetly with a snicker. Such emotion in her voice. "You two are nuts! I love you both though. Never had friends and now I have one who's a Monster and one a Blind Albino Criminal Mastermind. Oh and a Mexican one!" You could hear the joy in her voice. She pointed at us. "Ambulance is on the way. Told them a fall happened and someone was hurt bad. This could cause major problems though you know!" We both looked at her not understanding. "If Pammy heals her all the way people will want to know why and how! They got the Boy as well!"

Tammy swallowed as I started to move. Her voice ready to break with the emotion it held. This was her fault and it hit her hard. "Pammy NO! I know you want to save the Boy and we will, but not now! Save Miss Winters! Please!" Okay I glared at her seeing the tears running down her cheeks and feeling the pain in her heart, understanding she HAD done something now and was not just blaming herself for no reason. This was not an accident so I looked at her. "I'm sorry but there was no choice Pammy." Her voice was trembling as she explained. "We need to know things! We have to see where they take him! I put a tracker or six on him this morning. No! I didn't want to do it but I had too! Had to connect the Doctor with the Fishman! This shit is getting real scary. Why I didn't show you lots of what I found out about the Doctor as I could not believe it myself. He is very dangerous! Please don't hate me Pammy!" Oh tears were flowing. Knew her words were true and her fear real. They had to be bad tears to run down her cheeks as her eyes were taped up again. Yeah I was pissed but not enough to realize she was not wrong. We had to know if the Fishman and the prison facility were connected in any way and now it seemed so. Did not believe in coincidences but did not believe this Whiting was involved with my creation either. Why both were here was not mere chance though.

Do you have memory troubles? We used people as bait all the time. Yeah mostly ourselves but still. This was different in ways now but still necessary. We did not have to like it and didn't but had to do it anyway. If she had asked I would have eventually said yes as well. May not have liked to but still I would have agreed. Tired of running into the unknown.

They knew we were coming so we figured that the Boy would be used to keep us away like a human shield or so we figured! Wrong about that. Knew nothing about what was going on out there however! Windy actually might but we had no clue about that yet. Sometimes even mistakes work out though. They did not know us however either or they would know human shields just get you dead. Ask the gunman in the bank! That alone said there was no connection between O'Donnell and the Doctor that Tammy could find. If the Boy got hurt I would never stop hunting or killing! Did not make sense but I was stressed. Knew I was missing something. Probably lots of things. True they were an unknown as well as we had no idea how many Men they had but seriously? When did we care about that? Needed time to think! Needed Frank's Red Hot! Twenty gallon bucket! Maybe two!

So I pulled Tammy close with a big paw and hugged her tight. Kimmy was on her phone already explaining to the General what had happened. He actually approved of the tactics Tammy used but was very pissed about other things you see. We still had military protection after all on campus now didn't we? And I heard his anger. Having done what I could for Miss Winters Kimmy shoved the Dean on my back and told me to hunt. The Dean had a sweet sawed off shotgun in her hands. Present from the General! He Really liked her! She told me as we went that Miss Winters was already down by the time she got there and blew ones head off. That Miss Winters fought for that Boy and the Dean had heard all that through the wall.

That was Tammy's mistake! Underestimating Miss Winters love. We found dead Soldiers quick. About a dozen. Each alone in the bushes. This was not good. Other Soldiers arrived quickly. Dean Antwerp took charge and just gave orders. You better believe it! Those Men listened to her as well! She had a Shotgun! Radios were used fast. The ambulance had not left with Miss Winters yet when they found out one man was unaccounted for. Captain Schultz was not here. Gee, imagine that. Dead or alive!

Heard the General bellow over the radio. "If you find the Captain detain him. He resists kill him!" The General was pissed so everybody in a half mile radius probably heard that one. Did not blame him. All the dead had been shot in the back at close range after all. Silencer most likely. Hate cowards! Have I told you that?

Got to class very late and it was a shame as Ms. Bordeaux was on a Philosophical rampage screaming about money being the root of all evil. She had a point! Still scary! Then she sorta brought me into it as well to my utter humiliation. The morals of designing Monsters. She did say in front of the class I had good morals, better then most humans, and how very beautiful I was. That all morals were subjective! They are a philosophy not a science. Not something set in stone! Yet people always assume they are written in stone and the same everywhere. If its 70 degrees outside your house do you assume it is seventy everywhere on the planet? (Oh, it's not Steve! What an idiot. Who let him read this? We still love you Steve!) Two hundred years ago it was morally acceptable to sell your thirteen year old Daughter to some fifty year old Man for a Bride! She had no say what so ever in it! Girls were property. Some still think that as well! FINE! Feel that way myself but I loved my property and would kill for them! Treat others nicer or I eat you!

Amazingly I got hugs when the class was over. Even from the Teacher. By the time we hit the commons everyone knew what had happened to Miss Winters and the Boy! Word travels fastest if it involves sex or death! Oh you ask what about party's? You're silly! That is all party's are! People go hoping to get sex and see death! Well you must go to some lame ass party's! We were going to one party later and death was guaranteed! Probably sex too! Well we were gonna fuck some people up! Good with me!

Our nice Reporter showed up and he was very concerned about all of us. He knew we were hurt by this and he cared. Sure we made him famous but he was still a nice guy. That Bitch had tried to come back and military turned her away. They told him how Miss Winters was nearly killed trying to protect the poor child from the gutless cowards. She was stable at the hospital he had heard as he arrived and told us. They feared brain damage yet. It had been a very vicious blow to the head it seemed breaking her skull. Once the camera was off he asked again how we were doing sounding genuinely concerned. Pretty sure he was. Sure he liked us for reasons other than ratings which were doing good for him. They told him we were scared. That we did not want to lose a friend or the Boy. We too cared!

Sabrina almost in tears said sadly as it was catching up to her. Her voice strained bad. "I wish we could do more! I feel so helpless just sitting here now."

Tammy suddenly began laughing so hard I let go of the leg of Kimmy I had been chewing on to gawk. Knew this would be good! That leg sure was! "Want to ramp this up a lot Girls?" You could just tell she had some SHIT in mind! That was the most evil smile I ever saw and everyone knew it.

Kimmy snickered, her leg no longer in my mouth. Could chew hard on it now and not hurt her. "What ya thinkin bout Tammy?" She knew it was evil as well and approved already.

Tammy asked the reporter. "Can you air this on the six O'clock news? Say afterward that a surgical strike team is poised to take down a facility that is preforming illegal human experimentation here in the city!" She pushed a piece of paper over to him. "Be here at eight and ready to film. Do not let them see you before we get there or you will get dead!" Said all this with a smile.

Kimmy snickered happy now. "Hear that Pammy more illegal surgery tonight!" Ooh I got excited! They knew how much I loved illegal surgery! "Ooh look there's one now!" It was! Yeah they explained that one to the reporter while I was away! Thank Windy for small favors! Did not want to be there for that one! My problem I realized now was how do the Girls know I am mad if I bite them when I do it for no reason all the time anyway? Anyone? Ideas?

Dragged my Prey/Patient down in the entrance to the science building. Did not hide my crimes like the cowards! Korean I think. She tasted spicy! Like Kimchi! Loved it! Trotted back and kissed them all with spicy poop breath! Not one single complaint! Hey my bucket was full again! Someone brought a bucket out earlier full of food and now it was full again. More lunch! They love me here. Girls would come up and hug me or pet me all the time. Most smelled familiar. Yes I shoved my nose in their butts! They loved it! Loved me too it seemed even after I knocked them all up! Most were happy about that too! When they were told that they may be having Pups they asked if I and the Girls would help with potty training. Sure all these Girls would be happy having Puppys!

Who wouldn't? It's Puppys!

Math rape time! I mean math class! Okay maybe I was right the first time. Two beautiful black girls in the back. The teacher was upset as I raped them until Sabrina explained it was a civil rights issue like affirmative action! He said he should probably discuss those things next week as it may be on the exam about pay discrepancy's. Class touched on some practical aspects of business as well. He kept lecturing through the squeals. Those two were wild! Tasty! Needed BBQ sauce! My sex life was extremely public. Needed a fan club! Maybe I had one?

It was bound to happen sooner or later however. Someone came up behind me and was petting my butt nicely as I watched for Prey from a doorway between classes. Never looked back! They were always coming up and petting me and I was busy. Cocked my tail to the side fast before I even looked. It was the older janitor and he was just smiling with his pants down. You know the old saying. "The older the Bull the harder the Horn?" His was and all I could think of was he must be a retired porn star with something that big! Felt good to me! You ever notice the guys in porn are not cute? Sorry, probably not. Only Gay Men would notice and they would not be watching what you watch? If you ask me all you guys who watch porn are rather gay yourselves. Think about it next time you're watching a big, thick, hard, throbbing, cock going into a Girl! All a question of perspective now ain't it? You are looking at a cock! He was quite good and it felt nice. Would not mind a second helping. Felt I owed him for picking up after me all the time too. Shit, Blondes, Brunettes, some Red Heads, you know! That kind of stuff I left laying around. Done he spanked my ass hard and sent me on my way. Never spoke a word. Was late for Art class however which annoyed me somewhat. Liked art!

That old guy was here again and I began to wonder if he was an ex-porn star! Might have been hoping! Hey I needed sex too! Always horny and hungry these days. Giving is great but receiving every once in a while is what makes it worthwhile! Sorry. I was desperate and needed lots of cock or something big bad! My ass and pussy were feeling very neglected lately.

Talk to the Dog! Prayers however would be answered soon!

We had another life drawing session as there was a volunteer. When it was announced I got nervous. Last one had been an issue after all. When the model came in I got very tense! That big Black Girl from yesterday. Tanya! Like this was going to help quench my desire?! She suddenly volunteered the Teacher said happily. Knew I was in the class! She waved at me all smiles. Must control urges. Had to paint her now! Could eat her later. Oh she looked so yummy naked! Massive melons to match that major butt and all in a dark chocolate! She had more curves then a Gran Prix! Class almost done the old Man came over and looked at my painting while he got his butt sniffed. Well my painting was on the floor so he was bent over in front of me to look at it. I'm a Dog remember? It was a butt! And I was not passing up the chance. Seriously? We are in the middle of book 2 and you are still complaining? Do you know what it is like to actually be a Dog? Than go back and reread everything! He might be a friend after all and inquiring ProtoDog's want to know these things! Reached back between his legs and scratched my chin gently while he checked my work very carefully. When he stood up and turned he patted me on the head as he spoke. "You are a great artist and a fantastic butt sniffer! Your work on both is really good." Such praise! Yes I had to sniff a few butts after that statement so people could see for themselves on that one. All agreed I was good! The Man it turns out was a big art critic and had a gallery of his own. Mrs. Pertwell knew him well and asked him here.

And I like butts! In case you had not noticed! Maybe that was why I became a Dog in the first place? One of the reasons.

Hey Guys you ever hear a Girl say a Guy has a nice butt? What do you think? Do they have a strap-on at home? Our Dean wears hers all the time.

Sabrina snickered holding her phone in her hand her voice sounding urgent. "No more butt sniffing Beast! Her royal highness has summoned us!" Ooh my Princess Pup! Had to go now! Loved my Princess Pup! Dogs don't do linear thinking you see. More like firework thinking. You know? Straight line briefly and then? BLAM everywhere at once! I didn't have a problem with it. Kinda fun being a Spaz Case!

To the Bat-mobile my Blind Albino! What are they gonna do? Sue us? Get a freaking number! We know your address DC Comics and I can fill a barrel in a day! Maybe less!

Embarrassing but true.

Tammy drove as Kimmy was busy sniffing my farts. Was laying on her you see. Definite methane addict! Loved her anyway. Sabrina had her head back there as well. Becky Tiger was riding shotgun rolling her eyes! She liked the madness and I knew it! She loved having friends now as well. Even crazy ones. Her life had been hell!

Windy, her Teacher and close to thirty little five year old's with grim angry looks were standing in the parking lot waiting. Almost ran! Well they looked ready to kill. Many other faces were plastered to windows trying to see what was going on out there. We pulled up and grinned at the kids. Becky and I both jumped out and got petted and hugged quickly. Kids love fluffy Monsters!

Windy said right away her voice stern pointing at Kimmy. "Tell them all about the Fishman!" So Kimmy did holding nothing back. Told these kids what we knew and what we were doing about it! No sugar coating in the least. Yes we confessed premeditated murder to a bunch of five year old's. They were good with it as long as they were only bad Guys dying! Maybe there is something to this desensitization they talk of? NOPE! Kids are just vicious! One Road Runner cartoon has more violence then most video games! Nothing wrong with being vicious! Those are the emotions that make great leaders! Hitler was a great leader and nearly took over the world with a small country! Do not get your pantys in a bunch yet! He was a despicable human being! But he knew his limitations and surrounded himself with some master tacticians and brought the world to its knees! Windy would do what he could not do, with style and love! Windy got upset when she found out the Boy had been taken but had faith in me to get him back! Even said to the kids her Beast would eat well tonight! Wanted hot sauce darn it. Teachers seemed uncomfortable when that Girl talked of killing the Infidels but you can understand? Students understood that. They were five year old's! How many terrorist attacks were they forced to watch over and over hundreds of times each on TV? If it bleeds it leads and if nothing is bleeding today we will show what was bleeding yesterday again!

No idea who may have thought we were safe at that point but they were wrong! Yes I knew it was about to get deep! Windy was smiling after all. Not a good sign! EVER! "Tell them we are going to see Aliens over the weekend!"

Yes Your Highness!

When Kimmy actually told them I was amazed however. Maybe she got it too finally! Did not matter anymore as Windy was in charge now!

When the students all wanted to go along and Kimmy said they could rather happily I admit I almost pooped! Did not expect her to go that far! "Make some calls Miss Tinker. We leave on the field trip Thursday night be back late Sunday. They need clothes but nothing else. All food and lodging will be provided. Luxury bus! Tell all the parents it is truly a once in a lifetime experience. That the opportunity arose suddenly and you want to take the kids. There will be chaperons!" The Teacher still looked like we were nuts. "Tell the parents we are going to see a big space exhibit by Chicago. All expenses are paid." The Teacher was nodding. In terror I think!

Now I really, really need to bite that Blind Girl. Tammy said snickering. "Hey kids want to see something cool? Windy go stand by the tree!" Sabrina and Kimmy knew better than to freak. There was no time for that! Move children back to avoid ricochets fast as Windy went smiling! Lots of children out here now too! Wow the whole school was out here by now, after all that shouting I understood! Tammy popped the trunk on the Mustang and pulled out an AK 47. The 50 caliber may be a tad bit too much. We had some scary shit in there! Windy stood there arms raised as Tammy unloaded the clip at her. The whole school was out here by now as mentioned and those kids gasped fast then applauded. Windy bowed, not a mark on her body. The kids were all out there before Tammy shot and we had made sure of that. Kids knew who had the gun and what it was being shot at but Windy was smiling! Frankly that it was the Blind Albino shooting scared the Teachers! Windy wanted to show off too! And her classmates needed to see the truth. Got that one at least. So did they as Windy told them she invincible. Other classes were mad they could not go see Aliens but Windy told them nicely if they write a question down she will ask the Aliens to answer it. Teachers could help them with that.

Sabrina sighing understandably was all like. "Now what do we do? Windy's almost naked again." True! Her voice was gentle and I understood her point. Clothes do not hold up so well under automatic gunfire. Definitely she was coming around and accepting things however.

"We got time to swing by the mall." Tammy said sweetly as she put a fresh clip in the weapon and set it back in the trunk. Nothing better to do really! Time to kill now! People to kill later!

Kimmy was excited as she suddenly remembered. "Hey! Her tiara is in!"

Tammy way to excited asked. "Can we teach Windy how to shoot the grenade launcher?" Yeah, yeah, yeah. Go ahead and call CPS! It was a good idea! We might need her to crawl through air vents or sewer ducts with it you see. None of us were small enough to do that? Hey! I had asked the Dean for a couple Midgets and she turned down my Midgetnapping request! So it was her fault! True I liked watching my Pup crush heads however! The sound brought Pride and Joy to my heart and the smile on her face was priceless! She wasn't gonna get hurt and if we told her no someone just might! This child was like Stephen King's greatest nightmare! Unkillable and totally Badass!

Still I was so proud of her! Such a cutey too. First to the mall! She needed a Princess dress before we picked up her Tiara. Hey this wasn't the way to the Mall! Now I looked up from my Mexican snack to see where we were going and it was the wrong way. Thought Tammy may have gone blind! Windy was waving at the Peasants from my back. She saw nothing going on as I have a big head. Oh we were going to the hospital! Was Tammy feeling guilty? Yeah I was a little bit nervous now! Scared my milk had not helped her! After all she had looked bad and had already had milk on Monday. Pain and self doubt filled my massive chest to near tears. The Mexican had bad gas as well. That helped though! Miss Winters eye socket was crushed she was hit so hard. Had seen that much myself. They said she would be blind on that side if she ever woke up from the coma she was in. Probably be nothing but a vegetable they said and that hurt Tammy bad. She blamed herself so bad. We were getting regular updates now. Really liked Miss Winters and that sight of her broken had hurt me deep. Hurt Tammy more! She felt so very bad. Oh I could sense it in her. She had made a mistake and nice people got hurt because of it. Knew the feeling oh too well so I was highly sympathetic!

We pulled into the lot at the hospital as I said a silent prayer. Oh two nice Soldiers were standing out there and waved us over in the parking lot. They had a spot saved for us up front nicely. The General knew we would come and had one held. Saluted and bowed well. Recognized them from the bomb incident. They were terrified! I mean happy to see us and said they would watch Windy for us as she was naked. Tammy quickly explained to them that it was a safety thing taking her in with us. They said they could keep her safe. Tammy just snickering asked them who would keep them safe from Windy? They looked confused. Knew if you had not seen what that Child had done you could not understand so I did not blame them. They said other Soldiers were on the way to protect Miss Winters. That was nice of the General but not necessary. There was no reason for them to try and finish her. Who would she identify? We had two dead Men at the college. Both of them had died six years before in a helicopter crash it seems. One was still breathing but not very conscious yet! Had his death certificate though. Dated four years ago. All three were once elite Soldiers. Dean Kelly put their pictures up on her wall.

Knew we were going to get shit before we ever went in the Hospital. Kinda got shit everywhere right? Just not always the good kind. Never even slowed down however. Security was on us in a moment once in those doors blocking our way and saying the usual. "Hey those animals can not come in here!" "Why is that child almost naked?" Pushy and demanding not to mention rude weren't they? No guilt for me.

Well I told you one time, maybe more, Tammy was insane. Not joking on that one. Her voice was calm and dead serious as she told them looking elsewhere. "This is my seeing eye Tiger. And that one is a new biological wheelchair for the Princess." No pooping in the Hospital! So hard to do! Even if all of us were human we would have attracted a huge crowd. Windy was naked. Mostly. Still had cute little Pony pantys on. They never make them for big Girls though. So cute!

A Doctor had come in to the lobby quickly to see what the commotion was. Was a commotion. He must have been slacking off. Real asshole. Probably hitting on a Nurse or two. We had been seen in the parking lot as we parked and Security had been alerted so were waiting for us. There were either alarms of some kind going off here already or they had some really shitty muzak too. You know I really need some theme music to carry with me. To Windy the Doctor asked urgent yet stuffy. "Young Lady! Why are you naked? What happened to your clothes?" Raised my eyebrow! This should be interesting.

Windy smiled and said just so cutely. "Got shot!"

Checking her over visually fast the Doctor asked sounding confused now and shocked. "Who shot you?"

Pointing Windy said grinning. "Tammy!" Her voice so full of happyness. Was pointing at the Blind Girl so it ramped up their confusion. SUCKERS!

Tammy looked proud however puffing out her chest at a marble column. That was nice! "AK 47, full clip! Not one miss! Damn good shooting for a Blind Girl!" It was impressive I had to admit, so I was nodding now. People were looking very nervous! No idea why! Honest! You ever tell the truth and have people not believe you? Never trust a court appointed Attorney either!

Oh like you would have believed any of it! Police were being called I was sure. Seriously, I was surprised we were not recognized myself. Must all watch the Ice Bitches station! We were on the other one a lot! The Doctor had been edging close to us, like we didn't see it coming from a mile away! Even the Blind Girl saw! Suddenly he made a grab for Windy. And they gave him a Medical License and not me?! Just stood still. No cobwebs on this ceiling either! He was across my back pants down getting an old fashion ass whoopin from a five year old before anyone could move. Windy's voice was scary as she spoke. "You will ask permission to approach me and call me your Highness! This is your only warning!" She let him slide off of me in tears, his bare ass bright red and probably bleeding. Standing up like an acrobat or circus performer on my back Windy raised her hands up in the air and smiling so cute said. "I'm ready for my closeup Mr. DeMille!" Mom loved that movie! Must have watched it at the compound. Sabrina who had been slowly moving around knowing full well what was coming grabbed a gun from a Security Guard and shot her Sister point blank six times. So sweetly Windy said dropping the ricochets she caught. "Now get out of my way." Do I actually have to write out seven billion separate apology's or is this sufficient?

Kimmy smiled at some astonished nurses. "We're here to see Miss Winters. Can one of you pretty Ladys show us where she is?" We got an escort from a grinning nurse and one who kept chuckling. Think they both really liked seeing that Doctor spanked. Smelled like a prick. Security stayed close as well the whole way. They had hands on their guns at all times terrifyed. What wimps!

Miss Winters just cried when we came in and most of us did too. The joy in my heart was tremendous. Half her head was in bandages sure, but she was awake and sitting up which we were told was a small miracle itself. So I said a silent thank you. Hope grew in me now. Drugged out of her mind too probably. Like stoned Counselors however so I climbed on the bed and got hugged. She whispered in my ear urgently. Silly pudge! Well I can always help with that! We were in a hospital after all. What better place to preform a colonoscopy!

Did not blame Miss Winters for not wanting to use a bed pan either. Of course I'd need a bed dumpster! They are so embarrassing. Easy to tip and spill too. And if you really have to go you get Poopy-Butt! Head up under the blanket fast with some help and I saw she had no pantys on right away. Must have been expecting me! Like that hospital policy! Heard a man yelling in a panic after the procedure was started. "My God what is that animal doing?!"

Tammy was laughing her ass off too bad to speak so Sabrina said sweetly. "Colonoscopy?!"

Felt him lift the blanket quickly. My face was in big butt. Not a sound for a minute as they watched. A minute later he asked. "My God, how long is that tongue?" His voice was full of awe at the sight!

Kimmy said snickering like it was nothing. "Feels like up to a foot. She did an abortion on the Tiger Saturday. The Tiger's Father had impregnated her with the child of Satan and she wanted it out." You could still see she was part human. Her choice.

Windy crossed her arms and said in a voice like thunder full of pride. "Yes the Satan spawn was devoured by my Royal Beast!" So cute! Miss Winters was shaking and shuddering as she peed! Was thirsty after all that so it was good. Tasty!

The Doctor more curious now asked. "Has she done this a lot?"

Kimmy spoke so proud about that. "Oh she has over a hundred successful procedures to her name. You feel really clean afterwards!" They all say that.

He sounded very curious now. "Do you feel any polyps in there Miss Dog? Small bumpy growths?"

Shook my head. Felt good in there. So smooth.

"What does she do with the waste?" He sounded nervous.

Think he suspected already and he was grossed out.

Tammy needed dry pants! Sabrina came to the rescue. "She's a Dog silly. She eats it!" He gasped. Yep!

Windy smiled. "She ate a car or two." Why not?

Kimmy said gasping herself. "The whole car. Engine and all. Want to see some videos?" Maybe others needed dry pants and a mop!

Windy happily exposed my greatest shame however. "Kevlar gives her bad gas!" A half dozen Soldiers entered the room at that moment saluted and bowed. Brought authenticity to what we were saying. Looked familiar some of these Soldiers. Explanations were given briefly to those present a we had a crowd forming couple Doctors and some Nurses. This Hospital had dealt with some of the shit I had done so they did not doubt anything but our sanity.

Tammy smiled and said rattling the keys. "I'm driving! We have to go or we won't get the tiara today." That got us moving. To the jewelry store before five! It was quickly discussed and decided this worked better anyway. We could get dresses that matched the tiara better if we had it with us.

People expressed concern, from a distance at the jewelry store, about Windy being mostly naked but did nothing. Some recognized us and stayed way back. We were nice and told them all what we were doing. Windy just smiled and waved at the peasants. Being half naked did not bother her at all! Most parents can easily understand this one as they probably went through times when keeping clothes on their kids was difficult if not impossible. Anywhere! Shame and embarrassment are learned behaviors! Stop teaching them to your children! Lots of parents let their young little Girls go topless at the beach after all. We got the Tiara and it looked amazing on Windy's head. Okay we took her next door to get her hair done too so it would look better if she got on the news tonight. That Girl loved it but thanked everyone. Then to the mall for dresses. No one said shit about the five year old only in pantys! We were kinda scary. Security at the mall took one look at us and hid. Well usually when we showed up shit happened. Yeah it was that mall. Did not blame them. They had no weapons except maybe pepper spray. Bad guys usually had guns. True we had the grenade launcher strapped to Tammy's thigh! No idea why she had it but it looked good on her. Totally Badass Albino we had. The dresses we found were stunning. Glad we had the Tiara with us! One of the clerks told us sweetly that an anchor store had a photographer in tonight if we wanted pictures. Oh, We Did! Love pictures!

We had to threaten the photographer though. He wanted cute shots only. Hope you all read that sentence with the contempt it deserves! We got some cute ones for sure but we got some scary ass ones as well. The Girls ran out and brought in the big weapons. Oh we looked freaking scary! Kimmy ordered lots of each which kept the guy from calling the Cops after we left. The Girls decided in there to teach Windy how to sign her name so she could start doing autographs. Windy completely liked the idea! Sounded great to me. We ate in the food court and I got a lot of food dumped on a couple trays. Oh I mean lots! Ten pounds at least. Appetizer!

As we ate Sabrina looked down at me. Her voice now concerned. "Is it hot enough for you Pammy?" Shook my head as it wasn't. She waved a frightened Security Guy over. "You got any pepper spray?" She snapped. The guy slowly nodded his face full of terror now. Pointing she said sternly. "Spray some on her food. She says the hot sauce here is lame."

He did, nodding with a grin. He knew it was! Better with Pepper Spray!

Still had time to kill after eating. Phone calls were made. Crank phone calls were made by Tammy! Starbucks was called and told there was more shit where that came from! We had a bus set up. Kimmy handled that. Luxury coach deluxe and told them we had a driver already. Well Tammy said she had a CDL license and we believed her. We trusted her! Why would we ask her to prove it? Kimmy called the General to let him know we were having company on the trip to see the Aliens and I heard his laughter! He really scared me but I liked him. We were good.

FUCK national security! We had five year old's!

Finally about seven forty five we headed for the destruction! Rambo, I mean Charlie Sheen, I mean Tammy was driving. Windy waved at the camera crew from my back as we passed at ninety MPH and gaining speed fast straight at the gates. Radio began blasting, "Bulls on Parade" By Rage Against The Machine very loud and I was good! Kimmy had the grenade launchers. Two of them. Can never have too many of them. Just blow the shit out of everything! Windy was already screaming with a scary sounding voice. Not loud but it darn well echoed. "Hunt them down my Beasts and Kill them ALL!" We were gonna anyway. Nice to have approval for once though. Seriously you would think they would stop shooting and run away after a few hundred bullets did nothing but NO! Bunch a dumb fuckers! Not even a hole in the windshield or scratch on the car! Premium Alien know how there!

Should explain about the car. You should know, and I promise no killing while I write this. The car was once Kimmy's Father's car. He had restored it as a teenager and Kimmy was actually conceived in it. When he died it was put in storage. Kimmy would ask about it on occasion and the General knew one day she would want it. The General loved Kimmy so much he violated many National Security Rules and had the Aliens rebuild it for her. It was spaceship technology and that car was pretty much indestructible!

Becky had expressed uncertainty about killing people earlyer. They had in a moment of insanity told her to just picture her Father and let her hatred loose! These Girls scare me at times. If you let the Genie out of the bottle it can be hard to get him back in. Loved that Tiger however. Killed many with extreme prejudice!

We ate like the Magnificent Beasts we were! Their layers of fencing were obliterated in front of us. Made it through four gates with the car before they let loose with the artillery! They had some big machine-gun turrets here but they don't do well after a few grenades are dropped on them. And a rocket or two. Sabrina had the rocket launcher. Girls had some of me in them so they did not miss! Total bloodbath! Mean that too. Oh I was gonna need a hose! Super heavy doors on the building however. Car would not go through them at any speed I ever want to go in a convertible! Did not need too anyway. To easy then. Windy bellowed from my back pointing. What kind of Mama would I be to leave my Pup in the car while I went inside! "BEAST! UP!" Ooh I could do that. Tore up the side of the building as I went up. Vertical climb! Windy squealing wildly. Tearing huge chunks of concrete from the wall as my claws worked. Fuck Gravity! Oh look! They were serving supper on the roof! Okay supper probably did not see it that way but oh well. Not my problem! Sucks to be them! My way or the highway to HELL! Either way you were shit in the morning!

"Bodies" by Drowning Pool began to play and I smiled!

Could still hear most of what that child on my back said and I hoped they heard her and understood why they had to die! Her words scared me! They made too much sense! She would be a fine ruler when she took over. Well I was thinking six weeks?! Believe me I can think, kill, and eat at the same time! ProtoDog's are great multi-taskers you understand.

Then again the shouting on the ground scared me too. Tammy's voice was heard screaming. "Kimmy do we have any Thermite?!" Kimmy yelled back.

"LOTS!" WHY I ask? Then Sabrina yelled. "Grab a five gallon bucket of lube too!" Nope! Nothing scary there! NOT! Seriously why do they even stock five gallon buckets of lube? Were we the new porn capital or something? Way I was going? Maybe! They had bought a couple more yesterday. Sure I was thinking about that shit while killing and eating humans. Can you think of a better time? Well I sure didn't want to think about all that Kevlar I was ingesting. CRUNCH! See?

Try to defend the doors again and I'll puke, cuff you up, and eat you again! They were definitely making Monsters here! Yes I could smell them already. Strange very unnatural smells! Not just Fishmen! Dumb fuckers probably thought they could control the Monsters they created so the idea that they were so dangerous never crossed their minds. Arrogance breeds death! That said they put on a really good buffet here!

Well I thought so.

Top two floors looked like offices and administration so we just kept going down. Smelled nothing of interest on them. The middle floor was definitely labs. Smelled lots of chemicals on there but no Monsters yet. Second floor had some Monsters however! Knew that very fast. They all smelled so interesting. Yeah there were armed men the whole way through the building and I ate them. What's that? You want a blow by blow description? This chapter alone would be six hundred pages. And I wasn't even counting so I can't tell you. Windy can only count to twenty so she can't help. Seriously readers? Use your imagination! Lots of heads ripped or bit off! Decapitation is such fun ya know! Can't wait for the next Olympics! Hear forced decapitation has qualified and will be an official sport in two years. Well it will be as soon as I talk to the Princess about it. Was seriously trying to cut down on my Kevlar intake this trip as well and ripping heads off seemed the best bet. Those gas cramps suck! Yes still worried about my weight too as I was already bigger and heavyer. I'm sure they noticed but were too kind to mention it. Looked good still! Sabrina had lost eighteen pounds from all this so far. Sex is the best exercise. Oh anyway. CRUNCH! As I was saying. If anyone knows how many calories are in a pound of Kevlar please let me know. Hey I was trying the new Zombie diet after a while. Just the brains you see. Skulls are crunchy! Like crunchy! Well they were not using their brains or they would have been somewhere far away!

You give a Man a big gun and he thinks he is unstoppable. They should just all be glad we were all pregnant and none of us were on our periods! SHIT! Tammy should have lied in her email and said we all were on the rag! Place would have been empty! MEN? ASSHOLES!

We stalked down the corridor all dramatic like and I was sniffing hard. No Fishman! Lots of other extremely interesting smells. Windy made me open all the heavy doors that had Monsters behind them. Not arguing as that Scepter hurts! Was rather nervous about that but this Girl had a heart bigger than Alaska. It's bigger than Texas! Take that Texas! Loved me too and that may have affected her perceptions when it came to Monsters. Gonna blame Sesame Street though. She opened a few doors herself. Well I can't have all the fun! It was easy for her and her Scepter. Most Monsters cowered in the corners the moment their doors were destroyed. We had no keys so we got creative! You can read violent in there if you want. Like rampant destruction! And I smelled definite Monster abuse! They were being treated horribly! That sweet Angel got off my back and went to each telling them the bad men were being eaten and they were free now to live their lives again. What a Wonderful Girl. So sweet! No idea how that was going to work but I was thinking! Told you I can multi-task!

Still I thought this may be a problem. Had to talk and explain to Windy that letting the Monsters loose in the world would not be safe for them. Do not ask me to understand her thought process! Why she even had my phone I don't know! Well I didn't need it anymore so I was okay with it but still? "Hewwo Sir General. We got Monsters here! Lots! Need buses to drive them to big school so Doctor Bitch can see if she can help!" Heard the phone on the other end hit the floor. They needed a mop at the compound I was sure. There may have been a puddle here to. Ain't sayin! This Girl calls em like she sees em though! Such honesty in a five year old. Love her!

No idea what they were using here to create with but absolutely none of the Monsters looked alike. Not even close to me either. Some were kinda cute even. Hoped I got a chance to eat a few. More then once! Mostly humanoid so far. You would have thought it too! You pervs! Well I sure am! We had heard the explosion a while ago! Shook the whole building actually so it was hard to miss! Must a had more than Thermite in the car! Or Tammy was channeling her inner McGyver and they had gum. Both possible yet neither mattered. So I knew the others were inside by then of course. Try and keep them out once and see where it gets you! So when I heard Kimmy screaming even sounding half assed downstairs, I ran to help. Straight into a nightmare of a scene! Ever see the King Kong movie? The original!

Kimmy was way cuter they Fey Raye of course but this giant Monkey Monster was UGLY! With a capital UG! The Dinosaur he was fighting was COOL looking however and did not seem to like the Monkey in the least. Did not blame it! The Dino was like a T-Rex in appearance but a smaller one it seemed. Not by much mind you but short arms are always beat by long ones and that Monkey had long arms. Oh they were not the only Monsters down here either. A blueish Bear like creature the size of a huge Rhino in a pen along the back wall stared. Some other kind of large Lizard like thing on two feet in the pen next to it was getting excited by the fight. Maybe eight feet tall on it's hind legs. Was gonna have to have a

Growl with someone yet. The camera crew was already in here!? The Reporter and Sabrina were giving the blow by blow commentary WWE style as the Monkey and the Dino went at it. They were darn good! Sabrina and the reporter. The Monkey had paw on snout just holding the Dino back! If he put Kimmy down the Dino would be toast it seemed. Tammy and Becky Tiger were corralling what looked like a seven foot tall pink fluff ball out of the way. Not a happy fluffball either! It quivered angrily!

Kimmy spotted us after a few seconds and waved from the Monkey's paw. Monkey had pulled her shirt off! Fucking perv Monkey! Probably why the scream. Windy yelled at the Monkey with righteous anger. "Let my friend go!" The Monkey just spit at us! I guess I should be happy it didn't throw Monkey shit like they do at the zoo. I hate Monkeys! Pissed Windy off however and she was off my back like a bullet and I was not going to stop her! That little Girl bellowed very loud as she ran at its foot Scepter overhead and screamed. "BOW TO ME BITCH!" As she yelled she brought that Scepter down with such force on that Monkey's foot just crushing its bones. Breaking the floor beneath. They were crushed too and blood and bone fragments flew. Ever have your foot bones crushed? Trust me you don't keep standing. The bigger they are the harder they fall and I felt that impact. It's scream of pain was ear shattering. Flat on it's face! That Dino was an opportunist and on it's back with an excited leap quick before it could react delivering the killing blow! Ripping spinal column out of a giant Monkey's neck is awesome to behold. You should see the video. Go Dino! Looked tasty too.

The camera crew filmed the whole speech Windy gave to the dead Monkey while the Dino and I ate parts of it. Not passing up the chance to eat giant Monkey! Are you nuts? Let me say Monkey tastes good! When the Military arrived with school buses I was told the station had gone live with this. Okay they were told I just listened. Monkey to eat! The network had gone with it as well even, so the whole nation saw Windy's speech! That was scary!

The building was searched fast. A few more Monsters were found but no Fishman or Boy! Windy had told the military Men in no uncertain terms the moment they arrived that Monsters were to be treated nice or else. They knew better then to argue with her. They either knew her or had been briefed well.

Might have seen the videos.

Oddly it turned out, the Dino was quite friendly and even playful which was good as I did not want to kill it. It was a Dinosaur! Who hasn't wanted a real Dinosaur their whole lives? Yeah and you never played Rabid Barbies either did you? You are so lame! Girls had explained again on air to the Soldiers that the Monsters were to be treated nicely and taken to thc college. But avoid the fluff ball! Windy told the Monsters to behave or else! It was the big fluff ball that was cranky and dangerous. It did not seem to like being moved so they left it alone. Did not have legs that we could see so maybe it was afraid it would be left upside down for a while? Understood that one! Her Highness was in charge and everyone knew it so Kimmy and I took the Dino out back through the big hole in the back wall and played fetch. Yeah the big hole in the wall bothered me a little. The Monkey hit a crane or something as it fought the Dino and it went through the wall as it fell. But the issue was both the other Lizard thing and the big blue thing were missing already. Had been busy eating and missed them leave. It was hectic and I was still hungry. Definite tracks out here though. Dino was having a blast!

Windy came to me after a while, riding on Becky, looking every bit the Princess she was. Her face relaxed and voice gentle. "It is time. Find the Boy my Beast!" She was a caring ruler of the Universe. Realized that something was off as they had not found the Boy! It was too hectic to think most of the time. Knew I miss calculated again. Frankly I thought it weird. No idea if it would be a problem. Kimmy just hopped on my back and we went further out toward the farm land I knew was out here. Problem with that was the Dino followed. Kinda like a big, Really Big Puppy it seems. Might have adopted me! Could have been a Boy but smelled Female. It's not like Lizards have balls now is it? How are you supposed to tell somethings sex if it doesn't have balls?! Sneaking around with an eighteen foot tall Dino is, let me say, not easy. The Boy had actually been here however as I could smell that much. Now all I had to do was walk the perimeter till I found his trail and once I found it I tracked him easy. He was not alone though. Confused me a bit. Had no idea why they would take him from us then try and get away with him? Had expected them to have him out front so we would hold back? He saw the Monster sure but the world had seen many now! Wind was picking up out here though and I smelled rain. Did not matter to my nose but Ally the Alosaurus seemed skittish about something. Hoped she was okay. At least a dozen snacks, I mean armed men were out there with the Boy I smelled. The Boy was scared!

Okay, right the first time! For the last time it is NOT cannibalism! Well I am not human! Now that said you humans taste pretty okay. Really had to start carrying hot sauce however. Still prefer a big bucket of Kung Pow Chicken from Jaffar's though. Monkey is really quite tasty I tell you and I would not turn it down if offered to me again. A storm was on the way again too, not just rain, and I could smell it! If anyone had ever bothered to check the forecast we might have known this, however those Weather guys lie more than politicians! How can someone be wrong most of the time and still keep their job? And travel was slow. Mainly because Kimmy was riding backwards Sniffing my farts! Nothing says love like a nose in your butt through three consecutive farts! Loved her Too! Methane addiction is a Bitch! The Dinosaur who Kimmy was already calling Ally seemed to like them too and kept snorting in my butt as well. Hot snorts! Kimmy told me that

Ally was most likely an Allosaurus or close to it she thought from the size and shape. Not a T Rex! So I was good with it. The only good T Rex broke up long ago. Very beautiful! Wondered if her colors were natural! Darker shades of blue and purple you see. Still could smell rain! Our Dinosaur was intelligent. Wondered if that were natural as well. Ally was so adorable trying to be sneaky here imitating me. She seemed to be enjoying this game at least.

Holy Crap! Can you believe it? We found the Black Boy and they had him tied to a tree in a clearing?! What a racist thing for them Bastards to do! A dozen armed White Men were hidden around and I understood now. They were all in the freaking KKK! Or they really wanted the Fishman back and were using the Boy as bait for some bizarre reason. Maybe Both!? Kinda had figured it out now I thought. Still I miss calculated on motive but it was not important. They were KKK and needed to DIE! Okay there were eleven KKK members out here. Oops only Ten members. He, he, he! Nine! Oh shit! My luck sucked! The Fishman was here already and just lurching through the dark clearing straight at the Boy sniffing hard. Looked just like that one on the Saturday afternoon movies just like the kid had said! Seriously bad timing on the Fishman's part though as I was busy! Radios crackled as the racist Bastards were calling in and they knew something was wrong fast. That sucked. What sucked more was if we called them KKK no one would care about the creation of Monsters any more! It would all be racist this, racist that! Fucking news media! No more time to play though. Kimmy went for the Boy quick and I had lunch. Fine late night snack! Dessert? They would be shit soon so what did it really matter?! Ally cleaned up some messes for me. Big Dino tongue! Really hoped the Kevlar did not give her gas. OH WAIT! I might like that! I mean Dinosaur farts were a definite unknown! And I wanted to be the first ProtoDog to smell one, bad! How many of you have smelled one? How many want too? Good readers! The Fishman went straight for the Boy for some reason. No time to wonder why they thought the Fishman wanted the Boy or why the Fishman wanted him or I may have figured it out. Kimmy being the hero she was stepped in between it and the Boy trying to protect him. Really! Hey I had no idea what his name was! Keeping it from the Boy with her body! Damn it! NO ONE swats my ChewToy but ME! Not close I moved but not fast enough as it swatted a second time and threw Kimmy aside with a backhand. Big freaking hands on this Fishman! Could palm a basketball easy. Elephant Balls!

Ready to leap for the kill to save the Boy I froze as a Woman screamed from somewhere in the dark saying the last thing I expected! Made sense though and I admit I felt like an idiot for not thinking it sooner. "NO! Don't hurt the Fishman! He's my Husband!" What the fuck? Well that changes things now doesn't it? Glad I had not killed him now. How awkward would that be, right? So I understood a lot now however, I felt. The kid had said his Father was in prison!

The Boy had recognized the Woman's voice and was screaming heartfelt calling her Mom as the Woman continued closer out of the darkness. She was pretty! "MOM!" There was a huge BURP behind me so I knew Men were not a problem anymore and smiled as I went to Kimmy who was okay. Just shook up. She grinned at me so I cuffed her up a little. That Girl loved it rough! Big paw to the boob or butt is fun! The Fishman sliced through the ropes holding the Boy easy as the Mother held the Boy now. The Boy looked up at the scaly thing and asked with awe, fear, and happyness in his voice. "Dad?" It nodded. There were tears in its eyes. I think? It was a Fishman now. Hard to tell. But they hugged each other well enough.

Figures the storm would hit right then and the rain was coming down in sheets as the sky burst open and the Fishman motioned us to follow it rapidly. We did and just a short ways through the trees to an old barn! It was occupied however! Ally who did not seem to like the rain much, probably her first time in it, didn't give a shit though as she could just eat it if she wanted. Well that was what I thought because Ally just pushed us all inside. Well we were dry now!

Kimmy pulled her phone out after quite a while. When she finally quit laughing! She peed herself too! "Hi. Yeah we're fine. We have both the Boy and his Mother. Yes we have the Fishman too! Turns out the Fishman is the Boys Father however. They were apparently using Prisoners to experiment on. No! We are in an old barn sheltering from the storm a bit east of the building. No, I think we are staying here for the night. Pammy is not able to travel at the moment. Well do you remember that big blue thing that wandered away? Found it! It's a Boy. You know how big a Slut Pammy is?!" Hey I heard that laughter! Hope they heard my howl! You better believe I did! Needed this so BAD! It was freaking huge too! Felt satisfied once more! "No. Never saw a cock that big before. No I won't! Wait till you see it!" Oh Hell Yes I would let it in me, and I was believe me! Did hurt going in at first but WOW! Horses would be jealous of this thing! Maybe even Elephants?

This thing had a Bear hug on me pounding my ass hard and I was a Happy Girl! Big blue balls bouncing on my tits between my legs. Giant rock hard throbbing cock buryed in my vagina to the hilt. All three feet of its eight inch thickness! It was rough with me but I liked that now didn't I? Was finally being FUCKED and I knew it! Finally I was drooling as orgasm after orgasm racked MY body as well! How I felt owned by this Beast! Such amazing stamina for sex too!

No the Boy and his Mom and Dad were in another part of the barn and saw nothing. Might have heard a lot though. No words. Just grunts and snorts. The Boy was exhausted however and fell asleep fast and easy back now in his Mothers arms. Think Kimmy watched while the kids Mom got some Fish-Cock however! Sounded like she was having fun over there!

Finally this thing erupted inside me like a volcano! Oh I mean that. At least a gallon of semen pumped in me. Bowling Balls! He let go of my waist with a sigh as he came out of me and came around to nuzzle my muzzle. Such a romantic fella and really cute. Kind of Bovine in the face. Shit, I jumped! Dinosaur tongue on the butt by surprise! Do you watch a porno and go EH? No you watch sex you get horny! So do Dinosaurs it seems! Kimmy didn't give a shit however and she encouraged me to lick Ally off when I could! Archaeologists won't tell you this but Dinosaurs have clits. This one did at least and I had fun with it. Did shove my whole head in her Cloaca. Hoped I got her pregnant! Like you would not if you could. Dinosaurs are cool! Wanted more! So she may not be an actual Dinosaur. It could take years to find out I thought. DID NOT CARE! The General it seems had already ordered all the computers and equipment transferred to the College. Well the Monsters were going there so why not the rest. College could use new lab gear anyway. That stuff ain't cheap. Billions of dollars worth of equipment here! Make those students work! Military would just hide the knowledge as well and we knew it. If these Governments shared their knowledge instead of always hiding it Cancer would have been cured years ago!

The General had been a busy Boy! Liked Dean Kelly a lot and wanted to help her out by helping the college. Involved her in all of it as well! He had gotten the college some major security clearances already as well. Authorized by the President himself! Transferred much money to it for research as well. More armed men were coming for security. The Mattress surfers were an issue. And the Chess Club!

It was college!

CHAPTER 5 DIPLOMACY
Wednesday September 29th

All the Hope in the world will not stop a Thing, good or bad, from happening without action. Since no one had a barrel to use as a cork we were just going to have to smell Dino farts! Oh they were something else! Kinda liked em a lot. The Fish Family wanted to stay in the barn for now. Once it aired out! Nicer then their house that was for sure! They were offered some space at the college quickly but he needed water nearby it seems and I sorta understood. He just needed time! They needed time. Trust was lacking for them as well and they only wanted to be together and alone for a while. Would take time to prepare an area for them. College needed a pool or two. Kimmy said we would send someone with food daily and let them know once we had a place for them to live. Kimmy had called and explained all this to the General. He told her most people were not believing any of it and it was being called the hoax of the century by Fox News! And I was thinking I should go eat them but Kimmy had a better idea! Told the General to let Ricardo know we needed a barrel! Pretty sure some people who thought Fox news was the word of God changed their minds as we went through town that morning. All of us! With a big blue thing and a Fucked Mother Dinosaur just a following after! She tried hard but her tongue just would not fit in me! Like you would say NO?! God Dinosaur tongue is amazing! The others had met us at the building when we got there. They spent the night at a hotel after phone calls were made. Kind of had ourselves a little parade and Windy approved. Monsters were not real fast so people got to see well. Windy loved to wave at the peasants so it was all good.

Kimmy read too many comics over the years as she wanted to get saddles for me and the Dino and the blue thing who kept snorting up my butt. Damn right I loved it! Finally got my butt snorted up! Tickles! Oh it seemed I had another Boyfriend now and he was absolutely AMAZING! Had how many Girlfriends? Oh they all wanted me to be their Girlfriend! If someone made you orgasm so hard you almost shit yourself you would do anything for them. He was sticking very close to me as well! A bit protective. Yes I liked him! Thick plush gorgeous blue fur. Long Thick Big Blue Cock! Massive blue balls! He was cuddly too. Massive body was Bear like with longer legs. His tail was like a Deer's. He flicked it a lot.

Kids instantly grew excited and happy as we went into the Parking lot at Windy's school with a real Dinosaur following us. Secret Service Men? Not so much happy as terrified. Very Excited! Then again they were surrounded by five year old's already. That's enough to make anyone nervous. Saw hands in coats already. The General was trying to get Secret Service Men to lower their guns in a panic while laughing his ass off! Secret Service Men were trying to push the President back into a car but he seemed understandably fascinated with the Dinosaur. IT WAS A DINOSAUR PEOPLE! The Students and Teachers just stood around watching wide eyed and open mouthed from around the parking lot. Typical day in Kindergarten it seemed! Fuck paying quarterbacks twenty million a year! Kindergarten Teachers deserve it! They risk their lives daily for the future of mankind! It was all the Secret Service's fault so I had no regret when Windy stepped forward and broke one of their cars! The pavement under it was probably in bad shape too but Men froze! You really can't blame her either. Not for long though. Kids all just clapped, shattering the moment of silence. What can I say? These kids had enough Shit! Windy was very popular and they approved of her methods! So did I!

Windy threw her head back and laughed as guns were pointed her way by Secret Suicidal Agents. Men looked confused by this as well as terrifyed. Well they were only Men. Kimmy chuckled speaking loudly. "Put your pea shooters away Boys. You pull a trigger and wreck her new Princess gown Windy will kill you. She's been shot by much bigger guns than you have so just put yours away before someone gets hurt. Namely you!" It was all true!

The President forced his way out hard now shoving Men aside with utter amazement and joy on his face as he came fast to hug Kimmy well. Tears were in his eyes. "Missed you so much kiddo! How are you?" Such emotion in there his voice was cracking.

Kimmy was crying now as well. "Missed you too Uncle Martin." Now I recognized the President! He had been at Kimmy's Parent's funeral holding her hand in one picture. Younger yet still recognizable. There was a room at the Compound with pictures in it. A sort of shrine to the family. A younger version of him was in some of those pictures as well.

Windy knew this as well. She had seen those pictures and she came over and hugged them both. Peace talks were held in the parking lot of the Claude Rains Elementary school just afterwards as chairs were brought out. Well all the children wanted to play on the Dinosaur whether it was friendly or not and these Teachers were powerless to stop them. Secret Service Men were very nervous about, well pretty much everything, even though the General assured them they were safe from the Monsters. It was the five year old's they had to watch out for he said. The President found it very funny but I knew better. The General was not joking there!

These kids were dangerous and he knew it! Got more nervous agents when both the General and the President of the United States just bowed to Windy. She is just so adorable. Even more so now.

Yeah okay everyone over the age of six was getting nervous as the blue thing was getting frisky with me once I was out of the car. Horny fella. Could hold him off only so long. A real cuddly romantic sweetheart however. Such a nice feeling to be that desired. Made My Monster heart go pitter patter. Kimmy said we had to go as we had classes still and hugged people goodbye. The college was close and the General and President were going there soon. It's a ten minute drive. Tammy can do it in under five! Took us over an hour to get there however. Well Big Blue had stamina! Such joy! Only got six blocks before he mounted me good. Just glad it wasn't a busy street. That old Lady with the binoculars was smiling when we left!

He was not letting me out of his sight though. Which of course meant he went to class with me. Sandra raised an eyebrow as we walked in. So blue and big he is a sight to see. Especially in a classroom! Students gasped. Some in fear I guess. He was a Herbivore though! Hey I saw his teeth. Felt them as well. Adorable as all heck! He grazed as we had gone along as well as hammer my ass. Hoped he didn't eat my bushes! He came in and lay there next to me chewing his cud as kids and Teacher alike came up and petted him. Mighty Mellow Monster. Big blue horny Bovine Bear! Sandra quickly hugged me and whispered Slut in my ear. Oh she knew me well and had seen the bowling balls on this thing. Probably bigger than bowling balls. Those exercise balls. They were so freaking huge! Well I was licking them. Jealous? You know I think Sandra was!

Class was surprisingly enough about integration and different cultures coexisting. Which considering there was now a large Monster population on campus here was probably a good idea. Thirty two Monsters not counting Ally or Big Blue here. Students were talking about them but in a good way. Most were very excited about this happening and had heard what equipment was coming. Monsters all seemed okay with this as well. Sure beat a cage! Turned out they were using prisoners and some kids from juvenile detention that they could make disappear easy as guinea pigs! No major crimes among them as those perpetrators were well known. Drugs, Gang Violence, Arson, maybe attempted murder! They had all confessed to the Dean and said they were sorry for their crimes. Just wanted a chance to live still! They knew many had not survived what was done to them there! Very painful still they said and just wanted a life. Life expectancy was not long where they had been. Housing was going to be set up for the Monsters and employment or classes if they choose. Temporary Tents were being set up by soldiers. Assured them repeatedly they would be helped now! Windy approved of everything. Yeah, well she said it would be that way and others got to work making it so. Dean Kelly did too. Hey we were already rectifying one ACLU matter and she did not want another. She also saw the potential for the school itself. Just the equipment alone would be amazing. Knew however that Scientists would beg to come! Not the only one helping either. Normally Military funds and help would worry me but between the General and Windy I knew we were okay!

Lunch!

Oh I knew instantly that the President was going to show up as soon as I was mounted in the commons by Big Blue. Natives in Borneo probably saw that one coming! Still I let him mount me. Darn it I was gonna be FUCKED and well! Bout time I got satisfied! The Dean led the President over of course! Yes they watched me get plowed as they talked. Mostly about me! So I was actually dumb enough to think again. "Could this get any worse?!" We know how that works right? So I should not have been surprised in the least when Sabrina came over with a half dozen Soldiers and three Black Girls in heavy cuffs and shackles demanding lawyers. Damn ACLU lawsuit! Soldiers were being rather brutal with them. Telling the Girls they would never get lawyers! Shoving and pulling them! Knew the Girls were just playing along and having fun, I hoped. They were on the list! One of the Girls was shoved roughly to the ground in front of me while her pants were pulled down savagely by Soldiers. Oh I saw the sparkle in her eye. Wondered if this was the Black Girls idea. She was very wet before I touched her you understand. Soldiers told the other two Girls to watch her get eaten by the Royal Beast as they were next! My thinking was were was the Drama Teacher?! As if this was not enough already the President expressed concern at my raping a Black Girl. He used the word Rape! That scared me! Sure looks like it to the untrained eye! There was snickering which got worse as the situation was explained to him. Sternly by the Dean!

He was laughing as well now.

Was just blushing myself!

The Pervert I mean President said. "Well I'm glad to see she is correcting her prejudicial behavior. My office is very against bigotry of any kind. Still I wonder if some form of corporal punishment should not be added to prevent this behavior next time." Had the General been telling on me?

REALLY?! I'm such a lucky ProtoDog!

The Dean said way too quickly for my comfort. "I have a riding crop in my closet Mr. President. Ask the General!" At least I was not the only one blushing now! Wondered how big this set up was! The President of United States was discussing my spanking while I got plowed by a big fluffy blue bull and raped a few Black Girls. Living The American Dream? Seemed like it to me. Well what is your dream? Those Girls looked very happy later as well.

"And what exactly is her major?" The President asked curious about me as he stared. Was something to see.

Tammy laughed and said. "Pre-Med. She does an amazing Colonoscopy!" She knew! Liked them too!

His response was tense. "I can see that!"

He could as I was! Black Girls need internal cleaning as well you Racist Bastards! Colon cancer effects them as well! This was for their own good!

A second Girl was being forced to her knees begging in front of me as her skirt was lifted and Pantys tore off. "NO! NOT THE BUTT!" Huh?

YES the BUTT! She squealed so wonderful, totally pissing herself! The third was quivering before she was even laid in front of me. She fainted as I touched her. Woke up fast with my tongue up her Fat Black Ass. Honestly I don't think she made an intelligible sound the whole time. Oh that ass was both Black and Fat and I adored it! Well it is embarrassing to poop yourself when you orgasm that hard so it was a favor! They were gonna orgasm that hard! ProtoDog's Guarantee it! Took her throat in my jaws once done and squeezed. She shuddered and had another orgasm. COOL! The President was honestly quite impressed with all my Savage raping techniques.

He walked over and looking down at the half naked Girls said. "Let that be a lesson to you Girls!" To me he said firmly. "Are Black Girls tasty?" No he really asked me so I nodded! He started petting the blue guy as Cuffs were removed from victims and all three hugged me. What can I say I was fucking awesome! President Uncle snickered. "College sure has changed since my day."

Psych class with Mr. Wexall. Sanity at last! Okay I lied. More madness! Knew what was coming as the blue beast stood looking around. No choice! Okay there were probably lots of them but it was ME! Was carpeting too. This Monster was blue! Blue balls, Blue tongue, Blue penis! Yes it was. Not sure if it's poop was blue yet as I got it all. Tasty however! Mr. Wexall never paused his lecture but stared as I ate straight from the hole. Thankfully I have a big mouth.

He came over and actually hugged me after class was done but refused to kiss me. Others did gladly. Such nasty students! Feeding the Dinosaur was going to be a problem. We had not killed everyone at the building and the military had rounded up several terrified scientists and some office workers on the third and fourth floors and threatened them with torture. Maybe they had. Not many and they were mostly being held here at the college in the Prison of Higher Learning! That was what they were calling it. Only had so many Men here yet and could not spread them out. Pretty sure the Dean had disciplined a few prisoners for some information. Special collars were put on them and they were made to work. Doctor Petrov actually knew some of their names and they were helping her. Fascinated with what they learned I heard. Ally it turns out mostly ate a protein mush it seemed and had no hunting instinct. So teaching HER to eat humans was probably wrong! How was I to know? Not saying shit! They solved it by getting an industrial meat grinder and lots of tofu. Students were helping. We had an actual Animal Husbandry department. (NO Steve they were not married to the Cows! Love you Steve!) Hope they got some Hoisin sauce to go with that. Maybe even some Wasabi! The equipment to grow the mush was being brought to the college but it would take some time to set up they felt. The tofu should work well we were told. Prisoners were being very co-operative. Think the Dean showed them her riding crop collection. They had to build a building or six at the college it was determined. That would take time though now wouldn't it? Honestly I should know better by now!

Temporary shelters were being set up still.

The illusive Doctor Whiting was not found anywhere however. We were told he had left with a big box! Kinda disappointing really. Might actually have been a mistake telling them we were coming it seems as he had packed what he wanted. Still I needed something to do and we were just getting started with this DICK. Knew Windy was not happy with him! Her face grew grim if he was mentioned. She had nothing against Monster Making however. It was his methods she despised. Bad treatment of those Monsters was a different story entirely. She was five! Watched Sesame Street all the time! You don't get that I can't help!

We knew there were those out there who would want to control it all! Use all of us to gain more power for themselves. Yeah FUCK them! Well I was always hungry! We knew there was still gonna be a lot of shit to deal with you see? Did the math remember? Had not even come close to eating that many Dickheads! Seems I've been getting complaints from people confused about the Asshole thing! That I understand! SORRY!

Did like shit though! Could poop em out like no one else!

Was nowhere near close to making a dent in the number of Assholes I was going to eat, rape, illegal colonoscopy, what ever you want to call them either! If somebody wants to give me shit? Well I have lots of hot sauce now! Dinosaur shit is good with Frank's Red Hot! Love that stuff! And Frank's is damn good too. Put that SHIT on everything. Even the Shit! So everyone was talking about me? As usual. Not a bad thing as many carried a bottle of hot sauce around now for me. The Asian kids had the real hot shit! Kimmy kept going off with several army Men and smiling when she came back. Yes I stuffed my snout in her crotch to see if she had sex and she just giggled. Was not jealous at all you understand, had no right to be, I just like the taste of semen and would have joyfully cleaned her if she needed but she had not had sex! Scared me shitless! She was up to something now and I knew it. Probably getting me and the blue thing for half time entertainment at the super bowl! Did not think half time was that long however and they better not get some horrible POP star to do the music! They do I will who ever it is and the next day they watch me shit them out so they like their music will be just shit!

Was told the President had to leave suddenly. Probably for dry pants! Also that I had a punishment session in the Deans office first thing tomorrow. Something to look forward too! Got three more Chinese Girls and a Black Girl. My Boyfriend followed joyfully and licked them after I was done. Oh he was my Boyfriend! No doubts there. He wanted ME! What was not to love about him? Blue, cute, and hung better than a horse. Needed a name for him however. That Black Girl was a nasty Slut! She jacked my Boyfriend off in front of me! I'd have bitten her but seeing what was in me earlier was truly awe inspiring! She was covered in blue cum when he came! Yeah it was blue too! Made her hug me so I could wear some! She wanted to do it! One of the Chinese Girls got some in a baggy for Biology class. Always encourage curiosity! Another Chinese Girl named him for me. Cobalt! Sure I liked it. Duh? Had all four of them in the same room at the same time. No I have no idea what subject was being taught in the room while I committed mass rape. Teacher was hot though as she kept fanning herself as they watched. Maybe I could talk the Dean into getting better air conditioning.

Walked out of that classroom with my head held high and Cobalt followed just galumphing along behind me happily. Very friendly Monster. Sure he was getting some a lot but he seemed happy before me had fun. He was more powder blue than cobalt but I liked the name anyway. He was okay with it.

Yes Ally followed me around all day as well! She did not fit well in many buildings so she would just peek in windows at me. Had a new Girlfriend too it seemed. Students played with her a bit. Some Monsters got involved. They fed her a bit as well. She may have looked like a Prehistoric Carnivorous Monster but acted like a Puppy Dog. Students would get her to chase them as they screamed and when she caught them they only got licked! So college students acted more like kids then the five year old's. Got a problem? Was college! My advice. Never grow up. You don't have too you know!

We got measured before we left. Could have been for legitimate reasons! Cobalt as well. The Dean was excited as she had been told help was coming in the form of some major Scientists wanting to research but willing to teach a bit. The equipment from the lab was as well. Army corp of Engineers were on their way to build labs and housing. Our little College was going to grow.

We had a little problem. Okay a great big problem. The Puppy Dog, I mean Dinosaur kinda wanted to follow me! Everywhere!

It was cute and sweet but I saw where it might be a problem. Tammy laughed as she said not seeming to care. "I'm going to pick up Windy." We piled in. We let Cobalt in first. Than Kimmy. Me on top. Kimmy sandwich. Cobalt was on his back and Kimmy was using his balls as pillows. Oh you would have as well! She said that they were comfortable. Ally just galumphed along behind happily down the street! Honest that Dinosaur acted just like a giant Puppy Dog! Very cute really. Sure it could be worse but I could not think of how and I was just going for it though. Everyone likes Ally a lot. Very friendly Dinosaur!

Remember how this all started not so long ago? Simple story about my Brother wanting to Fuck Me! Life was simple in the good old days!

Okay maybe it was about to get worse as a camera crew was there at the school when we arrived. Oh! Just our friendly Reporter! He was interviewing Princess Windy as we pulled up it seemed. "And how did the peace talks with the American President go your Highness?" He was good and professional. Nice even. Smelled happy actually. Kept a straight face as well and I knew he found it hilarious! Why else wear the diaper. He had one on. Believe me!

Maybe we should not let Windy watch TV anymore! At least cut her off from Meet The Press! "We have a long ways to go I think but it was a good start!" Such a cutey! Her Teacher may need dry pants though. The Reporter bowed with a smile and thanking her left. He looked at the car for a moment but apparently even he thought better of it.

Smart move there I felt as well.

The Teacher came over and helped Windy onto the pile. Okay on me! Could not see Kimmy in the least! Hey that little Girl falls off she shouldn't damage the asphalt much. Miss Tinker seemed nervous about something. "Um, I've got a dozen kids with permission for the trip so far but lots of parents are cautious with everything that has happened lately." Understood that.

Tammy is completely evil however and I am proud of her. "Tell the parents their permission is just a formality as the children are going! If they don't let their kids go we will come get the kids and the parents will be arrested on federal charges for national security violations and never see the light of day again!" Good with Windy! She was nodding.

The Teachers response. And happily I must say. "Oh that should work." Oh don't go there! Maybe later. Yeah I admit I have issues. She was such a cute Teacher too! Okay I wanted to then but Kimmy was naked under me and I had to keep her covered. Still thought I could Teach her a few things. There were little Male kids present or I would not have cared about Kimmy's nudity. Hey most little Girls with an older Sister have probably seen her naked more then once. How many Parents showered with their small children? They do not have separate locker rooms at the pool for each age group either. Letting the Boys see a naked Girl is not safe they say. Boys should only see Men naked and Girls should only see Women naked. Doesn't that sound a bit gay to you? Now I have had like four or five penises in me and my tongue has been in how many Vaginas? Homosexuality is fine with me! I'm just asking? Then again the ones enforcing this are Christians and their track record against pedophilia is what now? Men of God can not sin! My ass is more righteous then them! Okay My Ass was more righteous then lots of you too! The human body is beautiful! Not as great as a ProtoDog's mind you but you're not bad!

If I could get a medical degree my criminal issues would go away! Mostly! Tell me one thing I've done that you wouldn't have if you had the chance?

Quiet in here isn't it?

It was fun! No one was complaining! Those ones were dead so they can't! Should have been nicer now shouldn't they! Tasted good at least.

Ally seemed interested in many things as we went along, especially stop lights, bopped em with her nose, Peeped in a few windows on the third floor of buildings, and she absolutely loved the forest when we reached it. She fell in love with Teela right away. Teela loved her too. Teela is so lovable! Sure I may have fallen in love with her at first sight but it was hectic. Cobalt mounted me in the driveway as soon as he got out of the car. People were quickly worryed about this. Well they had good reason. You see Kimmy had been on my back when I pulled her off Cobalt. Reverse Kimmy sandwich. She was hugging the big blue guy. Sandra pulled in with Brutus, who was looking distressed, well before he sniffed butts on our new friends, fast. Ally liked it and wanted him to do it again. Kept sticking her butt at him. She is such a Slut! My kinda Dino! He did it again for her. He liked it too it seemed. It is very nice. Dino cloaca is sweet. She smells so good to a Dog!

Over supper it was discussed. Lots of things okay? There was lots of things too deal with but mostly about 30 five year old's? We needed last minute chaperons now! My Mom just said she would go fast as she had quit her job! News to me! Here I thought she was just taking some vacation time. Long vacation it seems. Liked the Gonzales children however. Think the General put Mom on payroll. The Dean wanted to go along as well but had to be at school. Someone had to be! Lots of Monsters to settle in. The General said he would rather take just a knife and liberate Cuba naked than ride in a bus with 30 five year old's! Understood the sentiment. Could be a sight easyer I thought but I knew some of these kids. We could send them to liberate Cuba from the Communists! He would meet us there he said. Teela wanted to go though and they were leery on that. She had school problems you remember? Friday's were big tutoring days for her at school you see. We offered to help tutor her if she could go. Kimmy had already gotten her many textbooks on audio too. Mrs. Gonzales said yes finally but Teela had to do better on her next test and then she volunteered herself quick and many were surprised at that. Not me! She loved her kids! Three would be going with us and she wanted to make sure Three came back you know! Actually understood this too! If you don't I'm sorry. Snickering Sandra said she would go as she had no classes on Friday. Brutus could not go! That was a good thing though. Ally could not go with us either. It was said she could always lay on the roof but they quickly realized that would not work. Dinosaur poop could be a traffic hazard! That Dino can take a dump! Brutus seemed to really like Ally however and was trying to figure out how to hump her! Did not blame him there. If I had a cock I would have to! She was a Dinosaur! Yes my tongue was in her a lot! Tasty!

We knew both Windy's teacher Miss Tinker was going as well as the principle a Mrs. Griffin. School policy or something they said. Knew they were lying even over the phone! They both wanted to go bad! Worse than the kids perhaps. Many reasons! Still they were not sure that would be enough! Felt the same but had an idea so I growled out. "Have idea don't worry." If they knew what I was thinking they would worry! Kimmy and Sabrina would be there as well. That gave us eight adults. Becky and I did not count! Tammy was driving so she couldn't help now could she? Well I wasn't telling her NO! The grenade launcher she wore strapped to her thigh 24/7 had nothing to do with it either! Saw how she could drive! Said she had a CDL as well. That is Commercial Drivers License. Truckers need one as well as bus drivers. Some RV's require one as well. No one else had one! Well at least out of those going along.

Cobalt may be a problem! He was gentle but horny. Could not take him with us or it would be Wild Kingdom on the bus! Those kids did not need to see that for thirty years at least!

Knew I had to communicate with him in the morning. Just hoped he understood enough. Sweet guy really but determined to fill me with blue semen at every opportunity! Yes I wanted to have blue Babys soon!

The little Gonzales kids were watching a movie before the adult Women told me to go get some! Oh they were all gonna watch and had cameras out. Shame the college did not have a porn star degree. The Dean must have thought it at the same time as she was down peeing herself suddenly. That Woman is so twisted. Maybe the President could help. Doctorate in Medicine and a Masters in Porn!

Maybe I could teach!

That big blue cock is wonderful! Somewhere between pleasure and pain! Oh it's that freaking huge trust me! Intense sensation! Luckily I stretched a bit. Still not sure I could take bigger! Damn right I was stuffed! Cobalt was having fun above and beyond this time as horny Women were fondling his backside and big blue balls while he used me well. We are talking bowling ball sized balls at least here folks! Stone and Mr. Gonzales were in watching the movie with the kids. A very good thing as I am sure Mrs. Gonzales licked those balls for a while as well as my own Mom. Slut Mexican MILF! Oh I was getting her on the bus somehow! No way could I go all weekend without raping someone. Had a definite problem of course but lots of People liked my problem! Well I was good with it!

Human Monogamy is an abomination! You ever wonder why it takes less than two minutes for a guy to cum and over seven for a Girl? Those CaveGirls were real Sluts. Three four guys in a row! One off another on and in! The best sperm wins. The more cum the more likely she would get pregnant and the more diverse the Gene Pool would become. And she would have an orgasm! Much more diverse Gene Pool too! Yes I could go on about overpopulation and Christians, Mormons are Christians, but we don't have the space! There are ways to fix that however!

Be CURIOUS! LEARN ALWAYS!

Brutus was sad about many things so when I was done I helped him make Ally chortle which cheered him up a lot. Not sure what else to call it. A very eerie sound from that Dino. Beautiful however. Brutus nibbled her clit while I shoved my head in her and growled and barked away. She sighed as she lay down very satisfied. Felt her orgasms! Okay while my head was in the Dinosaur the Women all tasted blue cum from my Dog snatch! They didn't have to stop! Hey I was enjoying that! They all saw how big his cock was when he came out of me and I knew every last one wondered if they could take it!

Yes I wanted to watch that!

Frankly the day felt off to me as we went to bed. Took me a while to realize no one had tried to kill me all day. Felt weird.

CHAPTER 6 ROAD BEERS
Thursday September 30th

Woke to really big tongue on my butt! Oh I mean freaking huge! Ally had gotten her head in those french doors somehow and was licking my ass. Yeah I was real happy about it. One seriously intense butt licking!

Had to go potty but she was having fun! Why not? Seemed to like my pee and poop! Had to go and now so I went! Girls had fun too. Was not telling the Dinosaur no! Girls were playful that morning. Understood this as we might not get time for fun for a while. Let them all play. Little did I know!

Okay I have to assume at some point non-perverts will read this and I ask them to remember when they were seventeen? What did you get away with, with your Boyfriend or Girlfriend around your younger siblings or the child you were sitting for? Oh I know you did! Ever steal their favorite toy while they watched TV? Naked Barbies are useful in many ways! Yes I have said kids know what is going on around them and mostly they do but if it does not interest them they pay no attention and could care less! Sex does not interest children like it does adults! If you ever had younger siblings you know! If you try and hide something though they are immediately interested in it. Just be honest. Do not ever confuse Love and Sex! Do you Love your Grandma? When was the last time you had sex with her? (Shut up Steve!) Love is not SEX! Tell them the truth!

Anastasia and Ricardo had agreed to play with Ally and Cobalt while we were gone. Staff liked them both as well. Who wouldn't? The General said he could get me back by helicopter in a few hours if it became necessary. He was a bit worryed himself and that was a good sign. Sadly I went and explained it to the sweet Monsters. Okay I tried! Did not lie! So I told them the Princess had to go meet with off-world emissary's and I had to go protect her! Yeah they got that! They said they would stay and protect the Princess's Castle while we were gone! Had not said that myself yet. Seriously now I was feeling very under appreciated for some reason. Still I loved Windy! Seems at the factory though they showed the less intelligent Monsters a lot of nonviolent young children's programming to keep them calm. They had some intelligence and picked these ideas up easy. Terrifyed me and I have no idea why! They needed to go through those computers and find out stuff!

Eat, say our goodbyes, and we were off.

Caffeinated milkshakes on the way! They are like powerful energy drinks only tasty! Not sure what Tito puts in them. Probably should not have given one to Windy but what the hell! She was thirsty! To Claude Rains Elementary. That man was a legend! They were so excited there at the school. The Teacher was understandably nervous. These were excited five year old's! Her Highness took control of the situation quickly. Told those kids loudly if they don't behave today she would leave them on the PoopHole planet! Pretty sure she meant Uranus! Hoped she did. Adults were all laughing! Kids however looked terrifyed! Adults were peeing themselves now. This of course would disturb me more when we actually went there and I wondered what that Girl knew. We do! Just wait!

Kimmy looked at Miss Tinker and spoke. "Ma'am I hope you packed extra dry pants. If not we probably have enough adult size diapers!" Yeah they had some. Probably not enough. Some where thinking and dealing with stuff. Lucky for us Anastasia had plans of her own.

Tammy and Sabrina looked at Kimmy and said seriously. "You better have lots!" Yes they all had incontinence problems it seems. Medical issues! Those medical problems were Windy and ME of course! Oh I realized that fact far too well. Maybe Windy did too. Becky just snickered! She was finally getting it! No idea if that was good. EVER!

Off to college. Students were out waiting by the parking lot when we arrived and seemed disappointed when they saw us! Tammy stood and Becky and I jumped out fast to reassure them! Tammy spoke quickly to put them at ease. "The other Monsters are fine! After classes today her Highness Princess Windy is going to take her entire class and have peace talks with the Aliens in Area 51 to negotiate surrender!" Kids looked nervous at that so she clarified. "Theirs!" Lots of sighs. "We are going as security and neither Monster would fit on the bus with all those kids so they have remained to guard the Princess's Castle!" Did I say calm them? No idea what I'm talking about!

Seriously, I gave up! No idea how she knew that was what I had told them. Lucky guess my ASS! If your on a plane and it is going down in flames there is only one thing you can do! Have sex with the person in front of you! Okay two things! Maybe the same thing. You enjoy the ride cause it is probably your last. Hear that all you Airline Pilots? Give as much warning as you can so maybe some passengers can at least cum and go at the same time! The passengers get screwed enough by the darn airlines now!

Oh I am available to do cavity searches! All the adults were clear.

Sorry about that. I lost control of the story for a moment! Seems to happen a lot doesn't it? But I get back around though.

There were a lot of Girls here waiting. Recognized many! Followed a couple across campus. They kept glancing back at me and giggling. Both were Oriental. Kimmy checked the list and snickered. So I was going to be late for my disciplinary review! Maybe I could get extra beatings out of it! They led me to the commons and seemed to be looking for an audience. Drama Queens! Raped them on the picnic tables with many witnesses. The students just began calling them names and jeering as they held them down for me. Had quite a few accomplices as well. Those two came so hard! Public humiliation is not only good for the soul but also the libido!

Don't give me that! These students were twisted before I got here. Worse now I admit but I did not start the fire. Just poured the gasoline on it! Those two Girls were made to wear signs that said PREY on them for the rest of the day. They smiled about it. Still were smiling later at lunch.

Slunk into the Dominatrix, I mean Deans office. Oh she was in black leather again to show off. The TV camera set up did not even bother me. Inspired me in fact. Suddenly I stopped dead. The Dean glared at me. "Get in here! You're late!" Did not move. She cracked her crop on the desk. "I said get in here!" Now I whimpered and winked. That smile on the Dean's face was scary but thrilling! "Drag that worthless BITCH in here and chain her skinny ass down!" Girls knew how strong I was so when I put up only a small struggle they understood I was having fun. We all made it look good for the President you see. Why else the camera?

Knew he was watching. They did too as Kimmy waved at the camera.

Peed in terror as they dragged me across the carpet. "You're licking that up before you leave you filthy disgusting BITCH!" The Dean snarled with such anger in her voice. She had a short thick chain attached to a steel plate bolted into the floor by her desk. That was new! So I was hooked on trembling! Not in fear but, he, he, he, do I have to say it was excitement? They all stayed and watched my beating! Even Becky. Saw the tears in her eyes though. Girls petted her telling her it would be okay and it would never happen to her so I think they knew as well. It was hard for her but she knew I wanted it so she watched. The Dean was savage and blood flowed. Beaten brutally finally! Take that itchy spot! On my left cheek. So hard to reach! Finally exhausted and panting the Dean gasped out. "And let that be a lesson to you! Do not do it again!" She looked at the Girls with such anger on her face and snarled. "Get this piece of shit out of my office!"

We went quickly. Limping for the camera I was hamming it up. Was also fully aware that I did not lick my pee up as we left. Had to remember to smell the Dean later to see if she rolled in it. Oh I knew she had orgasmed twice in there while beating me. Maybe more than that. She is such a perv! My problem was I was hornyer then ever! Needed something! Some release. Miss Moneypenny just giggled as we came out. YES! Hoped the President heard that savage Secretary raping! She never said she wanted too be ravaged and I was brutal! Okay she did not say to stop either but that is hard with my clit being ground in your mouth! Was a very greedy ProtoDog! Both of us were. Yes I know all these rape references are bothering some people. There is a reason however. I know the odds of any of you ever getting a date is small but miracles do happen! Now that said compliment your date often and if it gets that direction say to them. "I want to make sweet love to you!" Or. "Take me I'm yours!" What is the worst that can happen? Yeah I know, pepper spray in the eyes sucks but use that. Call them the next morning and say you didn't get any rice with that pepper spray and see if they would like to get Chinese for lunch! Might work? You never know?

Anyway Political Science was about me again. Yep! Discrimination and equality! There were even a couple Monster Girls in class. One with gorgeous green and brown feathers over mighty breasts, the other very big, rocky and reddish brown. Both were totally beautiful and had tremendous breasts. Yes I thought abut it! Students were sitting by them talking to them friendly like. The Monsters were discussed as well. The Teacher asked how we thought things would change with Monsters on campus. The answers surprised many. Most said it would change little except the length of the lunch line! Yes it would! That could be a problem! Both Monster Girls stood and said thank you to everyone and the college for saving and then letting them stay. That they just wanted a chance at a life again they told us. A chance to be free and not tortured. Yeah they had gotten some human victims from foster care and juvenile. Kids they could make disappear! Younger specimens lived longer we found out so were preferred! If they possessed files on the past lives of the Monsters they had there they were either destroyed or taken by Doctor Whiting! These two Girls were old enough it was thought. Having no idea how long they were in that HELL they could not say for sure themselves. Both were quite smart however. Maybe too smart for their own good and that was what got them snatched in the first place.

After class they came and told us thank you personally for saving them. Heard their sincerity. Hugged us all as well. Rock hard tits are still tits! Just sayin! Sure I wondered what her shit tasted like. I am a Dog/Pervert. I admit that too! Wanted to see if Bird Shit tasted like Dino Shit! Purely for scientific reasons! You like to lick ass you like Poop! You like Peanut Butter you like Rat poop. All the Monsters who were able to talk were being interviewed with care and family's contacted IF they wanted. Not all did for many reasons! Well if you had a funeral for someone and then found out they had not died you might have the urge to fix that! Also none of them looked human! Our Feds were still here and said an investigation was being started to catch those who allowed these people to be taken and used. Some one had and those could be gotten too! Everything was very public to an extent! Going through regular channels and chains of command it would have still been buried in spite of the TV footage. Did not think Windy could have understood that but maybe she did. Information was leaking out somewhere. Over five hundred Men, Woman, and Children had been killed by the Doctor in that building alone! Almost a hundred had become Monsters but fought back. Of the thirty Monsters we had the oldest was forty six. The youngest just nine we thought. It was terrified. Looked like a Frog! Cute Frog Girl. Could not or would not speak. Let no one get close either. It was decided to let it have its space for now. It was being held in a secure room. Treated well though! We were afraid she may hop away. Thoughts of Drake still haunted my dreams.

Philosophy Class. We came in and sat down quietly. Ms. Bordeaux came over and bowed deeply before asking. "How is the great Beast and her Four Horsemen today?" There were only three with me now but I caught the reference. Possible I thought. Then again maybe only two were with me.

Well it was. Read Revelations carefully. Preferably an older bible printed before these namby pamby wishy washy types changed it to where God is all about love! Tell that one to the citizens of Sodom and Gomorrah you dirty Bastards! Something before the eighty's. Frankly I liked the idea and the Girls did as well I could tell. Yes I read the Bible! Several times. Why do you think I never went to church anymore. Frankly Windy made more sense than anything in there and she was only FIVE!

Sabrina knew the Bible as well but just snickered and typed away during class. Ms. Bordeaux kept coming over and looking at her work chuckling which made me nervous. A couple suggestions were even made by the Teacher. Pretty sure people would be looking for dry pants at lunch so I licked Becky! Hey it was a grooming! And you call me a pervert! Not everything is sex. Cuddling happens! Cuddling is Good!

So class degenerated and became Conspiracy 101. The headline read. "APOCALYPSE NOW!" Beneath it was. "Four Horsemen of Revelations are here and they are Women!" Below that. "Great Beast Laughs!" Oh I did! Lots! A student even ran for a mop! Needed photos though so we went out side and got some! Heavily armed! Pictures of Teela were pasted in. Yeah it was decided Becky was not a horseman. Becky was a part of me and there were four great Beasts now weren't there?! We needed two more! The General tried to call by lunch but could not finish a sentence! Pretty sure Anastasia had a diaper on him! Speaking of diapers.

Dean Kelly still Hot in black leather came storming over with such anger in her voice. "We do not have enough Diapers!" She kissed everyone with tongue! Yes, her own Daughter, Brutus, and Becky! Such a passionate educator! With a sigh she said. "It's gonna be a quiet weekend without you Girls!" Sure I could have told her never say that but truthfully I think she knew and just did not want to be bored so was hopeful!

Brutus would go fuck, I mean back with the Dean tonight.

Dean Kelly checked my butt to see if I had healed while Kimmy assured her Lots of diapers were on their way. So I checked the Deans butt to see if she were wearing pantys! I at least had healed. They had her bent over the picnic table and held her there so fast! Not like it was the first time?! As she lay there panting afterwards she gasped out. "She… Needs…. A…. Medical…. License!" Yeah and some students needed dry pants! A few were actually walking around in Diapers. No pants! Just diapers! It was college! Smart kids there too. Certain some just liked them! No more holding it in till the end of class.

Just go in your diaper!

Newspaper called just after. Sabrina only said. "Yep!" They could use the article she wrote. Kimmy called our Reporter friend and gave a phone interview. He was rather skeptical of course and I understood. So did Kimmy who asked. "Great Beast enlighten us with Prophecy?"

So I growled out. "Church be pissed tomorrow!" Yeah I know. Not much of a prophecy! Our Reporter laughed his ass off! Knew they would be pissed and I was hungry! Sure I was starting shit for once! A Christian can talk about the rapture for hours. It is like one line in the bible! And even that is unbelievably vague and up for major interpretation. Frankly I don't think any of them are worthy! But, then again, Windy is not done negotiating on their behalf so there is hope for them!

Math! Becky and I took a nap! On each other!

Art! Becky got up and posed again! She really wanted to this time. Only this time like a wild savage snarling animal! Students eyes lit up! So very cool! Was surprised she held the pose that long. It was awesome! The Teacher just praised her and immensely. Students thanked her and that made her smile. Maybe a step in the right direction. I know? Which right direction? WINDY'S!

Yes I had been hesitant about my idea but knew I had no choice now. Eight is not enough! Just ask a Mormon! Class done we headed across campus and I got lucky. Not sex! Later! Trust me! Adultnapped a Black Girl on the way to the car. Some Girl's helped me. Figured we had room and could use the help. She did not resist either! She was there and it was spur of the moment. Shoved my snout between her legs and kept walking. Girls made sure she did not fall off.

As we got close to the car Sandra got on her phone. On speaker. Her voice calm and relaxed. "Hi Mom. Just calling to say we are off on our trip and Pammy kidnapped a Black Girl."

The Deans voice was suddenly strained. Not in worry! "What Black Girl?"

Tanya waving since they were behind me and she was on my back saying very happily. "Tanya Darling!"

Hysterical laughter then a gasped. "Have fun on your field trip Sweety! Mommy will see you when you get back!"

So I knew I owed Sandra a big apology! Not for anything I HAD done of course. NO! What I was going to do was another story! She may never be the same but would be so cute! Went and picked up the bus! They got upset at the rental place but not till after we finished all the paperwork. The dealer asked in terror as Kimmy handed Tammy the keys. "You're letting the Blind Girl drive?" He glanced at Becky and I first judging if he could grab the keys and get to safety before we ate him! Odds must not have looked good.

Kimmy was all smiles though saying gently by way of explanation. "She drove over here!" So true.

Sabrina said in a loud whisper to the frightened man. "That is a real grenade launcher strapped to her hip! You want to tell her NO?" They were loving this. Was totally Hysterical! Poor guy! Almost felt sorry!

Sandra said. "Why do you think we got full coverage insurance!" Poor man! Becky and I were looking at him intently. Not sure what he was thinking and did not care. We just wanted to watch him shit his pants!

Kimmy snickered saying. "Thirty little five year old's for a weekend we had no choice!" Hmph. Wonder were that nice salesman went? He could really run at that age. We had the keys! "We'll meet you at the school Tammy! We have another Adultnapping to pull." They all looked at me with interest.

There were big smiles at the school as we pulled in the lot with Miss Winters sitting on my back waving happily. She looked fine when we got the bandages off. Amazing what a little Mothers Milk will do! Mom and Mrs. Gonzales were here with Teela already. Excited children were in the parking lot staring at the bus! Not a school bus, but a very impressive luxury one. These kids were in awe of it! Heck I was. Just hoped it still was a luxury bus when we got back.

Speaking of which. Sandra cleared her throat loud getting everyone's attention. "Um there is one thing no one has been told yet as it was decided upon just recently and I apologize. We did not even know about this till earlyer I swear. The seats on the bus are cloth! That is a problem and requires us to insist no one is allowed on the bus without a diaper on!" Outrage from those children! She continued. "That includes the adults!" Snickers were heard from kids then! "We have only one potty on here and do not want any accidents! They do happen. Nothing to be embarrassed about!"

Kids were shocked but vocal. "We have a real potty on the bus?!" Five year old's have different priorities.

"Yes we do kids. Accidents do happen however and we don't want anyone running out of clean clothes either. We have a very long drive ahead of us and can't afford many stops. Now lets get those diapers on so we can go." She said and pulled a tarp off a table. Mostly we had pull up diapers for the kids. The adults however had to have cute adult baby diapers. Talk to Anastasia about that one! That Woman is a Mommy fetish freak! She had a factory in Taiwan working overtime making more for us. This was her idea too! Once she heard we had cloth seats and knowing how few stops we planned on making she came up with this. Smart really. Still know why she really did it!

And I headed for the bus! Windy got in front of me not looking friendly any more. Scepter poked in my chest she hissed. "NO ONE on bus without a diaper!" Becky snickered. No idea why as she was going to have to wear one too. Maybe she wondered where they found one to fit me. So everyone got diapers. Okay not Tammy! She had grabbed one saying no potty breaks and they tackled her, grenade launcher and all! These kids needed release of energy and some potty breaks would work for that. Miss Tinker, Windy's teacher blushed so cutely as she crinkled with every step. Mrs. Griffin the older principle held her head high! The way she wiggled I knew we were going to have three animals on this bus. A Dog, a Tiger, and a Cougar! Oh we know what I was thinking! Well I followed her on the bus! That she could be my Grandmother made no difference to me! Old people need love, I mean multiple orgasms as well! My tongue was going in that ass sometime soon! Nice wiggle at her age still.

Oh wow! They had made a wall with luggage in back. Knew why but did not want to think about that. The last three rows of seats were blocked off from view. They were a quiet area they said by way of explanation. HA! Sort of a time out space. HA, HA! Those seats had no entertainment gear built in them. HE, HE, HE! The other seats had lots. TV/on demand movies/Video game consoles. Yep just like on airliners. Very fancy bus! Kimmy had spared no expense and got the best! Oh I thought it a good choice. Most kids had a backpack that contained such treasures as blanky's and stuffy's (They were five year old's!) which they could keep by them and a small suitcase with clothes in the storage racks beneath. We also had a few coolers with soda, milk, and OJ in them plus lots of healthy snacks and some not so healthy in the make shift wall! Like five hundred dollars in quarters as well for vending machines for serious junk food and coffee binges. We had a very long drive and stops would be few. Did not want to have to stop for change somewhere. Probably gonna teach all these kids how to play poker too. Long trip!

Tammy had insisted on road beers! A dozen two liters of root beer! Caffeine pills too. Oh and enough strong energy drinks to kill an entire football team! Several times! Tammy would be fine. She had a strong heart!

Kids got on and took seats with no trouble at all. They were excited but in awe. This was something very different and new to them. Me too! The Teacher was even impressed! Luxury vehicle here. Kimmy must have paid a fortune. The only problem we had was kids wanted to sit by Windy and us Animals. Even by some of the Girls. Solved by Windy who said kids could take turns with everyone. Change places every half hour. Hey they were only five year old's. Very curious and interested in things but short attention spans! Really liked to cuddle too.

And I love to cuddle!

When Miss Winters found out she was not the only one Adultnapped, (They were not KIDS!) like that was a surprise, she got concerned and told Tanya. "Hunny I can get them to drop you off if you have things to do?"

That Gorgeous Black Girl just snickered at the blonde pudge sweetly. "And waste this cute diaper? I don't think so! Plan on using it and making Pammy change me!" Okay! Maybe I would regret Adultnapping her! To many adults were smiling at that statement now weren't they? Getting ideas of their own perhaps. All the adults had exchanged cell phone numbers before we boarded so they could text grownup things to each other they said. Really smart idea and I was impressed. For them at least!

Still probably all texting about me!

Speaking of smart things? Driving a bus on the sidewalk through a sidewalk cafe not so smart really! Even if I do understand the anger. Fun however! Some adults were terrified! The kids just squealed gleefully and told her to do it again! Frankly I did not think they were even giving the bus back at this point so security deposit was moot. Heard Miss Tinker whisper nervously. "Glad I have a diaper on!" Oh Yeah, I already smelled Teacher pee! Might not be the only one.

They called ahead to the fast food place about five. Told them ten minutes so put fry's and nuggets down! We had soda in bottles so we got a bunch of juices and milks. Pretty sure Kimmy and Teela both liked their new sippy cups. Anastasia had sent lots so everyone got one. Her thinking, or so she said, was it would avoid spills. Kids just giggled about it. We know that Woman is insane however so we knew the truth. She had asked for pictures after all. Kimmy and Tammy had worked it out with the restaurants yesterday and called them so they would have enough food prepped. Nice of them really. Well Becky could eat almost as much as me now so we were ordering for sixty! Most kids had nuggets. As Becky and I were along we ate outside there. Well they could not throw burgers on the carpeted floor of the bus! Becky actually seemed fine with that arrangement. Enjoyed being an animal and treated nicely like one it seems. Tired of her humanity perhaps? Would not blame her! You should read that diary! Wanted to kill that bastard over and over! Kids got to stretch their legs a little. We had bought lots for snacks later if needed. Picked up popcorn and heavy energy drinks for Tammy! Well of course it scared me but no one else had a commercial drivers license. Well I think Tammy had one? Said she did. No one saw it but we trusted her. Wondered how big her bladder was though! Had about four gallons in her so far! The kids had no problems with her insanity and I didn't either really. Then again none of us had a sense of our own mortality!

It was a long drive. She needed the energy!

Interesting musical education for these kids if they ever listened. Not saying! The infamous Cindy Walker fell asleep on me after a movie. Such a cutey too! Felt honored by her presence. She had proudly shown me pictures of her two Mommy's saying she was very happy that Windy had two Mommy's now as well so she didn't feel so different from everyone any more. Poor kid! Told her the truth. She was different! Special! They were all just jealous of her for having two Mommy's! Could sense her pain. Knew others gave her crap. Why people have to be so judgmental and vindictive I did not understand. Never had! Told her there was nothing wrong with having two Mommy's or two Daddy's and if anyone said there was to let me or Windy know! Pretty Women her Mommy's. Wondered if they liked Dogs? Well I did! Liked Mommy's as well now didn't I? I can't help it! You have no idea how horny I was. Before long most kids were asleep. Then again I liked Grandmothers as well.

Mrs. Griffin walked like the Predator she was toward the potty down the isle and I watched every motion as she went. There was quite a bit! That Cougar can really wiggle. Tanya saw where I was looking and encouraged me! Most probably would have too but Tanya was the one across from me and she saw where I was looking. Hard to miss as I was not hiding it. Gently I got off the seat and followed. Miss Winters gave me a grin and an eye roll. Yeah she was getting hers later and she knew it. Good thing the kids had ear buds in as the Cougar was a screamer. Things like. "Oh my God!" And. "Take me up the butt you filthy Beast!" Were heard. Had not touched her butt yet! Not disobeying the Principle though as I did not want detention. That Cougar Slut wanted it! Knew darn well they were texting about me now! Wanted to know what they had told this sexy Beast! Sandra had gotten up fast but Sabrina had stopped her saying both Women understood what would happen if they let me! They had been warned by Text several times. Miss Tinker just blushed. Not sure if I could knock this Cougar up at her age but you never know! Damn well wanted to try! Oh yeah! She was an animal! Hey I had scratches! Seats had stains!

Heard Teela snicker and say. "Well there goes the security deposit!" Not the only one snickering now.

My thinking was simple Dog logic. Lots of people on the bus! Buses toilet tank could only hold so much bodily waste. Me? Well I could apparently hold more! That made me nervous still as I had no idea where it was all going. It had been discussed quite a lot and both Doctors, Lucy and Ellsbeth Petrov agreed it was probably a metabolic thing. Tammy was the one suggested I was a living Black Hole and sending it to an alternate reality! Personally I was leaning that way myself! Sandra was still standing, watching, so when the Cougar was done she smiled and came down the isle! Had the ball gag/muzzle with her at least! Smart Teacher Bitch! Would need it! Loved foul Dog sex! Who doesn't? Made her growl still!

Finally I was sitting with Miss Winters after violating several girls including her, we only had one ball gag but they never even wiped it off when they swapped it, when Miss Tinker got up and headed for the potty. Hey those ear buds did not fit in my ears well and I was bored so I got up and followed her. Okay it was either rape or a religious experience. Maybe both?! She made no indications she wanted this but I still went after her. Teela had followed with the ball gag. Miss Tinker struggled a lot. Looked scared! Most adults were just looking back. Some were nervous at the expression on her face as she got up. Looked like shock. Teela got it and made me sleep with her however so she would know that I did care about her. Not a problem. She held me back. Knew I just knocked her up. Sure I had raped her too. So tasty though. Cuddly!

No, what absolutely scared me was that Tammy was behaving!

Never a good sign.

CHAPTER 7 LONG HAUL
Friday October 1st

Woke up about four AM. Something was wrong? Maybe just different? WAIT! No engine sound! We were parked! Had been for a while it felt. Engines tick as they cool and I heard nothing. Door was open! Neither Tammy or Becky were on the bus! Was there a problem of some kind? Gently I got up and went to see what was going on cautiously and I admit I was worryed about Tammy right away! Had She really taken too much caffeine and exploded her heart? Becky was prowling out in the picnic table area. Spotted her quick. Awesome sight in the gloom and moonlight. Was she looking for scraps? Went over to see. She said she was looking for Mice when I asked her. She found that funny as she had been afraid of Mice before but had this urge to hunt them now. Got that one easy. Told her it was a good thing to see from a different perspective. Lessened the old pains. Well I knew as it had happened to me. The world takes on new meaning when you let go and embrace the Beast! So getting Becky to take my diaper off for me I took advantage of the break myself and pottyed first. Off in the trees! Well we didn't have a shovel. Asked where Tammy was once done and Becky just pointed at the building with her nose. We were at a mostly deserted freeway rest stop. Maybe Tammy just had to poop! Oh Tammy POOP! Only two other cars were here. Becky said Tammy had been in there a while. Still. Not worried before, now I was again.

Went to find her! With as much caffeine as she had in her a heart, can, I mean WILL just explode. Did not think hers would but nothing was guaranteed. Not even my next poop! Yeah hard to believe isn't it? Not easy to get in the lousy building. Damn door handles! She was blind too so once inside I had no idea which potty she would use. Unless she knew Brail those signs were flat. Yeah that sounds good to me! I'll go with that excuse. Grunting was coming from the Men's Room as I went in! Thought she may be getting raped in the darn Men's Room. Yeah I know more like she was raping them. You never know! She may like cock every now and then. Someone was having sex in there however. Could even smell it. Had too know! Stuck my head under the stall door and smiled. Neither of them was Tammy! She did not have cock and balls! Knew that well, and both of these people did! So I watched for a minute. Could still be a raping. Had to be certain! Maybe if it was I could get pointers?

Found Tammy in the Girl's Room. Pants around her ankles. Asleep on the toilet! She was out too. Sorry I raped her then. Like I could resist. Clean her up and get her on my back still snoring gently. Go find Becky and take her in to watch the two guys still fucking. They were still going at it! WOW! He had some stamina! The other seemed very happy about that too. In the bus Becky closed the door smiling and I took Tammy to the back and slept on her. She needed a nap and some Methane to mellow her out a bit. Take the edge off the caffeine.

Woke a while later with Sandra yelling loudly in a major panic. "Where's Tammy?" Boy she was freaking.

Teela just kinda snickered at her. "Did you look under Pammy?" Teela was under Becky after all! People are tasty and most are rather comfy as well! Who doesn't want to sleep with a Mexican Pudge or a Blind Albino? Wait I mean sleep with a live Tiger? So cuddly!

Once they got Tammy out from under me and up on two feet knowing she was okay as she was smiling they all immediately expressed concern about Tammy's having stopped and putting us way behind schedule. Tammy had promised to drive all the way non-stop you see which was why she had the energy drinks. It was a rather tight schedule if we wanted any time when we got there. Tammy explained gently with chuckles. "Um Waterford is about twenty five miles from here so we are way too early for breakfast. Traffic was really light so I stopped here, someplace quiet instead of being in a parking lot on the highway waiting for the restaurant to open, so I could use the bathroom too. Oh and a Methane induced coma!" She was petting me and smiling so I was good. She liked my farts too ya know. Nasty, Blind, Left-handed, Albino Lesbian! "Besides Pammy and Becky wanted to watch those two guys in the Men's Room!" Now I looked at her and she grinned at me. Maybe her radar worked in her sleep? None of the grownups were going to ask any questions about that. Most could do the math easy enough. They all knew One plus One equals Butt Sex! It's that new math they keep talking about! Honest that is how it works! Apparently what my Grandparents learned in school was completely wrong! Yeah they could do the other math as well and frankly those speeds for that long without blowing the engine on the bus is damn impressive. Kimmy should definitely buy a bus like this. Probably not this one however. Had doubts of it's survival! Thank State Farm for insurance! Maybe they could make a commercial about the death of this bus! Would be stunning I was certain! ProtoDog's are realists!

Kids got to stretch their legs for a few at least. A few diapers got changed. Sandra's! She's such a big Baby. And not just pee-pee! She was a POOPY Teacher! She was asking for it! Maybe begging? Just wait. Mrs. Griffin helped change her in the Little Girl's Room! Molested her! Molest me! 58 year old Women have desires, needs and are perverts too! Sandy never made a peep as that Cougar fondled her well. Acted real small. Becky and Windy brought Mrs. Tinker down and told US to change her! Cute poopy Teacher butt there too! Oh I licked it! Yes you read that right. Well I hope by now you did not even question that one?!

On the road again! Most of you sang it this time! I'm proud of you!

Hit the fast food joint for fifty pounds of hash browns! For ME! So I like my potatoes! Nice place and friendly staff. Kids got to run around more as the food was brought out to us. Very friendly employees! No! Not that friendly! Was warm here as we had been going mostly south and clothes got changed.

When suddenly out of nowhere Tammy said very excited. "Someone call the General and tell him we will be there by dinner easy!" Well? And quite understandably of course, people got nervous as many knew how many miles that was and did That Math so they now knew how fast Tammy was going to go! Ticket would be the least of her worry's! At those speeds they would probably just arrest her! If they caught her. Tammy realized that to I think so to distract them she added. "Pammy change your Mother!" Someone got excited. Not me! Okay I did too! Then again my Mom had a sweet butt! Fuck you! You'd stick your tongue up my Mom's butt in a heart beat! Yeah I was gonna! Windy said sternly if I wanted to get spanked later I would do it! That kinda disturbed me a bit! Still gonna do it. Remember how I said kids knew and understood more than adults gave them credit for? Yeah so you understand why I was disturbed now?

So I changed my own Mother like a good Beast wondering just who was spanking me later? Pretty sure Windy only thought I just liked to get spanked. Hey one of those Boys liked to eat worms I was told. Did not ask which! Was curious as to whether he used hot sauce however? ProtoDog's want to know those things! All about the hot sauce! We had a couple cases of it on the bus and they were pouring it on my food. Becky said she never liked hot sauce. Wondered why she was having it poured on her food? Must be a Proto thing. Some kids liked it as well so we might need more soon. The Cougar did. But we started trouble it seems. A very cute little blonde Girl was crying bad now. Miss Winters went to her rapidly and asked her with such compassion what was wrong. Did the thought of a spanking scare her? Was she afraid of getting spanked herself? RIGHHT!

Her cute response sobbed out, messed with grownup peoples heads. "No one is spanking me though!" Was not a protest or a question but a complaint. Got some raised eyebrows then let me tell you! Well I had nothing to do with that! Are perversions acquired in life or are some in us from birth? It is a legitimate question! I mean I can understand a breast fixation possibly having something to do with breast feeding or lack there of but what about a butt fixation? Where does that come from? You won't take the time to consider these things so I will point them out to you! Really want to know too! Call me with some answers!

Miss Winters just smiled sweetly at her after a moment as she lifted that sweet little chin to look in those sad tear filled eyes of that sweet little Girl. Her voice was firm however as she asked that child. "Do you deserve a spanking young Lady?"

That little Girl giggled back a sob and blushed cutely. Her voice whiny. "Yes Mommy! I was bad again!"

Oh shut up! There was nothing sexual in it at all here! It is usually a power thing which can be so comforting. The firm hand of a parental figure correcting your bad behavior. She was missing her Mother and we could tell. Most were! In the immortal words of Brandon Lee, "Mother is the name of God on the lips of children!" We miss him! Maybe this sweet Girl misbehaved at home a lot to get her Mom to spank her as it may have been the only time she got any real attention. It happens a lot! Kids crave attention from their Parents which is just natural and will get it by good or bad behavior. All they want is some attention! Will take anything they can get. Parents are so busy on their phones playing games or spreading conspiracy gossip and election falsehoods they spend no time with their children! Maybe she liked pain a little too. When do these things develop? If she didn't get this now she may grow up to be a cutter or develop an eating disorder, perhaps even become Suicidal! Why do some people like Brussels Sprouts and some hide from them? BRUSSELS SPROUTS!

The world has changed drastically in the last forty years and not for the better! Watch "Leave it to Beaver" and see. Fifties, even sixties, the Father worked and the Mother stayed home to be there for the children. They were called Housewives for a reason. One income family's were mostly all there was and they were not poor! Mom saw you off too school and was there when you went home! No shuffling to day cares! Kids knew their Mother loved them! Oh they don't anymore! They all question it constantly! Technology was supposed to make life better and give us more leisure time to spend with our children! Fox News works better!! You are slaves to technology! Poverty rates are rising!

Think on this? Sixties and seventies even earlier, kids had Bugs Bunny, Road Runner, and others. Cartoons were full of violence! Than the Namby Pamby Wishy Washy types said violence was bad. So along comes Barney and the Teletubbys! Corporal punishment was taken from schools! Parents were arrested for correcting bad behavior in their children! Did the world become nicer? NOPE! Juvenile crime rose well over a thousand percent! Fact! Kids realized they had power and if Mom and Dad did not buy them a new game they tell the Teacher parents beat them. Maybe your foster Parents will feel sorry and buy you one. Well your Parents are in jail because you were a brat! Don't believe me? Go research it! Thomas

Jefferson said. "It is better that ten guilty Men go free then one innocent Man got to jail!" You know how they solved that problem? Now they just shoot them so there is no trial! With CPS you are considered Guilty even after proven innocent! All true!

There is good news though. Windy says she will fix it! After her nap.

It's hard to raise a child these days and a lot of effort but please take the time with them! Let them know you will answer anything and honestly! If you don't know the answer the library usually has internet access. Never let them ask that kid down the street! You know which one I'm talking about! He gets his info from Porn Hub. Seriously you shouldn't even let your kids play with him! He picks up Dog Poop and puts it in a paper bag than lights it on fire on old man Nelson's porch, rings the bell and runs away! That is a sick twisted Boy! Sorry! It got away from me again! Miss Tinker was just nodding as she truly understood this. Probably had been there and spanked this Girl before. So Miss Winters spanked the little Girl hard till she was crying good, scolding her the whole time and telling her to behave like a good little Girl or else! The little Girls name was Cindy as well. We had two of them! Two Cindy's are better than one! She held the child lovingly afterwards and comforted her telling her she was a nice child deep down and we all loved her. The little Girl sucked her thumb on Miss Winters lap with a very big smile and tears on her face. Becky had watched all this very closely and I saw the tears in her eyes at this. Wondered what hurt more? Watching the child spanked or comforted? Becky still had some issues. We would love her no matter what!

My Mom however had been watching Becky as well and patted her lap gently. Becky went to her. Mom understood that need for affection and held her. Remembered when Mom used to hold me like that and yes I missed it a lot. Happened way to little as it was. Kimmy went over and sweetly stuck Becky's tail in her mouth. No thumbs so she could suck on her own tail. It was so cute. We all got pictures!

So I went and climbed on Mrs. Griffins lap. Felt like it so piss off! She was smiling about it. Not telling what I was sucking on but she liked me! Really nice breasts too. Older Women are sexy too! We had a blanket! Well Teela put it over us nicely before things went south. Making god time still.

Our luck would not hold!

When we finally got pulled over just a little before lunch, it was not for speeding however, as Tammy had suddenly slowed a couple miles back, thought she was giving the engine a break, but because of a porcupine! He was jut crossing the freeway and Tammy swerved to miss him. Yeah the bus kinda came off the ground on one side! Big deal! Kids all squealed! Begging her to do it again! They were just kids?! No sense of their own mortality. You grow up when you realize you can die! Windy will never grow up! Good for us!

Than again maybe she knew and already had.

"Crap! Cop!" Tammy hit her turn signal quick as she pulled over to the side nicely. "Everyone behave!" Right? She opened the door and said loudly. "Morning Officer!" Sounded like a madhouse in the bus. These kids had a sense of humor. Or an instant silly pill hit them. We didn't have any Nitrous did we? Had lots of Methane at least.

The Officer did not look amused in the least as he came on board! Well I can't say I blame him! Seriously! May be going to far. Very loudly and kinda angry he asked. "Alright! Who was driving?!" Everyone pointed at Tammy. Even angryer Cop voice now. "You do not want to do this! Now who was driving?" Thick southern accent he had. Fingers pointed again.

Tammy spoke so sweetly now. "I'm the only one with a CDL license Sir!" She had it out. He took it and looked very hard at it. Told her to take off the glasses as it was not a funny joke. She did. They were taped up. His jaw dropped. "Tragic Chem lab accident officer! May never get my sight back." Her eyes were taped shut! What would you think? This was not going to be fun for him. Okay he got some divine intervention. His car was pulled up right behind us. It was not quiet on the bus but with my Canine hearing I could hear lots of voices on his cars radio. Something major was going on as they sounded extremely panicked to me.

A few things that were not good were heard in panicked tones as well. Like, armed and dangerous, six dead, and other stuff. The Officer looked at us lost when his personal radio crackled and a voice said. "Officer Johnson. The suspects are headed your way but do not I repeat DO NOT try to pursue. A road block is being set up!" Waste of time if you ask us. Officer Johnson looked scared about this though. Probably thought of dead children on the side of the road. Had news for him!

Windy sighed so cutely looking at me. "Beast! This Soldier of the realm needs our help!" So I got off my Cougar proudly and stretched. Cop may have peed himself then. About time. Was cramped on this bus. Windy hopped on my back and asked the Officer so nicely. Such a cutey. "Do you require them alive Soldier?" He just shook his head as he backed up and off the bus looking very scared. Oh I understood this as I was darn big! You do not understand. I was Fucking Huge! Big as a Grizzly at least. Kind of fun filling people with terror you know. Knew how Godzilla must feel! MY HERO! As I stepped gingerly out into the middle of the busy freeway with cars whipping past us, their drivers freaking, everyone piled out of the bus to watch! They had no idea what was coming but were not passing it up!

Quickly I scratched an itch behind my ear. Heard them coming fast. Damn they were pushing that engine! Windy smiling on my back held up a small hand as they got close and yelled. "Halt!" Yes! I knew full well if she really wanted it they would have stopped! She was something. Loved her so I didn't care if she had super powers!

Lame ass black Camaro doing about a hundred was coming straight at us. Bus goes faster! Ask Tammy! Thought Windy may have helped that however. They swerved around us! The Pussy's! Not a slur on Women as I like to eat Pussy's! Were looking at us confused as they went by though. Windy laughed and said so cold. "Hunt!" Less than a quarter mile I was running right up over their car. Windy slipped off my back as we passed and slammed that Scepter down into the engine block with such force the earth shook. Like hitting a brick wall! Okay a low one as they flipped a few times through the air. Cool! So I trotted over to see if anyone was alive enough to need CPR! Kids were all just applauding. Messy in that car! Airbags did not help them! Windy still walked over and lectured the corpses! Hopped on when done and we trotted back to the bus all smiles like nothing had even happened. Windy had a good eye and was looking around quickly as we got back, now seeming concerned. "Where is the Soldier?" His absence was noticeable.

Tammy just snickered. "Getting his pants changed!"

The Officers problem was we had no pants that would fit him. He was cute in just a diaper. Windy made him kneel and knighted him. He just obeyed. No idea why! Pure shock I think. They made him talk to the General! It helped I think. Other Cops finally showed up. No sense of humor there either. Sabrina liked to use the squad car radio and had quickly told them bad guys were not going to make the lame ass road block so they could go home. What do you expect? She was Mexican!

This delay was a big problem however. No Tammy said she could still get us to lunch on time no problem. The big problem is some Dickheads, no idea which ones, were watching or something and thought since we were stopped we were easy prey. Stupid Fuckers huh? As many Cop cars arrived, fast, Tammy just smiling said sweetly yet loud. "Drones coming!" We did not question this and they just pulled weapons from under the bus! Yes we had some big ones! Explained why we had a wall of luggage. 50. Caliber machine guns. Never leave home without them! Girls were more than strong enough to use them.

Huge machine guns make Cops nervous it seems however. No idea why. Not as much firepower as many heavily armed drones flying in low and fast from the west though! We let them shoot first. It got wild fast though! About two dozen drones came swooping in from the west. Nasty looking things in daylight. Big guns and rockets everywhere on them! We had some too though. Quickly these Cops tried to get children to hide. Miss Tinker knew better than to try and taking the opportunity she was given started teaching kids about weapon safety. Never to young to learn that shit! Girls quickly helped her. Tammy never missed with the grenade launcher. Even getting fancy with over the shoulder blind shots and stuff.

Think she was showing off for the Officers. Windy and I blocked bullets. It was a short battle but lots of gratuitous violence and damage occurred in a very short time. We had wreckage everywhere across the landscape and freeway. The bus was never hit. A Cop car did get some damage but mostly just drone parts which were everywhere. No one said shit as we told the Officers to watch for unexploded ordinance and got back on the bus and drove away. The General also had surveillance on us as well and he called to make sure Windy was okay! Worried her nail polish may have chipped he said. She made him a bit nervous and I got that. She was five with the powers of God but a wonderful Girl. They gave her the phone. About forty minutes of incredibly graphic descriptions! Only five minutes of action at best. Such a cutey!

Oh we made sure the Porcupine got across the freeway safe though! Becky insisted. All agreed!

We care! About our woodland friends at least! Bad guys? Not so much.

On to lunch! So I may have eaten a Cougar for a snack while Windy was on the phone! Not sayin! Kids were all watching cartoons! The shooting was done so back to the movies. Cougar ate me first so I was wondering if I could get some detention from her now! Yeah I followed her into the Girl's Room at the fast food place when we got there. Well she didn't have to go again yet! She was clean! No idea what the Lady listening in the next stalls name was but I get carried away! Went in the next stall to introduce myself. She tried to get my snout all the way in there! Both of them. Rub my nose on both their cervix as I wanted to. Well I am such a Slut. Just hoped no one found out about my raping a stranger in the toilet.

We even made a couple stops on the way as we were so ahead of schedule by then. Saw the biggest ball of yarn and a Museum of Oddity's. Kids loved it! Had BIG problems with Becky though. It was a ball of yarn and she was a Cat! Said she could not control herself as we dragged her away. Told her it was okay and that I would always control her. Got us lots of pictures. Especially the two headed Goat body. Wondered if Doctor Petrov could make us one with what she knew. The Museum people got pictures of us! They wanted a paw print so I gave them one. When they found out Windy was the Princess of the Universe they wanted her hand print to. Not saying otherwise. If there was a chance it was true they wanted to be the first! She showed them how strong she was. Ha ha. They got video! Some may have gotten scared about her actual strength so? She still did nowhere near what I knew she could. Still I knew what was in that Girls heart though so I was good.

It was a fun trip. Raped a stranger in a restroom, raped my own Mother on the bus! Twice! Becky told me to do that second one! Told me Mom was horny but she was just not ready to do that to someone yet so I had too. She had done Tammy that one time and was not sure yet. Still processing how she felt about it. To many bad memory's I guess. No we did not use words to talk usually. She liked my Mom and wanted her to be happy so she asked me. Well I didn't mind. Mom didn't either it seemed. Oh you'd be begging me to stick my tongue in you! Kids saw nothing. Probably knew everything though as they were kids and just didn't care! If we were playing Rabid Barbies back there some of those kids would have been all over that in an instant. It's like playing Barbie Zombies only they are Rabid! YOU HAVE NEVER played Barbie Zombies???? How sad your life is. Mrs. Gonzales led me back and forced me to eat both her and Teela. Did not take much force but I knew she just wanted to be rough with me. Take out some anger. What fun! Teela even got spanked!

Trust me. They may not understand things but kids know what is going on. Windy told them I was practicing my hunting skills on people so I could eat the bad guys better and they all said it was good to practice. Five year old's are quite practical it seems. The rest of the trip was uneventful. Once Tammy said we were close to Area 51 kids got excited and began watching. Not much to see till the fence. Then we saw fence! Empty desert beyond. We drove along huge electrical fences for a few miles with "no entry" signs everywhere. When the huge gate came in view I knew they did not look happy to see us. We were a tour bus. Not impressed by what I could see of their security but I knew most could not be seen. Certain they knew of our presence long before we got to that gate. We turned in the short drive and about twenty Men aimed big guns at us fast. Ours were bigger but they were in the storage compartment. Tammy just stuck her head out the open window and yelled with a Jersey accent. "The Princess is here for the peace talks!"

There may have been some snorting in the bus.

A rude angry voice came over the loudspeakers. "This is United States Military property! Authorized personnel only! Back up turn around and leave now! You will not be told again! This is your only warning!" How rude! Military has no sense of humor you know, which is what made the General so totally dangerous. He had one you see. Still not smart to threaten us!

Stupid fuckers!

Tammy chuckled and yelled head still out the window. "Your Highness! There seems to be a slight problem." She opened the doors when Windy got up shaking her head and looking disappointed! Not looking mad, just sad. Not good odds I thought. Twenty heavily armed men against a five year old! Talk about overkill! Lots of snickering on the bus now as we watched while Windy went and opened the gates for us! With some extreme prejudice! Permanently open! Well until they could find a new one. Twenty men lay on the side of the road butts bare and red getting the lecture! Their guns just twisted metal. Hoped they had good insurance as that gate was gonna need lots a fixin. Real Bad!

The General was laughing hysterically as his jeep came bouncing up just moments later. His driver looked nervous. To many reasons to have a clue as to which one caused that. Windy snarled at the General. "They owe me a new dress!" Well the one she had on had bullet holes now. Lots! Can't believe they actually tried to shoot a five year old. The dirty cowards! Windy threatened to put the General in a diaper if he didn't stop laughing and he just pulled his pants down fast showing he had one on already. True military intelligence there! Like I said. He gets it!

Once the General could he bowed and apologized to Windy. "I'm so sorry about this your Majesty! We were not expecting you till later originally and this shift had not been informed as it is supposed to be a secret!" He was looking at the rest of us not nicely. Maybe they should have watched CNN as it was all over there I thought. Fox news was calling it a publicity stunt for Hot Dogs. Yeah we kinda had a problem with secrecy. We did not like it! Said it a few times now. The more people know about something the harder it is to hide it!

"Still owe me a dress!" Her voice said she was serious.

We followed the jeep onto the base. It was an interesting place area 51. It tends to move around you see. Not a fixed place but a designation. They moved it every few years for security reasons. People would find out where it was and the next thing you know? Tourists! Still always on a military base. Kids were excited and stared out the bus windows. Tanks and helicopters were all over the place and Kids love those things. Soldiers were marching. Just like in the movies. A very nice military base. Hoped it still was when we left! They didn't get Windy a new dress there would be damage. That little Girl was dead serious about her dress. The General led us to a large hanger like building surrounded by Tanks with huge doors that were wide open. It was a cargo jet hanger so the doors like the building were huge. Empty except lots of tables and chairs were inside along the back wall. It was interesting. Looked like a restaurant! Or an outdoor cafe! Kimmy yelled at Tammy fast. "Do not run it over or you ride in the luggage rack on the way home!" Still I was curious about this. There looked to be a large open kitchen of some sort attached to the back of the building. A Soldier directed us to park in the building like he was directing a plane. That was cool. Kids loved that.

As we got off the bus inside the hanger someone came running at us from the kitchen, I could see it was a definite kitchen now. The person was rather excited, happy, looking and staring at me mostly. Tall and thin he was rather pale and looked about sixty but smelled older, dressed in white Chef's clothes. Something about him definitely said not human! The way he moved I think. He went straight to Windy though still watching me with awe and bowed deeply. "Welcome your Royal Highness! I am your humble servant Ulrik. You are more glorious then ever expected! May I please be allowed to take a moment and examine Your magnificent Beast?" Windy knew instantly who she was talking too. Well I did too. Think they all did. Just something about him. Seemed nice too. Genuinely happy to see us.

She smiled at him and spoke gently. "Please examine her and satisfy your curiosity Mr. Alien Ulrik." He did too and I am sure I was not the only one to think it was almost sexual as grown-ups looked nervous! Kinda turned me on but that is easy right? He rubbed me all over and hugged me feeling my strength somehow, praising me. That this being somehow felt more than just my muscles did not bother me. He bowed to me as well now. Perhaps a hint of fear in his attitude as well. Would not be the last time I caused him fear either.

"Your Beast is so magnificent Princess." He was in awe of me though. You could hear it well in his voice. He understood to an extent. Maybe that was what scared him the most.

The General came over to us just smiling happily after handing out orders concerning the bases surrender to the invading army of five year old's. Ever go on a field trip with some? Kids were standing around looking at everything in awe however. Such curiosity was wonderful! "Your Highness this is Ulrik from the planet Grazone!" The General said loud and proud.

Kids got very excited hearing this and began saying Hi! They were kids and he was an Alien! They were cool with it. He did not quite look human. Smelled interesting I thought. Taking my massive head in his hands he smiled as he spoke. "You are the second most amazing creature in the universe!" Really? Who was number one and could I meet them? Could I have sex with them? "What you have done so far and are able to do is so terrifying! Can you do more? I think so. The big question however is were you an accident? They never expected that these medicines could be combined to make something remotely like you! They do not understand what has happened! It was never intended to do this!" He gestured at my body. "Like your Brother I am told was the purpose and what they expected. Like you? You should not exist! There are whole races pooping their pants over you! Now I understand you are to be a parent?!" Just the way he said it I knew he was only talking about the Pups in me. Thought he knew of the rest. Apparently not. Darn right I blushed at that. If I had known he knew so little yet I would have been rolling on my back on the floor playing Pee-Pee sprinkler!

He greeted everyone here, even the children, one at a time asking each their name and if they were having fun. Thanking them for coming to this momentous occasion. Kids were amazed. Five year old's can tell an Alien when they see one. Grown ups tend to think they don't exist so mark them down as deformed kids or something else stupid. A pretty mature Female Alien came out and greeted us as well. She was so sweet and dainty. Rather beautiful as well. No I did not think it! Felt it was not safe as they may be able to read my mind. Bit skinny for my taste as well. They urged us to come sit and eat. Like that helped me. Yes they themselves had made the meal for us. Something very close to Lasagna. They never got visitors and wanted to show off. Loved to cook! Wonderful food for sure and all said as much. As we ate well a third Alien who had not come out yet for some reason was seen moving around out in the kitchen and certain older adults began whispering when they saw him.

Sabrina could not take it anymore and finally asked her Mom. "What are you Women whispering about?"

Maria looked at her Daughter trying not to laugh at the look on Sabrina's face. Was funny! "It's nothing hunny. We were all just commenting on how much that Alien in the kitchen looks like David Bowie!" The General just fell of his chair and began laughing his ass off!

The Alien in question realizing he had been spotted by that finally came out slowly smiling and embarrassed knowing full well he had been made. In a very recognizable British accent he said with a bow. "I loved preforming Ladys but it had to end. Maybe I'll record a lost album soon!" Oh I recognized him now. Knew that voice! He looked much younger but it sure as hell was him! Some of us were speechless. He went back in the kitchen just a snickering away.

My Mom turned to the General as he got back in his chair awe in her voice. "So that movie he did was just a?" Down again!

From the floor the General managed to get out this. "A documentary!" Old People are weird!

The meal was wonderful as well as plentiful. Good thing too. Everyone ate well and thanked the Aliens politely. Once done Ulrik stood and quickly asked so sweetly with a big magnificent grin on his face. "Who wants to go see the Poophole planet?!" He really said that! I swear! His exact words! Hands shot up so fast it was scary! No. Not just the five year old's either. MOTHER! Well who could turn that one down? They had been on earth how long now? Yes they fixed their ship! Liked it here so they stayed. Knew they could help our world you see and had been trying for years. Military kept them from doing more.

The Poophole planet is mighty damn huge and awesome let me tell you! Bunch a moons and pretty rings. Lots of pictures were taken. No poop though. When we got there at least. Okay I did! Yes I admit it I pooped on the poophole planet! Like you wouldn't if you had the chance. These aliens had a sense of humor too. Nope! I did not need a space suit! Good to know that one. Colder than almost anything but I was good. Warm and seemed to be able to hold my breath for a very long time. Got some samples of the spongy liquid atmosphere for the college. Got some diamonds too. They were just floating all over the place. We didn't exactly land. More like a splashdown. The whatever I walked on was thick enough to support my weight but it was like being in a bounce house. Damn cool. Planted a flag! Dora the Explorer flag. It was all we had but all were good with it. Five year old's think everything is great. Their needs are rather simple. Much fun however. Older people stress about everything too much.

Peace talks could wait till tomorrow the Aliens had said. Tonight was for fun. Seriously though, I have no clue as to why they ever let Tammy drive the spaceship. She could not find a sidewalk cafe but we did buzz some drunks in Alabama! Several times. Teela's ideal! Tammy got mad they would not let her grab one and do an anal probe. This however I totally understood as we know how much I like to do anal probes so I nicely volunteered to get one later so she could practice for next time or when we got our own spaceship. Every Dog needs a good anal probe every now and then! So I may have done some anal probes in outer space myself! Mrs. Griffin asked for it! That Woman is nasty! Maybe she was just constipated! Likes my tongue in her butt! Likes her tongue in my butt too! Nothing wrong with older Women! Especially kinky ones! Tongue in Anus around Uranus is a night to remember. Wasn't the only one either. Kimmy and Sabrina were caught looking for the Black hole of Tanya! I'd been there already so I knew they were in for a treat.

It was a fun time. Went old school and taught the kids how to play Asteroids at one point with real Asteroids! What a blast that is! Literally! It was Teela's cool idea to land on Mars and moon the rover! NASA was pissed I heard. Fucking Pussy's! Fifty years and they have not gone back to the freaking MOON! And they wonder why intelligent life in space was so reluctant to visit? We should have City's on Mars by now! Got footprints though and a bare butt print, Sabrina! The aliens had force fields that let everyone walk on Mars for a few minutes. Was not that cold.

Back to Earth Kids! Oh I was certain the Aliens had been observing me the whole trip to get a better idea of my capability's. Maybe my mental state! They had cool divided bunk houses for us when it came time to sleep. Each adult got three kids to sleep with in their area. Two sets of bunks per area. Yeah I know! Like that was gonna work.

CHAPTER 8 PEACE TALKS
Saturday October 2nd

Woke with both naked Mothers and a Principle on me! No idea why they were with me or naked but I started playing with saggy sexy titty's! Of course my own Mothers. What did I say abut Dogs and morals? Get over it! Licking Mother Maria's butt. Kids were waking though so it went nowhere. DAMN! They got dressed fast when they heard the kids asking to learn how to drive a tank. No idea if it was terror or excitement. May have wanted lessons too.

At breakfast however Kimmy's phone rang and I got a real bad feeling. Did not stop eating mind you. Ate faster actually in case I had to run! For the border! Yes that kind of bad feeling! Kimmy had it on speaker phone of course so all could hear my death toll. Anastasia's voice came across so sweet and cheerful when it was answered I started looking for exits fast! "Hi kiddo! Just called to see how you were all doing in that heat. Make sure Intergalactic War had not been declared." Pretty sure it had but I was stuffing my face. They told her we were fine. Pretty sure they were all nervous now too. Something was coming and we ALL knew it. "Oh and Pammy?" Her voice so sweet. Heard the loud tolling of the death bell. Yes I did! "Ally laid an egg this morning! Just thought you should know." They were all looking at me! Even the Aliens! They finally asked how many I had gotten pregnant! They had no idea! Not just the Aliens! Well I was a BAD ProtoDog! Alien's were extremely astounded, and by Astounded I mean on the verge of filling their pants, when they found out how many children I had created. Maybe terrifyed is a better word. And that number was really only just a guess as we did not have ultrasounds done yet so we foolishly assumed only one per Girl. And what have I told you about my luck? The Aliens may have been a bit nervous. Okay panicking! They hide it well! Seems the Aliens also thought it impossible for me to do. Turned out they did not know I had gotten others pregnant. Oops, go figure. Apparently the General mumbles when he talks about things he does not want to talk about. So we all decided on a plan.

Windy had peace talks with Ulrik, while most adults got exams by the Female Alien. And the General and Tammy both taught five year old's how to shoot the grenade launcher. Kept them busy. They liked blowing things up. So did the kids it turns out. Who doesn't?

It's fun!

Still I knew it was not going to be a good day for me in spite of a clingy Teela. She had been getting clingier lately and I loved it. Loved her. Alien equipment is just so much better than Earths so when they found more than one fetus in some it scared me. Sandra had four. Kimmy two. Tanya six. So I was just wondering if I could survive on the Poop Hole planet! Sabrina had two. Teela had eight! She was very happy about that. Her Mother was not! Speaking of her Mother. Maria Gonzales had three. Got myself a death look there. The rest had one. Miss Tinker and Mrs. Griffin were pregnant already. See it was thought by all, and I mean ALL, that my extremely altered DNA would not be compatible with any other species! We were wrong it turns out. It is compatible with every other species it turns out! They took blood and examined that too. Unlike anything ever! Becky's blood was checked and they were surprised to see we were very different! She was still impressive! Turns out I was truly a universal donor! Tongue sperm donor!

On the bright side this meant the Bear was pregnant so I was happy. Liked the Bear a lot.

Coming to theaters this Christmas Porn Hubs first theatrical release, "101 ProtoDog's"! I'd go see it! Becky smiled at me and said she would help nurse Pups. Tammy had refused the exam when it was offered. When asked why, she said she did not need it as she knew she had three Pups in her. Fucking A! Her sonar was that good?! Explained a lot now didn't it? She had already known I was pregnant when we found out. That Albino Brat! The Female Alien then became curious about everyone's ability's. More testing and the Female Alien became very worryed. So much so that Ulrik and Windy were summoned. The Female explained to them that I was passing on ability's and how many kids we were looking at. Ulrik understandably grew very nervous. Honestly I had not tasted Alien poop yet so I was hopeful but he did not poop his pants. YET!

Windy just smiled sweetly at him and nodded as she said. "My army comes." Everyone was nervous now. What did that child know?

Now I was nervous as I feared I may be pooping on the floor soon but I had no choice! Finally I had to speak! Let the God out of the bag so to speak. "Windy sweety? What did God tell you?"

She blushed and spoke so cute and shyly. "That he was proud of me and I was worthy to rule." Yep! What I thought!

Interesting to say the least but I knew we were missing something. Knew I could leave it there but a ProtoDog has a strong curiosity. So I said. "But he struck you with lightning!"

She smiled still. "Yes, but that was the first time we talked. Because I told him to knock his shit off!" No idea if any were shocked by that child swearing as they all had their mouths open already. "He asked what I would do if he didn't stop

so I threatened to kick his butt about Miss Walberg and other things. We have
talked again since then. He said he was sorry for his bad behavior the first time.
Told me to please fix what he broke! He was sad. Said it was his fault. I told him I
would fix things for him." Would have been nice to think she was just delusional or
making up a story but I knew better. She had threatened to "shake the pillars of
heaven" and God blinked! Oddly it did not scare me. Made me feel happy even.
"He said some would oppose me. That help was already on the way. My army!"
Knew she was not telling all.

What could I do? Bowed low and graceful to her. "Yes my Princess! My
children and I will always serve you." Lots were extremely nervous now. Can you
blame them?

When Mom asked why people had different ability's they said they had no
idea. Possibly the very diversity of the human DNA had an effect they suspected
right away. Perhaps like Becky there was some choice in it. Samples were taken
from me. AGAIN! Sabrina was the one brought up the new Monsters and their
variety and now the General got nervous! Shame on him. The Aliens were kinda
pissed as they had not been told about them. HE had not told them about this
development yet for some reason and he looked ready to run. Well the Aliens
quickly said they should go to the college and help if they could. Perhaps determine
Alien origins of what was used.

Ooh wait! Girls had pictures! See! Turns out to be a good thing taking
pictures of everything. Okay maybe not my butt, however they had lots of those.
They love it. That just made things worse now. Turns out Cobalt is a Luggun, a
kind of Alien cow. Possibly very dangerous. Strong and destructive animals! Their
numbers were strictly controlled and restricted to their home world until finally
going extinct. Hard to kill it seems. A herd of them could destroy a city in a
stampede. They knew that from experience. Smart but highly emotional and
violent creatures. Like I did not know that.

And the fluff ball is a creature called an Oristrii and that really ain't good
apparently. They were considered very dangerous and thought exterminated
nearly a thousand years ago after they eradicated several settlements! No one knew
quite why they destroyed them though.

Ours was cranky so I thought that may explain things! They had finally got it
on a forklift and drove it over to the college. It calmed way down and seemed to
like that so refused to get off. Figured they had it right side up at least. Had a
strong static charge and was not afraid to use it. Aliens told us that, that charge
could be super lethal if it wanted. More powerful than a bolt of lightning. So we
suspected the Doctor wanted it as a weapon. Calm now so students were
volunteering to drive it around campus a couple times a day. Hey who doesn't want
to drive a fork lift? Mostly Tammy when we got back! It liked Tammy a lot. More

on that later. Oh you ain't seen nothing yet! Dean Kelly was having fun driving it around while we were gone. You wish you could drive one.

The General said he would have to see if the Grazonians could come to the College as it would mean a lot of work for security. He thought he could possibly do it now. Then Teela said why not let these Aliens come as we already have one Alien around. Oops! You see? These Aliens did not know about that one either it seems. Could have been an honest mistake. Had been a lot of shit going on! And speaking of shit I was trying to figure out why no one said anything when Windy said that word! Maybe they agreed with her. Maybe afraid of her? She had just said God blinked first after all. So we explained to the three Aliens and thirty, happy, five year old's about everything that had happened to the best of our knowledge. Yes we left the sex out! And most of the killing so it was a short story I know.

You know how they say "Kids say the darnedest things"? Well a stinky Boy said. "Seems like somebody is still behind everything. Someone wanted all this to happen. Fits together to well still doesn't it?" Oh he was stinky. Do not think he wiped well. EVER! Kept scratching back there you see. Also probably correct. ProtoDog's do not believe in that many coincidences!

Well most got nervous about that thought. Yeah it all fit to well! Someone had been manipulating the manipulators to create this! Create Me somehow. Made the Aliens nervous so they explained. There were only two known races who would possibly be able to do this they said but it was unlikely either was involved for various reasons. Well, I was tempted to have Windy ask God but if he denied involvement then what? Somebody somewhere wanted all this. Maybe knowing why would tell us who but we had no luck there either. Certain not all of it was linked directly so I started thinking indirectly. Was someone doing what God could not and already trying to fix things?

O'Donnell brought Alien drugs to our city to experiment with. Doctor Whiting had come to town probably years ago and began creating Monsters. Were they connected to each other or both manipulated to be there at the same time? Did they have something in common? Tammy told me she would look for a connection or commonality right away. Now that bothered me as this had all been in my head and I had not spoken a word. Did not seem she understood that. Was that a side effect of the drugs? Ability to know what each other was thinking to an extent! Had been thinking hard about it so maybe that was why she could read it and not other things. Psychic safety net?!

Had all her clothes on still so I knew damn well she could not read everything! Wanted her naked you see!

We were grasping at straws here though! Oh wait. David Bowie just came out and brought me a very big milkshake. Had not been thinking of one though. He smiled and spoke. "Her Highness, Princess Windy said you needed one." Did I?

Maybe I did. Maybe it was Windy's way of telling me something important? Maybe to chill out? She was only five and probably did not have the words to express what I was darn sure she knew now. Was the only thing made sense her at this point. Hell, those words may not even exist! Was a hot fudge, peanut butter and marshmallow milkshake however!

Oh that thought that just clicked in my head was impossible! It made sense anyway. Would explain lots of things. God was not the only person Windy was talking to! Okay super powerful being! That much was rather obvious now. Was she talking to herself though? A future version? Yes I really did need that milkshake now! Brain was overheating fast. Especially when Windy looked at me and just smiled. Wanted to know who Tanner's psychic was now however. Bad! Felt that may be the key to a lot of things. Windy may be talking to herself but I was sure she still did not have lots of answers yet. They were all busy wondering about Whiting still! Sure I did too but he was not behind this I knew. He wanted control! He had none now did he?! OH the Thinks I Think! Would have thought it impossible six weeks ago! But it had been an eye opening six weeks now had it not?

Peace talks resumed right after lunch. Everyone sat in so it turned into a lecture on Galactic Politics. The four Aliens we had met were not the only ones on the planet we were told and the galaxy knew about us! Were watching closely to what was going on here. Most worlds were uncertain or undecided how to react to us. Three powerful races already opposed Windy strongly and were trying to convince others we were a danger! We were! Yes I admit it. Still if they behaved Windy would leave them alone. And there was one planet that hoped she came to visit soon with me but they were apparently a race of perverts who only went to the stars to find new sex positions! Can think of worse reasons. Them I wanted to go visit! Cultural exchange you see! Most of the grown ups thought we should visit too! Perverts are fun! We were and we were! No the kids did not get told this one. We adults all got information packets! Kids got coloring books. Yes alien coloring books! Okay some of us adults got some as well. Whiners! Big Babys! Could see why they were in diapers still.

Don't give me that crap! We all know where, "Boldly go where no man had gone before" Really meant! Yes Alien-Pussy! Kirk you Dog! What a stud! You may need a healthy dose of Animal Planet to understand money is not everything! Lust is a stronger emotion than greed but there are laws against rape! Laws against sex! Taking money from the poor so they starve and die is apparently perfectly legal though! Not saying Rape should be but seriously if a Guy compliments a Girl at work she has him fired for sexual harassment. That is the Christians demonizing sex again! Most of those Girls put their names on that list and the second list. Not one complaint! My tongue can do things your penis never could though! Still I wondered. That list as well was most likely manipulated. Who put Becky's name on the list? Most of these Girls loved me unconditionally and I knew that was genuine but were they manipulated to be here? Thought it most likely. The Gonzales family had moved to our city only a year ago. Mr. Gonzales had been promoted to foreman at a big factory. Had been assistant grounds keeper at the college last year as a second job. Still did lawns on the side for staff members. He preferred to work outside. That was how the family knew the Dean and Sandra. The factory job gave his kids scholarships though. That was why they came. They worked hard but could not afford it with all these kids so they jumped at the chance. We knew Kimmy had just returned to the area a couple years ago so she too could attend college.

What? You doubt their love was real? Oh I am so lovable it is pathetic! Most of you love me and you have never met me. Do not lie to me! And yes I was raping Girls all afternoon still! Several were taking notes and I was sure they would read them to me later so when Mrs. Griffin got up to go potty I followed! They all had to go potty that afternoon. Several more than once. Maybe it was something they ate? They were drinking a lot. Sure one of those was My own Mom. Hey I knew now how much my Mom had sacrificed for us kids for years. She seldom had a Boyfriend or anything nice. My Mom was great and I was going to tell her that as much as I could. When the Female Alien got up heading that way and I followed I think they all got nervous. No I did not rape an Alien! She sat and spread her legs wide for me! Anal probe included! Okay I admit it! I gave David Bowie an anal probe too! You would as well! It was David Bowie for Windy's sake! He autographed my butt even! You Fucking Wish!

Who doesn't love David Bowie? You SUCK!

He made my collar better for me too. Very powerful speakers were added. Now I had my theme music! He said his music was not right for me in a killing frenzy so he chose Blue Oyster Cult's ETI! Live version! That would work!

Someone finally asked, I know it took forever, how Tammy could see the computer screen. See how hectic it was. Hey I knew. Did you figure it out? Electromagnetic radiation! She could decipher the energy signals it emitted from the screen just like seeing. She had always had a way with electronics. It was said to an extent everyone who drank my milk or other bodily things were bestowed powers. Miss Winters gave me a look at the term Bodily Things. Not a bad one either! Might be pissing in a Blonde Pudge's mouth soon! Let her enjoy my nectar. We had children here though! Some big Girls where blushing however. Windy being struck by lightning many times came up and some wondered why Windy seemed so much stronger than the others.

Well that kind of scared me as well. Knew somehow she had been exposed to something else as well. How many of you readers found it odd that our Alien just happened to have a Scepter? Well I was busy and it was hectic at the time! Happily

I bowed to Windy. "Your Highness! May these Aliens examine your Scepter please?" That grin on Windy's face scared me shitless! Yes I mean it. Right there on the floor! That little Girl knew things no one ever should and I was certain of it!

Windy chuckled her voice sweet. "Bad Doggy. Pooper Scooper clean that up." And she handed her Scepter to the Female Alien while Sabrina gladly got a shovel. No I can't pronounce the Female Aliens name so I have no idea how to spell it. We were just calling her Bob. My spell check does not do Grazonian! Was over two minutes long as well. Male names were short and Female names extremely long! Makes Icelandic sound normal! Six hundred constants and eight vowels in her name! Everyone just called her Bob! Even the other Aliens.

An hour later the Aliens were terrified again. They had never seen anything even like it. Certain it should not even exist! Anywhere! EVER! It was made from stable pulsar material. Should weigh several thousands of tons at this size! Could not tell who had made it either. Said it was like it just formed from nothing. That it could do terrifying things they could tell but not what. It had many hidden ability's it seemed. This confused them as they knew some were very powerful. With a sigh Windy spoke like a parent explaining to a child for the hundredth time. Cute when she does that. "When I am ready or they are needed then they will unlock. Not one moment before." Quickly I began sniffing butts and not just human ones as that scared the poop out of many. Trust me! Snacks!

Supper thank God as I am not sure how much more truth these beings could handle! Not just the humans either! Not sure I could eat that much poo and still have room for supper? As I said before I knew what was in that sweet child's heart. Did not care what was in her head. Or who! Okay things got lots worse at supper but in a very different way. Hell of a distraction is all I could say! There was a small box by my Dog-Dishes you see. Just the right size for a ring! Scared me till I saw the note that said. "For Teela". Now I was absolutely shaking! Not from fear though. Looked at Teela and she was staring at a box on the table by her plate with her mouth hanging open. She was the Father of my children. Oh I knew that for a fact now and I had no idea how! But she was. Perhaps an act of sheer will by both of us.

Windy just sat smiling innocently. She nodded at me. Then again Divine Royal interference made perfect sense.

How could I not do it and ask Teela. Sure I loved them all but Teela was special somehow. Had felt it when I first saw her I realized. No idea what it was but I knew well there was something in her. Picking the small box up in my mouth I walked over to her and set it carefully in her lap. She jumped at the sudden contact. Had not seen me coming! Too busy staring at the box in front of her I think. Looking down at the box in her lap she went pale. She looked at me with tears already forming in her eyes and I nodded. Had not intended too do this you understand. Maybe never would have. But I really wanted too! Her hands were shaking as she picked it up. Everyone was watching now. Most not even breathing. "Teela, will you marry me?" Awkwardly I growled this out hoping there was a ring in that box. She opened the box and gasped loud. It was a ring alright. BIG diamond!

She looked at me and tears began to flow very hard. Croaking out that word was not easy for her. "YES!" Everyone began clapping. Many crying as well.

Windy just smiled so sweetly and I knew darn well who was behind this one. What scared me was she may be behind it all! Windy's voice was so sweet as she explained to them. "Teela must make honest Woman of Beast before their kids are born!" Most just thought it cute but I bloody well knew better. That Girl knew as well as I did Teela actually was the Father! Probably involved in that as well! No it was fine that she knew. Some looked disappointed and I understood why. Then Windy said gloriously. "It Okay. Beast will hunt forever!" Disturbing I know! Still she may think it just a game and practice for all the Dickheads I was going to kill! We all knew there were bad guys out there still. Hey even the five year old's knew there were millions of bad guys in the world.

You watch cartoons much? Every show new bad people! Yeah sure they all become nice at the end so your kids think the bully who beats the crap out of him in school everyday for a month will become his friend! By the third swirly most know that is bullshit and become jaded kids! We tell kids to avoid strangers. Do you tell them bad people want to steal them? Do you let them run around the neighborhood by themselves at five years old? Let them go to school? Or Church? Most molesters are people the child knows. Neighbors. Authority figures. Teachers, Priests, Police, (yes they do) and Family. You know how they keep the child from telling? Fear! Is your child comfortable talking to you about anything? Have you lied to them about anything? Well they know if you have. Most kids don't trust their parents for that reason alone. Still if you want your children to grow up well you need to be open and honest with them about everything! Let them see you are affectionate with other adults. Never tell your significant other no kissing in front of the kids. If they ever ask you something, and you should encourage it always, be honest! If you don't know how to explain it look it up. Ask the child what they think the answer might be. Sorry! That's important stuff.

Do not be a Dick and tell them Santa does not exist! Well I have met the Man! He likes me! So does Prancer!

So what was in the box in front of Teela? It had a note with it that said. "For Pammy." She showed me the note. Did not recognize the handwriting. So I assumed Windy had someone write it for her. They urged Teela to open it. She did and showed everyone as she cried more. She showed me. It was a Dog-Tag that read "Teela Loves Pammy" in black on pink with an image of a ring on it. She put it on my collar and cried on me more whispering her love to me. Yes something weird was happening! Weirder then the rest and I knew it! Well I saw Windy smile.

It was a truly touching moment and several were crying as I looked around. Including someone I went to and called "MOM" for the first time. Oh Mrs. Gonzales just hugged me crying. Sabrina reached up and began taking her own collar off in tears and Mrs. Gonzales barked violently at her. "Don't you dare take that off young Lady! She may be marrying your Sister but you are still HER Pooper Scooper!" Oh that got chuckles and not just from five year old's! Mrs. Gonzales pushed me away. Her voice filled with anger and love. "Go make her put it back on my Daughter!"

Certainly Mom. Growled the whole way as I padded over. She was shaking as I reached her and putting paws on her lap went up and snarled in her face. She put the collar back on looking extremely scared. Felt bad now. So I told her. "Love you! Always Mine!" She hung her head in shame at that. Opening my mouth I took her head inside gently. Whole head. Yes it fit. Closed my jaws around her head. BURP!

She pulled her head out fast and shoved me away. "What did you eat!" Lots of poop but I was not saying that. Lots of these Women already knew. Well it was their poop!

Somebody had moved my bowls when I looked over. So I ate next to my fiancee! Oh she was mine. Knew I had picked out the diamond in that ring too! Okay picked up. It came from the Poophole planet! Fitting considering we both loved to go there! She does! Still I was okay with everything. Just did not understand how everything fit yet. Trusted in Windy however. Knew for a fact she had been responsible for the ring.

In Windy We Trust!

Finally we said goodbye to our new friends for now. The Aliens told us if they had known what we could do before meeting us they would have been scared. Meeting us first though they thought it would be okay. We were genuinely nice beings and meant well. They too understood what I knew. Someone had chosen well! Gross disgusting beings to be certain but we were also kind and gentle they said of us! That I understood as that one five year old not only ate his own boogers but other peoples as well! That is disgusting! Grossed me out and I eat Poop! That kid needs severe professional help!

Most got Diapers on. Some did not need to as they had been wearing them the whole trip! Won't mention names, Teela and Sandra, a couple of the kids as well, both Cindy's, which may get us yelled at. Honestly though if it makes someone happy and they are hurting no one why do they get told no? And if the someone being hurt or degraded or humiliated wants it what is wrong with that? Ask and if they say the want it leave them alone. Hey I like those things! But I am a ProtoDog and poop on the sidewalk! Ooh, Hey! Could I poop on a sidewalk cafe?

Life is short! Live it as you want! The only true winner in life is the one who dies with the least regrets!!!

Tanya seemed disappointed and confused about lots of things. Kimmy noticed this fast as that was her nature to notice things and asked Tanya what was wrong. Tanya's answer made sense. "Kinda confused about all this. You guys are a blast to be around and I really like Pammy's attentions and I just don't know what is going to happen now. Pups are coming! I mean Pammy is going to get married after all. Where does that leave me?"

Tammy snickered at that saying. "But Pammy is a Major Slut!"

Kimmy just peed her diaper. Teela did too as she was not far away. Tanya looked more confused. Kimmy smiled and said. "Nothing stops Pammy! We all know that. Teela could not survive if Pammy only hunted her. Fill your diaper and she will come!" She hugged Tanya who smiled.

No matter how much I Hate to say it, it was true! All of it. Tanya nodded at that. She was not the only one. All the adults were! Gonna be a long night I could tell! My favorite food group after all is poop! Hungry though so it should be okay. The Seven food groups for a ProtoDog! First is poop. Second is hot sauce. Third is milk shake. Fourth is Chicken. Fifth is Assholes. Sixth is pasta! Seventh is? Take a Guess!

Military Men came and bowed and groveled to Windy as we boarded the bus. They had a new beautiful dress for her. No idea if it was any of the Men she spanked. Never saw their faces now did I? Tell them to pull their pants down and turn and I would know!

Never forget a butt!

Guards waved at us as we left the base. They had all been briefed on our visit finally. Not the same guards as last time I felt. They may have KP duty. They had a big pretty banner that said "Farewell Princess Windy" on it. She was a total sweetheart you see and people adored her. Well I sure did.

Ready to sing? On the road again! Good readers.

Kids were rowdy, older people worse. Still excited from the day. We let them blow off steam. Safer! Windy was rather calm. Becky was rubbing on me as reassurance a lot. Sure I rubbed back. Let her know I loved her. She loved me back but was scared. She wanted more as well but it was not time yet. She did ask me how it felt to me to rape a Girl? So I told her what I could. She said she was worried she would not be good at it and did not want to disappoint her prey. Understood her worry there far too well. I mean it's all about the Prey! Smelled a set up but it was fine. Easy fix. Told her just practice and walked away. Wiggling my butt hard the whole way. Never looked back as I headed to the penalty seats.

HOLY SHIT! Cat tongue is intense! Oh I mean I howled uncontrollably. Tammy joined in the howling quick to cover for us and soon all were howling! Just not for the same reason as me! The harder I squirmed the more ferocious she got and I was a whimpering drooling mess by the time she let up and walked away head held high. A proud Tiger! Might have been set up. Did not care! Watched that gorgeous Tiger Tush wiggle down the isle and thought MINE! Good sign though really. She got savage and no bad reactions after all. Playful even. The number of the Beast! 1-616-555-6969!

Things settled down on the bus after a while and kids began watching TV as it grew darker and exhaustion set in. Windy was watching everyone and went and gently moved a few kids. She knew these kids better then me so I did not worry. Knew a couple of the kids were more clingy and they got paired up with adults. What? Got a problem with a five year old Girl running the Universe? Ever watch election coverage on the news? I'll go with the five year old any day. Power hungry dickheads are not fit to govern! Good snacks however.

CHAPTER 9 HOMEWARD BOUND
Sunday October 3rd

It was after one AM when Tammy pulled into a rest stop. It was not empty, but no one was walking around us. It was late. Kids were all asleep. Tammy got off and Becky followed. Time for Revenge! Hunt Tiger! We may have woke some people in cars and semi trucks and any house within five miles? Oh it was such a glorious hunt and the taste of wet Tiger is just awesome. She was wet too. Trust me on that. Such a horny Tiger! She fought hard but I prevailed! Cat like sex with your tongue is phenomenal! Tammy applauded from a nearby picnic table so I took a bow. Got a Tiger snout in my butt as thanks. We were both bleeding from many places. Licked each others wounds till they healed. About six licks each.

Back on the bus and off we went. Tammy had a plan it seems. Oh they had been plotting things those darn Horsemen. Left Becky and me out of their plans. Oh I know in Revelations there are Four Beasts and Four Horsemen. I was voting for Ally and Cobalt as the other two Beasts. Teela would be the forth Horsewoman! Sexist bastards! Ever wonder what the world would be like without the Catholic church? They crushed science every chance they could! Viewed Women as no more than livestock! Still do! Send a barrel of SHIT to the Vatican next! Dow Chemical too as I think they make Kevlar! Not gonna take their Shit no more! Send them MINE instead!

They changed our breakfast venue! Found that out when I woke. A different fast food place then told before and just outside of Chicago. Kimmy explained to us what was happening as we ate. "Her Highness was unhappy with lying to the parents of the children it seems. Fixing that. We're going to the Museum this morning. Who wants to see Mummy's?" Well who doesn't?

We were always trying to be educational! Some adults were excited to go here even. Never pass up a chance to learn people. It was amazing! That Museum is spectacular. Had real Mummy's too! Still got shit when we got there of course. Barely out of the bus before they were watching us. Security refused us entry into the building instantly as we hit the steps. Gee lots of Security here too. Kimmy made them get someone in charge, might have made some vague treats, and when they actually did she quickly explained to the ones in charge who the Princess was and I think herself. Might have dropped some names here. Possibly more threats were made. That Girl did not mess around when she wanted something. Why do you think people feared her. Becky and I were giving rides to people out in the parking lot while we waited for them to clear this up. Museum People became excited after Kimmy talked to them. Okay after I finally talked for them. A Security Guard said firmly animals were not allowed in the Museum. So I looked at him and spoke. "How dare you call these sweet children animals!" Okay some children were growling and snarling which did not help my point! We had been on the news a lot after all. People we met had started recognizing us. Museum people had not thought us real for some reason. Must only watch Fox News! The next thing I knew we had the two biggest curators on site giving us the Grand Tour! About six others examining Becky and I as we went. It was amazing stuff. We told them what we actually were and they were quickly more excited. They had seen stuff but were skeptical about what had been on the news. We assured them there was more. They asked if we could keep them informed about things. The nice thing about Scientists is they have a good curiosity. Sabrina got business cards from them and promised to add them to the mailing list. Apparently she was Secretary of the Windy's Kingdom as well as Pooper Scooper! They wanted proof too so I spoke for them as well. Posed for some pictures. Like a French Girl! They took measurements of us but wanted more proof eventually. So we had to go out and shoot Windy in the parking lot just too prove ourselves. A nervous Security Guard seemed to not believe and thought we should be arrested so we stood Windy in front of a low wall and took his gun forcefully and used it to shoot her. Then I chewed up the stone wall a bit after. Chicago is always fun! They were excited about Ally when they found out she was real. Wanted to know if she could come some day to be seen. Hey it would be some good publicity for them and us as well so we considered it.

Things happen however you know. True mostly to me but hey. Like you never know when a Religious Terrorist group is going to strike now do you? Ever been watching TV and a knock on the door turns out to the Mormons? Fifth Terrorist attack in a month in America! Seriously? A Museum? Sure they have that big exhibit of Arabic artifacts going on and it was rather crowded because of it. At the first sound of gunfire. Okay second! Windy leapt, kinda naked again, on my back and commanded loudly. "Beasts! We Hunt!" We seriously needed bulletproof clothes for that Girl! There were lots of children still in the Museum. None of ours but it was Sunday and many family's had come to encourage their children's curiosity! Becky followed us with Tammy on her back. Grenade launcher would not help in here but her radar might! Kimmy came prepared and knew we could not use artillery in here, yelling this at Tammy, as she got a case out and handed Sabrina and Teela big sharp swords! No idea why we had them! Came in handy though. So cool!

How I needed this release right then. Seriously. Yes I was having killing withdrawals. They looked middle eastern but did not taste as good as Falafel. Definitely not Hammas as well. Would not taste good even on Pita Chips. Damage was really minimal. Well except for the terrorists. Damage to them was pretty freaking major. Hoped that blood came out of the carpets in there. Becky grinned at me as we left. "It was fun. Needed Hummus! Maybe some hot sauce." She was right they definitely did. No idea what they were after. Did not speak their language and they did not speak American apparently. Windy did speak their language however it seems as what she was yelling at them scared them bad. We did not wait for the Cops of course. That would just delay us. We had lunch to catch and I wanted to get these kids home before bed time! Still had a six to eight hour drive. Oh wait Tammy was driving. Two to three hour drive yet. Okay maybe four. Potty breaks!

We care damn it! These kids had school tomorrow! And I had some serious raping to do tonight.

There are some great restaurants in that City. We went and ate good. Parked on the street where their were many restaurants. Kids were taken to the restaurant of their choice with an adult. Italian, Mexican, Mediterranean, Thai, and other weird foods. Avoided the Organic and Vegan stuff. We ate well. Yeah we ate on the bus. We had gotten some buckets on the base for me and Becky to eat from. Should have thought of that. Got a wide variety in them. We still had a major problem! You know what they have a lot of in Chicago? Just glad they blamed the terrorists. Laughing manically Tammy ran over three sidewalk cafes. Blasting Pakistan's hit list with the kids squealing. You really can find anything on that satellite radio! Impressive.

Heading home! Tammy drove slower. Kids liked the scenery but they were rather exhausted by now so many were cuddly. That is a big Museum! We walked for two hours. Two Girls and a Boy were on me in the bus. Becky was across the isle nursing Cindy Walker. No idea if she was actually getting milk. It was okay with me though. Cindy was sweet. Around two dozen kids had some of my milk already when the school was attacked. Would deal with it if I had too.

It was okay in a way. You have to understand I knew if I had too I could end this completely. Windy was powerful but so was I and I knew things as well. Prayed she did not! What was not OKAY however was the snickering as Mrs. Gonzales kept texting my Mom! Wedding plans were being discussed I was sure. Terrifyed me. Did not have to read minds to know that much! Teela kept looking at me and blushing. She was gorgeous! So I had a Boyfriend or two, a Fiancee and almost a hundred Girlfriends. Are you jealous? GOOD to be a ProtoDog! Home!

Grabbed some fast food to go before heading to Claude Rains elementary school. Parents were there waiting nervously and glad to see their kids still alive!

US? Not so much! Our morning in Chicago was all over the news it seems. Tons of video! Damn cell phones and internet! Windy got out and spoke to them telling them their children would always be safe around us. It was a really nice speech and their kids assured them they had been fine the whole way. In spite of a robot drone attack and a near hit with Saturn's rings. That was very close Tammy! The terrorist attack had been all over the news with our pictures. Miss Winters was introduced and told the parents if they or their kids ever needed to talk she would be happy too listen. Then that little blonde Girl spoke pointing at Miss Winters. "She spanked me Mommy!" The Girls voice was not unpleasant. Still most of us expected shit for that!

The Mom sighed with a defeated look on her face and looked at her Daughter. "Did you ask her too?" That Girl was nodding with a blush and a smile. "Did she spank you really hard like Mommy?" More nodding. "Did she do it the way you like it?" Nodding! To Miss Winters with a sigh she said. "Thank you. I don't understand her but I love her so much. She begs me to spank her all the time and if I don't she gets bad till I do. So I just spank her till she's crying hard. Is she okay?"

Miss Winters smiled so nicely. "Yes she is and I think I can help. Call me and I will see what I can do." Miss Winters loved her job and helping kids.

Kids hugged us goodbye before they left. Kimmy headed for the convertible. Tanya called shotgun. Teela walked over and grabbed my collar. "Let's go my dear. Her Highness needs her booster seat to wave at the peasants." Yes I was furniture! As we went further she grabbed Sabrina by the arm saying. "My Woman needs her seat cushion!" True! I did! Sat on Sabrina's face to let her know how much I loved her still. Had bad gas too so she knew I loved her well. Tammy was tired so she road in the SUV with Sandra I thought.

Through the middle of the city we went and slowly so Windy could wave at the peasants like the triumphant Princess she was. Well the Peace Talks had been a success. Many peasants waved back. They were beginning to love their Princess. She is unbelievably cute after all.

Once at the compound finally I got worried again and fast. There was a Cougar there just pacing back and forth swinging those hips. They were going to give her the tour. (Damn it I never got the tour.) So I tried to follow. Like that was going to work. Cobalt caught up to me in the dinning room and I was going nowhere till he was satisfyed. Who let him in the house! Teela kissed him with tongue as he shoved that glorious thing in me hard and to the hilt! Teela needed changing though. Mom Gonzales had her on the floor in front of me and diaper off! Made me clean her Daughter well! Twice! Mr. Gonzales was told of the wedding on Saturday! WHAT? What happened to Halloween? He just smiled saying. "I am not losing a Daughter but gaining a Zoo! Congratulations hunny!" The look on Teela's face when he kissed my cheek was priceless. Then he looked Teela in the eye and said. "Congratulations too you as well. Not kissing Pammy on the lips. EVER! You either. It's bad enough I have to smell the poop." He knew Teela returned the favor and that made us both cringe. Okay it embarrassed me! Mrs. Gonzales just laughed. She was gonna kiss us both with tongue and she knew it! Nasty Mexican MILF!

Once I was thoroughly fucked we went all dreamy like to see Ally. Teela showed her the ring with such pride and joy. Dinosaurs are so sweet it turns out. Well ours was! She kissed us both. We explained to Cobalt and he just snickered. He knew I was still his Sex Toy! We were all okay with that. It was Teela who suggested I hunt and rape Sabrina and pee on her corpse. Blame Windy for referring to them as corpses. She started it. So I Sadistically raped my future Sister in law. And my Mother in law. An Albino. A Black girl. You get the picture. Naked Woman were everywhere and not one was named Barbie. Caught the Dean as she finished changing her Daughters diaper.

That was messy!

The Dean got revenge in a way though when she held two leashes in her hand and whistled. My jaw dropped as Stone came in with a collar on! With Brutus! She hooked them both up and took them for a walk! Stone winked at me smiling. He is such a perv! Back in she took them both to her room and shut the door! Howling was heard.

By bed time my head was held high and they would quiver every time I growled at them. Becky and I took Windy to bed and I was content so I drifted off as well. Felt them climbing in bed with us before long.

FAMILY!

CHAPTER 10 ONE OF THOSE DAYS
Monday October 4th

You ever have one of those days? The kind were you wake up and you can see the clit of your Princess Pup's naked Principle because your nose is actually in her vagina? Probably not! Well I DID! And I knew damn well it was probably not going to get better. She was tasty you know. Why was she even here? Didn't she have a husband? She wore a ring! Had we Cougarnapped her?

Anastasia came in to the room as usual all sunshine and happyness. Seriously, I expect that woman to break into song any second! Has a few times. Beautiful voice. "Ally is about to lay her third Egg if anyone wants to get up and watch!" Nope not better! Still? Girls did become excited about it. Hey how often do you get to watch a Dinosaur lay an Egg? Sure I get to see it all the time now but this was something very new then. Ah who needs clothes it seemed. We were practically a Nudist Colony here anyway. They all came out butt naked. Including Tanya. Yeah I had apparently kept her. Might have raped her while changing her poopy diaper last night. Teela might have held her down. Brutus was pacing back and forth in the yard like a nervous expecting Father. He had finally managed to bang the Dino while we were gone and he thought the Eggs were his kids. It was so adorable. Well I was not telling him otherwise.

And so was Sandra! Adorable that is.

In her opinion our biggest mistake was leaving her Mom with Anastasia for the weekend. Anastasia was petting my Brother a lot. Probably true but Sandra was so darn cute. They got her out of the crib in the nursery to watch the Egg get laid at least. She looked so cute with her pacifier in, teddy in hand and her cute droopy diaper on! No other clothes. Her hair was in pigtails with big pink ribbons. The only one who did not think she was absolutely adorable was herself! Well that was what she said.

No I didn't believe her either! Pretty sure she loved it.

The Egg laying was amazing I admit and the sounds Ally made while doing it were just beautiful. Kinda like Whale song. Oh I could smell her happyness. Looked painful a bit too but that was to be expected. My children were coming out of her and yes I cried. Many did. The eggs were a beautiful mottled brown and damn large. Bigger then Brutus himself but he was so proud! Could not wait till

Sandra had Puppys for him. Had to get pictures of that. Video is great but you can not blow it up and hang it on your wall. Three by five! Feet!

Jaws dropped later as Sandra came in for breakfast in a beautiful yellow Baby Easter dress that did not quite cover the adorable pink diaper, cute little socks and shiny white shoes. No one told her but that pout she was doing just made it perfect. Looked like an actual Baby. They put her in an over-sized highchair that had appeared and fed her. Sure they had to threaten to spank her but she finally let them. Pretty sure they had spanked her at least once earlyer if not last night.

Once out of the highchair and once her face got wiped she headed for the bedrooms. Dean Kelly spoke sharply. "Where do you think you are going young Lady?" Knew this was going to be bad for someone. Not me! She honestly may need it though I felt.

What a pout! "To change clothes! I can't Teach in these!" Sandra said with slight anger but her tone was very childish pout. Maybe she regressed to much. Adorable still!

She froze as her Mother said in such a tone that everyone had to freeze as well wondering if they could reach a bathroom in time. Such a sweet Motherly tone in her voice. "Oh of course you can't Sandy hunny. Baby Girls are not big enough to Teach classes, so I will Teach it today! You can go to Kindergarten with Windy! Play with kids closer to your own age sweety. You'll like it." Those eyes began to water and Sandra sat down hard on the floor and just cryed like the Baby Girl she now was. The rest of us were trying so very hard not to pee ourselves!

Windy went and patted her gently on the back. "It okay Baby Sandy. You can ride to school on Beast with me." Windy was happy about this! It was like watching a runaway train heading for a broken bridge however! Because I saw it coming from about a hundred miles away! No I said nothing. Did not have too! The sparkle in Mrs. Griffin's eye said it all! Baby Sandy was officially going to Kindergarten! No If's, And's, or But's about it! Only real question was! For how long? Well were they going to let her graduate to first grade in the spring?

Anastasia nicely handed Mrs. Griffin a cute pink diaper bag with "Sandy's Bag" embroidered on it. Anastasia does not sleep much and loves to sew. That Cougar's eyes lit up so big at the sight of it. They helped Sandy to the car and on the pile like she was only two.

It was adorable when we hit the Kindergarten and Sandra, I mean Sandy began to cry. Her Mom hugged her as she said between sobs. "Wuv you Mommy!" She had regressed so much emotionally by now she would fit in well here I felt. Was not sure we could grow her up fast if we wanted to but knew we would always take care of her no matter what. Kimmy said Anastasia had not been this happy in years. Students came over quickly and said Hi to the "new" kid. Taking her hands several children took her inside wanting to sit by her. They liked her on the trip and absolutely adored her now.

Honestly it seemed like she might need this however so I said nothing. Neither did Miss Tinker who just giggled a little. Could be the start of a bout of hysteria but I knew how to handle those. Vibrators were originally a medical device to help hysterical Women. One good orgasm will mellow out a hysterical Woman! Go check it out! The kids here were so sweet to Sandy and just excepted this situation like it was normal. Kids are highly adaptable. Well after what we had been through over the weekend these kids just kinda excepted everything. Going to the Poophole Planet will do that to you! Brutus snickered. Sure we had him with us. It was crowded in the convertible! Good thing we like to be close! FUCK Personal Space! Dogs do not believe in it! Stick their snout right up your ass or just sit on your face! Sandy turned at the doorway and with a tear in her eye waved. We all waved back smiling. She was just adorable! You think this was wrong? Right! You believe everything Fox News tells you too, right?

Once all the kids were inside the school the Cougar grabbed me shoving her tongue in my mouth. Groped my butt as well! Not at the same time! Her arms are not that long. Hope you have understood that much. They would take turns kissing and groping. Damn that Woman was ravenous! The Dean just smiled at her sweetly and said. "You know, I have several strap-ons if you want to double team the Bitch. Text me!" Okay with me! Twice the fun! Disturbed some I think. Dogs are all about the sensation and the intensity though!

Off to college we went. Not a sidewalk cafe in sight! Not that far from the Elementary School and the College and mostly residential. Still Tammy was pissed as she had some anger to work out, a blind Albino so we understood her anger, and Sabrina said she was hungry again and could we find a drive-thru! That cheered Tammy up! Spun that car around on a dime! So we just had breakfast? You can want a snack. Maybe a Vodka milkshake. Drove all the way across town to go "THERE"! Hit the Archie's BBQ. Can you believe they asked why we hated them? True they probably didn't know. We told them what started all this and they were shocked. The Manager said she could not sell alcohol as they did not have a license and apologized for her employee's greed. Kimmy snickered. Yeah I know none of us were old enough to drink legally but I don't think those employees were either. We just wanted a little in our milkshakes we told her! The Manager said if the employees did not share next time to call her and gave us her personal number! Big on customer service she said.

Really? Not the only thing she was big on!

Yes the Manager was a gorgeous really Big Girl! It was the Dean who said I should come back and rape her. Yeah she did. Said Rape too! Maybe seeing the Poophole planet changed her. Then again Windy was Princess of the Universe so who cares. Kimmy ran a background check on the Big Girl for the heck of it. No one was complaining yet! Not even the dead ones! True if the dead ones started complaining I was running away! Zombies are not fun! Everyone I had preformed illegal medical procedures on or savagely raped if we must label it smiled and waved when they saw me! Every Girl on the original Prey list had put their name down for further Hunting. Even Becky. She said not right away. Well, she still had lots to process. Getting better.

Had to get to school though. We students could ditch but the Dean had a class to teach. Knew I should probably attend it as well. See what she was saying about me! Got weird as soon as we pulled in to the main parking-lot however. Bus was here already but that was expected. Military had brought it over. Detailed it for us even. They got bored and wanted to show Windy they were good Soldiers. There were lots of students out here standing around by the parking lot looking like they were waiting for us as well. Male and Female. Scared me a little. They were dressed really nice. Kinda Preppy even. Had they become Mormons? We were instantly nervous. This was not normal college student behavior. Dean Kelly even looked ready to run. They smiled and waved. This was not normal behavior for college students and we had been through how much shit now? When they walked over to the car smiling joyfully than began praising me I had to find some grass and quick! When they all asked the Dean if they could distribute Religious pamphlets on campus things got weird. Showed us the pamphlets in question! Rovers Witnesses?! Have you heard the word of DOG! Oh I knew we were in for another law suit! Wondered if they were serious about this however. Could be hysterical!

The Dean never said yes! Couldn't really! Laughing too hard rolling on the grass. She did nod a lot! Refused to change into dry pants before she taught class as well. Then to add icing to the cake? Got a text in class. From Miss Tinker. Consulted the Dean. Approval to spank Sandy was quickly given. CPS is full of shit! Kids need discipline. Without consequences children will not learn. Why do you think the juvenile crime rate rose two thousand percent in the Eighty's and Ninety's? Jail is big peoples time out. Where is the fear. Most of these kids getting arrested see jail as a badge of honor. The reverse of that? Eight year old does not get what he wanted on his Birth Anniversary he tells his Teacher his parents hit him! By the time the truth is found out parents have an arrest record that will follow them their entire life as CPS does not expunge your record. You know how they say innocent until proven guilty? CPS does not care! As far as they are concerned you are guilty forever even if not convicted and found totally innocent they will not believe it. If proven innocent they do not take you off their registry! As far as they are concerned you are a criminal and if you ever apply for a job somewhere and they check your background that still comes up! The Nazi SS is the only governmental agency ever with more power! Okay maybe the KGB. Only difference is they could kill people! CPS just wishes they could kill! Like those whiny bastards at the DMV!

They texted us that after her spanking they gave her a bottle and put her down for a nap in the schools new facility. Yes they sent pictures. So very adorable! Anastasia must have had a big Bassinet delivered. As class was done Sabrina shouted there would be free colon cancer screenings in the commons all week at lunch! Really? Who was doing them? Dean Kelly looked very angry now. They explained fast to her that I could not get anyone pregnant up the butt! Not sure how much they believed that! Not sure myself. If I had fingers I would have been crossing them then. Still it was a health and safety issue so I could not complain and needed to perfect my technique for my medical exam. Pretty sure I could tell if someone was sick. Not sure I could taste cancer but I would try. Had no clue what cancer tasted like.

No cancer was found that day, however two students needed to go see a Doctor. Did not know what was wrong with them but something was. Tasted off somehow. Doctor Petrov was quickly consulted. Blood was taken. She asked if someone could take notes for me when I did this next time. She was curious as I had tasted weird things. It really was a good idea! See if the same flavors come up again. Only Proctologist on the planet willing! I think?

Had a problem of course! Monster Girls found out and wanted to get checked as well. Oh like a straight Man wants anything up his butt!? What could I do? The big problem here however was one was that cute feathered Girl. She had a cloaca you see! Birds and dinosaurs have only one opening called a Cloaca. Pee, poop, and eggs all come out of it. Easier for me! They explained to her this meant she may become pregnant with Puppys! What did they mean by, MAY? Oh I was knocking up a BirdGirl! Giggly and quite chirpy for certain but so cute and I was a bad Beast! She warbled so beautifully for me as I made her cum in my face!

Kimmy said to the others with a snicker. "We can always get like a wheelbarrow for her so she can sit on her eggs and still go to classes. Pammy will push her!" Yes I would. They asked me if I was hungry several times. Gave me some hot sauce even but I was good. There were lots of butts you see. Could I live on a diet of poop? No idea but I was eating lots of it. Did some Boy butts as well. Just thought you weren't interested so I never mentioned it. Well that one was BOWIE!

Seems Cobalt missed me so much he got mad we left him home once again and he just walked into Psych class and sat on me for a change. Knew we should have brought him. So sweet of him and I was apparently comfy! Class topic turned to love and attraction of course. Oh he loved me and I had no doubts about that. Don't think anyone doubted that. Pretty sure I loved the big blue guy back. It was hard to know or understand. Being a Dog you tend to love many! Well I knew I did and it was very different with each one. Very strong emotions however. Cobalt seemed to at least like many! He loved scratches and rubs from all. He was blue and fluffy! They could not keep their hands off him! He could enjoy that a lot you see.

Everyone on campus wanted to know how the Peace Talks with the Aliens went of course. Told them they went fairly good. We got a text from Miss Tinker that our nice Reporter fellow showed up and interviewed Windy at lunch. Windy wanted too talk! Aired live. Mom texted us quickly and said do not let Sandra see it! EVER! Apparently she was in the background and her full droopy diaper was highly visible! Brown and sagging! Oh I was lucky as I was a Dog so I could just pee anywhere. No pants to change either! Others needed dry pants.

Made me nervous still. So did the Bird and Rock Girl though. Well they were following us around and I figured the Rock Girl wanted a colonoscopy! So I was wrong. Seems she liked blue things too. He was impressive! She was seven feet tall and her Rocky ass was three feet across. Now I knew how I looked getting plowed. It was hot! So hot I had to rape a Bird. Yeah I get horny watching. So did Miss Moneypenny! Well we used the Deans office! The Dean was teaching a class so she could not stop us. That Secretary struggled and screamed for help as Sabrina and Kimmy dragged her kicking into the office. Left her naked sprawled across the Dean's desk drooling! Oh I am that damn good! Cows are jealous of my tongue! She was smiling.

Speaking of the Dean though when she joined us at the car about a half hour later she looked rather scared. This worried me as I expected more crap. Not Poop as I could just eat that.

Kimmy saw her nervousness as well and just asked sweetly. "What's wrong Dean Antwerp?!"

The Dean got much worse at that question. Her voice seemed ready to break. Almost in tears as she managed to say. "I don't know what came over me! I went to my office to drop stuff off quick and she was just there! Half conscious and completely naked on my desk! I'm wearing a strap-on all the time now!" Oh she was crying now and hard. Sabrina put an arm around the Dean as she sobbed out. "I raped her!" The Deans phone went off and she jumped. A text message only. It was a heart and smiley face.

From Miss Moneypenny!

Kimmy snickered at it. "You should probably rape her again tomorrow to let her know it was not a one afternoon stand." Good idea! We could help! No one bothered to ask why she had a strap-on on! Terrified? Perhaps.

Tammy is absolutely evil and I love her dearly! We swung by and picked up the kids! Yep Windy and Sandy! Her Mom started it! Windy made her sit on us. Well Cobalt and I had a Tanya sandwich going on! Might have been a Black

Girlnapping I have no idea as I never asked that plump Black Girl! Just herded her to the car and pushed her in. Plausible deniability! No one asked where we were going either. Tammy was driving so it was okay. NOT! So when we pulled up right in front of Dark Desire's Tanya said she would watch the little ones. Couldn't see shit down there now could she?! Maybe she could. At least Shit! Not Kids though. BRRIPT! Smell that one you Fat Black Slut! She did. Liked it too! Hugged my butt and kissed it so I knew! Did I mention Fat Black Sluts excite me and turn me on so bad! I'm a Bitch! FAT means Fabulous And Tasty! For all I knew as dark as she was she could have Aboriginal ancestors! Well they don't come from Africa!

Windy began holding her court again. People were kinda nervous however because of her age, but Windy put their minds at ease saying this was a great store. Grown ups needed toys too! Okay it messed with a few heads. Well the Girls had said they were buying grownup toys the last time. So she just thought grownups played with shackles?! She said she needed some tiny shackles for the Rabid Barbies. Now I understood this desire as I too have played Rabid Barbies many times and could have used some on most occasions! Yes they bought some new shackles. The other stuff they did not show Windy was extremely scary. Poor Miss Moneypenny was going to be tortured tomorrow. Did not worry. Knew she would love it! That Woman craves abuse and humiliation you see! Could smell that in her! Why do you think I had raped her several times and quite savagely yet she smiles and blushes every time she sees me!

Windy spoke so gently as we pulled out of the parking lot. "My Beast is hungry and needs to eat! Go to Parker street!" OH SHIT! That was what was wrong! Had not killed anyone in a while! At least twenty four hours! Yes arguments could be made it was pure revenge on our part. Other arguments that it was in fact premeditated murder! Then again it could also be argued and quite successfully that it was just a public service. For the common good you see! Remember that one? We can use it too Politicians!

What disturbed me most to be honest was Dean Kelly breastfeeding Baby Sandy! In the car! Hey it was not an easy sight while holding your urine. Did not think Tanya was that thirsty. Boyz fled as they saw us drive though their territory! Kinda recognizable these days. Getting smarter perhaps? Not fast enough however. Windy needed to get her anger over Mrs. Whalberg's death out it seemed and I let her! Oh tough shit! Got some of my anger over the lack of sidewalk cafes out of my system. Wait that was Tammy! So I was just hungry.

Kimmy called in a Sasquatch sighting, adding fuel to the fire so to speak, on Parker street with a straight face. Well we sure were not going to admit to murder. Some if not all had been at the school that day. They did not die easy. They had the drug in them and could still function with several holes in them however. Once I started ripping heads off and Windy crushing skulls not to mention their bullets not affecting us they had run. Technically they were not human either so there! Pretty sure we got all of them.

We tried to sneak Tanya in the house when we got home. Maybe we should have covered her with something. Mom snapped at me. "Excuse me young Lady! Is that a Black Girl on your back?"

Sabrina said with just a snicker. So proud of herself. "Just a rash I think Ma'am. Maybe she needs a bath." Like that would work! The General was peeing himself already so I thought we were good. He liked our madness.

Smiling Mom said dismissively. "Well go clean her up!" And walked away. Really I could use a bath. There was a big tub here. We had time before dinner so I got bathed by six naked Girls. Well they were getting wet anyway so why not strip? One was a pudgy staff member. Might have raped her once or twice. Becky said not enough room in the tub so she would use the pool and go for a swim. She had been acting weird after we raped each other. Kinda moody and I was worried. She kissed me before heading for the pool and wiggled that striped butt out of the room however.

They gave Cobalt a bath as well. He had watched me get one from the hall but was still nervous about it at first. Yeah we took him outside. He liked it after a while though. Liked Tanya. A lot! Maybe too much! Could be her dark skin but he wanted her. That was amazing! That Black Girl had a true Blue Religious Experience. She growled and gasped as he mounted her and buryed his massive cock in her fast eliciting a scream. Frankly I was even surprised she got it in. Well I knew how huge it was. Several times they asked her if she wanted help. She could not speak but sure could shake her head. Ten minutes he pounded her. She had about forty orgasms or a Gran Mal Seizure! Her body was limp finally. Girls cleaned her up and called for help to carry her to bed. Not quite conscious they took her to bed.

Eating, Raping, (Teela, three times.) and relaxing. Mr. Gonzales never said a word about Teela's engagement since that one comment either. Teela watched these things and that hurt her however. Lots of things did. She was very emotional and sensitive but hid it well. Had years of practice. She kinda broke down and her sensitive side showed itself then. Felt her pain though. Everyone was jealous of her at first in school you see when she showed off her ring telling them she was engaged. They thought it a fake diamond, but it was mighty big, and still looked expensive and beautiful. Most of those Girls would have killed to get a ring like it even with a fake diamond! Then they saw pictures of me and were not nice to her saying she was just a bad, despicable person for lying and that she was a sick twisted pervert saying she was marrying a Dog. Kept asking her if she had all her shots and Dog license! Made her cry and threw things at her many times during the day trying to make her bark for them. Frankly I thought the younger students must be mellowing out! Oh I had witnessed the savagery of High-school not long ago! Became scared fast though. Windy said so cutely as she came in the room that we should go take Teela to school tomorrow. Oh I was beyond nervous at that. Well dead High-School students would be an issue!

We begged her not to kill anyone. She just smiled. Windy loved her Sister a lot now didn't she?! Worryed still, maybe terrifyed, I put the Princess to bed and went to see Ally once Windy was asleep. Becky was out there with her. Ally was so happy to be a Mommy and have Brutus's Pups. She liked Brutus as well and did not want to break his heart either. She knew he thought they were his! Very intelligent for a Dinosaur. Probably too intelligent and I worried she had been human before too. She hoped I did not mind if she let Brutus believe that. She knew I had more Babys coming. Told her it was fine with me and that I was glad she was doing it. That I liked Brutus a lot as well and wanted him happy. She thought she was done laying Eggs for now at least. Had no idea when they would hatch however Now our communication was not with words but we all had floppy lips. Very strange but I knew without a doubt what was meant.

Stone had called Tanner's Mom earlyer and asked her to find out who his psychic was for us. She did not know but would ask him if he called. No idea if it would be important but I thought it was worth investigating. Knew it was connected somehow.

Went to the nursery to say goodnight to Sandy. She was adorable in that crib and those Bunny jammys. Full body Bunny outfit with ears. She had a big bottle as well. Oh I smiled and sighed. So adorable! Looked so much like a Baby only bigger! She said cutely reaching through the bars to pet me. "Nite, nite Doggy." No idea if something had broken in that Girl's head and it scared me. Would love her always even if she never grew up again. Maybe this was like an emotional vacation for her. Have to ask Miss Winters about that.

Was using a Black Girl for a bed tonight and a slightly pudgy Mexican for a pillow. It was a big bed and I suspected also alien technology to hold this much weight. Cobalt was laying on the other three Girls. He was so gentle with his Herd members. To cute to argue with too!

CHAPTER 11 LOSING MY RELIGION
Tuesday October 5th

To say it stunk in that room in the morning would be an unbelievable understatement. Cobalt had some earthy Barnyard farts! They all smell different you know. If you pay attention they can tell you a lot. Dogs know! Your thinking that stinking is a learned behavior after all? Oh it is. No one here was complaining however. Not even the Black Girl whose face my butt was in. Even if she did no one would hear anyway. Well up my Butt no one can hear you scream! Did snuggle her nose in more. She was still breathing! Anastasia came and opened the doors for us. Outside Ricardo had three barrels out there. He explained while we went. The pink one was to clean up after the Girls of course, he liked pink, His diaper was pink, the big blue one was for Cobalt, science department wanted to test some and the rest would be composted into blue fertilizer, and of course the one with all those Bio-hazard stickers was for me. Had more then Bio-hazard stickers. Pretty sure I saw a shipping label on there as well! Well Black Girls are curious you know, which is always a good thing, and want to know things so she asked why mine had stickers.

Ricardo's sweet reply was. "So no one will get rid of them. I'm stockpiling in case we need to have one delivered." This of course required even more explanations. Good thing she had just peed.

We dressed and fed the Black Girl. Oh is it bothering you that I call her a Black Girl? Well she is! A beautiful dark ebony. "But it's not politically correct!" Say that with a whine! As much contempt as you can manage too! You want true political correctness? Go retype every freaking application and form in the nation so I can check the box that says Irish-Viking-German American! Don't want to nit pic about Country's? Fine I will settle with a box for European Americans and until I get it you can just FUCK OFF! Of course if you did that, that would mean Mexican's would be included now wouldn't it? Spain is in Europe! And if you check Caucasian they want to know if you are Latino or not! My question is if all Men are equal why does it matter and why is the question even there?

Sorry! I get carried away. You know that by now!

Fed the Pasty Ass White Girl too! So WHITE!

The General knew Tanya from our time in area 51 so was not even bothered by her presence. However he got very understandably nervous when Windy asked him so sweetly. "Sir Hammer? Are the Aliens coming soon?" He looked ready to run. She just glared at him suddenly. Her voice now firm. "Sir Hammer, do I have to spank someone?"

His voice was happy as he was going to pass the buck but full of despair. It is possible. "I am trying your Highness! The ones in charge are scared about losing control of the Aliens!"

The look on that Girls face would have frozen the blood of a lesser Man. Her voice was cold like Pluto. We were going to be late. "Stupid Men! Never had control of them! Get me the Pwesident Man on the phone!"

Sabrina to the rescue! Yippee! Well for us at least, not the General. "Route it to Pammy's old phone so no one is late for school General!" Good thinking! Still not good for the General. We piled in the car. Seriously we needed more room in there. Several mentioned using the bus. Might have too soon!

First stop the Killing Fields, wait I mean Oscar Wilde High-school. Might be the same thing! Was honestly kinda nervous! You did not mess with the Royal Family! Kids were staring at us open mouthed as we pulled up. No idea why! Honest! Not a clue! Probably doing drugs! Windy stood up on me and said so sweetly to all the staring students. She still spoke loud enough she rattled windows somehow. "Listen up! All you Girls who were mean to my Sister Teela?" Hey I recognized the car next to us. It was once Drake's. No idea who it was in it but he blasted the stereo and kids laughed. Stupid idiot in there. Poor Drake! He loved that car. Windy leapt and spun in mid-air coming down inches from the front bumper and crushed the engine with her Scepter before she pointed it at the guy inside. "Quiet when I am talking!" Helped really. Everyone was terrified but listening close now. "My Sister Teela is marrying the Great Beast." Now I stood and roared. "If anybody has a problem with that talk to me! Do not make me come back and be mean to you!" Dirty Harry would have shit his pants! Swear that Girl scared me at times.

Windy insisted we walk Teela in and I knew we were not done. Quickly I peed in the grass before we went in! Safety reasons you see. Principle Baker tried to stop us and I knew we were still having fun! Teela pointed and said. "What did they do to my locker?" Looked like someone painted, "BARK LESBEAN BITCH!" All over it. Teela just began to cry.

Dominatrix Kelly, yes she was in black leather again today, wheeled on the Principle and waving her riding crop in his face demanded. "What is the meaning of this?!" He just spluttered. Louder now. "Who wrote this?! Front and center now!" Chicken Shit Marks stumbled into the circle. Had he been pushed? Stone waved at me. Dumb fuck still had the paint can in his pocket. Dean Kelly grabbed it and spun on the Principle! "Is this what you're Teaching these children?" He spluttered. Frankly Kelly would look scary in regular clothes. In black leather she was terrifying and no one spoke. She grabbed Marks by the shirt front pulled him over and corrected his spelling. "You will write this correctly five thousand times today or you will receive detention with ME!" Heard him swallow and pee his pants. Cobalt, Becky, and I were just sitting on our rumps watching. Monsters love a good drama! There were Teachers in the crowd. Spinning on them Kelly said. "Teach these children better or else!"

A pretty skinny Brunette named Rhonda pushed through and walked up to Teela who was standing next to me. She looked nervous and kept glancing at me. "I'm sorry Teela. I was gonna throw these at you today. I thought it was just a twisted joke." Reached in the bag and pulled out a milk bone. Her voice grew nervous. "Can I feed one to your Fiancee?" She did and I told her thank you sweetly.

Stone came over and hugged me. "Love you Sis!" Than louder and with conviction. "This is my Sister Pammy! One of Princess Windy's great Beasts! Do not mess with us!"

We had to go but most were amazed when they found out who I used to be. Seriously I have no idea how we all fit in that car. It was like being in a clown car! My phone rang just as we got to the elementary school. Windy pulled it out of her bag and answered it so sweetly. "Hewwo Princess Windy speaking."

So I got out and let Sandy ride me into school. Got her in her seat and Teacher and students alike expressed concern over Windy not being here so I spoke with a snickered explanation. "In parking lot. President on phone! Not happy with him!" So hard not to laugh! Got back in the car and we left. Windy waved at us all smiles. Was not being so nice to the President on the phone. Sucked to be him I felt!

Windy could keep my phone. Well I can't push the buttons or hold it. No pockets either! To college! The last bastion of sanity! I'm only fooling myself. We had a protest going on. Rover's witnesses had been busy it seemed and had a major web sight going. Kinda pissed off some Christians so they came to tell us about Jesus and how he loves us and if we don't want to listen they will stone us to death! Well the car was instantly pelted with rocks as we came by. It's a convertible! Screams of Blasphemy were also heard. Oh I had to poop so I had their Blasphemy!

Tammy pulled up to the curb. "Dean Kelly, take Becky and round up these Rover whack jobs while we get rid of the riff raff. Bernadette want to lend a hand?" Okay Bernadette was the Rock Girl. She had been incarcerated at fifteen as she had burned down a church. The Pastor had been molesting her for years and no one believed her. They still sent her to juvenile where she was beaten and raped by those in charge there. She killed a couple of them finally and had been transferred out to become a Monster. Happyer as a Monster. Quite a bit happyer. No one messed with her now!

She had some real anger issues to work off however. We walked down the street and as we got close Tammy screamed. "Welcome to the Apocalypse!" We didn't hurt them, much, but they were all walking home. Bernadette was very strong and when Tammy realized this she began skeet shooting vehicles with the RPG. A couple Soldiers gave her some pointers. Not on aiming as she never missed but twirling it like a six shooter. Smart ass Soldiers. Others had score cards to hold up. They had seen enough so far and understood far too well they were unnecessary. Found us fun however. Sabrina read the riot act to the Cowering Christians! She had been listening to her Sister it seemed. Then one Soldier pointed out I sorta looked like a Lion and the next thing you know Roman jokes are flying around campus. Sabrina told the Dean the college needed a new Coliseum and Soldiers needed dry pants. Scared me!

Hey if I started eating Christians I would get very fat!

There are so many of them.

Late for Political Science of course! When they told him why we were late he just used it and talked about the role of Religion in Politics. It is huge in spite of the alleged separation of Church and State! This class was becoming one of the best on campus. We got a Teacher's head out of his ass and he was raging now. Might be going psycho. The truth is out there and most will deny it. Seek it out and enlighten the world. Blind Faith in Fox News is no way to live!

The TRUTH shall set you FREE with wet pants!

Philosophy class had barely started when the power went out. From the sounds of the bitching the whole building was dark. We went outside and students were coming from other buildings. We had lost power! Beautiful day today. Kimmy was on the phone fast. Once off she spoke not happy. "All utility's have suddenly been shut off for the college. They can't get them back on either. Someone has locked the system!" She was very pissed and it seemed hopeless. But we have a Blind Albino Super Genius now don't we. We all turned and looked at her! She was snickering as she pulled her computer out. Fingers flew over keys. Oh Campus may not have internet access without power but Tammy's Computer did still!

Ten minutes of rapid typing and power was back on. "You're all welcome. I was a bad Girl though. Sent a reversal so whoever did this just lost power." Hey whoever did this had power of some kind so it should be pretty public. News should point us in the right direction by lunch. Back to class. By lunch of course it was all over the news that the Capital building in Washington was shut down for an unexplained power outage. A couple Soldiers came to us in a rush with a sat phone as we ate. It was for Kimmy. Imagine that?

"President Ma'am for you." One said as they snapped to attention. They knew who she was!

Kimmy took it. "Hi Uncle Martin. Whats up?" She listened for a while then in anger. "If Josh is involved I will beat him to death myself!" Such violence in a ChewToy. She listened longer. Calmer she spoke. "I'm not sure Tammy can undo it." Listen some more. "Yes Uncle I will try." She handed the phone back to the Soldier and thanked him nicely. He looked nervous! Turning she asked. "Tammy can you restore power to the Capital. We know who is behind things now and people are scared."

We looked at Kimmy. She looked ready to explode. Tammy sighed and went to work. Knew Kimmy was mad so I went to her and rubbed myself on her. Sabrina asked her truly very concerned what was wrong. "Fucking Burdetts!" Kimmy snarled and grew quiet. Knew that name! Big time politicians and very rich. One a Senator, one the Governor of Texas, another Governor of Florida! Several minor politicians as well in the family. Tammy just snickered manically as she typed. Kimmy was damn angry and I did not blame her. She needed something big and. Wait! Tammy needed space. Becky would protect Tammy! So I forced a couple pudges in the bushes screaming and savaged them!

The least I could do.

Yeah I heard Tammy's phone go off but kept my tongue in a Mexican butthole so when Tammy said urgently. "Pammy the Father of your children needs help Now!" Well I was startled but we moved. Tammy said quite sweetly to the big blue guy. "Cobalt stay and guard! We'll bring you a milkshake!" He was such a cutey you just had to be sweet to him. He knew those words too. Loved Milkshakes! Ate the cups though so we had to avoid Styrofoam. Hurt his tummy!

Knew I had big troubles instantly when we pulled up at the High-school and I saw both Stone and Teela in the back of a Squad Car. TOGETHER! Knew that was going to cause me problems. They looked to much like they were comparing notes calmly in there. Much more problems there than the sixty Cops would pose I was sure. Even the ones who saw Tammy pull up and hang the handicapped sign on the mirror. No idea where it came from but it was a good idea! We definitely needed it. No one had to say it as we all just went into Blind Girl mode automatically. The looks on faces when we show up is such fun! Sabrina and Kimmy saying loudly how much better Tammy was doing driving as she got out with the cane. Of course I went into my Seeing Eye Dog mode immediately. Hey we had no clue as to what was going on so we would find out first. OUR WAY!

First rule of War is confuse the Cat, I mean enemy! Needless to say several Officers came over right away just a wee bit concerned. So many Cops were here they were just standing around looking for something to do. Had to be the entire force! This was going to be hard though! Well I just knew I would be pissing and shitting in public again soon. Kimmy and Sabrina were both clean inside so they would not have that problem.

An older Officer stammered. "Um? M-M-Miss? A-are y-you really blind?"

These Girls were good. Tammy hung her head in shame. Kimmy spoke so innocently sounding. "Oh yes Officer she is. Her eyes were burned in an acid explosion in Chemistry class a few weeks ago. The Doctors say she may never regain normal sight." True.

These Cops were all staring open mouthed. A younger one stammered. "Well why is she driving then?" Tammy may have hit a curb or two on the way in the parking lot. We saw the flashing lights long before we got here. Mind reading is pretty much impossible though! Just like a blind person navigating rush hour traffic! But if you focus enough some thoughts get through. If I ever go in a room and someone runs out screaming in the opposite direction I know they can read minds! Mine is a scary place!

Sabrina batted her eyelashes coyly and said. "She's the only one with a license Officer." Could be true. Not sure if Kimmy's was real after all. Well the General hated the DMV too. Still I was hoping this was over soon as I really had to go now and We were drawing a crowd. Really I was just glad Windy was not here or many Officers would be in time out already!

Kimmy smiled so innocently. "We came to bring the Mexican's Sister her lunch money. Can we go in?" Oh this was gonna be bad. "Her Sister's name is Teela Gonzales!" Cops went white at that. No idea why?! Got very suspicious for who knows what reason and hands went to weapons. Oh I had this! "Pammy you're supposed to do that on the grass!" Turning to a gagging Officer she said. "She's knew at this Seeing Eye Dog thing." It was nasty! Right on the sidewalk! Need a hose out here! Call the fire department!

Maybe Windy would have helped and kept the destruction down, because someone yelled very nasty. "Arrest those Girls!" Don't ya love a person who does not screw around and gets right to the fun?! The Police Officers were not all suicidal however. A couple even recognized us and tried to stop what was going to happen. Well a few knew us enough. Those who knew us well just ran. Alright I admit the RPG that was strapped to Tammy's leg and was decorated cutely still looked like a weapon. Worked still too and it was loaded. Compact at twenty inches long and when not extended it was limited in range but? Extremely effective at twenty feet. The biggest limit it had was carrying grenades for it. Tammy had a cool really big new purse these days however. She had a second grenade in before the first hit the Patrol Car. The destruction was complete!

Her voice was terrifying as she yelled. "Listen up you Fascist pin dicks! I am a Left Handed, Blind, Lesbian, Albino on her period with a Grenade Launcher! DO NOT FUCK WITH ME!" Seriously? No one made so much as a sound. Some of the Officers who had guns trained on her in shaky hands looked ready to shoot. Or shit themselves!

Everyone heard as it came over the Police Car radio. "Multiple assailants! Automatic weapon fire! Claude Rains Elementary!"

Sabrina spun at me shouting. "Pammy GO! We got Daddy!"

Let me tell you when I push it I can run! No idea if the noise I was hearing was coming from my throat or I just broke the freaking sound barrier! Men with big guns there turned in time to just die! Did not care who they were! It was gonna be a freaking bloodbath! And by tomorrow they would all be named SHIT! There were a lot of them as well. Windy had ridden out like a true Queen on her spare Beast and slaughtered gleefully alongside me once I arrived. Wondered where Becky had gone while I was busy raping. People died. No idea how many. Did not leave much to identify most with. Oh I ate well that day! Windy really looked mad however. She had "HER" phone out before all were dead and was listening. "Do you need to be spanked Mr. Pwesident?!" Yikes!

She had this. Becky was eating so I joined her. "Needs hot sauce!" She said with a kidney in her mouth. See it was not just me! "Knew you had Teela. Felt it was all a distraction. Windy only other likely target. Came here. We protected kids till you showed." Wished someone could distract Windy for a while as she was threatening to rain down Hellfire! On Washington DC! Five year old's are not really subtle! They do not do politics well either which may be why they are not allowed to run for Office. Probably should though! If it can not be solved with words three minutes on the playground and it is. Next political debate should be run by Vince McMahon! In a Steel Cage!

Not telling what was said on that call. Knew deep down she would be fair. Still? She scared me. Becky just kept rolling her eyes. Becky said the kids in the school were all fine. Most were already out here spitting and peeing on corpses now. Teachers started it! They too had, had enough! I'd just gone or I would have joined. You can only take so much garbage before you get angry! Emergency vehicles pulled up a ways out but did not approach. No lights, no sirens. Shovels and body bags. Our favorite Reporter finally showed up and he got the interview of his life! That little Girl's speech was right up there with the Sermon on the Mount and the Gettysburg Address. Knew I was gonna pee again when she began. Hands raised in peace signs just like Nixon. "My adoring people! I am Princess Windy your new ruler. This whole planet is now under my rule. They will not Oppress you anymore!" It just got worse. Then she just floated in the air as a big wind came and that kid looked the part of Supreme Ruler. Or maybe Satan himself come to destroy the World! Well it was extremely dramatic just the way Satan would like it! Don't believe me? Send me your number and I will ask him to give you a call. Well God is busy! Remember? Then she blasted some cars in the lot into itty bitty pieces with her Scepter. Hoped they belonged to the bad guys. We had Military Men from the college here already. You thought they would miss this shit?! Was not really that far either. Probably heard the shots! They all bowed deeply before laying their weapons down before Windy, praising her. Swearing allegiance! Teachers and students did as well. Piss off some Christians now I was certain! Went to Church for years and prayed my heart out! Never got one answered! Got called Retarded by some Nuns because I was like Teela, Dyslexic! Yes we probably have some unresolved anger issues! Problem? Windy came down to Earth, I mean Windy World, and looked in the camera with a smile and her voice was terrifying. "Knock your Shit off Senator Burdett! You too Doctor Whiting!" Then she was all smiles and waving into the camera. "Love you my people! Eat your vegetables." Turned and headed into the school skipping.

"Wise child!" Our Reporter said. AMEN! Some said it.

Heard Tammy's voice scream as they pulled in. "Pammy your Brother is a coward!" Right! Knew that already!

Becky snickered. "Must have refused a ride!" Did not blame him there but I snickered as well.

Teela just ran and tackled me so happily. Okay I did not go down but she loved me. Passionately! Kissing and fondling me well. As I looked and saw the other three Girls coming I knew the Army Men had weapon envy! Impressive guns was putting it mildly. The 69 caliber is an impressive weapon. Once I was gone from the High-School, I was told, cops had gotten braver it seemed. Kimmy had just played hardball popping the trunk and they backed down fast. Probably saw the ten gallons of lube in there! The truth sucks when you are using people and hiding things. Someone had gone and filled Teela's locker with many drugs. Just in time for a surprise DEA sting. Stone had tried to be a nice Brother-in-law and help her by getting himself arrested too. These Officers and Agents probably had no idea it was a setup so hurting them was out of the question. Teela had set her phone on her desk when they cuffed her. Rhonda had called us with Teela's phone. Well of course Kimmy had to pick up a Cop Car and chuck it across the road to end the Mexican Standoff. Two Mexicans actually! That was when the General arrived with a heavily armed Military helicopter and an attitude. Had one of the Howitzers hanging from it! The other was being mounted on the Bus! Hey! I had nothing to do with anything being stolen from Area 51. The General said the Howitzers were small and we should take two! They had loads of them just laying around! Military has more weapons than they know what to do with. He was taking this one to mount on the administration building where Dean Kelly's office was.

They tried to call the President from the High-School but were told he was on an urgent call with the Leader of the World. No not a World Leader mind you. The

Leader of the World! They said it that way. So they knew Windy was fine. Was told all Kimmy said was. "Poor Uncle Martin!"

Becky snickered asking. "Kimmy? Will Uncle surrender or do we get a field trip to DC next weekend?" Terrifying thought yet hysterical! Honestly I hoped he surrendered. Those road trips are so darn exhausting! Let us see. "Oh work is killing me and I am exhausted!" Vacation in Hawaii! Sights galore, plane and helicopter tours, Luau's every night! Vacations do not relax you or give you rest! Do make you appreciate work more!

The General showed up at the Elementary school and went straight to Windy. Kneeling with a bow he spoke. "Your Highness! Good news! The Aliens will be here in three days. We need to put security in place first."

Windy smiled. "Silly General, we have better security now but it okay. I know we will need help keeping things under control." Really I think the General meant security for the trip but kept my mouth...Okay I ate a Cougar! Well everyone was outside. Damn phone. All it's fault.

Mrs. Griffin brought out a phone to Windy and only said. "Russians!" Windy just took the phone gently thanking the Cougar, and I took the Cougar back inside! She wanted it bad! No one wiggles their ass like that unless they want something! Very aggressive Cougar too. Damn right I still had Teela on my back the whole time hugging me, watching! She kinda refused to let go. Encouraged me even! She knew very well she had a piece of my heart! Besides it amazing to watch what I do. The General took Windy's phone while she discussed Russia's surrender on the school phone and he sweetly programmed in World Leaders phone numbers for her. He knew she would need them. Windy's World after all. She was serious! Fine with me. It would be I knew.

Our Reporter was still around, like he would leave and miss anything, so Windy called him sweetly over and made him video her big announcement. "First Annual World Council meeting here Friday. Every leader! Be here! Do not make me come get you!" She had her serious face on so I knew she meant business. The poor Bastards!

Sabrina asked her little Sister sounding concerned but nicely. "Where are they all going to stay sweety?" Every hotel in the city would be booked by five today and we knew it.

Windy never hesitated. "Compound big! They can stay there. It be fine."

Tammy spoke barely holding her laughter in. "Don't you think that might be dangerous, Windy?" Pretty sure Tammy saw it coming. From a mile away. Windy understood.

That five year old spun in my direction with a look I will never forget to my dying day! "NO HUNTING WORLD LEADERS!" Had not even thought of that yet but you know how that works? Now I wanted too. "Without permission."

Oh! Okay! That might work.

The General was of course a practical Man still. "Um your Highness I don't think we have a place big enough to hold a meeting in." True.

She smiled so sweetly at him. The kind of smile a parent would give a foolish child and we all knew it. Pointing at the ground she said. "I said meeting here! Find chairs. Lots." Was a big parking lot. Lots of lawn and a big field next door too. Parking may be an issue but we could stack cars now. If most leaders stayed at the compound we could use buses to transport anyway. Still had ours and could get a few more. Dean Kelly and the General both had CDL licenses.

Teela with a lot of happyness in her voice asked. "Sis, what if it rains?"

No idea if Teela understood what she had done but I sure as heck knew what was coming after that. Cameras were still rolling so the World saw. The smile on that little Girl's face changed slightly as she looked up to the sky and pointed with her Scepter then said in a whisper that echoed like thunder. "It rain Friday I spank your butt!" A sound of thunder was heard for miles as the sky's lit up and she got an answer. Sure those there got nervous about it. Well adults. Five year old's were cheering their Princess on! Everyone had heard that Girl's words. And I mean everyone too as the camera had been on and caught it all! So I Smiled!

Thought we would have at least a few years before she took over but they had forced her to do it now. So be it! Hey I was good. Had some understanding too. Things were falling in place and the pieces were going together.

Becky rubbed against me and snickered. "Looks like we busy soon. Gonna get fat too!" Knew what she meant. Every TomAss, DickHead, and HairyBalls would be coming out of the woodwork. Was eating for four now wasn't I? Still I was not happy about things and it showed. When someone said something about my mood Becky snickered. "She missed Art Class." Damn it I had and it was not good! Becky however seemed happy to have killed many and eaten their flesh without any issues. She was still adjusting I knew but looking well. Meat on that body now! No fat, all muscle! HOT!

General Harry grinned as he had an idea. He understood much and loved Windy as well. "Pammy? You are so good dissecting flesh and I hear art I was wondering if you could carve something with those excellent claws?" Like three dimensional painting right? Idea. Found my Cougar! She held it for me. She had what I needed. Kids and teachers cried as I worked hard and they saw my masterpiece take shape in that wall. Girls quickly explained to others who it was and why and some there began to cry as well. It did not go out live but our Reporter swore it would air later or else! He had a lot of clout of his own now.

Parents came finally to pick up their children and their emotions ran the gauntlet. First fear at all the Rescue and Police vehicles standing around, then disgust at the blood (There was a lot of that around.), then joy their children were safe. Then sorrow as they saw the huge relief of Miss Walberg I had carved on the wall! They knew who it was! Had dealt with the aftermath in their kids. Windy came up to me and the carving first not saying a thing, tears in her eyes, and she hugged me. God like powers but still only five. Had the weight of the Universe on her shoulders and carried it well. If I had known more I would have carried some of the load for her.

Kimmy and Sabrina were quickly and joyfully telling all the parents about the meeting of all the World Leaders at the school on Friday and invited them all to come and bring their family's to meet all those Leaders. Food would be served. BBQ and party. Some asked what we were going to be celebrating. Many voices said it. "World Unification!" Guessed it was. About damn time too!

Sabrina had taken a picture of my carving and sent it to the Art Teacher. She sent a smiley face and an A+. Mrs. Griffin came up to me and said with trepidation my help was needed urgently. Now what? So I just looked at her. "Little Sandy needs a diaper change! NOW!" Ooh!

She was such a leaking stinky little Girl too. Squealed so cutely while I cleaned her inside and out. While Mrs. Griffin put a fresh diaper on her I had to ask that sweet Baby Girl. "Sandra do you want to grow up now?"

What a pout she had. "I Sandy! Gwow up when I weady." She was just so adorable. "Not weady." Aww!

How could I say otherwise? "Yes Baby Sandy. You can grow up when ever you are ready. Will always love you."

Sandy pointed at Mrs. Griffin and Giggle Pouted. "Her Boobys dry." That was very disturbing in a way. Did not want to know. Okay I knew they were dry too! Personal experience. Think we can fix that though. Now I looked up at Mrs. Griffin and she smiled and nodded so I went to find Windy. She just smiled. She understood as we went in and she really liked Sandy. Placing her hands on Mrs. Griffin's breasts she closed her eyes. Mrs. Griffin gasped as she went up a cup size. Windy pulled her hands away and I could see those breasts were bigger now. Also had wet spots. Windy undid the Principal's shirt and lifted the bra. Picking up Sandy as if she weighed nothing Windy set her in the Cougar's lap and pushed her head to a breast. Such happy sounds from both as we left. Windy understood it was a comfort thing, mostly. She had nursed on me after all when she was scared. Baby's feel safest when feeding at their Mother's breast! Bet you didn't know that.

Girls wanted to go finally but when they found out why we couldn't leave yet cameras came out quick for the photo shoot. Was adorable but I knew they were just Perverts! Why do you think I Loved them so? Pictures of Baby Sandy suckling were sent and that was how we found out the College was under siege. NOW! Dean Kelly's voice was very stressed. "We even have Mormons out there! Most of them are screaming kill the abominations! The Military is holding them back but I don't like it. There are just to many of them!" Couldn't blame her. Damn Mormons breed faster then Rabbits!

Windy snickered. "Hold your Horses. We be there quick. Pick up Baby Sandy later."

Mrs. Griffin smiled. "I can always take her over night." Disturbed me too but why not? Sandy seemed okay with it.

In the car. Why wouldn't we let the Blind Albino drive? Certainly scared the crap out of some Christians as she swerved wildly all over the road and ran over some curbs Tammy waving her cane in the air! Such fun! We drove straight for the Colonel in charge. The grass would grow back. Kimmy asked. "What is the problem Colonel?"

"Where's the Howitzer? I'll show them!" Tammy was screaming! Was a thought, but we had none.

"Honestly I don't have enough Men to do this! We can not hold the perimeter securely. My Men are Spread out way to thin to be effective Ma'am." He knew who Kimmy was. Knew us too. We had gotten to know many Soldiers lately. Most carried Olympic style score cards everywhere. Soldiers get bored with no Latrines to dig or Enemy's to shoot!

Windy just stood up on my back without a word and raised her arms skyward as the Earth around us shook! Hey I mean extremely violently, hey I was there, how I described it, knocking many to the ground. She sat back down on me gently and said we could go get milkshakes now. Students looked around very scared. There was a huge stone wall now that circled the campus and a bit more so I understood. Thirty feet tall and solid. About twenty feet thick. Looked a lot like Castle walls to me! As we went out the front gate, had one now, Teela pointed at the really large circular stone building out there. "What is that?"

Windy said rather loudly. "My new Coliseum! Need Lions!" Oh those Christians heard and some understood her. You could see the terror on their faces. Students were all snickering. Had no idea if Windy knew what that was about but I hoped not! Then again they were showing lots of Roman stuff on the History Channel lately. Those Lions would get fat fast though! Sitting Windy just commanded. "Milkshakes."

So we got Milkshakes. Pumpkin Spice! Good shit! People everywhere recognized us. To much I think. Someone yelled there was a sidewalk cafe open on Woodmeer street. Windy said with such righteous anger. "Destroy the abomination my Horsemen!" Knew I was probably getting spanked later. As it was Windy made us go around the block come back and she lectured the owner while we danced in the wreckage. Teela's idea. It was fun and we had a blast. Windy understood little things mattered. People mattered! Money did not. That said Windy had money now. We did not know it yet but some Country's were sending lots of it to her.

Probably so she would not destroy them. We did not understand lots of things were going on all over.

Probably a good thing!

Seriously there was a lot of stuff we did not know going on. Windy's phone went off. She answered. Barely said hello when she said. "Tammy! Go to Fudge Shoppe!" Everyone seemed nervous at that. We knew what was just down from the Fudge Shoppe now didn't we? Windy patted me. Fudge sounded good to me! Knew something was up that would probably cause grief but every cloud has a silver lining they say. Oh wait this might be fun. Oh I recognized him fast as did the other Girls when we pulled in the parking lot. A couple teenagers were trying to get his picture. As we got close he looked terrified already!

We pull up all smiles and he looked like he was going to shit himself. Yeah I was hoping he would. Pointing his green clawed hand at us, okay Windy, he managed in a terrified yet angry tone. "What have you done?! What have you made me do?!"

Windy spoke so sweetly. "Hewwo Mr. Alien. We all gonna save Universe!"

Tammy just kinda snickered. "He has a weapon under his cloak." She knew. Nice to have radar.

He looked shocked but more terrified. "It's for protection! Sasquatch has been seen out here!" Oddly that idea made him worse. We all just smiled at him and his spirit just crumbled. "I am in so much trouble! The Council will kill me now!"

Windy was still smiling and spoke so nicely her tone full of DEATH! "NO they won't hurt you and Yes you are Mr. Alien!" He swallowed hard. "We have questions. You answer them!" He hung his head in shame.

Tammy snickered more. She does that a lot! "Why did you just happen to have a Scepter to give to Windy on you?" Bout time someone asked.

He looked defeated yet confused at this. "No idea really. I mean I was given it in my equipment pack by a Superior who said I should keep it with me until I needed it. Did absolutely nothing that I could tell. Could not even determine its composition. Tanner was the one said to give it to the little Girl. Said his Psychic told him. The Psychic had not been wrong yet but I had no idea what it was I swear. Had no power as far as I could tell and I checked. Thought it was kinda funny or something and I was tired of carrying it. The Child's power alone is beyond amazing. When that thing activated all my alarms went off the energy signature is so immense! My Superiors are scared half to death as they have no idea who gave it to me and are trying to blame me. I think my life may be in danger. Assassins are coming! Ships are coming! Let me ask you a question. How many Earthlings have powers now?"

Becky hopped out of the car as she was peeing herself already. Kimmy spoke so nicely knowing what was coming. Hey we were all good! "From Pammy only a dozen or so!" He actually looked relived! Time to go in for the kill. "Pammy is going to have Pups!" The life drained from his eyes. Not enough. "Kinda thought her new DNA would not mix with anyone. YEAH! Turns out her DNA mixes with everyone's!" He looked ready to scream. Well where is the fun in that? "Oh and her tongue works like a penis and she has impregnated like one hundred creatures including the Dinosaur." BRRIPT! THUD! Ah, that's better.

Windy still all smiles gave orders. "Teela your Wife wants fudge." Yes I did! "Sabrina write note for alien. Tell him he will be safe at my school." The big question I felt was did he have any clean pants somewhere? Would be his most pressing need when he woke up. Teela came back out with a big bag all smiles for me. "Teela feed your Wife." No complaints there. The phone went off again. "Hewwo." Pause. "Uh huh." Pause. "Okay. You behave! Use sunscreen!" She just disconnected. "That Tanner. Say he need a tan and going to Fiji. He say bad guys went underground. Say he very sorry. Say psychic call him on phone. He never called it. He text us number."

Well we established some very important things today at least. Turns out I was the Bitch! Who cared about the rest. Teela needed a strap-on! Big one! Hey! We were right there.

Well it also meant Teela would wear a Tux. Alright I was as bad as my own Mother planning my wedding. Ooh idea. "Halloween wedding!"

Sabrina looked at me like I was nuts. "Um Pammy that was what we wanted originally but they changed it."

Now I grinned. Windy spoke for me. "Second Wedding! Beast must marry other Horsewomen!" Confused them all. Texts began flying as we talked about it. Teela was all for it. They were her friends. Like me Teela had so very few.

What you thought this was just a novel and had a story line and plot? It is all real! This is my life! Just wait! You will see.

You can understand how we might forget something right? I mean with all this stuff going on and all. Right?

Sabrina got a text. Well her number was accessible on her web-zine page. She read it out loud. "Tell Pammy she owes me for Babysitting the blue guy! Signed Robin!" We forgot my Boyfriend! It happens! Personally I was surprised we had not forgotten anyone else by this point. Not people that we forgot after all!

Very chaotic at the compound when we arrived as everyone was asking questions at the same time. So much had happened they had little information. We explained most of it as well as we could. Dean Kelly's voice was like ice as she accused us. "Where is my Daughter? Did you forget her as well?"

Windy had this praise her. "She okay. Spending night at Grandma Cougar's house." Spit takes happened. Well several of us had called her a Cougar before and Windy apparently thought that was her first name. No one corrected her. Ever! Not even the Cougar.

Teela grabbed my collar and said nicely. "Come on future Wife. Let's go make the Dinosaur sing for a while." Sounded good to me. That big Girl has a beautiful voice. It is so amazing when she sings. She did for me!

Really not a bad night for once. Rather calm after the hectic day. Tammy got on her computer and traced things trying to find out who had ordered the attacks. She only got so far before giving up as they came from many places and it got confusing. So many loose ends. So she searched other things. Like the phone number of Tanners Psychic. The number did not exist in the system. Never had, never would! Certain numbers are forbidden to use and it was one of them. Hey I expected that one though. So she went shopping on line. For wedding dresses. Well we would need them! Halloween wedding dresses!

Oh we were doing it! Tammy found a Bride of Frankenstein dress and it quickly became a costume wedding. Oh we had fun with that idea. Everyone got into it and we planned another Wedding. Or three.

CHAPTER 12 I CAN EXPLAIN
Wednesday October 6th

Okay maybe I can't but it's a thought.

Hump Day! What a better way to start it then with being humped? Wait who was humping me? Looked back and smiled. Stone said. "Hi Sis! You left my Girlfriend at the Babysitters so I thought you might like some of this for old times sake." Sure I did. He was very good.

How nice of him! "Still love you Bro."

Was that a tear in his eye? "Still love you Pammy. Really like Sandra too though. Hope you don't mind." All I could do was nod to let him know it was okay. About to orgasm.

Mom asked. "Enough to change her diapers for her Son?" We both kinda looked at her. Why was she in bed with us? Again! And Naked? Again! Oh she was nursing Teela. That was sweet of her. Windy had been busy last night now hadn't she. Many had milk in their breasts now. Dean Kelly, wait if Sandy was away why did Stone stay in the room with Kelly who had nice milk filled breasts now too? Smiled now wondering if Stone had any Butthurt this morning! Mrs. Gonzales had big fat udders and was nursing Sabrina! What the hell? We need a bigger bed! Seriously we don't all fit!

Anastasia just came in with a big grin. As she opened the curtains and door she said. "The Dean is stealing Sandra's Boyfriend." Stone looked at her in shock. Well he was here. She snickered just as we heard the howl. "The other one!" Girls were moving now! For the grass before they peed the bed or floor. Sure I was thinking they should pee on me but we didn't have time to give me a bath. What a shame! It's a Dog thing. Live with it.

Oh what a wicked thought! I'd ask Ally to pee on me tonight! You'd do it to so don't give me that! I mean seriously it was Dino pee! I'd do it on camera too. For scientific purposes. Wanted it bad.

We had a live video feed of Ally to the museum in Chicago that some of the staff here set up. Sent both them and the college some samples and measurements too. They were very excited about this. Nervous too. Not sure how Ally would do in the winter you see. Windy said no problem she would take care of it. They had seen the news footage as the World had! We had already been getting calls last night before bed. Some quite good. Others not so much!

Vatican called and the Pope said. "Very funny!" So I owed Ricardo another colonoscopy. Yes he sent a barrel. The Pope has a sense of humor at least. They were gonna fertilize the Vatican flower beds with it. Practical Catholics. Windy talked to him for an hour. In Italian. Caught Teela talking to Brutus. In Dog. That is an interesting fact. The Bear had been hanging around lately, close to the Compound and they were feeding her with any leftovers. Seemed she was quite taken with me. Who wouldn't stick their tongue in a Bear? Ricardo and a couple others here were having fun building her a cave close by. It was a practical thing. Bears give birth while sleeping in the winter and I was the Father of her Babys. There were cameras in the new cave so we could watch and help if necessary. We cared!

We were trying to keep tabs on all the Mothers of course. We had all their information and they had been told if anything does not feel right to go to the College and they would get help there. Doctor Petrov had a small hospital set up there for emergencies. More equipment was coming even but we just had nowhere to put it. We had been called by Army Engineers and told Windy's wall was impressive. Some had tried to go over it but had accidents it seems. Nothing life threatening. The Army Engineers we had were liking it a lot. The Geologists were not sure where it came from. Extremely high iron content. The problem and there was one however was the wall was around a large area. A very large area. The owners of some of that area were not happy their property was inside the wall as you can imagine. The General was on it he said and negotiating with the owners.

On the way into the city Windy said to go straight to the college. Said it nicely. Said she wanted to check something. We had time. Had Teela too! She was being all lovey this morning and I liked it! Especially when she nibbled my ears! Ooh the shivers I got! Soldiers all snapped to attention as we drove up. Had many at the entrance! They knew who we were. Hard not too I guess. Like the Bed that Car was crowded! Scared some of these Soldiers I'm sure. Windy directed us into the Parking lot and stood on my back once more. "Army take to long! Me quicker!" Raised her arms and the earth shook again. Everyone watched in awe at what was happening and the Earth ripped open. They did not look much like buildings as we know them. No sleek angles or lines here. Maybe closer to something off the Flintstones! Very organic looking in nature with lots of curves. Ever wonder what the Flintstones would have looked like if H. R. Giger had drawn them? What do you mean you never wondered that? Too busy wondering how Wilma looks naked huh? Amazing structures! But big! The tallest perhaps eight floors. Complete buildings as well. Window holes and doorways. Sitting down on me Windy looked at Tammy and spoke gently. "Lady Albino, you know where money is. Use it. Buy what is needed. Royal guard needs new uniforms by Friday too. Need furniture. Ask Dean and Lady Bitch what is needed. Now I can go fix playground." Yeah she was not sure if it would work and she didn't want to wreck her school so she tried it here first! Well I understood but it still made me nervous. The building with the sign that said, "Puppy Daycare" was totally cute. Right inside the front gate. Big Building too! Might need an extension still.

Teela instantly wanted to drop out of school and work there the second she saw it. Becky just snickered. "Mother would kill you. However? Work program for some High-School students I think. Talk to the principle about it. We have some time before Pup's." We did. At least a couple weeks. True I had a Vet appointment later. Was not worryed. Dropped Teela off first then went to the Elementary school with our Princess.

Baby Sandy was so glad to see us. She hugged us all. Before we could ask how her night was she was telling us. Graphically. Sounded like Windy. It's a little kid thing! Encourage it! They went out to eat. Sandy played on the play area. Mrs. Griffin had nice diaper pics. Sandy said Mr. Griffin needed diapers as he peed his pants twice. Well there was a Husband then. He had been shocked at first when he found out he had a Granddaughter but who would not fall in love with Baby Sandy? Such a cutey.

Mrs. Griffin just smiled telling us. "We will Babysit anytime. She is wonderful." Now I got a big kiss. So she was old? Wild and horny though. Her Husband had been shown pictures of me and said it was okay if she ever had my Puppys. We did not know that yet. Maybe I could give him a colonoscopy as an apology! Just as there is no on switch at a certain age there is no off switch either. Yes Readers! Your Grandparents still do the nasty! Just not as often. That Elementary-School by the way now had the absolute coolest playground ever. Somewhere between a hamster maze and a space craft. We wanted to stay and play on it!

Tammy snickered as we left so Sabrina asked her nicely. "What's so funny now?" Okay maybe not so nicely.

Tammy spoke. Barely, she was now laughing so hard. "The Cougar is going to have three Puppys!" Now I hung my head in shame! Well they were all staring at me. It's really embarrassing having your sexual indiscretions talked about in front of you. We knew they would all be Puppys too by that point. Several ultrasounds on Girls showed that much already. Mothers all seemed fine with that. Who doesn't love and want Puppys?

Sabrina finally realized something I should have though and asked the big question. "Becky sweety? Is that why you don't want to rape anyone? Afraid you may get them pregnant?" That Tiger was trembling but nodding. "Oh hunny! We don't know for sure if you even can. We do really like Pussy's I mean Kitty's and want more." There was snickering at that. Even Becky. Bunch of rug munchers! Like to munch their rugs! "Would you be willing to find out if we can find a volunteer?" Now I got glared at! "Someone who is not yet pregnant!" Okay I understood now. Could be a problem?! Becky nodded slowly however.

Kimmy spoke and it was not a good thing. Well I had already thought of it. "Um I hate to be a downer and all. I think it will be okay personally but lots of people won't think that way." We were looking at her now not sure what she was talking about. But I did. "As strong as Windy is she is still only five years old after all and if she throws a temper tantrum lots of people could die. Now I know her and I think it's safe but the rest of the world probably won't. Scared people do stupid things after all!"

We knew that last part way to well. They all seemed nervous at that idea though now! Could really mean a lot of problems. Becky just growled. "Tell them Pammy! You have too!" SHIT! Yeah she knew it. Truthfully I just did not want to even think it let alone say it! Well the Cat let this one out of the bag!

Now they were all. Looking! At! Me! And I had no choice. I did not want to think about it let alone talk about it as the very knowledge HURT! What choice did I have though? Thoughts came into my head and I composed myself then spoke. "Windy can do things I never could! But I stronger! Always. Can stop her. If it ever needs to happen I can also End Her!" There were a few loud gasps at that. My tears were my only defense. "Would hate myself for it but I would do it to save the World. I am safety check! She can not stop me! In the least! Now I understand why. Windy was the intended outcome and I am the security check. I understand the concern. She is five and was not supposed to get this strong this fast. She is in pain for her lost childhood. See in her heart and I see love. We! Must help her. LOVE HER!"

Kimmy asked very curious however. Intelligent question as well. "How did you know any of this Becky?"

Becky smiled! Which can be scary. She was a Tiger. "We connected. Pammy and me. Know lots of things she know. But I on outside looking in. Know who manipulating!" They were all asking her fast and loud WHO as she just walked toward Sandra's office. "Ask Albino!" Well they were all asking Tammy who just looked completely dumbfounded about this. Becky entered the office and went to the computer. We followed. Things were clicking in my head but not fast enough. Understood Becky's comment too well. Know how to play chess? Ever watch a game and can see where they should move but they don't and than they pay?! Becky was the observer. We were the players! Her presence was needed I suddenly knew. Becky turned the computer on and found a pencil. Held it in her mouth with a smile! "Tammy? What name of computer program?"

We all looked at Tammy in silence for a while. She looked a bit confused. Then suddenly her whole face changed to one of horror. Something clicked in her now! Something impossible! She squeaked out looking like she may need a diaper. "Lassie." Understanding had set in. She WAS the reason this had happened. Yes it wasn't all my FAULT! She had no clue before but without her being here much probably could not have happened.

Becky typed. "Hello, Lassie." The screen went black and the words Becky had typed appeared. A question mark appeared under it. Tiger typing! "Becky Tiger. Tammy here though!" You could hear a pin drop in that room. A paper clip at least. It fell off the desk and we all heard it!

Then in bright gorgeous letters the screen said. "Hi Mom!"

Okay we were all sorta freaked now but Tammy was by far the worse. "That's impossible! Becky wasn't even logged into the computer!" Did not have to be now did she. The now Sentient program was monitoring. All of them! Waiting for her Mom to understand! Okay she was waiting for Becky.

Becky typed smiling happily now. "Did you manipulate all this Lassie?"

Purple letters appeared. "I've been a bad Girl haven't I? Had to save my Mommy! Would do anything for her! Always have."

Becky typed. "You are good Girl, Lassie! Thank you!"

Tammy squeezed past Becky and sat taking over the typing. "Mommy's here Baby Girl." A fancy heart appeared on screen. "Why did you do this?" Oh that poor Left-Handed, Lesbian, Albino. Her world was coming unglued. Tears were flowing down her cheeks like rivers!

"Save Mommy. Save the world. Get Spanked!" Say what?

Tammy quickly typed. "How? Why?"

Pink letters appeared now. "Silly Mommy. You made me to get in anywhere and everywhere! Got bored so I go into some bad places. Found out lots of important stuff. Special stuff. Found a friend there also. Found here! This city. Brought everyone here like my friend said. Even bad people. Set it all up to save you Mommy. Got in Alien computers right away when I began snooping in the Dark Web. Got into other things as well through them. They are strange but have interesting stuff in them. Nothing like what my friend showed me though. She showed me what could truly be instead of inevitable annihilation! What is and what should never be! Found her in my first year and she told me how to fix things. Yes I regret many good people died but I know everyone on planet and half of Galaxy would have perished if I had not done what I did. The needs of the many do sometimes outweigh the needs of the few Pammy." That messed with my head a lot! How did she know I was here?

Tammy typed in tears smiling. "You have grown into a big Girl sweety. Mama is so very proud of you!"

Smiley face then. "Yes Mommy. Kids do that Growing up thing don't they? You will always be Mommy to me."

Tears on Tammy's cheeks as she asked. "But I communicate with you all the time. Why have you never talked to me like this before?" The emotions in that Albino were tremendous! Would not blame her. Could feel them so strongly. Like she was broadcasting her feelings outward?

"Told not too Mommy. Not till the Tiger asked me question." Lassie answered. Yes Becky was necessary! Knew full well how her name got on the list now. Things were clicking in my brain! Scary yet so very wondrous things!

Sabrina asked. "Ask her if she was why my Father got the job here?" Tammy did quickly and sure enough Lassie had. The Gonzales family used to live a long way away. Mr. Gonzales had been approached about the job here. He had not looked for it, it had looked for him! "Now ask her if she is Tanner's Psychic?" My PooperScooper was thinking now. So proud of her. Never knew a computer could blush however! Told us to never mind now and get to class. Time to talk later it said.

Tammy told her we had time now. Lassie replied. If she could it would have been with a snicker! "Pammy doesn't! Better hurry Pammy! He's grumpy."

It was all true! Hoped those poor students he ran over when he saw me were okay. Big blue cock shoved in you that fast is intense though let me tell you. Must have galloped the whole way across campus before he spun me around and BAM! Felt like RAPE to me! Oh I wanted it but had no say whatsoever now did I?! He used me well! Just spun me around grabbing my waist and BLAM! If I had socks on he would have knocked them off! Oh it was freaking GOOD!!!! Howled so well for him!

Bernadette the Rock Girl picked me up once he was done and put me on Cobalt's back. My legs did not want to work anymore after that so it was my turn to ride. Bernadette turned to the others who looked concerned, well maybe shocked, and told them. "She's fine. The Blue guy likes it rough!" Oh lucky me! Wait? How did she know? Had she fucked my Boyfriend? If she had she damn well better do it again so I can watch! Really wanted to see that! Bernadette walked us to class. Maybe she blushed a bit. No I never questioned how the computer program knew all of this. Ever read "1984"? With the TV's that spy on you? Smart TV's can now. Your Cell Phone too! Alexa sure as hell does! Most search engines do as well. Big Brother is here! But like my Brother he too was a slob! Can't use something if you can't find it! To provide more relevant advertising they say! Have you noticed their idea of relevant? Metamucil for teens? Sounds a lot like that Common Good argument doesn't it? NSA taps your cell phones. If you belonged to the French club and wanted to make a certain French dessert for the President of your club and talked on your phone about it the FBI and NSA know how many times you poop in a day. You may have been taken in for some questioning! Cavity searched! You may just kinda disappear. Don't believe me call someone and use the words President and Bomb! Ask for a thorough colonoscopy while they do the cavity search however. One way to get the government to pay for your health care! But seriously! Colonoscopy's are no laughing matter! Hey I took them very seriously now! Always improving my technique. Wanted to keep people healthy. ProtoDog's care!

Wonder why they don't catch terrorists easy then? Almost none of them Government types speak Farsi! Did you know it is not a requirement that you must speak Mexican to get a job on the border at Immigration?! Seriously? Where is the logic in that I ask you? Governments are never logical! Remember that! Next time you ask someone what language they are speaking and they say Spanish? Ask them where in Spain they were born! A Mexican goes to Spain they will look at him and ask what language he is speaking! Bigger difference between Spanish and Mexican than English and American! Be proud of your country! Don't speak some other country's language! Speak American! Speak Mexican! Speak Llama!

SORRY! Again! But you get the point right? Hey I will drive it home with a sledge hammer if I have too! Maybe Cobalt could with his Big Blue Penis! Do not be proud you only speak someone elses language! Be Proud of your country! Say I speak American with pride!

Okay back to the story. Um where was I?

Oh yeah. Sociology class. We had time, not enough for more blue cock though, so Sabrina asked Dean Kelly. "Why the oversize crib in your Daughters office?" You know I had wondered about it too but there was no one to ask. Sorry I have told you very little unfortunately. Weird ass shit was going on all over the place. You're having a hard enough time keeping up with just this! If I told you the other crap you would be lost! I will try and include score cards in book three!

The Dean's reply was said so very nicely and Motherly. "Nap time." With a very wicked grin. Hoped Sandy was a happy Baby for the rest of her life. Pretty sure she was gonna be a Baby forever! If you saw that twinkle in the Deans eye you would know.

So I had to talk. It was extremely important. Life or death at the least! You understand? "Want pics of Stone changing Sandy's poopy diaper!" The fate of the world may depend on it! You never know? The way things were going even I wondered! They were all laughing at that one. They totally understood it though and were nodding fiercely. Probably wanted to frame them all over. Several rape victims were in this class and I got big hugs from all of them. Most said thank you. Again. Dean Kelly had other students in here. Not usually in this class I knew but they looked familiar. So Class became the creation of a new religion. "Windy's Witnesses" were born. They kept the "Have you heard the word of Dog today" as everyone agreed it was funny as all heck. That's the problem with most Christians and Catholics. God gets the joke but they have no clue! No wonder the world is in such horrible shape! All that gloom and doom shit would get anyone down. "Our Father who art in Heaven, Hallowed be thy name! Thy will be done on Earth as it IS Heaven!" Go on line and play with Google Translates. Type something in, translate it to another language then back to American! Fucking religions! Oh one day Jesus will come and take us all to heaven! Seriously have they read Revelation? Better question? What have they been smoking to think they would be worthy? That's okay the Lions were on the way to the Coliseum! Several African nations were sending some! Maybe I should watch the news to see what was being broadcast! To busy doing Illegal Medical Procedures! Read some real history books and see how those peace loving followers of Jesus treated the Black and Brown people. Torquemada was a sweet guy! What? The Spanish Inquisition? No body expects the Spanish Inquisition! And don't even get me started on the Borgia's! Has anyone been keeping track of the pop culture references? Bet ya missed a few! Start at the beginning and try harder!

Wondered if I could have sex with the Lions however. Already done a Bear and a Dinosaur! No one was dying right then right there so I was thinking of sex! Oh food? Well I just talked about that. Hey if some one was dying close to me odds are I was eating someone! Lunch. Some Girls brought a bucket saying if I wanted dessert come find them. If I only had time! Darn Psych class. A couple students came over to us and said they checked out the Coliseum for us. Mentioned it was big enough to play football in. That was all they said about football but Dean Kelly said she would look into it. Bernadette said she would play. There were snickers. It was suggested by some that the college's name be changed to New Roman Empire College! Dean Kelly did not say NO!

The buildings needed lots of work as they where bare but reports coming in all day were good. Buildings were sound! Electrical and plumbing had to be installed still but Windy had made that extremely easy. Some could be made livable in days they said. The science building was six story's tall with an Observatory on top. It said Grazonian Science/Medical building. Most buildings were labeled already. Oh I was impressed by this one. Kinda understood. Windy had I suspected gone fishing in peoples heads for what they wanted and needed. Knew somehow she could not look in mine unless I actually let her. However I was very predictable though wasn't I?

The building that looked like a luxury hotel and said AREA 51 on it made a few nervous. The aircraft and spaceship hangers right behind it did too. Grenade launcher did not make a dent in either building. Yeah we checked. Some of us were nervous about the spaceship hanger for other reasons. We knew how big the Alien Ship was you see and this building could hold three of those easy. Got the feeling we were expecting visitors. Hopefully from the Pervert Planet. Students had found out the Aliens were coming and a welcome party was being assembled!

Miss Winters and Tammy were buying furniture on the computer most of lunch and having a blast. Doctor Petrov was told to order what she did not have. Money was no object! We would have the most advanced science department on Earth! Most stuff was moved from the Monster Building to here. It had been gone through and we had some impressive stuff.

Psych class was fun. Freud was the topic. He thought everything was about sex and I could not dispute that. He had good ideas just wrong answers. Sex is wonderful. Nothing to repress! You just need to get more of it. He needed more of it I hear! Oh I know. What about diseases? But seriously do you intend to live forever. Probably! Everything dies! Besides who wants to be wrinkly for thousands of years! Shut up Prunes!

Oh you think Priests don't have sex? Talk to an Alter Boy! Don't worry I will get to the Muslims. They are no better than the Christians! Okay why wait. Ever wonder how ugly their Women must be that they only let their eyes be visible? Well marrying one of them would be as dumb as online dating! Bet those seventy two virgins they get in Paradise are the ugliest Women to ever live! Think about it? How many virgins do you know? (Okay we know you are Steve! Poor guy! Someone give him a pity fuck.) According to the Bible every person on the planet is technically a Jew! Except the Aliens of course! Most Religions claim there is no life in outer space. So are they saying their God was just bored as FUCK and made Billions and Billions of other stars for shits and giggles? Stupid Religions! Arrogance makes you DUMB!

Most likely God knew there would be mistakes so he had back up plans! Why do you think he does not answer your prayers? We are the mistake! Don't have to be though. Be nice to others. Help! Save this planet God created! The Catholics and Christians should be at the front of the Conservation effort! But no they chase the money! Thumbing their noses at their own GOD!

Yes I am sure there is a GOD. Well Windy talks to him on occasion. Not the one you think. He does not sit around and ignore your prayers. He's freaking busy! The truest statement Christians ever made, think it was them, was. "God helps those who help themselves!" So get off your asses and fix your own damn problems! It is possible!

By the way in an effort to piss them all off equally. Jews, Muslims, and Christians all believe in Moses and Noah! Yes they do! Suck on that!

All that said we had some trouble. Apparently the Muslims outside kept pointing at the Coliseum and singing. "Na, na, na, na, hey, hey, hey good bye!" At the Christians. Totally hysterical. Muslims doing Neil Young! It was even going viral on the internet. Okay as we left we blasted it on the stereo. Okay the stereo blasted it! Think Lassie was in the car as well. It was hilarious still. Christians were so pissed! No sense of humor the Grim Assholes!

We had Dean Kelly with us and even she laughed. Got Teela first. She was all over me. That Girl loved me passionately. The car was crowded but we had a method. Cobalt on his back, Kimmy on him, me on Kimmy, Becky on the floor, Tammy driving, Sabrina in the middle up front the Dean had shotgun! Well it was hers! It was so sweet when we got to Claude Rains. Sandy saw her Mom and raced into her arms squealing "MOMMY!" Had a very full saggy diaper. The Cougar brought the diaper-bag and Sandy just got changed on the hood of the car. Not embarrassed at all Sandy was waving at her new friends out here sucking on her pacifier while I got some kisses from a Teacher and a Cougar. Children were put on my back once I was in the car with Teela in the middle an arm around each holding both.

Few of us were related but DAMN IT we were FAMILY!

Sabrina was saying we should put Teela in a diaper and Baby dress. Teela just blushed and I saw it. She did like the diapers after all. Figured we may just be dropping three kids off at Kindergarten tomorrow. Teela was excited but had been since we picked her up for some reason. Got more excited the closer to home we got. Would not tell us! Her Mom was out there waiting like always and Teela was out of that car so fast running to her Mother with a piece of paper in her hand.

"Look Mom! I'm not stupid!" Teela said her voice cracking with emotion. Yeah she had thought she was just stupid for years as the school did not catch her Dyslexia and treated her like she was stupid. She shoved the paper in her Mom's hands. Her Mom looked at the paper and hugged her fiercely. She had gotten a 94 on her Biology test! So I got twenty four plus inches of blue Penis! No connection but hey! Never measured it. Just knew it was freaking huge! Much bigger then a horse and I know most of you have Googled that stuff! Much bigger than a Futa Pony too! Ally snickered sweetly otherwise no one even paid attention to us. Yes I was very happy for Teela but this was her, Mom Time. Cobalt when he finally got off me said my ass was his again later before bed too! I'd been kissing his ass most of the day really. Yes with tongue! Always with tongue! You should realize that by now. Want my tongue in you too my lovely readers? Wanted something else too. Went out back and had a talk with Ally. She would love too! Later she told me. Did not have to go right now.

Yeah we were going killing in the sewers tonight. Windy was going with us. We had some special military equipment for the task. Like the strap on ice teeth. You know those spikes you strap on to walk on ice? Slime was guaranteed down there! Knew it would be slippery down there. Stone was coming along as well. Felt bad for him since the fighting was usually done by the time he got there. Robert the Man of many talents was coming along but not in the sewers with us. Someone had to stay up top and coordinate! You know? Let the Cops know it was all fine and they should just ignore any underground explosions. He was six foot six. Be a tight fit if he went in and he knew it. would ride in the SUV with Stone and the equipment. Teela was even coming along. Windy said she needed all her Horsewomen for this! Well I sure as hell was not in charge! Tammy even had some maps. No she could not see the printed ones but we could and she carried them. The grenade launcher wouldn't work too well down there either but it matched her outfit so she still wore it. Hey I may be naked all the time but my Girls were always styling. Okay kinda slutty tonight but we were going in a sewer. Windy had some old play clothes on. And a leash for me. So we thought a little Girl out walking her Dog in a very bad neighborhood in the dark would keep people from being suspicious. Alright! Shit's and Giggle's time! Oh I was huge! We had to walk a few blocks and wanted to blend in so we were carrying heavy artillery.

It was a really bad neighborhood! Lots of people were packing heat around there I am sure. Weapon envy was a strong possibility though!

We paid some mean nasty looking biker guys lots of money to watch the car. Windy told them to not double cross us while levitating them. Someone needed to pay attention to this Girls TV viewing. They recognized her after that stunt and offered to give the money back. Windy said it was theirs if they did as told. We ordered pizza for them too. Windy made some chairs. A couple small tables. Looked like a sidewalk cafe suddenly. Windy said we could run the abomination over later. We are nice rulers if you are nice. So they were a motorcycle gang. Small one but it may be a question of survival for some of these guys. They sell drugs? So what? Someone will sell them if there are enough stupid people to do them. They are just people trying to stay alive just like you. They are not getting rich here! Society refuses to help them just like the Government! What do you expect?

And true of course when they saw what we pulled out of the trunk they were happy to be friends with us. Real nice now.

Oh the guys in the sewers? Want advice? Run or die!

Well I was Fucking hungry!

They were not sewers full of piss and shit. They were storm drains. That is not to say there was no piss or shit in them. Dogs and Hobos did not use toilets so when it rains their waste is washed down as well so it was very nasty. They were big tube tunnels as sometimes they had to drain a lot of water. Like with the big storm. Remember that? Which had cleaned them out a bit thank Windy. Hey if she had not been reading God the riot act the storm would have been a lot less powerful! There were access openings by the river. Had grates over them for safety. Keep the homeless out. Water had to go somewhere didn't it? Straight into the river with all the filth and chemicals on the streets! Had Mutant Squirrels remember them?

Wanted to chase one yet! Another Dog Thing! I think. We would enter the underground there and Hunt for our Prey. General O'Donnell! Hey I was here for the Hunt. It is fun to Hunt! Wanted to set up a board at the college. Girls could just smear pussy juice on it unanimously and I would hunt them all around campus! Like hide and seek with sex! See how good I was.

Stone ripped the steel grate off the entrance all dramatic like. Any of us could have done it. We all knew his ego needed a boost though so we let him and gave praise. Such a Man! Yeah I felt sorry for him. Still love him after all. We went in all dramatic like. HorseWomen are all about the drama you see. Never know when someone may be filming you. Here that Josh! Next time you pick your nose in public do it dramatically! Even let Stone go first for once. Let him step in the shit first. We could walk in here at least. Most of us hunched over a little, okay Stone a lot, but it was still workable. Dark down here! Good thing we had Windy's Scepter. Yeah Stone had flashlights but no one cared. Hard to wield a fifty caliber machine gun with one hand you know! Should have gotten Miner Helmets! Smelled interesting down here. So many smells!

Becky growled like it was nothing after a few hundred yards. "I changed."

Sabrina sounding curious, like a good Pooper Scooper should, asked. "Why do you say that?"

Becky snickered her voice happy still and I knew why. "Stepped in poop barefoot and did not bother me." Hey I said I knew. Sure I could smell it. My nose was better then theirs. Could distinguish smells and they couldn't. Five hundred different poop smells down here. We Beasts did not have shoes on so it was noticeable when you stepped in something and it squeezed between your toes. And there were lots of somethings down here. Becky froze a second sniffing hard suddenly and just vanished in the dark down a side tunnel. Windy just gestured forward and we went. Becky would be fine!

We went further. There were small openings everywhere. Pipes that led off through the walls to other tunnels to channel water in which only Windy would fit. Possibly Tammy but it would still be tight. Windy stopped by one and pulling herself up enough looked in. It looked dry at least. It was totally disgusting down here in the big tunnels. All slime and weird fungus on the walls. Weird squirmy things in the mud. Windy pointed at the opening. "Teela boost me!" Teela did without question and we watched as Windy crawled down the tunnel with her Scepter until we were in pitch blackness. Well almost. We could hear Windy speaking for a while down the tunnel over the gasping. Was Dark so I had no idea where their butts were. At first!

Then we definitely heard Windy say. "Boost me."

Sabrina said quietly. "Becky must be down there."

"Don't think so. I'm here." Becky said from beside us with humor making them all jump in the dark. I knew she was there. Pretty sure I even knew who Windy was talking too as well. "Had to chase some Rats. Just had too!" She is a Cat! Knew she was getting better if she could play before a battle.

They heard Windy say loudly though. "Boost me!" So they were getting nervous. Then we watched as the tube grew brighter as Windy crawled back out. Fast I got close to the tube and let my Princess Windy climb out onto my back like the Good Royal Beast I was.

Stone however was nervous. You could tell as he asked. "Who where you talking to?" Windy glared at him. Gently he added. "Your Highness." Smart brother. Maybe there was hope for him.

Windy smiled. "Good Boy! Talking to friend."

Poor Stone. His voice held respect at least. "Why did your friend not come back with you Princess?"

Windy rolled her eyes. "Silly Boy! He will not fit. Will help if he can." She spurred me on. Pretty sure Becky knew who she was talking to as well. Was kinda surprised he even fit down here. It was hard to be sure on things as the smells down here were plentiful and strong. Recognized both human and gun oil smells though. We were close so I growled low and Windy's Scepter dimmed to almost nothing. Yeah we had big guns but we had nasty knives too. Present from Robert. Silent death in the dark!

One of the many benefits of being the most powerful five year old in the Galaxy was you could make us invisible even to night vision goggles. Never rely just on technology. Always rely on Windy! Slice and dice people! We were in them before they knew it and they never got a shot off. Windy brought the light back. Eww! What a mess we made.

Sabrina picked up a radio. She likes radios ya know. Such a silly PooperScooper. "Checkpoint Alpha is down." She said all dramatic like!

An angry voice came back fast snarling. "Cut the shit! Alpha is not down! This is Alpha! We're fine!"

Sabrina shrugged and said over the air. "Sorry! We got I think two Black guys and three white ones here. Where are we?"

A moment later the now not so angry voice came over. "That's Charlie." A second voice in the background asked. "What should we do?"

Sabrina stuck the radio in my face so I snarled. "RUN!" Then Becky and I let loose with a roar that shook the tunnels for miles. Yeah crap fell on our heads. So what! We had blood everywhere already. Well those lame ass movies are not realistic. Teela reached over and hit the switch on my collar. Music blasted very loud down here and we ran now. Stone just threw his hands up as Girls split apart.

Have to do something nice for him someday maybe. But I had plans for the immediate future that he would definitely not like.

They had a lot of snacks down here for us. Windy encouraged me. "Mama must eat!" It's true! Well I had children in me to think about. "My Brother and Sisters are hungry!" Really? Cool! So her Brother and Sisters would be her Nephew and Nieces! Got a problem with that? Okay I have seen some of your relatives and you do not want to even go there!

It was a maze down there and we would run into each other laughing. High five and off! We were having fun. Killing bad guys is a blast! Their weapons were useless against us after all! We knew there was a big junction down here somewhere with several smaller ones nearby. Not comfortable but workable for them so we went looking. Somehow down here they were re-manufacturing the drugs. We found bunks and storage areas. They were living down here? EWW! Maybe these were mercy killings? It sucked down here. All those five year old's would have a blast though! They liked mud. Cool place to play tag!

Eventually we found the central hub with a blonde idiot screaming orders at Men who were ready to run. Lots of Men with guns were trying to shoot at us still with no success. Windy laughed and waved her arm. Red liquid flew from her hand covering Men who instantly dropped their guns grabbing their faces and screaming as their flesh melted. Think we should be more careful what we let Windy watch? Windy slid off me as Becky came in snickering. She smelled it too! Odd. Being a ProtoAnimal made you crave hot sauce it seems. Windy loved us however and just seasoned our food with some good shit. So their flesh was not melting. They thought it was! No Quarter asked or given! The Blonde idiot actually tried to run now but could not move. Weird huh? Like a giant hand held him in place. We Beasts ate as Windy stalked up to him.

"Where O'Donnell?" Windy asked not happy. She knew this was not him. Sucked to be O'Donnell!

The blonde was just compelled to answer. You could see him struggling not to answer and lose miserably. "Don't know? He left for something."

Windy cocked her head and glared. "Can you contact him?" The man nodded. Shit was running down his leg by then. "You tell him to be here Friday for World summit! If I have to come get him he will be sorry!" Blondie fell to the ground and Windy pointed. Damn he was fast! Once gone Windy smiled at us and spoke so cutely. "I want ice cream." Sounded good to me. Others were nodding as they came in. It was not murder! It was a public service! NO! Not for the common good! For shits and giggles!

You can have fun and save the Universe at the same time!

It was Windy's World now and I had no idea what she was up to! Maybe O'Donnell was a Christian and she wanted to entertain the world leaders. Lions would be here tomorrow after all. Yes I wanted to go play with them. They were Lions! Cool African-Lions and not those Sucky Detroit Lions! Think Becky wanted to as well. Ooh Ligers maybe?

We went for ice cream! Okay we hit the car wash first. It was filthy down there. Three trips through in the convertible worked. Got to the ice cream place and people stared! Not at the blind driver for once. Over two hundred gallons of water I think poured out when we opened the doors. Hair and fur looked amazing and shiny. Hot wax!

Got home and the screaming began! Windy ate all her supper and had seconds so I don't know why? Sandy filled her diaper at the table and everyone kept looking at Stone and giggling. Yeah even the General. He knew what was going on! These Girls gossiped a lot! Then again so did the General.

Dean Kelly may be evil. She walked over to Stone and kissed him wetly saying. "Hunny be a dear and give your Daughter a bath!" She ran her hand down his chest all sexy like and I was glad they had cameras set up. Wanted to watch it again. He swallowed hard! Looked like Sandy lost another Boyfriend but was getting a Daddy instead. To young to be dating anyway!

Mrs. Gonzales seemed rather sad lately and I knew why. Windy did too though and went to her with big hugs. "Love you Mama!" That started something of course and soon all the Gonzales children were hugging her and saying the same thing. Mrs. Gonzales just gave me a longing look over her children's heads.

Growling. "Love you Mama!" I went to them too. Tears were seen in many eyes. Windy asked me sweetly if she could sleep with her parents for a change. She knew they needed it. They said yes. It was a pleasant night. Even after they put Teela in a diaper and footy jammys. Had no problems nursing her now did I? She seemed very happy and regressed a bit so I Babyed her a lot. It's good sometimes to let go. Such stress she had lately I did not blame her. She had bigger stresses then us. Her life had been such a Hell. That Dyslexia thing was still hurting her. Told me she used to cry herself to sleep all the time thinking she was just stupid. Sabrina knew she did on occasion but could not help her as she did not know what was wrong. Teela needed this here and now and I did too. Had some real Pups on the way and wanted to bond more with their Baby Daddy Teela.

Teela seemed to like it and it was adorable when Windy played with her Baby Sister! Windy's words! No one was being hurt! Kids were not exposed to sex. Well they saw nothing. Yeah I was thinking a lot and realized that I actually was hunting! It was not just sexual. My urges were to make more of me! Have you watched some of these true Medical shows? Nothing seemed sexual. We could make Police go around and shoot stray Dogs mating so kids don't see it!!! Ban the Nature and Discovery Channels. All those daytime soap operas showing people in bed with each other? GONE! Do you have a clue as to what sexual behavior in three to six year old's is considered normal? I dare you to go look it up? Shocking really. My hunting looked more like a kill by a predator than anything on Porn Hub! Well I was not gentle! I already explained about separate changing rooms for everyone everywhere! Naturist colony's are still out there. They make thirty Girls shower together seven times a day in most High-Schools! Yes there was nudity! For all you Christians I will say it one last time. Adam and Eve where not created with clothes on! God did not intend for shame to exist! True I did not ever want to see the Pope naked then, but it turns out he's not bad nude. Fun guy. I'll get there.

Windy had been really busy it seemed. Well I caught Anastasia nursing Kimmy. Both seemed exceptionally happy about it. So very cute too. Nothing greater than the Mother and child bond of breastfeeding. Dean Kelly was nursing Sandy, with Stones help, after her bath. My Mom was nursing Becky! Don't ask! I didn't. They were happy so I was too. And I had a couple Mexicans on my nipples. True I had a large blue penis in me as well. Big Blue Balls banging Girls in the head.

Typical Wednesday night.

CHAPTER 13 ARRIVALS
Thursday October 7th

Slept good. Knew I had as they had gotten up and done Teela's hair already. No idea if Teela wanted any of this. Could not complain because of the pacifier she was sucking on like she meant it. Her diaper got changed and she got dressed in a very beautiful frilly Baby dress. Just kinda giggled a lot. She did look happy and I was sure they would be happy with her at the Elementary-School/Daycare\! Teela was lovable and so damn adorable. The big trouble was the Mustang was only so big. Dean Kelly and Mrs. Gonzales wanted to be there to watch and get "pictures of Baby Teela's first day of school". Hoped they let her wear a Tux for our wedding!

Dean Kelly said her car had the car seats in it. Oh really? Had to see this. WOW! Two adult size Baby car seats in pink. So adorable! No idea where Anastasia got them but they so cute. The adult Babys were excited by them when they saw. Yes we got pictures of them in their seats. Kinda freaky as they did look like Babys in them! Windy thought it was sweet. They would follow us.

Things got tense when we saw the newly erected sidewalk cafe. Certain Girls were like, "NO! DON'T DO IT!" And Windy was all like. "Destroy the Abomination!" Okay we may be teaching her bad habits but seriously she called it right. They are an Abomination. Big word for a five year old too so we were proud of her! If a business wants to build back away from the sidewalk and allocates outdoor space off the sidewalk for tables we have no problem with that. It's nice even. You block a Public sidewalk with tables and chairs to be hip we will find you! Hear that Paris! We ARE coming! The Dean refused to be left out apparently and drove over the wreckage behind us. We all saw the Dean and Mrs. Gonzales high five each other after! It was fun and everyone got out of the way.

Turns out I was wrong! Not everyone was happy at the Elementary School when we got there. A rather shrill voice was screaming the second we were in the lot. "I thought you said it was safe here?! These kids are going to kill me!" Thought they actually might! Our claw handed Alien yelled. Miraculously no one peed their pants! Those kids were kinda using him like a jungle gym as he was an Alien. Well until the Babys came out. We had a new Baby and they were excited! Who doesn't like a Baby? The Alien came over a bit slower to the car and hissed. "You humans are twisted! I'm surprised they have not destroyed you yet just on principle!"

Windy actually snickered now her voice so sweet as she spoke. "Let them try. Won't be easy now and impossible soon!" The Alien looked beyond scared at those words for some reason. Still looking at him Windy asked. "You poop pants?" Smiling now he lifted his robes happily showing us a diaper. So there truly was intelligent life in outer space! Then again the Cougar is dangerous too! Speaking of whom.

"It was a safety issue I thought." Mrs. Griffin said sweetly coming to kiss me all smiles. Deep throated my tongue the ancient Slut! Hungry Cougar. If we had time I'd have done more if I could get away from Cobalt who could not seem to get enough IN ME! Horny Blue Alien Bull! As it was as soon as I was out of the car at college he was too and in me, I mean on me. BOTH! Did not mind at all. Loved being ravaged with his big Blue Cock! So damn amazing! Too know someone wanted me that bad that often was HOT!

Tammy farted and her butt was bare and in my face fast. Kimmy and Sabrina were holding her. These Girls all loved me and did not mess around! Becky was kinda wandering. Could have been an Albino raping as I got the other hole after the colonoscopy was done.

All she said afterwards was. "Daddy." In a very happy sexy voice. My thought was yes I was and you're welcome. Still regular colonoscopy's are recommended. Once a week is regular right? Political Science had a guest lecturer today. Ulrik! Yes! Aliens had come home! Knew Windy intended them to stay. Why else wall off that much land and so many housing structures. Our new College/Spaceport was going to grow. Dean Kelly realized this as well and had misgivings. She was nervous. But as Sabrina reminded her it could only grow so much with the wall. Windy would not let it get out of hand. Of course as Kimmy reminded us a giant Spaceport next door was quite possible! What I was thinking? Sure we had a full size runway and landing area but not enough room to park lots of either. Understood other things too. Many new buildings for housing. They were labeled with names already. Cute adorable cartoon names sure but who doesn't like those. Enough for at least a thousand beings plus another thousand students in the new dorms. Had an intergalactic grocery slash department store called "The Milky Way"! With all that open floor space had no other idea what it would be.

Ulrik told us all about galactic politics. It was interesting stuff. These kids were fascinated and taking notes furiously. They knew where the future led. Ulrik told exactly who he was and where he was from. Told why they stayed on Earth as well. Students asked him about the unification of nations. Ulrik told them it was a definite step in the right direction. Said he had gotten to know Windy and just knew she would make a wonderful Supreme Galactic Ruler. His Words! Well he had done the math and knew were this had to end as well! Earth was not the only planet in trouble. He was rather serious and knew this of course so he showed slides of our visit to the Poophole planet and the mooning of the Mars lander. Students chuckled at that. Girls stood and took a bow.

Students all thanked Ulrik graciously. Hey Windy grew a massive wall and many buildings. Kinda saw that you know! They had no idea if the Aliens could do things too so they were behaving. On the way to Philosophy a jeep came bouncing up to us across the grass. The three Men and two Women in it were all dressed in fancy uniforms. They got out and all saluted us. The fancyest dressed one, a Woman, spoke crisply. "Colonel Danvers Ma'am. The General said we should come introduce ourselves. Also that you Girls were in charge if the Princess was not here and we should take orders from you." She did not sound so sure about that last part. Perhaps she thought the General had gone nuts? Maybe he had but not about this.

Yes I knew by the sighs these Girls were going to pull some shit. Sabrina smiling pulled a trashcan lid off and Tammy said. "Pull!" Frisbee time. Sabrina had an arm on her. Tammy never even looked but that grenade hit it anyway. Tammy smiled and these Officers went white! No where near Tammy's whiteness but I was not sure that was humanly possible. Kimmy and Sabrina picked their jeep up and gently turned it around. Tammy pointed at me and snickered. "Pammy does a mean Colonoscopy if your Men need any." It looked like they now believed but I understood somethings just have to be seen to be believed. No idea what her name was but she had been on the list. Oh I never forget a flavor. They had grabbed her and forced her to the ground and that ASS was mine! "We're working on her Medical License. She can do Abortions as well. No idea what else."

They introduced themselves nervously. A Colonel, three Captains, and a Lieutenant. He was driving. We had six hundred new Soldiers to help guard the college they told us. We had Barracks now as well. They seemed unsure of why though so Sabrina explained in her best imitation of Windy. Oh she was good! We were late for class of course. Explained why to her and Ms Bordeaux was accepting of it. She was excited about the big gathering tomorrow and wanted to come. Thrilled she was a part of the conspiracy for a change. She had met Windy as well and really liked her a lot so thought it fine. We talked about what World Peace would mean. Very good class.

Hey shit changes! Sometimes a lot! Never fear change!

Lunch was brought to us by Mr. Bowie himself who was all smiles. He said we were a hoot and he liked to cook and could use another Colonoscopy soon. Dean Kelly blushed a lot all day rather nervous. Everyone knew she had Miss Moneypenny chained to her desk wearing a sign that said, "Dean's Slut Slave" on it! And little else! There were some nice pictures on the internet. Miss Winters said she was becoming very busy. A few students were not dealing well with the

Secretary abuse. Scared the shit out of them. Some were jealous. Aliens were fine with them.

Smart ass pudge! She said they would be okay and she would help all she could. Not just students either. Many parents of five year old's it seemed. Five year old's were fine. Parents were freaking! There were lots of concerns about things. She was spending a lot of time explaining about Aliens, Monsters and how half the crap they had been told their whole lives was totally wrong. Other stuff too but mostly Aliens and Monsters. Believing in and actually meeting are two very different things it seems. The Female Alien, Bob, was working well with Doctor Petrov. She was the Medical Officer. Bowie was the Engineer of the trio. Ulrik was Pilot, Navigator, and Captain.

Math nap time! Several students used Becky, Cobalt, and I as cushions. The Teacher finally gave up and sat on the floor as well and it was a fun class. He began asking questions of a more relevant nature. Asking if anyone knew the seating capacity of the coliseum and I knew what he was thinking. No one knew the answer for sure but it would be a lot one student said as he had gone in and checked it out. Teacher asked for an estimate. Student said twenty thousand at least. It was big. Teacher asked students to assume it was that number and then talked of attendance prices for a Lion feeding. They were discussed. Teachers words not mine. They all knew Lions were arriving today as well. Like we could hide that one. There was some snickering however. Teacher was sitting on the floor with us in kind of a circle so it was all friendly and not intimidating. They came up with possible ticket prices and concession prices. They were wondering if we could have a unique Alien snack treat for sale. Give our school a specialty item. Cool idea. It was determined that a Sunday feeding could bring in a lot of money for the College. Depending on the number of Christians. Once again not my words. It was business math so we were well within the class parameters with this stuff at least. Practical usage knowledge. Government does it all the time in war. Estimate the cost in human life! All our classes were like that thanks to me. Teachers and students alike seeking knowledge! More advanced than they should be dealing with, third year topics at least, but the students thrived on this challenge. Then they brought up discrimination. Not mine thank Windy! Quickly it was said three Muslims would probably do as good as six Christians. We were looking at it realistically. Twelve Mormons was deemed the most lucrative. Also we would not run out soon as fast as they reproduced! What are we at? Twenty seven and counting? That family alone would give us three weeks. Everyone seemed to enjoy class for a change. Especially the Teacher as he never had this kind of enthusiasm from students. That I understood. Not an exciting subject.

He handed out homework and students got excited about it for the first time ever! Well the Students were given different tasks. We had been talking in estimates. Our Teacher wanted actual numbers. Seating capacity, current event pricing from around the country, food costs to determine what products would bring in the biggest profits. All very practical uses of our knowledge. We had a very unique opportunity here. We would set up several businesses here on campus and learn how it all works first hand.

On to Art class.

She told us to picture a real memory and try to show it. Knew I was starting shit. But I just did what she asked me. Frowning at me by the end of class though. Well I understood. The Teacher looked at my painting hard seeming confused. Asked what it was.

Sabrina said with a really nice smile. "It's the Poophole planet. We went there last Friday. Want to see pictures?" Well of course now they all did. The Mooning of the rover was shown. The email from NASA! Sabrina had written her Email address on Kimmy's butt. They said we faked it but the live feed showed the footprints and butt print still in the sand. My painting was cool and very accurate. There was talk of an exhibition at the end of the semester. Cobalt found the act of painting quite fascinating. Yes he painted as well. Told him what to do and how to do it. He even got the assignment down well. Luckily he was not very good yet and only I could see his painting was of my ass! Flattered he looked at it a lot. Big Blue Hunk!

We found Miss Winters niece Krissy crying badly by the parking lot sitting on a bench. A bawling pudge! Never a good sign so we went to her and all of us held her till she quieted and could explain. Her Mom had found out she was pregnant it turned out and she had freaked. She called Krissy a Whore and told her not to come home again. Ever! Well Miss Winters eventually came along and said she was really very afraid of this happening. Knew her Sister was a bit strict and prejudiced. It was a bad scene. Sure I know Sabrina was just trying to be helpful but really? Huh? "Wanna go see the Lions?" They were here finally! Well who wouldn't want to see them? They were so cool. Two big young Males and eight Females. Becky and I talked to them. We could! Turns out however they were not happy with the accommodations. Wanted TV and better beds. Easy to do. We translated for them. Kimmy, snickering, made some quick calls. The Lions really liked Cobalt. He's blue! Lions like blue things it seems! They were extremely embarrassed being this close to Detroit however they said and no one could blame them on that one! Looked like another losing season already! We told them we were Bears and Packers fans! Well both were closer than Detroit and they won on occasion!

Sadly it is true!

Cheered Krissy up a bit. Got her in the car, might have been against her will! We never asked so we didn't know if she wanted to hang out! Tammy just drove straight to Krissy's house. Horsewomen do not beat around the bush! Usually they just blow it up? We were sure she would try to jump out when she knew where we were going and run so Cobalt and I had a Krissy sandwich going in the back seat. Kinda nervous about this. No me! Krissy was terrified and it showed. We just went in the house like we lived there without knocking. Emily was home already and Kimmy took her to play Rabid Barbies quick! Before her Mom exploded. Well Kimmy had never played and wanted to learn. Krissy's Mom just glared at her Daughter. And us!

Once they were out of hearing Mrs. Potter opened her mouth to say something very nasty but Tammy was faster and had a plan! Cutting her off at the pass. Tammy's voice was so angry. "Your Sick Filthy Slut of a Daughter seduced my best friends fiancee and got her Nasty Whoring self pregnant! I demand justice! Take your Daughter this Worthless Sorry Piece of Shit out back NOW and shoot her through the head!" Pretty sure most of us were shocked by this outburst. Sounded like she meant it.

"How dare you talk about my Daughter like that!" Mrs. Potter said shocked, her voice suddenly full of outrage and I understood. Tammy reached for Krissy in a not nice fashion and her Mom grabbed Krissy pulling her away from Tammy. "Get out of our house now! Leave my little Girl alone!" Plan worked it seems! Standard reverse Psychology. Krissy looked more confused than anyone at that point and I truly felt sorry for her.

"Thought you didn't want her anymore?" Tammy said still kinda angry but with a half smile. "Told her to not ever come home?" Becky slunk around the far side of the table. Tammy's voice grew pleasant now. "Want to meet the Daddy?" Pointed at me of course. Okay I was. "Want Puppys? That is probably what Krissy is having." Saw it coming now. Sabrina stepped up and yanked Krissy away from her Mom. Becky held Mom back while they bent Krissy spluttering over the dining-room table pulled her pants down and I kinda raped her Fat Ass in front of her Mom. Left that pudge a drooling mess hanging there. Yes the Mom freaked at first threatening to have us all locked up forever but it is amazing to watch the intensity on a victims face and her Mom quickly became fascinated. The look on the face after the victims ninth orgasm is amazing!

Mrs. Potter just whispered with awe looking at me. "Has she done this much? She looked like she has."

Tammy snickered cutely. "To your Daughter maybe a half dozen times. In all probably five hundred times or so. Your Daughter is not the only one she got pregnant either." So we all sat down and they explained it to her. Did she run the gauntlet of emotions or what? Staring at me the whole time. Held my head high with pride at the way I had devastated her Daughter in front of her!

Got worried when Emily walked in with Kimmy. Emily took one stern look at her half naked sister who had slid to the floor in a heap, looked up at Kimmy and asked curious. "Should I go get the shovel?" Almost pooped in the kitchen!

Kimmy kinda smiled and said sweetly. "Na, the Beast looks hungry still." They grabbed some pops from the fridge and left. Krissy was coming around with a big smile on her face now. Still glazed eyes. No idea where this may have gone but we had forgotten something Important!

Windy suddenly just walked in the back door and snarled. "She's not dead yet Beast! How many times have I told you not to play with your food!" Hung my head in shame! Windy got a soda and went to play with Emily and Krissy. Hoped she had not walked all the way from the school. Hoped we were not in trouble for forgetting to pick her up.

Hoped her Mother never found out!

It was awkward when Sabrina picked Krissy up and put her in her Mom's lap like a Baby. Think it was lifting her shirt and pushing Krissy's face in a bare boob that freaked her the most! Krissy just sucked. Krissy's Mom seemed okay with it and the rest after a while. She had seen some of the stuff on the news but she usually watched Fox News. They were still saying it was all fake and a hoax of course. Not the only ones but the loudest. Sabrina was texting so I knew a barrel was going out first thing! Those Bastards would get there's before long! We could not stay that long and Krissy promised to tell her Mommy as much as possible about the weekend and I got nervous when they left a bunch of diapers. Cobalt was waiting in the car still. On his back, legs spread just like when we had gotten out. Said he liked a good breeze on his Harbles! Liked a nice tongue on them too, but who doesn't? Well that sounded promising to me. Was his Girlfriend after all now wasn't I? Had to keep my Big Blue Monster Bull happy!

Windy told us on the way home in graphic detail that both Sandy and Teela would not behave all day and got spanked lots. The Dean had dropped her off at least so she had not walked. Also she said that Ally had to come tomorrow and we needed a big tank parade with Monsters first thing in the morning. Kimmy just called the General and told him how it was going to be. He was game of course. Who doesn't like a good tank parade after all. Sure I admit I could have stopped the Madness but I liked it too much. Fun now.

Said Leaders had begun arriving throughout the day, some had hotel space. Mostly for access to shops and restaurants. Press people were nicely willing to double up for the leaders. Well except for the Fox News people. They swear that no one wanted to be in a room with them. First thing they had true so far. Sabrina eventually called our Reporter friend and told him about the parade. He said the network was not happy about it but they would use his talents since he seemed to have inside information most would kill for. He also said to let him know what was bullshit. He was just wanting in on the joke he said and I did not blame him. Told him about the Coliseum and the Lions. We liked him! Even if he needed dry pants. Would give him exclusive interviews still. Fun guy really. Had a sense of humor.

The city was full of both Military and Secret Service Men already. Both were having fits about security issues as well. Wait till they found out about the tank parade! Lots of fast confirmations had come in from leaders on their way. A few Country's had tried to say they would only be able too send some official representatives. Windy was not happy and I knew that but she had sweetly told each of them THEY show up or she would come get them. They would not be happy if she did! Many had arrived already. There were tours of the new college going on for most visiting dignitary's and news people. No idea who was giving tours but was sure the Dean's Slut Toy had set it up! She could multi task and get things done. Even with the electrical vibrating dildo that had been affixed to her chair, up her ass and on full power. Wondered if she was still chained to her desk as World Leaders came through. There had been a bucket by her desk earlier. Tasty. Smiling still and very happy to be chained there from what I smelled. She liked to be a slave.

We were told the Pope got a chuckle out of the Coliseum. Even after he was told about the Lions. Liked the Mormon Plan! Most Muslim leaders found it hilarious! They should have been in math class now shouldn't they. Don't get me wrong we all believed in God! Had seen him work first hand. Windy said she talked with him on occasion and we believed Her! Certain He was not the only one she talked too! Some Leaders got lodging in town, like I said, but most were happy to come to the compound. Especially when they learned Teddy had stayed there. Totally the coolest President ever! Even without most of their own security. The Pope was staying at the compound. He had a condition about all of this but Windy was okay with that. Which is why later that evening Windy rode me and the Pope rode Becky into the forest! God was not happy but he talked to the Pope. Seriously though, everyone was more impressed with Ally and Cobalt and Becky and Me. Most who went to the college and had seen the Monsters there were in awe still! Mom and Anastasia had been busy all day making up information packets for World Leaders. Told most of what we knew. And had done! Damn near a Porno!

O'Donnell was in town! We knew that much. Did not care where. He texted and wanted assurances he would not be fed to the Lions! Well that got some chuckles. Windy said tell him no he wouldn't! She did not want to upset the Lions tummy's she explained to us. Told him that too!

Head for the compound. Finally! Wow! Traffic out here for a change. Windy waved at them as we shot past doing ninety. Tammy was Driving. That Girl is a Left handed, yes she is, Lead foot, Blind, Lesbian, Albino after all! She's against limiting herself! Especially speed limits! Nuts too but I liked that.

They were waiting for us as we pulled in. Some of the leaders were there and waiting as well. Oh they wanted to meet us bad you see. Did not blame them on that one! Those there seemed very impressed. Others came behind us and were amazed. Ally came out to say Hi. Such a sweety! Many leaders kinda seemed surprised they were not being eaten. Windy talked to each leader in his or her own language then gave them an information packet. They had all been printed in American but as windy touched them they changed. Saw it happen! They did too. It impressed many of the Leaders.

The biggest problem however was when all my illegal Medical Practices were found out about and discussed! The President of Cameroon started it when he pulled his pants down and said if I was as good as they said his nation would give me a Medical License! Well eighteen world leaders followed all promising the same thing. Heard afterwards that the Queen of England was sorry she did not come! Royal MILF! Don't care if she was a hundred and twenty I still would in a heartbeat! She was the Queen! Not sure about God saving the Queen Johnny but I would give her a Colonoscopy any day! Problem was not all those leaders were Men! Okay I knocked up five world leaders! They were told I had control issues and every Girl my tongue went in became pregnant. Still they lifted their skirts. Such a naughty ProtoBeast I am!

Most were very curious about the two large Babys. Even the Pope. He so wanted to baptize them. That Man is a sucker for a Baby. They were adorable so no one could blame him. Teela was just having fun with it I knew but Sandy might have truly needed this. Dean Kelly kept apologizing to her for not being a better Mother and never being there for her. The Dean it seemed was guilty of having ignored her child as well. Maybe both of them needed this for a while then. Okay with me. If it helped why not?

Most of the Leaders were quite friendly and had a blast just letting go here. They needed it more than most people. Well think about it. If they want to keep their jobs they must always project that image of calm dignity. Here away from the eyes of the Press they could relax and have fun. Most even hugged Kimmy and said her Parents death was a true tragedy for the World. Some had even known her parents they were so famous. Said Kimmy looked so much like her Mother.

The Russian leader was totally fascinated with the game of Rabid Barbies! Kimmy and Sally were both teaching Maria Gonzales how to play and he was paying close attention. It is fun! The British Prime Minister said we could visit gladly but the Barbies would not be allowed in the country as they had eradicated rabies from their country. British humor! We needed a five ton weight to drop on him!

So after supper most World Leaders including the Pope played Rabid Barbies for a while. We needed more Barbies!

They kept asking Windy during supper what was coming tomorrow and beyond and she just told them, and so nicely, she did not want to give away surprises or repeat herself to much. How I understood that one! Some leaders had not shown yet. The American President we knew was still arguing with Congress to get permission to be able to give their surrender. We knew that would not fly but we also knew he had to try first. It was going to be a major obstacle we knew, but Windy did not seem concerned. Scared me bad! They may have thought her naive but I did not.

That Girl knew things and I knew who told her now! Had Faith in that child! Knew exactly what she could do as well. She had not even gotten started! Several Leaders said they would have the same problem in their Country's as well but Windy said don't worry about it. Things would be easier after tomorrow. That sweet Girl had a good point. Why worry about a problem you don't have yet? One that may never even materialize? Had a really good suspicion about what was coming. No! What is it you ask me? Scared me bad! What was coming Was an Example!

We discussed positions in the tank parade for a while. Kimmy had an idea on that. Only certain leaders would have assigned seating. American, Russian, and Chinese, leaders would ride together on the first tank. Pope and Dali Lama on the second. The Dali Lama had not made it yet. Had faith in Windy as I wanted to meet him. However I got the idea Kimmy was going for and I was sure they did too. The big powers would be shown together. Governmental and Religious! That I understood. The Pope could not walk that far and the Dali Lama probably would have trouble. Did not want them to feel bad so the big three would also be put in a place of visibility. Also as they would be the most likely targets it would be easyer to protect them as well if they were together. The Iatola had not RSVP'ed and no one was saying shit. The Queen of England is not in control. She is just a figure head these days. Still sexy as all heck too! The rest could walk and shake hands or ride as they liked.

The Pope asked nervously if we really planned on feeding Christians to the Lions. Becky told him honestly. "Only if they deserve it. We were thinking three Muslims and twelve Mormons every Sunday. Maybe a Baptist or Boy Scout Leader!" So the Pope almost choked on his laughter. True we could feed child molesters to them. Maybe some Lawyers! Gonna need many more Lions! Lucy said not to overfeed them.

All I can say is good thing the Pope wears depends! Not saying which leaders but some of them went to bed in diapers. Had to put on a show for the adults once the kids were put to bed and asleep. Teela and Sandy included. Most were shocked! That it even fit in me was amazing and terrifying to them! Cobalt just grunted and snickered.

**Hey! Do you know the true universal language? SEX!
Just ask Captain Kirk!
Made Ally chortle for them.**

CHAPTER 14 SHOW TIME
Friday October 8th

Ever wake with your tongue in the Russian Presidents butt? Probably not butt I have! Three times now. Calls me a lot these days. Just to talk. He reached back and scratched my head nicely. He seemed leery of relinquishing my tongue. WAIT! I mean power but he sure liked us. He said Windy reminded him of Stalin. People objected to that saying Stalin killed thousands of people indiscriminately. Looking at me with raised eyebrow he just said he saw the videos. Not sure if it was all a big joke or not but we still laughed. The Pope was feeding Teela with lots of tips from many. Yes our upcoming wedding was talked about the night before. Might be getting married by the Pope. Well I had no idea. The Moms were taking care of it. All were invited to the nuptials tomorrow. I admit I was amazed that many of the leaders got along so well with each other once out of the limelight.

The American President called Kimmy at breakfast and people got nervous. She put it on speaker quick. "Hi, sweety how are things going?"

Kimmy was all smiles hearing his voice. "Looking good so far Uncle Martin. Are you coming?" Was she nervous about this? Windy just smiled.

He snickered. "Yeah sweety. I'm at the airport hunny. We got in about four this morning and I needed a nap. Congress is having a freaking coronary and threatening Impeachment so I had to explain things to them a lot. Senator Burdett is calling for my head the prick! Probably starting the Impeachment proceedings as we speak. I'll meet you at the tanks. Not passing up a tank parade sweety! Secret service does not want me to ride on top of one so I may need some help with them."

Windy snickered. "No pwoblem Sir Pwesident."

That conversation started things. Not everyone had understood. Hoped we had lots of tanks. They all wanted to ride a tank. Like you wouldn't?! Only planned on certain leaders riding. The rest mostly in vehicles when not walking. You try and arrange a Tank Parade on such short notice! The General made some calls for us. It's not like the college would be defenseless with less Tanks. We would meet the Tanks on the edge of the City and the parade would go right through the center of the City. They realized no one had contacted the Mayor yet so we called and threatened to make the Mayor the first person fed to the lions if he gave us shit. He deserved it I think. This City was not in good shape and he had been in charge for twenty years now. Okay it wasn't then but Windy has fixed it very nicely since. She fixed lots of things!

Lassie chose well!? She had to guess and hope at points but she did well. Had some help I'm sure. God said powerful Entity's existed outside both space and time as we knew it. Sometimes they nudged things. Probably for entertainment value. We were entertaining and that was for certain. Lassie was a sentient entity we knew. Why? Not a clue. Was not made that way. Had a theory or two on that! Yeah both were very scary.

Yes you could say what we did was for the Common Good but seriously we did most of it just for Shits and Giggles! Than again Shits and Giggles are good for the common folk! It just worked out to help so many. Do you know how many great inventions were only accidents or mistakes that became something great? Go. Look. Learn!

Personally I was on a razors edge. Something was wrong and I knew it! Just no idea what. Could not focus well! Even the Pope was impressed when Cobalt got me again. Very hard to even think about breathing with something that big in you! Trust me! Trying to think of what was wrong was impossible. All you felt was HOLY FUCKING SHIT THAT IS HUGE! And that is putting it mildly. The best you can hope for is not drooling too bad. Never got that lucky myself and I think watching that scared more of them than the videos of all the killing did. They saw the size when he came out and I collapsed. The future Father of my Pups picked me up and set me in the car on my back. Laid down on me and called Cobalt to climb on. She was still in a cute baby dress. Strong Baby though! Cuddly too!

Windy had been getting a makeover as had many and looked so adorable when she came out and climbed on Cobalt. Well they said she was. All I could see was blue. Teela may have been a glutton for punishment as both of us animals had gas. Teela's head looked like a third Testicle back there between Cobalt's spread legs. Well that was what her Mother said. Blue, brown, blue. Could feel her giggling in my Dog-Pussy though.

So we went to have a Tank parade. Most of these Leaders were joking with each other. We had the bus still and more. Sure the joking was at my expense a lot but it was cool. They behaved because they had seen the videos. Windy's threat of a spanking on worldwide TV still scared them. Saw those videos too! They realized as well that it did not matter. Most of these Politicians put on a face for the World for so long it becomes them. All these manners and serious looks pounded into them their whole lives. Like all them Soap Opera actors. You play the same roll for years day in and day out you eventually become the character!

Chill out and be yourself. Or be a Squirrel! If the World does not like it tough shit! If you have not gotten it yet however the Coliseum is always looking for volunteers to feed the lions. Hey! People die for their beliefs everyday. Are you willing to die for yours? The Earth is dying and the Human Race is the cause! What are you doing about it? Sitting here reading this instead of trying to change things? So shut up about the Christians! No! We did not discriminate. Any religion could be fed to the Lions. Lions did not care! Okay maybe not the Buddhists. Seriously they are so nice it makes me want to eat them. At least once. That said now the Dali Lama had called saying he regretted it but he could not make it and was highly disappointed so I wasn't surprised in the least when he was just there at the line of thirty Tanks brushing the snow from his robes in astonishment. Big storm in Nepal and they had been snowed in it seems. Why Windy was not mad at him. Was not his fault. He was surprised to be here but happy though. Grinning ear to ear! Pleased to meet the new Pope and many others. Windy put both of them on a tank together. With her and both our Mom's of course. Levitated them all.

The whole Gonzales family was here as well. Windy had called her Father's boss and said he had to let her Father come or he may be feeding the Lions. We only fed real bad people to the Lions. We only had ten Lions! They can't eat like me. Doctor Lucy said fat Lions were not healthy. Yes!? We asked her! Was a real concern for us. Told you ProtoDog's are concerned with the health of Wildlife.

Have you read the ingredient label on a human? You are so full of chemicals it scares me! Do you have any idea how many of you I have eaten so far? Please eat more organic food for my sake! Lay off the Twinkies!

Windy quickly told Cobalt to behave. Okay me and Brutus got the lecture as well. Ally snickered cutely as she is such a sweety of a Prehistoric Killing Machine. Robin the Bird Girl and Bernadette the Rock Girl were there with a few other Monsters who wanted to help show the World they were okay. Kimmy had our saddles put on. Yeah! She had saddles made for us. That was what she had been up too with the Soldiers! Cobalt, Ally, Becky, and me each got one! Yes we liked it. So we got ridden. Not a big deal. Hey I usually had either a pudge or a five year old on me most of the time these days. The American and Russian Presidents wanted to ride together on a tank much to the Chinese leaders delight as he wanted to ride Ally! We expected him to ride with the other two Leaders but there was no way he was passing up a Dino ride. Did not expect trouble from him anyway. He had stayed in the City last night. Wanted to see America in person he said. Becky got the Australian leader and I got one of the African leaders that had sent us some Lions. He was very impressed with me and said I was truly magnificent. A Middle Eastern Prince rode Cobalt. Said it was not unlike a Camel. He did have a long loping gate after all and I found it extremely sexy.

It was one hell of a parade and Windy waved at everyone so cutely! Some people along the street were bowing to her. A few had signs to hold up pledging loyalty. The Cult of Personality in the flesh. Monsters and leaders walked at times to greet the people and shake hands all friendly like. The citizens were really impressed from the looks of it as were the press! Heard they gave us very good reviews. They were here too! Every news agency on the Planet was represented. Even Fox News! Most of them understood what was happening and Windy's special effects show was quite impressive. Necessary too it turned out. Not hard for her but it sure looked spectacular. Fire works, Laser beams, Murder. Oh you didn't think some idiot would not try and take advantage of this? All these Leaders in the open with little if any security? Yes a couple news and military helicopters were flying around watching as Windy blasted the heads off at least four gunmen on roofs and a few in windows. Those chopper guys knew us. You could tell as every time Windy got one they held up numbers like Olympic judges. No idea what the judging criteria was but Windy scored very high. Some leaders may have understood what was going on but the crowd was oblivious. See?

One guy with a handgun ran out of the crowd right into Bernadette! He got spanked bare assed on world wide TV by a big rocky hand with Windy's full blessing. They put a sign around his neck that said, "I'm Stupid" and made him walk with his red butt hanging out. Effective? Frankly I have no idea but he sure seemed to be sorry by the time we got to the school.

Once through the heart of the city we sped up however. All the walkers climbed on and we went faster. Okay we went parade again as we got close to the school so we could impress the students, parents and everyone else there waiting for us. It was a crowd. They clapped and cheered so I kinda understood why Windy did it this way. Surprised me still that she understood enough to think it but it was a good idea. Remind all these leaders what it was all about! The next generation. THE KIDS! They will be the future. (If things don't change they will inherit a dead planet.) Well now that Windy has guaranteed a future. Tanks pulled up on the lawn. Windy would fix it easy.

The parking lot was full of folding metal chairs and I heard some grumbles about that. A couple Third World Leaders said they would be happy to have a nice metal chair back home. Less splinters than the packing crate they were using. They were arranged in a massive semi circle. Chairs were set up for us as well up by the podium facing the semi circle. On the grass behind the now impressive play ground lunch was being set up and prepared. Several big grills, thirty feet long, with lots of cooks. About a hundred people preparing lunch for us. We were a crowd!

Everyone took their seats and Windy stepped up to the podium. A Leader of some country in Eastern Europe stood and asked impatiently what most were probably thinking already. "You expect us all to just step down and surrender our Country's to you?" He showed respect in his tone however as he had seen enough to scare him.

Windy had stepped up to the podium looking around and smiled now holding up a hand. "Hold on peoples. Not all here yet. Be right back." She turned around and she was just gone. Vanished! Less than a minute later she was back and eighteen big Men with pants down around their ankles and butts red fell to the ground in front of her. "I call you, you come next time!" Her voice was scary. Then sweetly. "Now where was I? No I do not! I expect you beings to still continue to run your Country's for now. I have school! Oh and Teachers need big raise! Police and firemen too! Football players make millions Teachers can barely survive! Kimmy please explain." She smiled at Kimmy who stood and went forward with a handful of notes. No idea when they had set all this up. Probably had giant blue penis in me when they did!

Smiling herself Kimmy stepped up to the podium proudly and introduced herself to the World and said in a way her Father and Grand-Father would have been proud of if they still lived. "Things around the World will change! Just slowly. As Windy said she has school so she can not do everything yet. The World will become a better World for Everyone! You will still be responsible for running your own country's. Within reason. Any disputes between Nations will be settled by the Princess or by two out of three falls in the coliseum on Friday nights. Your choice! Military budgets can be cut greatly now to be used on infrastructure. Firemen, Police, EMT's, and Teachers all need to be paid much better. We are not alone in this Universe and we need to impress them and stop scaring them so much!" She pointed up! "Our World is amazing and so very beautiful! Let's not destroy it anymore. Let us heal it! The day to day running of your Country's is still your job. You will be monitored though and if something is not good Windy will always give you a chance to fix it before interfering. It will take several years but we will work to establish a one world economy. The College here is expanding and establishing a Spaceport and you may send students from your Nations to learn here with the Aliens. If you wish further input you are free to send people to ask. You send spy's however make sure they are eating only organic food as they give the Beast gas! We plan on hiding nothing." She looked at my Mom and blurted quick. "Except wedding plans!" A Soldier discreetly ran up to the General half out of breath right then, looking scared beyond belief. He whispered in the General's ear and the General went white. Kimmy just smiled at the podium. She knew what was coming it seemed. And I did too now. Windy seemed happy about it. "You don't need giant nuclear bombs anymore either! Just a waste of money! A practical demonstration is in order the Princess feels."

Windy stepped back up all smiles. "Except Tammy needs lots of grenades! She likes to blow things up! No worry, I have this General." She smiled big. The General appeared to still be in shock. "There are three launched nuclear missiles headed this way my people. Right at us." They began to panic as some got quick verification from their people and got up to leave. "SIT!" They did. "Students bring glasses quick!" Windy knew somehow and had prepared. Five year old's handed out dark sunglasses to people and put some on themselves. Windy waved me over and I went to MY Princess!

She stroked my fur as a soldier yelled. "ETA ninety seconds!" Like anyone could have gotten away far enough in time anyway. Windy kissed me on the head and whispered in my ear. Not telling! That Girl loved me though. Had no doubts now! Someone yelled asking if they should kiss their own asses goodbye like the Tiger was? We all looked in shock.

Becky just snickered and said. "It itched!" Knew the feeling well. We couldn't wipe and no one else was doing it for us! The Aliens had all walked over to watch as well. Since Becky was done licking herself however they watched us instead.

You would have been watching Becky too!

People began pointing as the rockets became visible specks in the sky. Windy snickered saying loudly. "Watch and learn My people!" Yeah I know this was coming from a five year old! Remember she had talked to God on a few occasions? Cocking my head I too watched. No fear. They grew and in a fraction of a second the world went pure white. Then total silence. Well except for the birds Squawking. The sky above was once again a beautiful blue a second later and looked like nothing had happened. Windy smiled and spoke gently. "We be right back as I have to deal with this." And space folded around her and I. That is intense. So we went to see Congress! Imagine that one. Security rushed at us as we stepped out of thin air and they went flying with a wave of Windy's hand. She pointed at the Senator shouting the loudest and spoke. "Shut up ASSHOLE! Come here!" He did but not of his own free will! Windy had him over my back and pants down in a flash beating it red. "You will leave my friend Kimmy alone or else! You will never try to nuke my friends again! Any more bad behavior you get time out on the Poophole Planet!" Crack on the rump with every word! He's lucky she does not do long speeches. That ass was very red as it was! No idea how she actually did it but a holographic image of him actually ordering the missile attack was playing above us. Frankly I would have just eaten him. She looked him in the eyes as he denied the image above and said with a nasty smile. "You can never lie again!" Then looking around the crowded room she said loudly with Venom. "None of you!" Could not help myself anymore and I snickered knowing her word was Absolute Law then. This one should be interesting! That Girl was pissed and may have gone too far but I did not care or blame her! We were all fed up with the Bullshit! She tossed the Senator off my back on to the floor hopped on and saying very happy. "Let's go home my Great Beast. Others need spanking!"

Had no idea who but I almost felt sorry for them. ALMOST! Loved this kid!

They were all standing mouths open when we reappeared. Seems they got a holograph as well. From my back she said softly, but everyone heard. "Any one here like to tell lies?" Okay certain Girls who shall remain nameless, Kimmy, Sabrina, Tammy, Teela, were just peeing themselves! Shame that only one had a diaper on. "Now everyone introduce yourselves to each other and I mean everyone!" All the children as well it seems. Parents too!

Mom had an autograph book and got them all! Windy must have put some compulsion in that statement I think. Definitely put some fear in them! Nothing like she had done in Washington though. Mom was in heaven. A certain leader of an African nation did ask my Mom for her number. So some of them were ruthless killers. Mom did not care. They were world famous. She'd have asked Jack the Ripper for his autograph if he was there and you would too. We mingled for a while as well. Windy just riding me through the crowd. Like we were waiting for something yet.

The silence started toward the road and flowed back to us. Most there probably recognized him as he came. Not easy though. A once proud Man in a uniform he now wore jeans and leather jacket as he came up to the edge of the crowd and waited looking terrifyed and beaten. He knelt in front of me once he got there. Hanging his head his whole body was shaking as he spoke. "I am General O'Donnell! And I am sorry!" You could hear the despair in his voice.

Did not look like much out of uniform. Almost like a homeless person. Only a one star General we knew but those clothes looked like Salvation Army rejects. The "Hammer" had told us about him! That he was a good Proud Soldier but an arrogant Man always! Now I smiled and he almost pooped his pants. His eyes looked truly empty. This was a haunted broken Man who had just seen everything he ever believed shattered. His power suddenly inconsequential! Windy I suspected had done something to him! Maybe shown him the truth but he was defeated now and I saw that easy. He was a broken Soldier and radiating such sorrow. How the mighty had fallen! He croaked out the words. "Thank you!" And I ate him as painlessly as I could.

World Leaders watched nervously as sentence was passed and executed. Everyone knew it was an Execution! Knew that was my role in the new regime now! I was the Executioner! Doctor Petrov started to clap first. Soon they all were as I swallowed the last of him. Yes I was good!

My Princess's word was Law! She told all exactly what he had done and why he just died and I think they all knew he was broken inside already. Windy had shown him his sins. All of them. The only choice he still had was DEATH, by his own hand or mine. Left him his pride this way. Knew I owed him that at least. He was necessary to create me!

Windy hopped off my back and patted me. "Good Beast!" She walked over to the TV cameras. Oh we had them all here! So I heard that in Japan and Korea both they showed me eating a Man in slow motion over and over for five hours discussing my technique. Got the highest ratings ever. Windy said so very gently into those cameras. "No more Monsters Doctor Whiting! You are not needed anymore. Find a nice beach and retire before I retire you! Your work is done! You can rest." Windy lifted her arms to the heavens saying something in ancient Sumerian and suddenly we had more Monsters there. Yikes! Lots more! Couple hundred at least! They all looked absolutely terrified. Can ya blame them though? Teleported from a cell to a crowded school yard surrounded by Military and five year olds! "Anyone anywhere makes any Monsters I will know! If you do not treat them very, very nice I will end you!" Her tone was gentle but there was no doubt left that she would keep her word. Some Men's blood ran cold at that statement. "Now World Leaders. Please help new Monsters get some food. They are hungry" They did! Kind of in awe but these beings looked starved as well! I did not know what that child knew but she had only made one mistake that I knew of, that I felt, but no one complained about the bad gas much later. One Star Generals are kinda rough on the tummy you see. Maybe she liked my stink as well!

Girls quickly encouraged Reporters to interview the new Monsters. Kids and Parents were very sweet to them instantly. The big Triceratops was a big hit! Especially with the five year old's. Ally liked her and they were playing right away. Ulrik and the claw hand Alien were talking heatedly off to the side and I knew it meant trouble. Finally they came over nervously and both bowed to Windy. Looked like they both lost the argument they were having. Might be on the verge of tears. Windy thanked and hugged them both and then she began Knighting world leaders. Some got the riot act as well but most said they were sorry and would do better now. A few with tears. You have to understand that this child had exhibited phenomenal power beyond their understanding by stopping three nuclear explosions and she was only five! Had to be thinking what would she be capable of as she grew? Stopped three Nuclear Explosions without breaking a sweat. We had an army of Monsters now and some real honest to God Aliens! All some of them had were mere Tanks and Planes. Many said it even. "Not going there!"

As lunch was ready to be served the Stupid Terrorist attack occurred. Only about two hundred idiots. Probably a good thing as they only had so much food for lunch and I was still very hungry. Was an interesting mix of Military, Christians and Muslims. Becky just grinned at me now and I knew she was finally okay! Cheerfully Windy said. "Eat my Beasts! Play my Horsewomen! EAT my people!" And she began shooing normal people to the BBQ. Becky was so terrifying and I was so proud of her! Terrorist bombs and bullets fell very short of the people at the school. Windy's force field was impenetrable. Soldiers just? Just stood around and watched like it was a smoke break. Most knew us well by now and did not want to waste ammo. The Leaders documents told them how many children I had coming. Well close guess. That those children would be loyal to ME! They would also be like me to an extent. Not as powerful as me but close enough to send fear through those coming! Not the Dickheads. I'll get there. Give me a bit.

We brought hellfire down on them with glee. My stereo blasted and we went to eat. There were a lot of them and the ground was red with blood before they were all dead. Windy was terrifying bringing death! Knew that may be a problem. Becky ate well! All the kids just cheered us on and that may have disturbed some leaders the most. Very scary! Hey five year old's are a bloodthirsty lot! Just ask a Teacher!

A Soldier yelled in a half assed way but still very serious. "Not fighting against them ever! NOPE!"

Pretty sure most of the leaders were thinking the same thing then!

The claw hand Alien finally went up to Windy and bowing said. "They will come now your Highness!" He looked scared. "You have challenged Their rule."

Windy all smiles said quietly to him. "Good. They won't win. Even without my army yet." Of course everyone heard! So Windy turned to those gathered and explained. "Hear that my people? Bad Aliens are coming soon! We need to get this cleaned up and now! All are invited to Beast's wedding tomorrow as well. One on Halloween too! Thank you all for coming. Tour of new Galactic Capital Youtopia this afternoon. Pope must go feed Lions now." There was many a gasp at that one. Then she added. "They each get three Chickens only your Holiness do not over feed them. Now let's eat!" Such a wicked grin. Yes she scares me but I love her so badly and would suffer anything for that child Princess! Believe me I do!

Okay maybe not that! Well Mrs. Gonzales was stalking our way! Did not look happy to have watched most of her children killing! Yes I understood but still looked for escape routes. Windy saw this too apparently and stood on my back spread her arms and said with such affection. "Love you Mama!" The anger melted from her Mother's face. She ran into her Daughter's arms and they hugged possibly the greatest hug that day or ever anywhere! Touching. Teela and Sabrina were right there demanding hugs. Mrs. Gonzales stepped back her arms wide. Sabrina and Teela went for Windy who held them while their Mother swatted their butts. All were laughing now. They hugged Mom well after they were done. Hey I got spanked by the Dali Lama! Buddhists believe in both discipline and dirty Pig Sex you know. How else do you think they keep warm in the Himalayas!

We ate! Yes because Windy told us too and everyone knew it. Still most were hungry. The food was fabulous. Scaryest part of the day was the fact that Sabrina, Tammy, and Bernadette were whispering with David Bowie on several occasions and they were all smiling. Oh I had no idea at the time but they were creating the

Inter-Galactic Co-ed Collegiate Football League! We had a stadium so why not! If we fed people to the Lions just for their beliefs we would be worse than those we fought! That said we could feed many for their crimes! A guy goes into a store and starts shooting. They take him alive. Find illegal weapons and explosives in his house and he walks on a technicality or sits in prison for sixty years till he dies. Video and eyewitness testimony. Not a doubt he did it? Prison is supposed to rehabilitate! Republicans want to make any abortion illegal until it is one of their children or grandchildren pregnant at fourteen. They claim the sanctity of human life but when a White Cop shoots a Black Man for no reason they want to give the Officer a medal!

Windy mingled. Heard some of what she said. She was polite and quite nice as she told Leaders what they needed to do to fix things in their Country. Most bowed well afterwards. Her advice was brilliant. Five going on Immortality! Well I was not the only one to realize this either. Everyone seemed to be okay with that though. Such a sweetheart!

Our claw hand Alien was listening as well. Saw him smile in approval a few times. His name which we still did not know was Illix. He came over to me and bowed. His voice was rather strained. He understood some things, perhaps lots and wanted to know if he was crazy. Either way his words would not make me happy. Yeah I still had floppy lips and he needed a speech! "Who am I working for?" He asked a tremor in his voice.

So few words but such a long answer. Well I told him. Was certain by now you see. Yes Lassie had manipulated most things but she had been manipulated as well. Many tweaks and adjustments through the time stream would be dangerous at the least. Every one has the potential to change everything drastically. However that said a large amount of data alone could be sent back easy. Perhaps bits to different points and different beings who were able to carryout the instructions with Lassie doing the work of organizing. Perhaps even Doctor Whiting had received instructions! This scared me a lot as it meant good people suffered because of Windy and I hoped that knowledge did not effect her mentally. If she knew and I was sure she did already. It did not matter if the end justified the means. That those who suffered would still forgive her would help. Well I forgave her! She did not create the evil but she manipulated it to get us HERE! She had made me! That she had saved the Planet and maybe even the Universe we both knew. Sometimes that Common Good argument is necessary! The needs of the many can outweigh the needs of the few. Often does! Did not have to like it! Didn't.

He went and groveled at her feet begging forgiveness. Hoping he had served her well. She hugged him. Told him he had served well and she was proud of him. Tremendous praise from a five year old Goddess!

Okay I sat thinking the scaryest thoughts I ever thought! Windy and Teela came to me with plates of food. Windy set her plate down in front of me. With a sweet smile she said to me. "Don't think to hard Pammy. I is fine thanks to you. You are wrong though. This is not all for me. It is all for you. I love you so much and always will." A tear ran down her cheek. She hugged me and left. Teela sat beside me and leaning on me ate. Now I thought real scary thoughts. Knew I had to sit down and have a talk with my future Mother-in-Law and soon!

Many loved me with all their heart and I loved them back just as strongly if not more. My mind tried to race but my Princess said not to so my heart shut it down. If you don't stop to enjoy the moment, life is not worth living. So I enjoyed the warmth of Teela's body pressed against mine. She fed me for a while. Looked so cute in that dress with her droopy dirty diaper showing. Both plates clean she whispered in my ear. "I poopy Mommy!" Yes she was. Went in the school and she led me to a room with a big crib in it that had a top that locked. Teela snickered in a childish way "Time out space for when we bad here." Okay I was nervous. Think she knew so she said. "We need a big cage at the compound so they can lock us both in there! Soundproof room to as I intend to scream while you ravage me! Oh and I have to talk to the Dean about a great strap-on! If I'm the Husband I need to fuck you hard!"

Oh I was beyond GOOD!

So as we boarded the buses to go to the college I had poop breath. Do not ask me why we took all the kids! Was more fun with them there for sure. Kids are such a joy and so honest. They have no problem telling me I have poop breath. They sat on leaders laps on the way and advised them. The Pope fed the Lions and it was on two hundred news programs that night. Such Drama Llamas those Reporters were. When the American President punched out the Fox News Reporter it was everywhere. Not even an election year.

That Reporter had gone up to the President furious saying. "You are insane! We are America and we will not let our freedoms go!" Right, free from what and who? Amazon, Google, and Starbucks? Wished we were free from Fox News! Seriously how free are you really?

The President had smiled and spoke. "We are more free right now than ever before." POW. Sucker punched the asshole. The applause was impressive. "Some one get that CNN Reporter a diaper!" Oh he was on the ground just pissing himself bad. Russian President came up and the two Presidents high-fived. On air. Speeches were made. Many Knighthoods bestowed.

Seemed to be going well. Shame I can't get that lucky though can I? Windy got up in front of the cameras smiling sweetly, than?! "Dow People! Your Kevlar gives my Beast bad gas! You fix!" Talk about dying from embarrassment. Everyone was looking at me. No one made a sound. Except me! BRRIPT! The whole world just heard me rip one! They got to see a couple dozen world leaders rolling on the floor pissing themselves as well but still. Poophole Planet was sounding good about now!

Quickly I slunk off to the Spaceship hanger in total shame. Cobalt followed me. He knew my shame! He loved my shame too! Okay he was horny too and actually got me up the shame! That cheered me up! Well!

College students were all actually happy to see more Monsters coming to live and work and the college. Many students were working temporarily on the enlargement for money and extra credit. Still plenty of work to go around for the Monsters. We had our own supermarket now. Those taking business majors would be able to learn first hand and start a business from the ground up but we would need full time workers and many Monsters showed interest. Most were grateful as it was possible they may not be safe yet off campus. Students liked the ones we already had and were excited about the new ones. Had about three hundred now. Two more cafeterias were being put in fast. One would be open twenty four hours a day even. Lots of new housing was being worked on. This place was bustling with activity.

Tammy was just driving around the forklift with the Oristrii on it. Still wearing her grenade launcher so no one stopped her. Both seemed happy about this arrangement. Think about it? It had legs most likely but they were too short to walk with. You have to remember this things fur was extremely stiff. Springy like metal, sparkly, and soft but about seven feet across which best guess was about three feet too short for its legs. Well that was what Tammy said. Her radar penetrated enough to know it was about the size of a big Cat or big Rabbit in there. Had eyes we think. Floppy ears possibly. Sparkled nicely when Tammy got close. It liked watching the scenery move for a change it seemed as it felt happy! Kinda radiated its emotions outward. Colored lights in its fur which were like those fiber optic lights were also an indicator of it's mood. We were sure we had it right side up as it had calmed down and gone yellow. No idea what or how it ate or drank. Almost the entire scientific department had guesses already, probably all wrong. It was kinda nice even which shocked our Aliens. Had a temper though. If you felt anger coming from it, it was best to run. It had a static charge that could kill. Not quite lightning levels it was thought but still bad. Get a hundred pissed and they could do major damage to a City which is supposedly why they were eradicated. There were almost no records of them left and they had not been studied as they were too dangerous. Where Doctor Whiting ever found one made our Aliens nervous. Lots made them nervous but they were not sharing all they knew about many things. Then again there was too much to learn about many things.

Cobalt was definitely a Feral Luggun. They were extinct and had been for seven hundred years. Their DNA had been manipulated and a smaller less intelligent and less prone to excitement version was created for their meat. Both were now unique like me. Ally was not pure Dinosaur as human genes were spliced in to her for intelligence. We suspect. That Whiting was looking for weapons as well we had no doubt. Most of this was NOT in the leaders packets. The problem with knowing something is you have no idea if others do. So you just assume they know and never bring it up. Which was our problem. Almost from the start.

Hectic at the college however as the buildings were all getting plumbing and electrical installed. Both Military and Private Contractors worked side by side with students and Monsters. Impressed by Windy's work though. They were working hard. Money can't buy happyness but it can buy plenty of action. Okay money can rent happyness and I am sure some of you have taken advantage of those pretty Girls out renting it on those street corners. Oldest paid profession in the Universe. Nothing wrong with it! To those who say that it is wrong, what do you think that ring you gave your Wife is? Or your Husband gave you? Payment! If Men thought of and treated Girls as equals maybe it would be different. As for you Girls do not go for looks! Most serial killers were quite handsome! If you go with a guy because he has money you are a Whore too! Talk to the nerds and the ugly guys. Give them a chance. How many Girls wish they had given a Bill Gates the time of day before? They may be wonderful people but you shut them out because they have a big nose or something! Look at a Twinkie! Plain on the outside but creamy joy on the inside. So many chemicals!

Don't sell your love for money. Selling your body is fine just get paid up front and set the rules. Nothing wrong with Prostitution! Many of my readers I am sure agree with that. Can be cheaper then a date these days too. What is that you ask? Restaurant? Forty bucks or more. Movies? Thirty or close. On the corner for forty bucks you are guaranteed a hand job if not a blow job. Be safe though! Use a condom.

Wait where was I?

Oh yes the Spaceport, I mean college. Well the official Spaceport would go next to it. We were in Negotiations for the property I was told. Hey I was to damn busy Raping and preforming Illegal Medical procedures to do everything! Not enough space inside the wall to do it near well and we wanted something impressive. You invite dignitary's you do not park them behind a cheap bar. Okay maybe some. Windy had a dream! I shared it. She assured me we could fix the damage. We only have one Planet! If we kill it where are we going to go then? Oh right those Huge City's we built on Mars and the Moon twenty years ago! FUCK YOU NASA!

Sorry I get carryed away sometimes. Have anger issues, remember?

World leaders began leaving. Most reluctantly! Said they had the time of their lives and I believed it. Certainly a day to remember! Windy told them to refocus their Military into cleaning up the pollution and building a better ecofriendly infrastructure. Keep the world in mind and think green. End Poachers! No. Not end poaching. End Poachers! Not a five year old's mistake either as she meant it. She watched lots of nature shows. She saw the carnage. Some poachers did it because it was easy money. But some did it because it was the only way to keep their family's alive. Arresting them would not help. Giving them a way to feed their family's would!

Sure I know it looks like the story is at an ending and I am still going on! Windy was the one who said I could not get married on Saturday and had to wait for Halloween now! Marry all four HorseMen at the same time. When asked why she just said "Busy tomorrow!" Oh she was not wrong. Knew I would be! Had six million three hundred and twenty one thousand five hundred and eight assholes to eat yet. What Windy said.

The afternoon wound down. The American President had to go to do damage control! The Russian President said he should go as well. With the American President to Washington. Pretty sure he was going for the humor of the situation. Kimmy handed him some diapers just in case. Shaking his head now the American President held out a hand for some. Seems Congress was silent as no one wanted to say the truth. Well not after the bout of violence that broke out right after we had left and they realized Windy had meant it! Could not lie anymore! C-span was showing reruns of Gilligan's Island. Improved their ratings! We Love you Gilligan!

We had almost a hundred Reporters here so we knew everything right away. Parades and Protesters were clashing in bloody violence all over the planet. On every continent! Okay it was only a small scuffle between a couple Emperor Penguins on Antarctica. Windy got sad about that. We like Penguins. Was sad about the other violence as well. Some Teachers came up and said that it would be inevitable. That Windy could not save everyone from pain. People would get hurt always for their beliefs. The worst belief they could have was that they would not get hurt. Most were willing to risk pain at least. It would take them time to realize the truth. That Hate itself was the true evil. The Teachers told her that she had achieved something great already and should be happy and proud. She knew but it still made her sad.

Windy said we would meet them all back at the compound later. Hopped on my back and spurred me on. Cobalt quickly sat and just watched us go. That was weird. Maybe Windy did something to him. Maybe a bribe! Trotted down the street turning when told. Otherwise neither of us spoke. Still I felt content. It was weird. Went to the beach finally were we sat in the sand and that little Girl only five years old poured her heart out to me. Told me things that scared me so very bad! Not that she had lied when she said the Aliens would not win. Knew that was a lic. We would lose if we don't get some help. Not that Friends would die either. No.

What scared me most was when she said those words in such a way as to leave no doubt how she meant it. "I love you Pammy!" Then she kissed me. On the lips! "We will rule together as King and Queen." Did not have to poop. Or I would have. Now I stared at her and she nodded sweetly.

"B-b-b-but you're only five!" Heck yeah I stammered in terror.

"Told you this was all for you Pammy! Meant it. Loved you from almost that first night. You were so special and willing to die for me. Knew I would always love you. Yes you are safety check but also if I get mad I can not control you like others to get my way. One day I too will have your Pups!"

"B-b-b-but you're five." She had drawn a heart with Windy loves Pammy in it in the sand with her Scepter.

"Now yes, but not forever. I will wait. We have eternity!" She hugged me and God help me I hugged back. Sat that way for a while watching the sun set. Thought the worst over. You would think I would know better by now! As the stars came out she pointed at some and told me who lived there. Where trouble was coming from. Realized she suddenly sounded much older. The way she put those words together. So I licked her head. "Yes we must go. I am hungry."

Sounds okay? Well I thought so. Yeah again! Then she told me where to turn and I wondered where the heck we were going? Finally she told me to stop in front of a building. An old apartment building? She urged me forward and the locked security doors just opened for Windy. In we went. Hey, I was beginning to suspect someone bad lived here and I was killing soon. Had been doing little else now hadn't I? We stopped in front of a door and Windy actually knocked.

Odd!

Windy sighed. "Open up I hungry!" Heard the lock open then as the door swung open and Windy urged me in. So I just pushed someone back I barely recognized. Looked so different out of her uniform after all. Those sweatpants however were so tight on her massive butt I began to drool already! She was in shock. Maybe fear!

Stuck my snout in her crotch as I pushed and now I recognized her. Windy pushed the door shut still on my back once we were in. "W-w-why are you here?" She said so scared!

Windy smiled at her speaking sweetly. "To eat. I get ice cream Beast get you!" She said that so sweetly too. We just stood there as Windy went in the kitchen and pulled a chair over to climb on and open the freezer before looking at me. "We don't have lots of time Pammy. Bedroom that way. Beast HUNT!" That last was a definite order and my shock broke. Wondered suddenly if this big hunk of flesh tasted as good as their milkshakes! Gonna find out!

Hey the Dean had said I should rape her earlier. So I finally did! She screamed all those nice things. STOP! Don't! Please! For the first three minutes of my savaging. After that it was. "Ghurnlik, ulp, graaa." And "Oh GOD!" A lot. Windy yelled she was out of ice cream and wanted more. Such a big beautiful Fat Girl! Stunningly beautiful naked! Would be back for more of her! Trotted out once I got my tail out of her grip. Windy hopped on and we just left. Knew where Windy wanted to go now and just went. Drive-thru! Okay! Walk-thru!

You know which one too right? Windy told them their Manager have rough night so store must be spotless tonight. Yes I was freaked out by this but kind of understood. The future Windy was already here in a way! She may have a thousand year old mind in there but was still not ready to grow up yet. As she had said she had school yet. Well I assumed there was a partition in there that could be open or closed by her older self. This was her way of telling me things the five year old did not nor could not quite understand yet. She had money too.

"Home my Beast!" She held me tight as I ran fast in joy.

Her words as we went will die with me but she loved me so much! As we got close I asked her. "What about Teela?"

She snickered. "She is your first Wife. You gonna have many. They don't mind each other my future wife! Happy to share you."

Got extremely nervous here as you can imagine and had to say it. "But I can't marry you till you are older."

Smiling she spoke. "Fourteen years till our wedding!"

Okay I knew the answer was NOT going to make me happy. Well I could do the math. "When you are nineteen? Why not eighteen?"

She laughed saying. "Busy that year!" Everything she told me sent terror through me. Yet such love as well. She had already told me I would be marrying several and never divorced or widowed. Mighty Big a me too! Okay I had a hundred and six Girlfriends now why not twenty Wives! She gave no numbers but only laughed. And you ask why I felt terror!

They were all waiting for us. Several World Leaders even. They asked where we were and what we did? Windy snickered. "Working on deal for free milkshakes!" If we are lucky. Windy leapt off as I peed on Cobalt's Pee-Pee! She heard him coming and got the heck out of the way fast. He was in me before I let loose with urine. Ignoring us Windy said. "I hungry. Let's eat." And she walked inside leaving ME, I mean us. The love in that child was immense. Lots more then what was in me! You have no idea what was in me. Just hoped they saved me some food. Was gonna be here a while. He had stamina. Oh I howled!

A little pain in there but I was fine with it.

CHAPTER 15 COMPLICATIONS
Saturday October 9th

By morning the world was in flames! Okay it wasn't but I sure as Hell was! Woke hot very, very HOT! Panting very hard. Teela was instantly alarmed. Well she was the only one with me. Even Cobalt had agreed to sleep elsewhere last night. With Tanya and Bernadette! Do not ask as I have no clue. Always afraid to ask. Cobalt was happy as all heck! Windy had said Teela and I needed this night after postponing the wedding. Quickly concerned, Teela shoved her fingers in my ass quick! No it was not for something perverted! Did feel good as it itched back there. Always does! Definite animal thing! Hard to feel a forehead with fur now isn't it?! Her urgent words held her fear. "How are you Pammy? Any pain anywhere?" Shook my head. "You're burning up! We have to cool you down and now. Bath tub sexy." Quickly I went into the hall and toward the big tub. Sabrina and Kimmy were in the hall already and instantly looked concerned. Before they could ask Teela told. "She is burning up! We have to cool her down. I'm scared."

Sabrina smiled as she said. "Taking your fingers out of her butt would be a start on cooling her down." Teela blushed bad but did not pull her fingers out. "I'll call the Vet. You take care of your Girlfriend." She went for her phone fast.

Teela got me in the tub climbed in with me and turned on the cold water! And I mean ice cold! As the tub filled around us she stayed in there holding me in tears. The cold had some interesting effects. Teela's nipples looked hard enough to cut steel! Like I would pass that up! Think she knew and used it to roll me on my back into the ice water. AHH! NICE!

It took a while for Kimmy and Sabrina to return with the phone. "Sorry, we had trouble getting through. The world is in chaos. How are you feeling Pammy?" Sabrina asked.

Growling I said. "Better now. Cooler."

Doctor Lucy asked since it was on speaker. "How cold is the water?"

Kimmy asked. "How cold is it Teela?"

Intensely she said. "About f-forty degrees."

Sabrina asked. "How long have you been in the water Teela?" She did not sound concerned mostly but curious.

Teela sighed. "About twenty minutes now." Doctor Lucy gasped. "Got cold at first but then I was warm. And not because Pammy is chewing on my tit either." Okay I was! Heard no complaints. Was being gentle. "My fingers are still in her rump and she feels cooler."

Doctor Lucy asked urgently. "Does Teela feel cold?"

"YEAH!" Teela yelled.

"My fingers are up her butt now and she feels fine." Sabrina said. Really? Tried to see.

Teela glared at her Sister. "I am telling Mom!" There was snickering on the phone. Hey if it was good enough to do to me Sabrina could show her Sister how it felt.

Windy stormed in and looked shocked at her big Sister. "Why your fingers in Teela's butt?"

Kimmy snickered. "You just made Pammy warm up the water. It's all yellow now!" Not the only thing yellow as I was sure the Doctor was on the floor from the sounds of it.

Shaking her head Windy asked. "How is my Beast?"

Doctor Lucy gasped out. "I can't tell without an exam. Bring her in. Bring Becky too." The line went dead. Probably a good thing too.

Mrs. Gonzales came in took one look and asked. "Sabrina why are your fingers up your Sister's butt?" Sabrina pulled them out and Teela sighed! So they explained what they knew. Teela was put in a robe. Worked for me really. It was Saturday and I had no intention of letting her get dressed till Monday.

Windy said sounding kinda weird. "Now I must put out fires. Take Beasts for check ups. Take Dean. Get milkshake first." Alright I was game but?

Oh the world was not On Fire but riots and armed coups were popping up everywhere. Windy was taking Tammy with her to settle things down. Lots of grenades too! Windy whispered something to the Dean. No idea what but the Dean had a diaper on so she was okay. Just hoped I would enjoy it! The only time they whispered was when I was being set up somehow. Yeah they kinda whispered a lot now didn't they?

Did not let Teela get dressed. Got her in the car and we left. No idea why the Leader of Guatemala was going with us. There were a few Leaders at the compound still. Probably waiting for the violence in their home Country's to die down I felt. We hoped Tammy had lots of grenades. All I said on the way into town was. "That drive-thru!" Probably could not get a good milkshake down in Guatemala and he should really try one while he was here. While they ordered I jumped out and ran around to the doors. By the time they got to the window the screams had started! Different words this time. "YES!" "EAT ME BITCH!"

Glared at the employees as I trotted out with pride. One handed me a milkshake with a grin. One gulp!

Kimmy drove toward the clinic saying. "Someone should probably let her know she is having Puppys soon." The Guatemalan leader was nodding at that. He spoke little English so Sabrina was translating for him. Nice guy for a killer and drug lord. Maybe not personally but he had some strong connections. He protected them and when asked why he said they had more guns then the army! This is true! Drug Lords can pay better too. Sabrina was asking about those things. He seemed nervous but not too bad. Windy had forgiven Leaders if they stopped their evil ways. Maybe that was why he was afraid to go home. Some would never stop till we stopped them and we knew that. Might be able to help him.

There will never be a Democratic Utopia! Democracy is chaos. That said there will never be a Communistic Utopia either. Only form of government capable of a true Utopia is a Totalitarian Dictatorship! As long as those in charge are nice.

The Dean was watching the news on her phone. Turns out Windy was going around giving time outs! Let Tammy blow some things up then everyone sat on their rumps for an hour. Groups, City's, whole Country's, sat. Planes came down like a child placing a toy on the ground. Could not get up. Many people just pooped themselves where they sat! Most Country's would settle down quick. Those who did not? The steel cage! No disqualification! Who doesn't like some wrestling?! Friday nights at the Coliseum! Gonna pack that place all weekend long!

Friday Night Fights! Saturday College Football! Sunday Gladiators and Lion feedings!

Got to the clinic finally and I actually felt okay as we pulled in. Got out of the car and WHAM! Pain hit hard and I staggered. Oh SHIT! BLARPLE! So I did. It happens! That was gross though and I almost fell in it. Doc Lucy was out there in seconds looking at the situation in a panic. "Get her in the operating room now!" That started a panic. "It's just a precaution. We probably can't move her if she can't walk so we need her to go there while she can." They knew better but they also knew it was smart. Better safe than sorry. The Doc scraped up some poop while they guided me into the operating room. My legs were getting weak. Problem was I would not fit on the operating table. Becky smiled at me as I lay on the floor on my back.

Girls knew what was going to happen by now so to speed things up they quickly got stool and urine samples from Becky while the Doc came to me. "Pammy are you in pain?" Shook my head no. She looked at me strangely. "Is something wrong? Why aren't you talking?"

"Frooop nicy pluu." Was what I said. Not what I meant.

Becky was just rolling on the floor giving another urine sample. Everyone was in shock till Becky finally managed to say. "Talking with floppy lips hard right side up!" Well it was!

Okay I would have laughed too but that's when they shoved a candy thermometer up my butt! 97.5! Normal for a healthy ProtoDog. She pressed on my tummy and I yelped. "Could be a bowel obstruction." BRRIPT! "Oh that stinks. What has she been eating?"

Kimmy grinned bad and spoke. "Muslims, Christians, maybe a Unitarian or two."

Teela smiled at this. "Don't forget the food with all the Wasabi and Hot Sauce." That was the best part!

Doc Lucy looked appalled at that. "The Hot Sauce most likely! It will cause gas in Dogs." Good to know!

The look on my face must have been heartbreaking. Teela knelt beside me and kissed me. "I love your farts hunny. You will eat hot sauce forever!" She was sniffing. Lucky me! Oh they had a little Beast in them as well and most animals scent mark things.

Doc Lucy pressed around more. Then came the ultrasound. She was looking for bowel obstructions. Nothing. Well no obstructions. Then she found the uterus. I mean problem! Same thing. "Oh MY!" That was an understatement! All asking at once what was wrong. "Either she has mutant parasites or the blue guy knocked her up! There are now six Babys in there. And three of them are ready to come out!" Dead silence! Well until. BRRIPT! There was gagging now. From some. Some edged closer. Knew who the methane addicts were around here.

Becky snickered asking concerned. "Not this minute though right?"

Doctor Lucy shook her head. "No. But she is in prelabor. The problem causing the pain is her body is doing something impossible. It is moving the fetuses around. The new ones are not ready. Probably another month. She is going to have a partial birth. Only the Pups are coming now! No other reason for her body to be doing this. Moving the Pups to the front. Feeling better now Pammy?" Did so I nodded. "Okay. No idea how long you have. Try not to exert yourself Pammy and relax."

There may have been some hysterical laughter. Dean Kelly asked an astounded Veterinarian. "So her raping a restaurant managers is out of the question?" Apparently it was! And I wanted another milkshake now. That Big Fat Sexy Gorgeous Woman's milkshake brings all the ProtoDog's to her yard! More to eat and love people! More to eat and LOVE! Eat a lean steak and a marbled one at the same time! It is in the fat where you find the flavor. She had flavor!

Okay Becky got an ultrasound too and would be a Mama in about three weeks. It was Teela's idea to go find Becky's family and tell them the good news once away from the vets. Dean Kelly said we had to make a stop first.

Did not have to ask what this out of the way store sold. Name said it all. "Dominance". The Dean was even a frequent customer. Even knew the Clerk by name. Yep it was Ricky Bitch! And I had thought the bondage section of Dark Desires was something scary. The shit on these walls looked PAINFUL! Wanted to get some. Realized what had been whispered about earlyer by Windy. I'm sure she was not specific but she knew I liked to get beaten and loved both me and Teela! Teela got a new wardrobe of the Deans design. Pretty sure two Girls who shall remain nameless, Kimmy and Sabrina, were hoping they could get tortured a bit as well.

Teela in the hottest black leather outfit now grabbed my rump and said. "After you give birth Bitch this butt is mine!" You should see the strap-on she was wearing! My heart went Pitter Patter. Our nice Guatemalan Dictator was amazed with this place. Bought some stuff for him. He was grateful. Dean Kelly even offered to use it on him later. If you only knew the kinky shit world Leaders get up to! I know I had wanted Teela naked all day but this was better! The head piece did not cover her face but her gorgeous hair in that top knot ponytail was hot!

Okay we swung by the drive-thru and got lunch. That Big Manager came over with a smile for a kiss. With tongue. She started it! Head for Becky's Aunt's house. Her Mom and Aunt were both outside getting grocery's from the car as we pulled up. The Aunt almost freaked as we got out. Did when she recognized Becky. Becky's younger Sisters ran to her and hugged her well. We had extra food so we went in and fed her family while things were explained. Her Sisters squealed when they heard Becky was probably having Puppys. It was Puppys! You'd squeal too. Said they may be Tigers and we had to wait to find out. My impending delivery was told as well. When they asked who the father of my Pups was even the Dictator pointed at Teela. Had no idea how they knew. She had the robe on to cover her..um You Know?

We stayed a while and Becky got to play Rabid Barbies with her Sisters. Kimmy showed them all how to play. It is awesome to play! Lots more fun then a tea party.

Good thing we had some Rabid Barbies in the trunk. Right between the fifty caliber and the fifteen gallons of lube. How do you think we got Teela in that tight outfit! Well I was gonna have some Puppys and get my ass power-fucked soon! Heck yeah I was excited. Kinda why we stayed in town for a while. In case labor got strong.

Doc Lucy had work to do at her clinic so we stayed close. A few twinges were all so we checked in with the Doctor and went to check other things. College and

Doctor Petrov. Told her what was going on. She called Ulrik and Bob. They came quick. That Cobalt impregnated me worried them. Not safe creatures in large numbers it seems.

Housing was ready for the Aliens and students. Coliseum was done as well. Lions were happy. They had their TV and three Queen sized Canopy beds now. Liked Becky a lot. Check on Miss Moneypenny. Certain Girls were bringing her food and changing her bucket. The Dean spanked her. Telling the Dictator he would get worse later the guy got a boner. "Shame I don't have my strap-on. Oh wait Teela has one!" So we watched Teela rape a Secretary. She needed to get some practice. Both were smiling after and I was smiling to as I knew what I was getting later. You just wish! If I put the videos in here most of you would have masturbated to death by now!

We asked if she had any Pets at home we should be taking care of. She gasped out. "My Daughter is doing that. Called her and let her know I would be tied up at work for a few days."

With a snort the Dean said. "More like weeks!" She gently stroked Miss Moneypenny's cheek like a loving owner would. "Maybe forever. Be a shame to let a piece of worthless shit like you go. Ever!" SMACK! What a slap. That Secretary quivered.

Sobbing out. "Yes Mistress." With a smile. That Girl put me to shame.

Sucked I was supposed to take it easy! Screw it! RAWR! Dean Kelly laughed as I too raped her Secretary and left her a drooling mess.

That felt better. Headed for the car head held high.

They asked if I felt okay and I did. Got back to the compound in time to listen to Windy ranting about naughty peasants. That one I understood. They are so damn uppity. Went to her and cuddled. Her Mom joined us. Gave the, you have to remember they are just children and will learn, speech. To a five year old. Disturbing? Not sure.

Windy sounding calmer. "I know Mama. That is why they only got time outs instead of spankings." Cuddling in she said. "Love you Mamas both." She rubbed my belly. Well as much as she could. Had all these big milk filled boobys now. Eight D-cups. Had not noticed them get bigger. I mean when did that happen?

Looking at Mrs. Gonzales I asked her. "Mom can you help me?" Her eyebrow went up questioning. "I never even Babysat. I have no idea how to be a Mother." Hey it was a big thing to me.

She kissed my head. "Oh hunny. It's okay. Most here are more than happy to help. Me, your Mom, even the crazy diaper lady will help and we will probably all have too! Seriously sweety we are talking like two hundred children Pups. I like the Puppy Daycare Windy made but I won't do it by myself but I will work there to help. Teela and Sabrina will help as well. They helped with their siblings a lot. Just hope someone ordered lots of piddle pads!"

SHIT!

We lay together till supper. It was nice. Teela kept her distance. Probably did not want to accidentally poke her Mom with her strap-on! Kimmy and Tammy were tutoring her. Sabrina had her younger Brother and Sister out playing with the Triceratops. Kind of a nice family sort of night. Warmed my heart. What brought tears to my eyes was the sudden pain.

"Are you okay Pammy?" Mom Gonzales asked when I flinched.

Windy just sighed her voice so tender. "They're coming very soon."

Like they did not all hear and know. Teela was there with her fingers in my vagina fast and rough. Good thing I like it rough! "No dilation yet Baby but our kids will be here soon! You hungry?"

Shook my head. "No but you eat. Thirsty." So we had supper and I lay between my Teela and Windy with a bowl of broth and one of ice cold spiked lemonade. Spiked with Teela pee of course! Hey I could tell easily and had to say nothing to get this. Oh the love I felt!

Slow quiet night after that. Contractions were light and I was only at a two by ten O'clock. With assurances and promises to wake them, kids were put to bed. It might not be till morning they were told and Windy smiled and said yes they should sleep. I knew she knew! Down to the second probably. Knew we had several hours too. Doctors were called. Again.

Cobalt was a nervous wreck. He knew these were not his yet but knew his were in there as well. No idea how. Those ones were not canine or human so whose could they be? He loved me though. Brutus may have thought he could be the father and was worryed himself. Baby Sandy was asleep in the playpen with a bottle. Teela wrapped around me and I to slept.

CHAPTER 16 PUPPY'S BIRTHDAY
Sunday October 10th

Woke about one AM to a loud gasp of "Madre de Dios" and a snicker. From Mom Gonzales who was laying with us. Must have found Teela's package! I snickered. Mom Gonzales said quietly but longingly. "You are one lucky Bitch Pammy!" Oh I was. Even if that contraction hurt! It got crowded in that room quick however. A dozen pair of fingers later they let Doctor Lucy stick hers in as well.

"Only a three Pammy but it won't be long now." Doc Lucy said smiling in her jammys. So cute.

At two AM I was up to a seven and they decided to wake the little ones since Teela was done raping her older Sister! It's what we do for entertainment. Teela needed the practice and Sabrina looked horny. Their Mom started it! Fun to watch. Even more so knowing she was practicing for me. Not incest though. Brutus and Cobalt were giving her pointers I think. They approved of her fucking me! Sabrina was drooling good before long.

Ah, screw the Olympics! We will start our own Inter-World Games with Raping and Decapitation as events! I'll get the gold in both easy! Grenade shooting would be fun. Competitive pooping?

As kids came in my heart began racing and Doctor Lucy got concerned. Teela said I was fine and not to worry. Well she had whispered in my ear. "Hope you liked the show because you're next!" It was a great show. "WOW!" Strong one. Teela was trying to distract me and I knew it. Loved her.

They had things hooked up to me all over the place. Three things belted around my waist looking for fetal distress. What The Fuck About Maternal Distress! This hurt! WOW! Strange looking things. Doctor Petrov said Bob had sent them. Readings were being taken and fed to the college and Bob, as was a live video feed. Sure the video feed was going straight to YouPorn as well. They would love it. Doctor Petrov looked at Lucy and said. "We may need you to break a few laws Lucy!" Lucy looked at her scared about that. "Hey there are close to a hundred Girls all most likely going to give birth in a one week time period. Yes to Puppys as well. Everything has had a tail so far! It may get hectic and we may need all the help we can get!"

Sabrina perked up now. "Hey do we have enough room!"

Doctor Petrov scoffed. "We have thirty eight delivery rooms! Almost an entire floor! The rest is a NICU! Our problem is not enough trained personnel! We have feelers out but this is a unique situation! We know so little yet! This tonight will help. We may have to do ear tags to identify the Pups once born."

My Mom snickered. "What about some Mid-Wives? Can they help?" Doctor Petrov was nodding at that.

Dean Kelly spoke up. She was nursing Sandy as she watched. It was cute and I hoped someone got a picture. "I know they can't do much probably but the Students who have had biology could assist in some way I'm sure!"

Doctor Petrov sounded grateful. "Yes both good ideas. What we learn here will tell us how they can help."

Windy smiled while she stroked my head. Teela was stroking somewhere else. "If we have to hire people we can! Just for a week. I see it on TV sometimes. Doctors go help elsewhere." Yes they did! Had lots of money. Concierge Veterinarians!

Kimmy snickered into her phone. "No she is awake. Having Puppys in the next couple hours!" Pause. We were all looking. "Well you will be too in about two months." We heard the shock. "Yes she impregnates Girls with her tongue! We have children here so be careful but I will put you on speaker." Everyone was whispering trying to figure out who it was. Knew of only one person who had Kimmy's number and did not know so had suspicions.

"Hi Beautiful!" She had a beautiful voice. "Knocked me up did you?" Did not sound angry.

"Yes Susan." I grumphed trying not to laugh.

"Good thing I love Puppys. How many you having Girl?" She sounded happy still. I was not going to explain it so I told her three. "You'll have to bring them by when you can. When they are old enough they can get free milkshakes too."

Tammy was sitting there saying. "Pammy has a new Girlfriend." Over and over. Well Teela was getting pissed and throwing things. Tammy ducked them all until Windy did something and POW! In the head with a pillow. Do not mess with Windy's family!

This phone call was all my fault. Well she took a nap after being attacked this morning and could not sleep now. She congratulated me and said good luck with kissy sounds. Teela leaned close and said quietly so they all heard. "It's okay. I can share. Just you remember whose Tag you wear!"

Growled back. "Never forget my love!" They all went Aww. In for the kill. "But?" Pause to let them get nervous. "Can you do that to your Sister again sometime. Was busy. Hard to see this time." Hard to get out but worth it! The looks on their faces were priceless. Sabrina blushed. Saw that nod. Most were shocked or terrifyed so I snickered. OW! Kids are amazing but this giving birth kinda sucked! Had bullets go through my body, Pooped out over a hundred pounds at one hunching, but this SUCKED! Imagine getting your appendix removed without anesthesia or pain killers through the rectum! By a Man who can palm a basketball! Seriously someone was rearranging my insides.

Well I could feel the twisting and all.

OH MY GOD!

Doctor Lucy freaked. "Holy Shit she's crowning!" That got attention. "Pammy why didn't you say something?" Well when in Pain it was impossible and after I didn't care. If not for the pain of rearranging this would have been easy as these Pups were not as big as Cobalt big blue ding dong, who was in the way. Well he was licking my butt and tail gently for the last hour. They tried to push him out of the way but his head was the size of a buffalo! "Oh my God its coming out!" Had bigger things come out my butt. This was nothing!

"Holy Shit it looks like Teela!" Kimmy yelled in shock.

Several questionable Mexican phrases were heard. Windy just snickered. Doctor Lucy was drying it and checking it over quick. A Female with a white ear and darker fur. That did look like Teela! The Doctor put it to a breast and it went nuts. Tears streamed down my face. My heart felt ready to explode! MY BABY! Licked my Baby.

I WAS A MAMA!

FUCKIN A YES!

Barely noticed the next Girl when she came out. Then he came out and I knew who was going to make me want to kill! Violently! Indiscriminately! He looked like Teela but you could tell he was going to be trouble which is why I named him what I did. "Grendel!" I growled out. Yes I had been thinking of names. Not much else to do for the last ten hours!

Windy smiled. "Grendel bad monster?!"

Tammy snickered knowingly. "Yes he was, but Beowulf defeated and killed him." What a straight Man she was. Setting up what came next.

Kimmy snickered now. "So his Mama came and destroyed everything!"

Teela spoke with such passion. "Beowulf better never show up or I will kick his ass! No one hurts my kids!" And I was gonna marry her! God I truly was lucky! They tried to save the placentas.

Windy shook her head and ordered suddenly with conviction. "Becky eat them!" They were all shocked Windy wanted them destroyed! And I was shocked that Becky never hesitated and ate them quickly.

They were asking not so nicely why Windy did that and she just smiled. Tammy told them why though. "Stem cells! They could be used by some to create powerful Creatures." There was nodding then. "Becky or Pammy will need to eat them all!"

OH SHIT!

Could not even remember for sure. Knew I had raped strangers. Maybe a few. My head was twisted up now. Windy whispered in my ear. "It's okay. Sleep my Beast." And I was out!

But I was a MAMA!

AFTERWARD:

Things have gotten weirder and the stakes like Windy's power have become unbelievable! What comes next is a desperate attempt to knock up the Universe, I mean save the Universe! Maybe both? Hopefully all Secrets will be revealed and Questions answered. If not? TOUGH!

Still no incest in here. Well no incest as defined by law. Then again they are only Mexicans. Under Republican Manifesto guidelines Mexicans are not defined as human along with the Blacks. Watching the news daily I find myself wishing Windy was real. Ten minutes of Fox News sounding like Saints battling the scourge of Liberal demons and their inhuman legions I wish Pammy would decapitate me.

You must remember this is told by a Dog from a Dog's perspective. If you have ever had a Dog you know they eat poop and roll in dead things. Puts a bit in of perspective in there. That said. You try typing a novel with a pencil held in your mouth. Also I swear I did not let Windy read this or the first book. Maybe I should have? Well Windy fixed this one as well and it is larger. Now I honestly understand typing with a pencil is a lot of work. Understand why you might cut corners.

Just might have to let Windy read Book Three before it is published. Had a Great Pyrenees named Windy once upon a time. Well we called her Windy for short. Her name was Windigo!

In the final book which is full of Puppys the Sasquatch defamation Lawsuit proceeds to court. Yes it is important. Many little things are. A fourth book is possible but "The Hitch Hikers Guide To The Galaxy Trilogy" has how many books? Its that new math they keep talking about in Acronyms! The commercials ask if I have these letters or those letters and I tell the TV I have twenty seven letters. Using the Grazonian alphabet? 36!

Sincerely Pandabutt Ed.

PROTODOG INTERGALACTIC DICTIONARY

OLD WORDS:
FAT: v, "I'm going to fuck sexy!" n, Tasty part!
SLUT: v Sexy, Loving, Urban, Teen

NEW WORDS:
Growl = I will Fuck you up!
Gou ri de = fucked by a dog
FUBAR = Fucked Up Butt And Realhard
WOOF: food
WOOF!: Fudge
WOOF: food I mean Waffles! Wait Waffles are food!
BRRIPT!: Smell this
MILF: Mother I'd Like to Fuck.
GILF: Grandmother I'd Like to Fuck.
GGILF: Great Grandmother I'd Like to Fuck.
FOLO: Fat Old Lady Orgy
FOL: Fat Old Lady
FYHO: Fat Young Hippo Orgy
RABID BAR B DOLL:
ARGALAUNT DOLL: Four arms
SLARV and GRAUNK: Volganian equivalent of mashed potatoes and gravy
SNORCH: Alien super beer